UNTIL THE FALL OF '19

Howard Rayner

Until the Fall of '19 © 2021 by Howard Rayner. All Rights Reserved.
ISBN 978-1-7399241-0-2

All rights reserved. No part of this book may be reproduced in any form or by any electronic or mechanical means including information storage and retrieval systems, without permission in writing from the author. The only exception is by a reviewer, who may quote short excerpts in a review.

This book is a work of fiction. Names, characters, places, and incidents either are products of the author's imagination or are used fictitiously. Any resemblance to actual persons, living or dead, events, or locales is entirely coincidental.

Howard Rayner
Visit my website at www.howardrayner.com

Cover design – Intermedia LA

CONTENTS

Distant Explosions – March 2008 1
Revelations 14
A Smaller Splash 35
Misinterpretation 50
Layers 67
The Imperfect Past 81
Questioning 102
Visions 121
New York's Burning 142
I Want to Believe 163
Rock Breaks Scissors 184
Apotheosis 203
Fumage 213
Recto / Verso 229
Un Lunedi A Venezia 255
For Better or Worse 273
How Do You Solve a Problem Like Luisa? 288
The Weight of Souls 306
Neorealism 332
Thin Air 350
Memento Mori 363
Unseen 379
Ka-Boom! 398
Success d'Estime 420
White Shirts and Promises 435
Letting Go 465
When the Evening Comes – October 2019 484

Howard Rayner

UNTIL THE FALL OF '19

"If you want a happy ending, that depends, of course, on where you stop your story."

ORSON WELLES

DISTANT EXPLOSIONS — MARCH 2008

"I got off the plane."
"You got off the plane?"
He couldn't move. He couldn't speak.
An inert object lay across his chest.
"I love you."
"I love you too. And I'm never letting go of you again."
Who was speaking? Were demons in the room?
"Here's where I want to be. Okay?"
"I don't want to mess this up again …"

Who just said that? Explosions were happening in space. He didn't have eyes but saw flames. He had no flesh yet felt pain. He was drowning in an airless galaxy.

His fingertip tingled.

The bat squeak realization he needed to stop the words if he wanted to breathe again sparked his consciousness. He commanded his hand to move. Move. Make a fist. Fuck it. Move!

A studio audience laughed.

The pins and needles in his fingertip spread to his hand. Shit. Something sharp was stuck in it. Coming to life, neurons relayed messages along his nerves. The strange object on his chest was his arm.

Bang!

A real door swung against a solid wall.

"Time for your meds."

Through the foggy slits of his eyes, he saw the nurse backing in with the drug cart. He remembered where he was, Cedars-Sinai cardiac wing. Sensation spread up his arm. The stabbing needle was an IV cannula. Recalling what brought him here, his chest tightened. If he panicked, the crushing weight that slammed him to the deck after getting out of the pool would drop again. This time it may not lift. The fiery black nothingness he just experienced terrified him. Had he glimpsed the undiscovered country? The words and laughter carried on relentlessly. If he'd just died a little, it was horrible. He never wanted to go to that lonely place again. He willed his identity back into existence.

He was Alex Morgan!

He flooded his body with his mind. His belief system kicked in. Life did not continue after death. Better there be no country to discover than where he'd just been.

"It's you and me all right. This is it."

The demons were actors on a TV show. Their words had ignited the memory of a terrible event. He had to break free from that memory, but paralysis gripped him. He gasped for air like a fish out of water. The hospital room spun. Purple spots bloomed before his eyes. He forced his uncooperative mouth to move. "Maakke eet stawp."

Parking the cart, the nurse rushed to his bedside. "Are you having another episode, Mr. Morgan?"

"Caan't ... breathe. Turn eet awf."

"What?"

Alex's lips and tongue got in synch. "TV ... off!"

"Is that all?" The nurse hastily checked the monitor and IV pump by the bed. "I was about to call the crash cart."

Alex fought the agitation gripping his heart.

"Where's the remote?" The nurse looked around.

"I dunno. Unplug it. Toss it out the window! Just make it stop."

Fishing the remote from a pile of newspapers, the nurse clicked it. The screen went blank. The actors' words and studio laughter ceased.

Like a death row convict unhooked from the electric chair, the constriction eased in Alex's sternum.

Nurse Roberto DeLano went to the basin and washed his hands.

"Check this needle in my hand, will you? Who rammed it in, Nurse Ratched? She just get back from Guantanamo Bay?"

Coming to the bedside, Nurse DeLano's gentle fingers expertly checked the cannula. "You got tense. If your muscles clench around the needle it feels worse."

"That what your textbooks tell you? Wanna trade places and take the practical course?"

"Let's get you sitting up."

The bed's motor hummed. Alex doggedly rearranged himself into a shape resembling a human being.

"I won't tell Nurse Charles what you said about her cannula insertion. She's one of our finest."

"Finest, huh?" Alex wriggled the wrinkle out the surgical gown beneath his sweaty ass. "Came with a glowing set of references from Torquemada."

"I have no idea what you're talking about, Mr. Morgan."

"Kids today."

"Thanks, but I'm twenty-nine." Nurse DeLano passed over a paper cup of pills.

"Playing hooky the day they taught Spanish Inquisition?"

"Gee but you're cranky this afternoon." Nurse DeLano filled a beaker with water. "Now shut up and swallow."

"I love it when you talk dirty." Alex tipped the meds on his tongue and chugged the pills. Allowing his heart rate to slow, he watched Nurse DeLano check his care plan and fill in the observation chart. "Twenty-nine, huh? Whole chunk of life under your belt and plenty more in front."

"You got plenty in front of you, too. You're in great shape for a man of sixty-two."

"Great shape? Rheumatoid arthritis and a bum ticker."

"The RA meds you've been on may lead to plaque build-up in some patients."

"Now they tell me." Alex let out a sardonic laugh.

"Two days ago, you experienced a heart attack caused by a small blockage. Because you received prompt treatment your heart only suffered minor damage. Your rheumatologist will likely prescribe alternative meds to control the arthritis."

"Did my heart just stop back there? I felt like my heart stopped."

"I checked the readings. Your heart's fine. I suspect you had a panic attack."

Alex coughed and struggled to sit up.

"Let me help."

Allowing the nurse to assist him to lean forward, Alex waited while he plumped the bolster. "Once I worked as a lifeguard, now I need help to move a goddamn pillow."

"You'll get your strength back in no time. You have excellent muscle tone and low body fat. Like I said, you're in great shape for a man of your age."

"My age, my age! Must you add that to every sentence?" Resting back on the bed, Alex flexed his bicep and winced. "Guess I'll sit out this year's iron man." He swept his hair from his face, he wore it just above shoulder length as he had since his mid-twenties, although its waves were more graphite than chestnut brown these days.

"Finished with the newspapers?" Nurse DeLano asked.

"I only had strength to skim. Battles in Iraq, riots in Armenia, Bush waging the endless war on terror and some giant eruption in space. Most distant explosion ever seen from earth with the naked eye. Yeah, dump 'em."

Nurse DeLano bundled the papers into the trash.

"I shouldn't have yelled at you back there. Sorry. That thing on TV must've freaked me out."

Nurse DeLano went to wash his hands again. "I thought the whole world loved *Friends*."

"Those sitcoms reduce life's problems to a series of laugh lines tied up with a happy ending. In real life people don't make peace with the past, some misunderstandings never get resolved, some hurts are never forgiven. People die of cancer. They don't get off the plane ..." Alex apologetically shook his head. "You ever been in love, Roberto?"

Nurse DeLano nudged off the faucet's handle with his elbow.

"I don't mean to embarrass you. You were very open about your life and coming out when we talked yesterday, but if you've never been in love I don't think you can understand the pain of losing it."

Nurse DeLano tore paper towel off the roll. Drying his hands, he came back to the bed.

"The pain grips here, like a vice." Alex laid his hand on his heart. "I wouldn't wish that pain on my worst enemy, yet I'm sad for those who've never felt it."

The nurse's limpid brown eyes engaged with Alex's. "How so?"

"It's an exquisite pain. And the deeper the love, the deeper the pain. My wife died seven years ago. Neuroendocrine cancer." Alex allowed himself a grin as a look of surprise crossed Nurse DeLano's face. "You heard correct. My wife, Danielle Brown. She was an actress. May I say that? Or is everyone an actor these days? Guess a man my age gets to say what he likes. She was on that TV show, *Eddie's Girls*."

"Must've been before my time. I'm so sorry for your loss. Excuse me, but I need to get on with my rounds." Nurse DeLano kicked the brake off the cart.

"Maybe I've been lucky because I'd found a deep love before her. Back when I was your age and living in my grandma's beach house. I'd been scraping along trying to make it as an artist, on the verge of throwing in the towel I may add, when I met this guy on the beach. The summer we spent falling in love was unlike anything I'd ever known. But as happens at the end of every summer, fall arrived. He was an actor too. And just as his TV career was about to take off, a whole scandal blew up about him being gay. His dad, a movie producer, died suddenly. It was the perfect storm. Anyway, the press story killed his acting career, then he had to take his sick mother home to Italy. That was kind of the end of us. Without him, I hid away that part of myself he'd awakened. I'd nearly stopped thinking about him, but after Danielle's death guilt and regret overwhelmed me. I regretted letting him go too easily, that I hadn't fought to get him back. Then one lonely night, drunk on grief and whiskey, I summoned up the courage to search him out. And thanks to our old friend, the coin toss of chance, he was actually in this country. Boston to be precise. I tracked down his hotel and left a message. When he didn't return my call, I figured I'd blown my chances for the last time."

"So that was it?" Nurse DeLano asked, drawn into the story.

"A week later, he called. He'd been out of town and only just got my message. Knowing it was actually him on the line scared the shit out of me. I mean, over thirty years had gone by. What if I'd idealized the memory of a lost love? But the moment we heard each other's voices it was like we'd never been apart. Suddenly we needed to touch again, to love again. The crazy impetuous kid that he was dropped everything to hop a flight to LA the next morning."

"Happy ending then." With a relieved smile, the nurse began edging the cart away.

"That tomorrow morning was September the eleventh, two thousand and one."

"Oh, no …"

"You see, by leaving so long to find him I'd drawn him into the most dangerous place on earth. He'd booked to fly on one of the hijacked planes. And that's why… and that's why …" Emotion choked Alex's voice. "That's why the words from some scene in a TV show brings all that back to me. Brings back how weak I was for letting him go in the first place. And makes me mad too. Mad at him for letting his mother domineer him and split us up. Mad at him for not having had the guts to stay here and face his problems. Mad at him for running out on me, leaving me alone in that empty house on the beach when we should've been living in it together. And my heart breaks for the people who *don't* get off the plane. All the ones lost from being in the wrong place at the wrong time, the ones who don't have happy endings. And I grieve for the empty spaces left in the lives of the people who loved them and —"

"Don't upset yourself, Mr. Morgan. It's awful bad for your heart." Nurse DeLano stroked Alex's shoulder. "I haven't been in love. Not like you describe. I guess love like that doesn't come along every day."

Alex patted the nurse's hand.

Both of them flinched as the door flew open. A bunch of yellow flowers appeared, followed by three silver helium balloons.

"I'm late, I'm late, I know. The Conservatory Board meeting overran." Rick bustled in behind the balloons. "You'll never guess who …" His words died as Nurse DeLano snatched his hand away. Rick's eyes fell on Alex's distressed face. "What's up?"

"Nothing, I'm fine." Alex toughened his lower lip.

"Is it his heart again?" Rick asked the nurse.

"He had a panic attack. Something on TV upset him." Nurse DeLano wheeled the cart to the door.

"Something on TV gave you a panic attack?" Rick put down the balloons and flowers. "What could be so bad? They canceled *The Return of Jezebel James*."

Poised by the door, Nurse DeLano glanced at Rick and then back at Alex. The nurse gave him a knowing half-smile. "Guess he got off the plane. Take it easy, Mr. Morgan. See you tomorrow."

"I'll get that." Rick held the door for Nurse DeLano to wheel out the cart. "You've never had a panic attack before."

"I've never had a heart attack before. I sense a whole new world of infirmity opening up for me."

"These are from Tiffany and the kids." Rick looped the ribbons of three helium balloons with GET, WELL and SOON on them around the bedframe. "The flowers are from Letitia." Rick took a vase off the shelf above the basin and filled it. "I postponed all your interviews until next month. The Duchamp Stage is rescheduling the *California Icons* Q&A. They'll fix a date once Rod, Cayde and Allen get back with their availability. *Architectural Forum* wants the house feature to coincide with your MoMA opening for the June issue. They were the only ones to quibble a date change. But you've got a few weeks before it's scheduled. You'll be well enough by then, won't you? I'm afraid they'll drop the article if you can't solidly commit." Rick arranged the flowers in water. "Fuck it. I'm just going to tell them yes."

"Go for it." Alex gave a resigned nod. "If I die in the meantime, they can prop my corpse up against the pool house for the photoshoot."

"Good thinking. That'll also hide the crack in the weatherboard. Xander Chen's called several times about Art Basel. I made it clear you're not to be bothered by work for at least two more weeks. Chen doesn't like being told no, does he?"

"When you're about to eclipse Gagosian and Zwirner as the biggest art dealer in the world, you get used to people only saying yes."

Rick fluffed out the yellow chrysanthemums. "And I let Myrna know what happened."

"What'd you do that for?"

"Myrna's your sister. She's praying for you."

"She's had plenty of practice. Without much success so far. Last time I checked I was still in love with a man despite her best efforts with God."

"What that nurse said about getting off the plane. You told him the story, didn't you?"

Alex distractedly fiddled with the cannula in his hand. "Maybe."

"You need to let it go." Rick set the vase of yellow blooms on the table by the bed. "Your hair's all over the place." Going into the bathroom, Rick returned with a brush. "These pillows are a mess."

"The nurse just did them."

"Well, he didn't do them very well. Honestly, what do they teach them in medical school these days? Lean forward."

Alex obeyed orders. Behind him, Rick fluffed and smoothed the bolster and pillows. Still sitting forward, Rick wriggled out the wrinkles and pulled down his hospital gown. Much more comfortable after Rick's attention, he leaned back, closed his eyes and let Rick tease the tangles from his hair. "I'll never let it go. Imagining you on that plane will haunt me to my dying day."

"It wasn't that close of a call. I didn't get off the plane because I never got on the plane. I never even set foot in the limo to go to the airport. I texted you I'd switched my flight to the next day when momma got wind of me canceling that meeting with the Gardner Museum and ruled from on high it had to go ahead."

"And when I read that text, I threw my phone so hard it took a chunk out of the drywall. I was so mad you'd let the old witch manipulate you and were bailing on me again."

"When in fact, her interference saved my life. But remember, the day following the attack, when nothing was flying and it felt like the world was ending? I borrowed a car and drove cross-country. I didn't run out on you, I ran towards you. And we've been together ever since. So you don't need to ramble on to all and sundry about that day anymore. Must say, it all looked very lovey-dovey between you and Nurse Dreamy when I walked in."

"Roberto's a sweet guy."

"Roberto, is it?"

"We talked a lot over the past couple of days. He's a good listener." Alex gazed at Rick, nattily dressed in navy pants, putty colored Pima cotton crew and tan Harrington jacket. Daily yoga and healthy diet kept his body in shape, which combined with wearing his sandy hair in a longer style these days would lead most people to figure he was far younger than late fifties. "But I've only got eyes for you, babe."

"Can't wait for you to come home. Bella keeps staring at the door wondering where you are. Collapsing the way you did gave Manuela and me quite a scare."

"Didn't do a heck of a lot for me either."

"That's better." Giving a final sweep of his fingers through Alex's hair, Rick put down the brush. He shot a dark look at the helium balloons. "Of course, Tiffany's Googling heart attack symptoms. She's asked to be referred to a cardiologist."

"Still wiped out all the time?"

"She's constantly got one thing or another wrong with her."

"You think it could be more than physical?"

"Psychological? Could be. The divorce from Pav knocked her sideways. But Tyler's mental state isn't exactly stable, and they are twins after all. In the space of eighteen months, he's totaled two trucks and fallen out of a tree because he hadn't harnessed himself on properly. And those are only the screwball things Tyler's done we know about and —"

"Ty had a run of bad luck. He's a good kid."

"He's thirty-six but acts like a fifteen-year-old!"

"Ty's a free spirit."

"One way of looking at it. Frankly, Tiffany could do with some of Tyler's *joie de vivre* and he'd benefit from some of her gravitas. Those qualities were clearly not divided equally in the womb."

"Losing their father so young couldn't have helped. They were only three when Sid died."

"C'mon, dad wasn't a bastion of emotional stability."

"Sid had his faults, but he was a good father. Out of all his kids, they got to know him the least."

"Those of us who had him longer have more than our fair share of hang-ups. So that blows that theory out the water. Maybe neurotic behavior's in our genes. A study of all my half-brothers and sisters would've given Margaret Mead one helluva good book. *Growing up in Hollywood*, a case study of mental instability."

The entrance of the care assistant making their hourly checks stopped Rick from pursuing this train of thought. It also prevented Alex pointing out that Tyler and Tiffany had a well-balanced, deeply loving mother in Letitia, whereas Rick had the manipulative, self-obsessed Luisa D'Onofrio for his. While the charming Korean lady helped Alex use the bathroom, Rick tidied up the room, slipped off his jacket, dragged a chair to the bedside and made himself comfortable.

"Anyway, like I was saying." Once Alex was settled back in bed and the care assistant had gone, Rick carried on, "You will never guess who accidentally on purpose ran into me at the museum today."

"Boutros Boutros-Ghali."

"Wrong. I mean, you will never guess!"

"Nicolas Sarkozy. Cher? Barney the Dinosaur. I'm tired, babe. Just tell me."

Rick dramatically announced, "Tina Mason!"

"Eh?"

"You can't have forgotten Tina Mason, although she's Cristina Raban these days. Her husband's the top cosmetic surgeon in Beverly Hills, Dr. Harun Raban. He's just launched a skincare line."

"It's like you're speaking Norwegian. I have zero idea who these people are."

"Tina Mason was the co-star of the *Mystery Movie* pilot I was meant to be in, *The Brad and Carol Mysteries*."

Mulling it over, the name did stir a distant memory. "The tough cookie?"

"Correct, Tina Mason! She's angling for a position on the Conservatory Board. I get the feeling she wants to rekindle our association in the hope I'll put in a good word for her. She invited me for lunch to give my feedback on their art collection. They seem serious about broadening their scope. And they're absolutely loaded, which would mean a much-needed boost to the museum's coffers if she does get appointed to the Board."

"Beware Beverly Hills matrons bearing gifts."

"They live in Bel Air. And our Board seriously needs some new blood to kick the place into the twenty-first century. C.Z. Hulton should never have been made chair of a modern art museum in the first place, I mean, the woman knew Holbein personally. I propose shows of Latino art, street art, Black art, and every time she turns up her nose and waves them away. And her clique, who are either senile or deaf, always take her side. And none of them appear to have any intention of dying soon and …"

Alex yawned.

The light dimmed over the Los Angeles skyline outside.

Alex lost track of what Rick was saying but the sound of his voice was comforting. His eyes grew heavy. Part of him wanted to fight the descending darkness, fearful of closing his eyes after that disturbing vision of loss and death, afraid this sleep could be the one from which he'd never awake. But his body needed to heal, and he was tired.

His mind, in the last flickers of activity before going on standby, figured it was the randomness of life which really disturbed him. His artistic career was on a high. The honor of a major retrospective coming up at MoMA. Signing with the Xander Chen gallery for exclusive representation in New York and Asia. The professional validation and acclaim he craved was within his grasp. And just as his dreams were coming true, his heart threw a curve ball. Nurse DeLano was correct, he needed to address his mental state and avoid stress to regain his health. If you only live once, as was his belief, he needed to make the most of this ride.

The coming summer promised to be the best of his life. He hoped his heart would continue beating, and he'd carry on waking to the material world each morning from the maroon velvets of slumber.

At least until the fall.

REVELATIONS

Feeling like the Tin Man after having spent the night on a damp hillside, Alex's rusty joints creaked as he hauled himself up in bed. Through the voile curtains he saw Rick out beside the pool, morning coffee in hand, staring up at the overcast sky. Scratching his head and stretching his jaw, he dragged on the sweatpants and zip front hoodie he'd dragged off last night and dumped on the Eames chair. Shuffling to the windows, he slid back the glass door.

"It's started," Rick said without turning.

Alex followed Rick's gaze. A row of construction uprights jutted above the razor wire atop their Venice compound's nine-foot rear perimeter wall.

Rick sighed. "Goodbye sky."

"Vacant former industrial lots don't stay vacant forever. Once the residential zoning got approved, something was bound to go up there sooner or later."

"Three story apartment buildings. They're gonna overlook our hot tub and pool."

"We'll put up some trellis masking or have Ty plant a row of palms."

"I told you last year would've been a good time to sell."

"Set-ups with the amount of studio and living space we got here are hard to come by. Not to mention room for a forty-foot lap pool." At this time in the morning Alex would usually be in it, halfway through his hundred laps. "A few blocks from Abbot Kinney and the beach, we're in a prime location."

Rick reluctantly nodded. "How're you feeling?"

That was a loaded question.

The relief, joy and happiness of coming home following five days in Cedars-Sinai had rapidly been replaced by frustration, tension and anxiety.

There were the things he wanted to do ... take his daily swim, make love to Rick, and get back to work in the studio.

There were the things he needed to do ... take his daily swim, make love to Rick, and get back to work in the studio.

And there were the things he was afraid to do ... take his daily swim, make love to Rick, and get back to work in the studio.

The terms of recuperation from his heart attack, only a mild one the cardiologist reassured him, forbade all three for at least two weeks. Enduring thirteen days of gentle strolls on the boardwalk with Bella, Rick erecting a Berlin Wall of pillows in the center of the bed, putting his assistants on hiatus and locking the studio door, Alex was ready to combust from frustration on all three fronts.

Yet however much he wanted to do those things, they scared him. The heart attack had come as a shock, although he didn't remember much about it other than the pressure on his chest, falling to the deck by the pool, the meaty wetness of Bella's tongue licking his face, and Manuela banging a cooking pot with a wooden spoon to summon help. The fact he was only wearing a neon pink Speedo and swim cap added an almost comedic element to the mental picture he'd built up of the event. No, it was the vivid memory of that death dream he'd experienced in the hospital which terrified him. Being paralyzed, not knowing who he was, and the agonizing fear he'd lost someone precious in the flames about to consume him too had imprinted themselves on his psyche. For all the years he worked as a lifeguard, he'd never given his own safety a second thought. Preventing people getting into difficulty and diving in to rescue them if they did were second nature, his own death had been an abstract concept. He'd learned to live with the rheumatoid arthritis. Medication to alleviate the inflammation and pain, plus physical activity to keep his joints mobile, rendered it inconvenient but bearable. He was living with that disease. But there was no living with a heart that stopped beating. Every so often he'd find himself putting his hand on his chest to check it still was. So how was he feeling?

"Fine."

"Come on, I'll make your smoothie."

Alex followed Rick across the patio. Enclosed by the house's rear wing, the glazed double doors to the entrance hall, the back of the pool house and glass door into the living room, this courtyard functioned as al fresco dining room and short cut between the living room and master suite.

In the kitchen, Manuela stood at the granite countertop chopping ingredients for his allegedly health-giving morning drink. Bella watched intently, hoping something would fall to the floor. "*Buenos días*, Mr. Alex."

"What's on today's menu?" Alex asked nervously.

"Pineapple, spinach, cilantro, chia seeds, turmeric and organic honey," said Rick proudly.

"Is anti-inflammatory," Manuela added.

Rick tipped the ingredients into the blender, poured in some coconut water and blitzed them.

Bella's doggie kibble looked more appetizing than the foamy gray concoction Rick handed him. Restraining his gag reflex, Alex glugged his morning meds with the weird drink.

"Now you're gonna be okay while I'm out?" Rick asked.

"I promise not to play with matches or stick my fingers in any electrical outlets," Alex replied as they passed through the wood paneled dining area, entrance hall, and small gallery on their way to the master suite. Bella's claws tip-tapped on the walnut hardwood as she trailed after them.

"Or call Xander Chen or do anything else to raise your blood pressure."

Alex followed Rick through the storage area behind the master bedroom and into the walk-in. "Scotty's gonna swing by.

Rod might visit too." Leaving Rick selecting a jacket, he carried on through the dressing area to the master bath.

"Scotty and Rod, in the same room? That's like sticking two scorpions in a box." The jangling melody of Rick's cellphone erupted. He raced to the bedroom to answer it.

Alex ducked into the john to take a much-needed pee. He was at the double vanity brushing his teeth when Rick appeared in the bathroom doorway.

"My agent." Rick despondently swiped off his phone. "I didn't book police psychiatrist on *The Closer*."

"Bru wha abiow ehn shee ow es?"

"Uh?"

Alex spat out the toothpaste. "But what about *NCIS*?"

"I told Daisy not to put me up for that."

Alex rinsed and spat. "Why not?"

"Schlepping out to Valencia to lie naked on a slab for three days? No thanks. Once you start playing victims, casting directors only see you as corpse of the week material. I'm holding out for a lead, preferably recurring. Okay, I'm off."

Stripping off his sweats, and not ready to see how out of shape he'd gotten, Alex averted his eyes from the full-length mirror as his bare feet crossed the polished concrete floor on his way to the shower.

"Can't you just go to your studio and dabble?" asked Scotty. After accompanying him on Bella's afternoon walk, they'd settled in the living room with Rod who'd just shown up.

"If I set one foot on the bridge over to my studio, I have Rick wrestling me back to the couch to throw a blanket over my legs. Being treated like an invalid's driving me nuts. Xander Chen's chomping at the bit for new material for New York and

Art Basel. I can't afford to blow my chances with him." Alex raked his fingers through his hair. "I really need to get back into the studio to finish the work I have in progress."

"What's your vibe these days?" Rod slipped his phone in his back pocket having checked his messages for the tenth time in fifteen minutes.

"I got a couple of epic color field pieces underway, and I mean huge, plus a tranche of mid-size abstracts. I must admit, I've got a real hankering to do some figurative work again."

"Gonna set up your field easel on the boardwalk and slam out a few watercolor sunsets?" Rod asked with a guileful grin.

"If my fingers still worked the way they did before the arthritis, I'd be down there like a shot." He knew the contempt Rod and his contemporaries held for his plein air work and scenic studies. So much so that when he'd shared the Venice studio with Hank, Scoop and Rod in the seventies, he'd hidden his beloved *Cliffs of Mendocino* paintings from them out of shame. Alex flexed the misshapen knuckles of his right hand. "On bad days, I struggle to unscrew the tops off the paint tubes."

Rod dropped his eyes. "That's rough."

"Face it Rod, Alex was the only one of us who could draw or paint realistically." Scotty picked up her cup from the coffee table scattered with large format art and photography books. Draining her coffee, she broke into a coughing fit. Leaning forward to assist her, Scotty shrugged off Alex's concern. "Last dregs of Valley fever."

"I thought seniors moved to Palm Springs primarily *for* the climate," said Rod.

"You're three years older than me, Rod. If I'm a senior I don't know what that makes you. And I moved back to LA because I decided inhaling smog was preferable to inhaling fungus laced aerosol sand." Scotty grabbed her purse. "Anyway, I was going stir crazy up there by myself after Bob died."

"You weren't tempted to stop shaving your legs, adopt stray cats, pick up your brushes and become a lady painter again?" asked Rod.

Scotty gave him a fatigued sigh. "I lost the habit of painting." She pulled a Kleenex out of her purse. "I channel all my artistic drive into my event planning business now. At least I can make an income from that."

"You made money from your art." Alex recalled a time when Scotty's art career had eclipsed his own.

"That was over twenty-five years ago! Even established female artists struggle to get picked up by a gallery these days. And when they do sell, they rarely achieve the same prices as men. You guys rule the art market." Scotty coughed into the tissue. "Name one woman from our old crowd who's still working."

"Tina Seattle," Alex blurted.

"Man, did you see her last show?" Rod's unnaturally white teeth gleamed. "*Ten Porcelain Vaginas Hanging on the Wall*. And I'd hardly call Freedom Space a serious gallery."

"But it is a gallery, and she is working," countered Scotty. "Thank you, Alex. Good for Tina Seattle."

"And if one porcelain vagina should accidentally fall, she'll have nine porcelain vaginas hanging on the wall." Rod sniggered.

Alex chuckled along.

Scotty broke into another coughing fit and muttered, "Chauvinists," behind her tissue.

"Do you need water?" Without waiting for her to answer, Alex yelled, "Manuela!" Noticing Scotty's glare, he adopted his serious face. "I get the impression gay artists also sell for lower prices. When did the art world become so macho?"

"Maybe when the wealth managers and investment funds made art into an asset class." Scotty directed this at Rod.

Rod checked his TAG Heuer watch.

Carrying a pile of folded laundry, Manuela came in from the patio. "Yes, Mr. Alex?"

"We need water in here."

"Don't worry, Manuela, I'm fine," said Scotty. "I should be hitting the road. I'm scouting a wedding venue up in the hills at seven."

"Bring water anyway," Alex told Manuela.

"The pool man say you forgot to pay him last month," said Manuela.

"Did he replace the filters?"

"I don't know, Mr. Alex. You want I go ask him?"

"Yes. Tell him I'll check with Rick about the payment." Manuela put down the laundry beside a large golden seated Buddha sculpture and went outside. "Sheesh. I kept reminding Rick to make sure Tommy ordered new filters." Alex cocked his head to overhear the conversation out by the pool. "Sounds like he forgot the filters and forgot to pay the invoice."

"Can't get the staff," Rod said with a chuckle. Feeling a vibration, he pulled out his phone.

Alex saw Scotty staring at the Warholesque silk screen portrait of Danielle which dominated the wall over the fireplace.

"I need to take this." Rod went outside with his phone.

Scotty turned her gaze from Danielle's portrait to meet Alex's eyes. "Are her things still upstairs in the small house?"

"I'll get around to it."

"She's been gone seven years ..."

Scotty stopped as Manuela came in from the kitchen. With a tremor, she set down the tray holding three tumblers, a bottle of Evian and a dish of sliced tomatoes with cocktail sticks. "The pool man say Mr. Rick didn't tell him about no filters. But he gonna order them and come back next week." Manuela picked up a blanket off the floor. "Is Mr. Rick home for dinner?"

"He should be." Alex realized it was after five. Rick's lunch at Tina Mason's, or Cristina Raban as she was now known, had clearly gone on longer than expected. A flicker of anxiety crossed his mind, Rick usually called if he was going to be late.

"You want I should fix something and leave it in the oven?" Manuela went to drape the blanket over Alex's knees.

He pushed the blanket aside. "No, Rick can throw something together. Finish up for the day when you're ready."

Dipping her head, Manuela returned to the kitchen.

"This the new way of serving mineral water?" Scotty picked up the bowl of sliced tomatoes.

"Probably a health fad Rick dredged up on the internet. What joy if he discovered hot fudge sundaes and whiskey were miracle cures."

"Tim about my Tokyo opening." Rod turned off his phone as he ambled back in. "Good to see you up and about, Al."

"Reports of my death were greatly exaggerated." As soon as he'd said that a cold shudder made him wish he hadn't.

"I'm gonna swing by next door to shoot the breeze with Cayde. Rehash our halcyon days of Venice Beach, when making art was like going surfing, our lifestyle not our business."

"I still consider my art as my lifestyle rather than a business," said Alex earnestly.

Rod sucked a skeptical breath in through his uncannily perfect teeth, their white evenness emphasizing his tanned face's weathered creases. "Signing with Xander Chen's put you at the top of the major league. Takes one helluva lot of work to stay there. And I'm not just talking about art. Will we be seeing you and Rick at the County for the *Phantom Sightings* opening?"

"Not sure. I'll see how I feel."

Scotty's back stiffened as Rod rested his hand on her shoulder to kiss her cheek then swaggered to the patio.

"Rod!" Alex called after him. "Use the roller gate between the houses." Rod gave a thumbs up and went through the glazed doors from the patio into the entrance hall and out the front door. "I don't know where Bella is. She tries to dash out if you haven't got hold of her when the pool door's open."

"Goodbye, Manuela!" Scotty slung her purse's gold chain over her shoulder.

"Bye, Miss Scott!" Manuela's reply was followed by the clatter of pots and pans being shunted around cabinets.

"Rick must've emptied the dishwasher. Manuela's moving what he put away back to where she thinks they belong."

Scotty shot a glance at Danielle's glamorous portrait. "Back to where *she* thought they belonged?"

"Manuela doesn't like change," Alex said as they walked alongside the lap pool. "Running the house is a real battle of wills between her and Rick at times. I keep my head down and let them get on with it."

Hearing their voices, Bella padded around from the meditation garden. Her paws skittered on the paving beside the pool when she saw them.

They paused at the white door set in the nine-foot-high front wall, its cinder blocks softened by a covering of evergreen foliage. A little clumsily, Scotty extended her arms and hugged him. Bella jumped up to join in the hug. "Bob never forgave you for telling the police he pulled a gun on the mugger that night Rick got shot."

"I told the truth."

"I know. But carrying a concealed weapon without a license isn't a great look for a high-profile lawyer. Be that as it may, Bob was in the wrong and I shouldn't have let him drive a wedge between us over it. I'm so glad you forgave me. That was another reason to come back to LA. My social circle in Palm Springs were acquaintances rather than friends. My history is here. You're the best friend I ever had, maybe ever will."

"What about Rod?" Alex asked, a twinkle in his eye.

"Rod's a misogynistic dinosaur."

"An exceedingly wealthy misogynistic dinosaur."

"Rod hit the jackpot by making a single word into a painting. Do you think people collect them to make up a sentence?"

"Like classy fridge poetry?"

"Will they need to subtitle his work for Tokyo?"

"Bitch."

"Serves him right for putting down Tina Seattle."

"You always considered Tina Seattle pretentious."

"Any reservations I had about Tina's work were artistic. Rod's are sexist."

Alex opened the white door. Scotty stepped into the paved strip separating the pool house from the perimeter wall. Following Scotty, he pushed Bella back and shut her inside. He opened the turquoise street door onto Hampton. Scotty walked out onto the sidewalk just as the garage door on their left was lifting. Rick bipped the horn to Scotty as their white Prius pulled in. The lights on Scotty's black BMW flashed as she clicked the fob. She kissed him goodbye and got in her car.

He was on his way back to the house when Rick emerged from the garage's side door at the base of the three-story studio block. Bella skittered around the pool to greet him.

"You! Inside, now!" barked Rick.

Alex whistled to Bella. "Yeah, get inside girl."

"I was talking to you. You're supposed to be resting."

"I've rested up enough. I unilaterally declare recuperation over. I was just about to text Suki to come in, I need to get back to work."

"But —"

"It's decided."

Bella raced through the living room. Coming into the kitchen, they found her sitting by the cabinet which housed her kibble, expectantly wagging her curly golden flag of a tail.

"Where's Manuela?" Rick filled Bella's bowl.

"I told her to finish up for the day."

"Oh." Rick put down Bella's food. Casting a critical eye around the kitchen, he picked up a cleaning sponge and wiped the sink. "She leave anything for dinner?"

"No. I said you'd fix something."

As Rick rinsed the sink, he studied the glassware on the open cabinet to his right. Squeezing out the sponge, he put it in the sink caddy then set about rearranging the glasses. "I've asked Manuela a million times to put the short glasses in front and tall ones behind."

"Does it matter?"

"It's crazy reaching around a tall glass to get a short one."

"Good lunch?" Alex asked to change the subject.

"You should see Cristina and Harun's home. West Gate Bel Air. Ivory marble floors, gold faucets and overlooking the golf course." Smiling dreamily, Rick opened a cupboard and let out another aggravated sigh.

"You forgot to tell Tommy I wanted the pool filters changed. Seems paying his bill slipped your mind as well."

Rick shut the cupboard door with an unnecessarily loud bang. "Let me guess what's happened here." Rick went to the cork board beside the sliding glass doors out to the narrow barbecue area between the house and front perimeter wall. Unpinning a slew of shopping and to-do lists in Manuela's barely legible scrawl, Rick excavated a brown envelope with TOMMY written in his own super-neat handwriting on its front. "I told Manuela to give him this last month. With all the drama of you being in the hospital it never crossed my mind to make sure she'd actually given it to him."

Inside the envelope Alex found Rick's note requesting new filters and a check covering the invoice. "Are you telling me Manuela deliberately didn't do what you asked her to?"

Rick investigated the cupboards. "She's been moving things, hasn't she?"

"You know Manuela has set ideas about where things belong."

"And this is where a dirty skillet belongs?" Rick held out a pan with baked on food. Delving into another unit, he excavated an empty granola carton and a block of half-melted butter. He dumped the granola carton in the trash, put the butter in the fridge and set the skillet to soak. "Maybe you haven't noticed, but Manuela's been doing some pretty random stuff of late."

"How'd you mean?"

"I didn't want to worry you while you were sick, but if you can handle getting back to work I guess it's time. Let's go sit." As Rick went from the kitchen to the living room, Bella darted around his legs. "A few weeks ago, when you were in the hospital … Bella, no! Get down!" Having jumped on the coffee table, Bella had her nose in the bowl of tomato slices. Rick lurched forward to drag her off. "Hold her." Alex clutched Bella's collar as Rick carried the tray to the kitchen. "You can't leave cocktail sticks lying around, you know what she's like. Eating those could have killed her," Rick said as he came back in. "And what was the tomato in aid of?"

"Manuela brought it with the water. I figured it was some new health fad of yours."

"And what's that pile of laundry doing by the window?"

"I distracted Manuela while she was putting it away and —" The entry phone's buzzer interrupted Alex.

"Yo! Anybody home!" a man's foghorn voice bellowed from the street.

"I'll buzz you in through the pool door, Ty," Rick said into the intercom panel in the entrance hall.

"Yo, Manuela! I could murder a cold beer! Ricky, where'd you want this?" boomed the foghorn voice upon entering the property.

"We'll discuss the Manuela issue once Tyler's gone," said Rick.

Alex let go of Bella's collar. She raced outside and Rick followed. He sank onto the couch. Rick's, "We'll discuss the Manuela issue," had an ominous ring to it.

"Leave it on the deck by the bedroom windows," Alex heard Rick saying outside. "And take off your dirty boots."

"What's Ty brought?" Alex asked as Rick came in from the patio.

"Some giant rainforest plant that looks like a beanstalk. Maybe he sold the cow for magic beans." Picking up the folded laundry, Rick carried it across the patio to the master suite.

A few moments later, a six-foot three bundle of ginger-blond long-haired masculine energy, dressed in khaki shorts, sweaty t-shirt and soil-stained socks, bounded into the room. Tyler loped across the living room and hurled himself onto the couch, landing with a thud. He slung a leanly muscled arm around Alex's shoulder and clasped him in a sideways bear hug. "Uncle Al! How you doin'?"

"Good, good," Alex gasped. Tyler was practically squeezing the life out of him.

"There you go, one *Lite* beer." Coming in from the kitchen, Rick set a frosted bottle on a coaster on the coffee table. "Ty, go easy on him!"

"Why? Uncle Al's better, isn't he?"

"I'm fine. Rick's treating me like I'm made of glass."

"I was shitting my pants when Ricky told us you'd been rushed to the hospital. Thought you were a goner back there." Tyler grabbed his beer. Bella launched herself onto the couch then nuzzled into the ginger-blond fuzz covering Tyler's thigh. He played with Bella's golden ear, and she licked his dusty hand. "A heart attack. How'd that feel? Did you have a near death experience? Did you meet Jesus on a cloud saying come unto the light, my son?"

"Oh, yeah," Alex replied. "All of the above."

Tyler withdrew his stubbly chin. "For real?"

"As if," scoffed Alex. "The heart attack felt like a lead weight dropping on my chest. As for the other stuff ..." The way Tyler's green-gold eyes were gazing so deeply into his own was unsettling. He hadn't experienced any extraordinary phenomena during or immediately after the heart attack, but, despite assurances to the contrary, he was convinced that terrible waking dream in the hospital was the result of his heart momentarily stopping. That torturous empty feeling had felt like death, but he couldn't tell Tyler that. "Sorry I can't report back on any welcoming harps and clouds. Guess the non-believer's department just tell you to fuck off back to finish up your shitty old life down on earth."

Alex's comment cracked Tyler up, he broke out in rumbling guffaws.

Issuing them both with a withering eye roll, Rick returned to crashing pots and pans around in the kitchen.

Riffing on the indignities of sickness, stays in the hospital and assorted hard instruments being inserted into various bodily orifices, Tyler's oddball humor lifted Alex's spirits. Although Rick's half-brother was a grown man with a successful landscaping business, there was a goofy innocence about him which Alex found charming. Being with Tyler always made him feel young and carefree. Thirty minutes of dumb jokes and juvenile banter later, Tyler gave him another bone crushing man hug and got to his feet. On the patio, Tyler dragged a rattan chair out from under the table to pull on his work boots.

Alex admired the tall exotic plant with dark green glossy leaves and hanging seedpods. "What is this?"

"Moreton Bay Chestnut." Tyler tied his bootlaces. "I'll come over and dig it in next week. Figured it would sit well in the meditation garden. Some Butterfly Ginger will look good around it. Ricky, I'm outta here!" Tyler projected his foghorn voice towards the house's darkening interior.

"*Architectural Forum*'s coming to do an interview and photoshoot. The grounds need serious attention. Got space to fit me in? Standard rate, of course."

Tyler surveyed the oleanders and lemon trees on the patio, the shrubs and rock plants of the meditation garden across the pool, and the countless other trees and palms around the compound. Standing up, Tyler fluffed his long hair from his neck, ran his fingers through it a few times and tied it back with an ikat pattern elastic from his wrist. "I'll need a couple of days. Would the weekend after next work?"

Rick emerged from the double doors to the entrance hall, Bella at his heels.

"Perfect. Stay over in the pool house," said Alex, "save you driving back and forth to the canyon. We can see if Tiffany's free and get her over too."

"Family dinner, yay!" Tyler gave a lopsided grin. "And there's no need to pay me."

"C'mon, we don't expect favors."

"You guys have done plenty to help me. A little yardwork's the least I can do for Uncle Al and big brother Ricky." Tyler crooked his elbow around Rick's neck and squeezed him. Although only four inches taller than Rick, Tyler was built on a larger scale, dwarfing his older brother.

Rick acquiesced momentarily into Tyler's armpit before wriggling free. He fanned his face. "Go home and shower."

Tyler sniffed his pits. "Nah, good for another couple of days."

Shaking his head disparagingly while Alex snickered, Rick walked Tyler past the large porthole window set into the pool house's cobalt blue weatherboard.

"Is it okay if I have a guest stayover when I'm here for the yardwork?" Tyler asked shyly.

"What kind of guest?" Rick's eyes narrowed.

"Someone I've been seeing. We're getting kind of serious." Tyler scuffed his boot's toe on the deck.

Alex detected a flush under Tyler's tanned cheeks. "Sure, no problem," he said enthusiastically before noticing Rick's mouth was drawn into a tight line.

"Cool!" Tyler grinned. "His name's Jack. He's a real sweetheart. See ya!" Tyler crossed the sidewalk and jumped up into his work truck.

After locking the street gate and white inner door, they heard Tyler's truck roar off. "Are you crazy?" Rick asked. "A stranger in the house for a whole weekend? And you know Tyler's always favored quantity over quality in the romance department. Although I'm not sure romance is the correct word for his private life."

"Ty said this is getting serious. Give the kid a break."

Rick emitted a dubious grunt. "I'm not in the mood to cook. You up for Martin's?"

"You up for jump starting me if my heart gives out on the way?"

"I'll chance it if you will."

It was growing cooler as the sun went down. While Rick put on Bella's leash, Alex grabbed a chunky knit belted cardigan from the walk-in and met up with Rick in the decked passageway between the properties. A yellow light burned behind the kitchen blind of Manuela's ground floor apartment. Rick glanced up to the empty blackness behind the drapes of the small house's second-floor windows. After exiting through the wood paneled double doors between the houses, they crossed the parking space, which rarely housed a vehicle but was home to their trash cans and Rick's Roadster bike. Alex punched the green button to raise the metal roller gate onto the street.

Fifteen minutes later, having let Bella blow off steam in the off-leash park, they entered Martin's on the Beach, their favorite of the local casual eateries. Once through the green tile and walnut paneled entrance, they received a warm welcome from Martin, the proprietor. He swiftly installed them in their regular blue leather corner booth on the terrace. Local artists short on cash sometimes settled their tabs with an original artwork, hence the vibrant and quirky paintings covering the walls. The swoosh of surf and boardwalk hubbub mingled with discrete soft rock. Having tucked Bella under their table, Alex slipped on his glasses to peruse the menu. "Contains fat, salt, sugar, spice ... anything here I'm allowed to eat?"

Rick ran his finger down the menu then looked at the table. "One of the hemp placemats?"

"Ha ha."

"The vegetable tacos appear suitably spartan."

The server took their food order. "To drink?"

"Water," Alex sighed.

"Me too."

"You can drink if you like."

"Pitcher of adult style lemonade," Rick added as he handed back the menu.

Their order in, Alex removed his glasses and rested his chin on his fists. "The Manuela issue. Okay, hit me."

"The other week when I got home from visiting you in the hospital, I found her in the street."

"And?"

"It was after nine o'clock! The roller gate was up. I assumed she was taking out the trash cans, although I usually do that. Then I saw the doors between the houses were wide open. I came in and knocked on her door, but no answer. I got my keys out but didn't need them. Our front door wasn't locked! I went around calling her name but there was no sign of her. Wondering if I should phone 911, I went back outside. I was really starting to panic. That's when I spotted her heading up Indiana Avenue. I chased after her. She was distressed, hysterical. Because Danielle wasn't upstairs in the small house, she'd gone out looking for her. Thankfully, Bella was asleep in the den. I mean, Manuela had gone out and left our place wide open. Thank God I came home when I did. It's a miracle Bella didn't run off or we got robbed." The server set the pitcher of lemonade on the table. "I calmed Manuela down and got her back in her apartment. Next morning it was as if nothing had happened."

"Maybe she woke up from a nap and got confused?"

"Sliced tomato instead of lemon, dirty skillets in the cupboard, notes not passed on …" Rick poured himself a glass of vodka laced lemonade. "Babe, how old was Manuela when she began working for you?"

Alex shrugged. "Dunno. Forty, forty-five?"

"And how many years ago was that?"

Alex put his hand inside his denim shirt and scratched his chest. "Um … twenty-six."

"Do the math." Rick drained his glass.

The penny dropped. Manuela had gotten old. She'd been a fixture on his landscape for so long he hadn't even noticed.

"You need to speak with her son. I mean, Jorge never comes visit with her anymore."

"Okay."

"And you need to discuss her retirement."

Alex sat back in the booth. Manuela was devoted to the house, and to him. Merely the thought of broaching retirement with her was making him tense.

"And I saw lights on in Danielle's rooms."

"Manuela dusts and vacuums up there."

"At one in the morning? It was eerie."

"Maybe she heard a noise and used the back stairs to go up and check. Like that time the possum got in the attic."

Blowing off this possibility with a contemptuous shake of his head, Rick refilled his glass. "If Manuela's losing her marbles, having Danielle's clothes and furniture upstairs in the small house isn't going to help. Look, you need —"

"You've alerted me to the issue. I'll deal with it, okay." Being told all the things he needed to do was irritating him. Taking an empty glass, Alex poured himself a small adult style lemonade.

"You shouldn't be drinking that."

Alex knew he shouldn't but needed a hit of something pleasant. "Cristina's home met your approval, then. I recall your very vocal dislike of Bel Air when your dad lived there."

"That mock Georgian of Sid and Letitia's was an architectural travesty. And I hated anything dad liked on principle back then."

"Apart from floors glazed in marble and bathrooms dripping with gold, how was the Raban's art collection?"

"A Lichtenstein enamel with minor damage, an unattractive Richter, a late period Durant. All the right names but not the right pieces. The jewel in their crown's a stunning Basquiat. Cristina's prepared to loan it to the Conservatory."

"If she gets appointed to the Board."

"Art museums can't function without money. Or art. And Cristina brings both to the table. New acquisitions are at an all-time low. So's our endowment."

Taking a sip of his vodka lemonade, Alex thought the better of it and tipped the rest into Rick's glass.

The server arrived and set their food on the table.

"Sorry, I shouldn't have spilled my worries over Manuela on you like that. What with you being sick and everything else, guess I've been bottling things up."

"Everything else?"

Rick picked at his fried chicken. "I really thought I was going to book that role on *The Closer*. I'm beginning to wonder if I'll ever get decent acting work again. And I could really use earning some money. Black Monday slammed my investments."

Alex chomped his veggie tacos, wishing they were crumbed chicken and thick cut fries. "Don't stress about money. I've told you what's mine is yours."

"I know. But meeting up with Cristina's brought back the time I had a starring role within my grasp. I did a million readings with actresses when they were looking for someone to play opposite me. Cristina got cast because we had chemistry back then. We still do. I had fun with her today. With their last kid off to college, she's tried to break back into acting. And with no luck either. Anyway, from throwing political fundraisers and local charity boards she's got in thick with Ellery Pritzker and Augusta Kramer. Cristina's put a proposal together for TV show, a behind-the-scenes look at Bel Air high society featuring her and her friends. If the show gets green-lighted she'll be an executive producer. There could be a role on it for me."

"Why do I get the horrible feeling this is reality TV?"

"More like a documentary."

"We don't live in Bel Air. How can that work?"

"Cristina getting elected to the Conservatory Board would give me a relevance on the show. It'd be great publicity for the museum too."

The taco stuck in Alex's throat. Changing his mind, he poured a slug of vodka lemonade. "A part on her show would be Cristina's reward for you getting her a position on the Board."

"Not at all." Rick dipped a thick cut fry in garlic mayo.

Alex enviously watched Rick make short work of the rest of the fries. "You seriously think being associated with a show like that's a good idea?"

"Being on TV as myself will remind the industry of who I am. I need to get my name known again."

"And the potential for dragging up the past doesn't concern you?"

"My acting career got canned in the seventies because I was in a relationship with another man, namely you. The gutter press blew it into some kind of sordid scandal. I got treated unfairly. Don't I deserve a second chance?"

Alex studied Rick finishing his chicken and beckon the server for a second pitcher of vodka lemonade. Stepping aside from looking at his lover, he became the artist considering his subject. Rick's handsome face, his softly waving hair, the sparkle in his powder blue eyes ... familiar features of the man he first fell in love with. But looking deeper, and more critically, he saw crinkles forming around Rick's eyes, a loosening of the jowls and the beginnings of disappointment and defeat behind those saucer-like black pupils.

Reaching across the table, Alex placed his slightly misshapen right hand on top of Rick's perfect left one. "I have the feeling Cristina's using you and this could all blow up in your face. But if that's a risk you're willing to take, I guess you should go for it."

"You're right, Cristina's TV show is a dumb idea. I was clutching at straws." Rick screwed up his napkin and pushed his plate aside. "Maybe I'm having a mid-life crisis."

"You plan on living to a hundred and twenty?"

"End-of-life crisis." Rick laughed self-deprecatingly. "I got plenty to do looking after the house, sitting on the Conservatory Board, organizing your publicity and supporting your career. That's enough for me."

Rick's words kept repeating in Alex's head as they walked home. They sounded sincere,

But then Alex remembered Rick was an actor at heart.

A SMALLER SPLASH

Tucking his hair into the swim cap, Alex adjusted his goggles and looked down at his toes hanging over the pool's edge. After weeks of being bundled in jeans and cardigans and having blankets draped over his knees against his will, the sun on his bare skin and breeze ruffling the hair on his arms and legs was unnerving. Although unseasonably warm for early April, he shivered. Since there was no chill on the air, his goosebumps could only be down to apprehension about getting back in the water. Throughout his late teens and twenties, when he was working on the yachts and lifeguarding for a living, neither the roughest of seas nor deepest of pools gave him the slightest qualm. He hated feeling nervous about this reunion. But then he'd never felt unsure of his heart before. The attack had occurred immediately after his last swim, would the same thing happen again?

Poised on the pool's edge, hesitating about his dive seemed ridiculous considering the way his love affair with water had begun. They'd met by chance one summer day in 1949. Pop's promotion at the Douglas factory had led to the appearance of unfamiliar luxuries like stylish clothes, shiny household appliances and family vacations. The rustic cabin Pop had taken for a week on the shores of Lake Erie marked the first time Alex had been outside of Dayton. Also, the first time he'd seen the sea. Okay, Erie was a lake, but its vast watery expanse and tidal wash rendered it bigger than the Pacific in Alex's young mind. Mom and Pop were taking him and Myrna, his sister, to the service at Fairport Harbor's waterfront church. Holy worship was to be followed by a steak lunch in town. Mom had told Pop to take three-year old Alex down to the lake while she and Myrna got dressed in their Sunday best. He vividly recalled the short-sleeved shirt with whipstitch edging, short gray pants, and brand-new Red Goose bumper boots Mom had put him in on that fateful day.

 Pop immediately found a bench to sit. Chain-smoking, he buried his nose in the newspaper. Being seven years younger than Myrna, Alex had gotten used to playing alone. Ten minutes of drawing patterns in the sand with a stick grew tiresome. The isolated white building with a red roof and high tower at the end of the breakwater captured his attention. Looking over his shoulder, he saw Pop had put down his paper and fallen into conversation with a red-haired lady from one of the other cabins. He remembered seeing her sitting alone at the inexpensive diner they'd eaten in last night. Pop offered the lady a cigarette. She glanced towards the cabins, tossed her red hair and giggled before hesitantly accepting. She must have been telling Pop a funny story because he began laughing too when he leaned forward to light her cigarette.

 Seeing the adults were busy doing adult stuff, Alex's imagination wandered into the sturdy structure on the rocks. He loved Westerns. The white building would make a swell fort to play cowboys. Figuring he could make it there, fire off a few shots at marauding Indians, and make it back before Pop even noticed he'd gone, he picked his way along the breakwater.

 The distance to the fort was greater than it had appeared. The rocks grew larger with every step. Alex's small legs were scaling jagged boulders while the white fort was slipping farther from his reach. Realizing this adventure hadn't been such a swell idea, he reluctantly turned to go back to Pop. The brown algae covering the breakwall had slicked the soles of his new boots. Little Alex lost his footing on the slimy rocks. His arms flailed. He clutched at thin air. Painfully hitting his hip on the rocks as he fell, he tumbled into the lake. The surface closed over his head. Water roared into his ears. Although he'd fallen into a new world, he didn't panic. Underwater, time stood still. In that eternity Alex sensed an inherent knowledge of the viscid substance suspending him. He clawed his way up. Shaking off his hair and gasping for air, he heard a woman screaming. The weight of his waterlogged shoes and clothes dragged him down. Kicking out more strongly than before, Alex broke the surface again. Blinking water from his eyes, he saw Mom, dressed in her new blue two-piece skirt suit with daisy trim, white gloves and hat, hurl herself in the lake. Splashing towards him, she grabbed his arm. Then, half-swimming and half-staggering, she dragged him to shore.

Pop, Myrna and other folks from the cabins, including the lonely lady, had gathered on the breakwall. They watched Mom haul him from the lake. After slapping his legs for going off alone, she clutched him tight and thanked God for saving her son. Mom then vented her anger on Pop for letting the kid wander off. Growing increasingly hysterical, she'd lashed out at him. "Cool it, Clemmie," Pop had said with unwavering eyes as he clenched her wrist, "the boy was doing something he shouldn't ought to have." Then Mom hissed at Pop, "Why didn't *you* save him?" Pop had roughly pushed her away. "I don't swim, Clem. Thanks for making a fool of me." Pop looked at the lonely lady, who turned away. Without another word, Pop had dragged Myrna to the cabin and locked the door. That day changed something in his family forever. A bedraggled pair of outsiders, young Alex had comforted Mom in her wet clothes as she wept. The thought of going back into the cabin with Pop terrified him. But going back into the lake and exploring that new world didn't. The water was a place he could escape to, one where Pop couldn't follow …

This memory spurred Alex on. He'd never been afraid of the water before and wasn't about to start. Tightening his abs, he dove.

Splash!
He was in.
His arms were moving.
His feet were kicking.

He was gliding through the water, building speed at every turn. It took ten laps to find his rhythm. Completing his twentieth lap, he came up for air. Clinging to the metal ladder, he pulled down his goggles and blew snot from his nose. He put his hand to his chest. He was out of shape, but the swim hadn't stopped his heart. Music was playing in the main studio. He must've missed Suki arrive for work while underwater. He climbed out of the pool. Slinging his cap and goggles on a lounger, he wrapped a towel around his waist and pulled on a terrycloth robe. He slipped his feet into his pool sliders, crossed the patio and went through the doors to the entrance hall.

Rick was in the kitchen, still with bed hair and dressed in a sweatshirt and jogging bottoms from Bella's morning walk, pouring himself a coffee. "So, you survived." He chose a Danish from the bowl of pastries on the counter.

"Yep. Hard work, but good. *Buenos días*, Manuela." Alex enviously watched Rick eat the Danish with one hand and nervously watched him hit the blender button with his other. Moments later, Rick thrust another of his foaming gray concoctions under his nose.

Taking a sip, Alex winced. "What the fuck's in this?"

"Coconut milk, spinach, beetroot and pineapple," Rick replied brightly.

"This makes the reason those ingredients don't exist next to each other in the natural world abundantly clear." Alex grimly downed his morning meds with another swallow.

"Mr. Rick say is good for you." Manuela swept the beetroot tops and peel and the rind, core and crown of the pineapple into piles on the countertop.

"And I added an extra-special ingredient today," announced Rick.

"Let me guess." Alex had another sip. "Eye of newt?"

Rick indicated a glass jug of murky fluid with unpleasant grains at the bottom. "Fermented water kefir."

"Yum." Alex raised the beaker in a mock toast then glugged the rest. "I need something to take that taste away." He reached for a Danish, but Rick slapped his hand.

"No sugar, no salt, no fat!" Rick and Manuela chanted.

Alex reluctantly selected a red apple from the fruit bowl. Biting into it, he scuffed through the wood paneled dining area, entrance hall and small gallery to the house's rear wing. Rick followed him into the master bedroom.

"They posted fliers about the homeless man murdered on the beach." Rick tugged off his sweatshirt.

"Poor guy." Alex shucked off his robe. "What a way to go. Beaten to death then buried on the beach like garbage."

"You know the weird thing? His name was Morgan, and he came from Ohio. Who knows, he might have been related to you."

"Who knows." Alex tossed the towel over the Eames chair and peeled down his tangerine swim trunks. "What you up to today?"

"Nothing much. Just a Conservatory Board meeting at noon." Rick swished the voile curtains over the glass sliding doors that looked across the pool to the main studio. "Suki's back at work, remember?" Rick rolled down his jogging bottoms and undershorts.

"If Suki did glance over, there's nothing here she'd be interested in seeing." Naked, and fluffing out his cock and balls from his swimsuit's compression, Alex padded around to the master bath. Leaning into the granite lined double shower, he switched on the jets. Waiting while the water ran hot, he turned to see Rick come in. His eyes lingered on Rick's bare buttocks as he stood flossing at the vanity, the triangle of muscles at the base of his spine twitching as his arms moved. Mentally running his fingers over Rick's body, Alex stiffened. He'd knocked one item off his list of recuperation no-nos this morning, may as well go for another. He turned off the shower. Coming up behind Rick, he pressed his erection into Rick's butt crack.

"What're you doing?" Rick asked through the floss.

"Been so long you've forgotten?" Alex trailed his fingers up and down Rick's ribs then traced them down his loins. He savored his power to make Rick shiver and giggle. "I drank the slimy substance you gave me." He nuzzled Rick's neck. "Time for you to return the favor." He softly bit the scattering of freckles on Rick's trapezius.

Rick rinsed and spat. "Sure you're up to it?"

"Seems I am." Alex pulled down his erection and let it slap back up against his abdomen. "To be on the safe side, you can do the hard work." Alex rested his buttocks on the cast concrete vanity. Pulling Rick around in front, he gripped Rick's shoulders and pushed him down. In the full-length mirror, he watched the back of Rick's head slide down as he got to his knees. Seeing the reflection of his own arms, chest and stomach wasn't as depressing as he feared. He'd lost a little muscle tone, the tangle of hair in his chest's cleft had a little more silver in it and the pads of back fat had grown somewhat, but the hair on his arms, legs and belly was still dark, his pecs still perky and although his six pack was more of a four pack it was still a pack. Rick's ball sack dangled below his furry butthole as he spread his legs to get low enough. Alex tossed back his head as Rick's mouth went to work. Licking down the back of his shaft, Rick then flittered his tongue around his balls before taking each one in his mouth in turn, humming as he sucked and swirled his tongue around them. Alex glanced down just as Rick glanced up. Their gaze connected. Rick widened his eyes then dropped his jaw to consume Alex's meaty cock. Leaning on the vanity with one hand, Alex restrained the back of Rick's head with his other. His balls slapped against Rick's chin as he pounded his dick down Rick's throat. The deliciously warm wetness of Rick's mobile lips around his cock's root and three weeks of abstinence rapidly brought him to climax. The cum stirred in his balls. Reaching up, Rick pinched his nipples then roughly tugged them. Rick's exquisitely executed tit torture tipped him over the edge.

Pitching forward, he held Rick's head in place as his cock spasmed down Rick's throat.

Giving a sigh of relief to be off his knees, Rick got to his feet, running his dribbling mouth over Alex's hairy stomach and chest. Trailing his sticky tongue up Alex's throat and chin, Rick locked lips with him.

Moving from the vanity, Alex spun Rick around to face the full-length mirror. Standing behind him, he had to semi-squat to reach around. He wanked Rick's pulsing erection with his left hand, restraining Rick's balls with his right. "Aw, I hate seeing my hand on your body."

"Never mind how it looks, it feels good," Rick moaned.

Alex pressed his oozing cock into Rick's butt crack as he built up wanking speed. He adored the way Rick's cock felt in his hand, like it had been perfectly fashioned to fit his grip. Letting go of Rick's balls, he brought his hand up to Rick's throat. "What say I make this sexy guy in the mirror cum, huh?" Alex looked at Rick watching himself get masturbated through half-closed eyes. He increased the pressure on Rick's throat, clasping him to his chest. Rick arched his back, bent his knees and, stretching up, laced his hands behind his head. "Shall I make this guy cum, huh?"

"Yeah, babe, make him cum …"

Massaging the mound at the base of Rick's cock, Alex authoritatively wanked him. "Cum, then. Cum …" He made eye contact with Rick's reflected gaze. Rick's body shuddered. His mouth fell open as white liquid spurted from his cock. Once Rick's shivering climax had erupted, Alex gave his spent cock a few more strokes for good measure. With Rick's knees still trembling, he smeared his cum covered hand over Rick's mouth. Rick turned to face him. They kissed again, letting their sticky pubes rub together. Then Rick got down on all fours with a towel to mop any slippery cum off the concrete floor.

Savoring that vision, Alex subtly put his hand to his chest. His heart was still beating. He turned on the shower jets.

Stepping in, Alex wet down his long hair. The steam built up. Rick slid in next to him. They lathered and washed each other with bergamot shower gel.

Fully cleansed and well rinsed, they toweled off before taking up position on their respective sides of the double vanity. Always speedier in his ablutions than Rick, Alex had shaved, slapped on a shot of moisturizer and tied back his damp hair by the time Rick was only beginning his ritual of under-eye cream, concealer and tinted SPF moisturizer. In the master suite's dressing area, Alex donned his painting gear of jersey shorts, loose tank, neckcloth, paint splattered canvas slip-ons and his customary stacked leather wrist bands. Rick was still doing whatever it was he did in the bathroom that always took so long by the time Alex was ready for work.

Going out through the bedroom's sliding glass doors, Alex crossed the red metal bridge straddling the lap pool's mid-point. The bridge saved the fifty-foot walk around either end of the lap pool but, more than convenience, he liked the symbolism of crossing the bridge to get to his studios. The lap pool drew the dividing line between home and work.

Coming down off the bridge into the meditation garden, with its Buddha sculptures, bamboo wind chimes and hammock strung between the palms, Alex noticed Rick had brought Tyler's beanstalk over to this side of the pool and placed it against the tall, frosted window of his studio. Suki was hunched over the Apple Mac with her back to the door. Over the new age music playing through the sound system, she didn't hear him enter. He came up and stared over her shoulder. "What the ...?" He jabbed at the screen. "Zoom in. Top left."

Suki magnified the area he'd indicated on the photograph of a work from his *Red* series.

"What the heck's that?"

"Another of the red oils on loan from Harrison Wilde's got the same issue," said Suki. "MoMA's conservator spotted the damage while they were being unpacked."

"May I?" Alex put on his glasses. Suki moved aside to let him take her seat at the trestle table.

"Hey, nice to see you back," Rick said to Suki as he came in. "How've you been?"

"I moved in with Jess last weekend." Suki shyly stuffed her hands in the pockets of her paint splattered dungarees.

"Congratulations. Now the real fun of living together begins." Rick smiled knowingly at Suki. "Good luck."

Alex swung round on his chair. Peering over his glasses, he saw Rick looking particularly lovely in a white chambray button-down, DKNY dove gray pants and Tod's baby blue driving shoes. "I thought your meeting wasn't until noon?"

Rick fiddled with his watchstrap. "I need to run something by Thaddeus. Bella's asleep in the den. She seemed off this morning. Check in on her if you get a moment." Rick glanced at the Mac's screen. "Everything okay in New York?"

"Loans for the retrospective are arriving." Alex swung back to scroll through more photos.

"Wilde claims the paintings got damaged in transit," said Suki.

"That's not transit damage, look at the position of those bumps." With the full painting filling the screen, Alex pointed out raised areas in the top right and left-hand corners. "They've been hung on screws that weren't set deeply enough into the wall. Those raised areas are where the screw heads have stretched the canvas and cracked the paint."

"What should I tell the museum?" asked Suki.

Alex chewed the arm of his glasses. "Those pieces left my hands over thirty years ago, but for sure those bumps are *not* part of the original artwork. They have to be restored before they can be shown."

"Did Harrison Wilde get a condition report for insurance before they were packed for transit?" asked Rick.

"Apparently not," said Suki,

"That blows out any claim for transit damage then," said Rick. "I suggest the museum gets a quote for the restoration, offer to get the work done in-house and pass the charge back to him. If Wilde doesn't accept that, they return the pieces to him in the same condition they were received."

"Then they won't be in my show. The *Red* series comprises some of my most important work."

"Having them in the exhibition catalogue will increase their value way more than any restoration cost," said Rick. "Wilde will know that."

"When people invest big money in art, you'd think they'd take more care hanging it," said Alex with a sigh.

"At least Wilde had them on his wall. Some investors buy a work and put it straight into climate-controlled storage these days. Poor paintings, kept in the dark without a life. Okay, see you later." Rick patted Alex's shoulder. "Don't overdo it."

"I won't," Alex assured Rick as he left.

Ready to check off the last no-no on his recuperation list, work, Alex snapped on his blue latex gloves then added a pair of black fingerless compression mitts over the top. It wasn't scientifically proven, but he felt the compression gloves reduced swelling and prevented pain in his hands. They also distracted him from seeing his right hand's enlarged finger joints while he worked. He considered the blank boards, freshly gessoed canvases, aluminum sheets restrained by chains and works in progress stacked around the studio's perimeter.

"Could you put that one on the easel for me, Suki?" Alex pointed to an abstract work he'd begun the day before the heart attack. He'd already thrown down some blues and greens. It may not turn out to be a seminal work but making a little eye candy would reawaken his painting muscle memory and get the creative juices flowing.

While Suki was setting up the canvas, he went to the phone. Rehearsing what he was going to say to Chen, his heart skipped a beat. He touched his chest. His heart was fine, he was just nervous. Biting the bullet, Alex tapped his phone.

"Xander Chen," came the clipped man's voice.

"Hey, Xander, Alex Morgan."

"Alex! Great to hear from you. How are you?"

"Good. Back in the studio, business as usual."

"I'm in LA for one week from April twenty. I'll come to your studio. What day's good for you?"

"Um …" Alex hadn't been expecting a studio visit quite so soon.

"That a problem?"

"No. I haven't got my diary up. Can you hold?" Alex opened the Mac's calendar. He wished he had more new work to show, but a few weeks should give him time to finish what he'd started and get new pieces underway. "Does the twenty-sixth work for you?"

"Yes, that morning is good."

"Afternoon's better for me."

"Fine, Ysabel will confirm by email. Great news, the *Vanity Fair*'s interview's firm for June third. We've got an overlap going on in the publicity area. I'd prefer all your interviews and press to go through my gallery."

"Rick has things in hand here —"

"We agreed I'd exclusively represent your work —"

"In New York and Asia," Alex interjected. "Neroli Copley still handles all my primary sales in LA."

Chen fell silent.

"Xander, you still there?"

"A world-renowned museum's about to hold the first major retrospective of your work. Interviews with minor journalists and niche publications are unnecessary. In fact, they could be detrimental to your appeal. My clientele isn't interested in what student art bloggers think about your working methodology, what you ate for breakfast or what side of the bed you sleep on. I want our association to be a positive experience for both of us. But I need to control the way I introduce you, and your work, to new markets to make the greatest impact, give you the greatest cachet and get the best prices for you. Let me know if you have an issue with that so neither one of us wastes our time."

Alex understood where Chen was coming from. "It's okay if I go ahead with any press Rick's already booked, though?"

"If it's booked, okay. But don't let him contact anyone else before running it by Ysabel or me first. See you on the twenty-sixth. I look forward to seeing your new work."

The conversation with Chen played on Alex's mind as he squeezed acrylic paint onto his palette. He mixed Process Yellow and Hooker's Green with a palette knife then used the knife to hang paint on the canvas. Working with linear strokes, blocks of color formed. The squares pleased him. He squeezed out Cadmium Red Deep. Years of working his art had given him an instinctive feel for color and value, he knew the classical rules but wasn't a slave to them, sometimes even putting the subject in the middle of the composition. As he did now, placing a bold red square dead center. Willing himself to concentrate solely on work, he tried to stop his mind straying to practical matters. Applying a thick swathe of green, he tried not to think about the best way to speak to Manuela's son about her retirement and potential medical care. Changing to a flat brush loaded with red, he stopped himself rehearsing how to tell Rick to back off from organizing his public appearances and interviews. Picking up a hefty amount of yellow on his knife, he dispelled all thoughts of removing Danielle's earthly possessions from the small house once and for all. And just at the moment he'd banished all aberrant thoughts and entered the world where no other relationship existed other than between himself and his creation, a bright flash exploded inside his right eye. Dropping the palette knife, he clapped his hand to his face.

Hearing the knife hit the floor, Suki turned from the Mac. "Careful, Alex! You got paint on your hand." She snatched a clean rag from the table and rushed to him.

Peeling off the two layers of gloves, Alex tossed them aside to take the rag.

"Let me do it. Don't rub paint in your eyes."

Alex lowered his head to let Suki remove his glasses. Closing his eyes, he felt her wipe his cheek and temple. When she'd done, he opened his eyes. An odd waterfall rippling shimmered in his right field of vision. He looked around, hoping that moving his eyes would clear it. A sudden shock gripped his heart. A slim woman's shadow fell across the tall window's milky glass. She raised a finger. He heard her tap on the window. Although the frosted glass removed all detail, he instantly recognized her. "It's Danielle! She's at the window!"

Startled, Suki turned to the window then said, "Alex, there's nobody there."

Blinking repeatedly, Alex looked at the window again. Danielle had gone, replaced by the shadow of the Moreton Bay Chestnut. The wind was tapping its leaves against the window. Danielle's phantom appearance had set his heart racing. He felt faint. "I need to go back to the house."

"Do you want me to come with you?" Suki cleaned a smear of red paint from his right eyeglass lens.

"No. I must've overdone it in the pool. Guess I'm not Superman after all." Leaving Suki to get on with answering emails and other office duties, Alex crossed the bridge over the lap pool. In the kitchen, he filled a tumbler with mineral water. As he drank, he took in as much visual detail as he could to reassure himself his eyesight was functioning normally. The rippling had gone. Although blurry, he could make out the small chips of black marble, brown quartz and copper glass in the terrazzo floor, the red tulips in the green stained-glass window, and scattered beetroot and pineapple peelings around the sink. He rinsed his tumbler, swept the peelings into the sink, picked some scraps up off the floor and flushed them all down the disposal. He wiped the counter tops. The last thing he needed was Rick finding fault with Manuela the second he walked in.

Relieved that the visual disturbance was a fleeting event, Alex was on his way back to the studio when he came across Bella in an odd position. Her head was low, forward and she was panting. "What's up, girl?" Getting down to pet her, he spotted an unpleasant mound of vomit on the ecru rug. Dark red streaks in it resembled blood. He hurried back to the kitchen for some paper towels to clean up the mess before it stained the rug. Throwing up hadn't helped Bella feel better, he could see she was still distressed.

Rick was the voice of reason in domestic emergencies and always knew exactly what to do. After scooping up the vomit and dumping it down the garbage disposal, Alex washed his hands, picked up his phone and hit Rick's number.

The call went straight to voicemail.

Alex checked the kitchen clock. Eleven-thirty. He tried Rick's number again. Again, Rick's voicemail picked up. Waiting a couple of minutes, Alex gave it one last shot. He left a message when Rick's voicemail picked up this time.

Now he wasn't only worried about Bella, he was also concerned why Rick's phone wasn't on. Since the Board meeting wasn't till noon, Alex called the museum.

"Los Angeles Conservatory of Modern Art. How may I direct your call?"

"I'm trying to get hold of Rick Stradman. He's attending the trustees meeting."

"May I ask who's calling?"

"Alex Morgan."

"Mr. Morgan! Hi, how are you? This is Otavia."

"Hey, Otavia, I didn't recognize your voice. Good thanks. I've got a situation at the house and can't get through to Rick's cell. Can you track him down or put a call out for him?"

"Sure, let me put you on hold while I find which room's booked for the meeting."

Hearing Bella whimper, Alex went back into the hallway. The dog was in obvious discomfort. She retched. Brown foam dribbled from her mouth.

"Mr. Morgan, apologies for keeping you," said Otavia over the phone. "I checked the system. No Board meetings are scheduled today. Do you think Mr. Stradman could've got his days mixed up?"

"Maybe. Could you leave word that if anyone sees him, they'll have him call me back?"

"Of course. Have a great day, Mr. Morgan!"

He hung up.

Wherever Rick was it wasn't where he said he was going to be, and Alex had a sick dog on his hands who needed urgent treatment.

MISINTERPRETATION

Manuela dipped the sponge in a bucket of soapy water.

Alex checked his phone. Nothing. He hit Rick's name. "Did Bella eat anything from the trash?"

"Not that I see." Manuela scrubbed the stain on the rug.

Bella lay on the hardwood, her ribs trembling with shallow breaths.

"Rick, I need you!" Alex spat into the phone as voicemail picked up yet again.

"What did the vet say?" Manuela blotted the rug with a white towel.

"Just to bring her in as an emergency if she didn't improve." Although he could see okay now, the sudden distortion of his vision and disorientation which followed concerned him. Alex debated on asking Suki to give him a ride to the animal hospital. She came to work on her motorbike, so using her vehicle was out of the question. Rick had taken the Prius, which meant they'd need to take the SUV. Suki would do anything to help but asking her to drive a large, unfamiliar vehicle would be unfair. She performed enough tasks above and beyond the call of duty without chauffeuring him around too.

Going to the study, Alex did a quick internet search. There was another animal hospital not too far away, but Bella wasn't up to walking and he wasn't up to carrying her. He figured he'd have to call a cab. His heart thumped. What if he was with Bella at the clinic, fell sick and wasn't able to look after her? Not being able to contact Rick meant there'd be no-one to come to his rescue either. A thought struck him. Scrolling through his contacts, he hit call and got an immediate pick up. "Hey, Ty!"

"Uncle Al, you okay?"

"I'm fine but Bella's sick. Sorry to bug you at work, but Rick's out and not answering his phone. The clinic told me to bring her in, but I had this weird flash go off in my eye. It's cleared, but I'm worried about driving in case it happens again. Any chance you're this side of the hills and could help me out with a ride?"

Tyler hesitated.

"Look, I'm sorry. I shouldn't have disturbed you at work. Maybe I overdid it in the pool. It's my first day back in the studio and then this happens ... and I'm stressing. I've got no idea where Rick is, and I guess ... well, I guess I'm panicking ..." Alex stopped himself from babbling. "Don't worry. I'll call a cab or —"

"Uncle Al, I hear you. Give me five and let me get back."

Alex kneeled beside Bella and stroked her ear. "You think she picked up something in the yard?"

"You know Missy Bella, she eat anything." Manuela finished blotting the rug. Leaning on her knee to stand, she picked up the bucket with a sigh.

Alex's phone buzzed. He hoped it was Rick finally calling back. Opening the screen, he saw it was Tyler.

"Sergio can get along without me for a few hours. I'm in the Palisades. Be with you in twenty."

"You're a lifesaver. Thanks." Relieved that the cavalry was on its way, Alex dashed to the walk-in. He peeled off his painting togs, untied his hair then pulled on blue jeans and an Aztec print shirt. Glimpsing himself in the mirror, the shirt's upbeat vibe didn't sit well with the occasion. He swapped it for a taupe waffle knit Henley. Stuffing his feet into a pair of McQueen trainers with green neon laces, he checked there was cash as well as plastic in his Prada wallet and shoved it in his back pocket. He crossed the bridge to the studio. "I gotta take Bella to the animal clinic. You cool holding the fort?"

"May I put you on hold?" Suki covered the phone's mouthpiece. "No problem. You feel okay now?"

"It was nothing. Guess I'm adjusting to the new meds."

Suki tapped the phone. "I'm speaking to MoMA about the Wilde pieces. Kent called. He heard Jerry Weir's leaving The Copley Gallery for Hauser and Wirth."

"Wow, Jerry's been with Neroli longer than I have. Some parting of the ways." Neroli Copley had been the dealer for many of LA's most highly respected artists over the last two decades. She'd discovered and nurtured new talent as well as represented some of the biggest established names in town. She'd lost a slew of her star players recently, either defecting in search of higher selling prices or poached by the mega-dealers with their fat Rolodexes of high-end buyers. Neroli had been a loyal supporter of Alex's over the years. But when Xander Chen came knocking at his door, he'd gone with Chen for exactly that reason … more money.

"Kent asked if you need him this month," Suki said.

"I'll let him know tomorrow." Turning to leave, one of the metal panels stacked in front of the windows at the far end of the studio caught Alex's eye. Through the holes drilled in its top, used for the chains to restrain it to an overhead girder, points of light punctuated its dark solidity. The rainbow halos flaring from the dots transfixed him. The manner in which light reflected from his work fascinated him, but he'd never thought to play with light coming from *behind* his work before. "Suki, I have an idea. When you finish that call, could you source some surfaces?" He quickly outlined different weights of paper and card stock. "And research hardware. Tools that puncture, like a bullet ripped through. Brutal, explosive. A nail gun, something like that?" Suki took his instruction without questions.

Back in the house, Bella lay prone across the entrance door. Her collar was still on from her morning walk. Alex grabbed her leash off the hook. Stepping over her, he opened up the double doors between the main house and the small house. Crossing the vehicle parking space, he hit the green button to raise the roller gate. Halfway up, he ducked under it and hung out on the sidewalk. As soon as Tyler's truck turned the corner, he went to rouse Bella. She was reluctant to move, so he creakily bent to lift her.

Tyler, in camo shorts, khaki bush shirt and muddy work boots, stood poised for action beside his dusty pickup.

"Ty, can you hold her while I close up the house?" Tyler tenderly held Bella while Alex locked the inner doors and lowered the outer gate. As the metal roller clanked down, Alex opened the passenger door of Tyler's truck. "Let me get in, then pass her up."

Being super careful of how he handled her, and speaking reassuringly as he did, Tyler placed Bella on Alex's knees. Safely in, Tyler hurried around and jumped in. Careful not to slam his door, Tyler asked, "Where'd you need me to go?"

"Get onto Venice Boulevard. I'll tell you where to stop." They hadn't gone far before Alex's phone buzzed. Wriggling Bella around, he dug it out. Rick's name came up. "I've been trying to reach you for over an hour!"

"I just opened my phone and saw all the missed calls," Rick said breathlessly. "What's up? You sick?"

"Not me. Bella. Why weren't you answering?"

"Um, I put my phone on silent cause I didn't want to get distracted talking to Thaddeus. Then I put it in my bag and went straight into the Board meeting. And the meeting was real tense, so I —"

"I called the museum and asked the admin desk to page you." Alex's voice cracked. "Otavia told me no Board meetings were scheduled for today. What the fuck are you playing at?"

"Calm down, darling. The doctor warned you about getting tense."

"Well, *darling*, I wouldn't be fucking tense if you'd been where you said you were going to be, and I hadn't been left to deal with a sick dog!"

"How sick is she?" asked Rick.

"Looks like she's been throwing up blood, so I'd say pretty sick."

"I'm on my way home. I'll take her to the clinic and —"

"Too late. We're on our way. Ty's taking us."

"Tyler? What's he doing with you?"

Alex hesitated. Mentioning his eye issue would only lead to Rick berating him for not resting up longer or hounding him to put himself through endless medical consultations and investigations which he hadn't got time for. And since it seemed only a temporary glitch, he fudged. "I haven't been out for three weeks and thought I should have someone come with me. When I couldn't get hold of you, I called Ty."

"Sounds like you two have everything under control then," said Rick icily. "I'll meet you at the clinic."

"Fine." Alex tersely ended the call.

"Everything okay?" Tyler asked, warily negotiating Venice Boulevard's traffic.

"Miscommunication." Alex fell silent. He'd harbored the suspicion something was up with Rick for a while. Had other Board meetings and Conservatory business also been fictions? Rick was fit, agile and several years younger than himself. Was being saddled with an old man with creaking joints turning into a drag? Was Rick having an affair? Why else would he lie about his whereabouts? Fears multiplied and fermented in Alex's gut. Missing their easy banter, Tyler attempted to instigate conversation… without success. "This is it," snapped Alex. "Pull in when you see a space."

Slowing past a thrift shop, cycle repair shop and pet food store, Tyler nabbed a spot directly out front of the clinic. Tyler swung his long legs down from the truck and opened Alex's door. "I'll take her. Come Bella, there's my good girl." Tyler cradled the dog.

Alex clambered down and reached out to take Bella.

"It's fine, Al. I got her." Tyler carried the dog inside.

Alex fumbled in his wallet, fed the meter then followed Tyler into the clinic.

"Aw, poor baby, you do look sick ..." The lady on the front desk was stroking Bella's head.

"Hey, sorry. Here now." Alex outlined the details of how he'd found Bella. While checking Bella in, the lady on the front desk called for a vet tech who was at their side almost immediately. Priscilla, the vet tech, a sweet-faced, rotund young woman in teal scrubs, ran through a bunch of questions. However, he couldn't identify any particular substance Bella may have eaten or come into contact with which could have had this effect.

"She was licking my hand last night," Tyler told Priscilla. "I hope there wasn't anything on it that could've hurt her."

"Like?" Priscilla asked.

"I do landscape maintenance and arboreal work. I handle fertilizer and stuff."

"Even if you did, I doubt it'd be enough to make her so sick. But I'll pass that on to the doctor." Priscilla smiled sympathetically at Tyler then said to Alex, "It's good that your son mentioned it. Every detail helps."

There was no doubt Tyler's style - the long hair, laid back manner, latter-day hippie vibe - did mirror his own. And Tyler's age made it possible he could be his son ... his son ... shit, today's emotions were not doing his heart any good at all. "He's not my son." Alex's throat tightened. "Family friend."

"Sorry, I just thought, er ... we need to get some fluids in Bella. I'll call you through when the doctor's ready." Summoning a nurse to assist her, Priscilla took the dog.

Watching Bella disappear through the double doors to the treatment area brought another lump to Alex's throat. "I'm good from here on in," he said to Tyler. In the waiting area, a variety of dogs, cats and something in a shoebox with holes in it sat with their human guardians on blue plastic chairs.

"Bye, dad." Tyler gave Alex a lopsided grin.

"Suppose I should be grateful she didn't think I was your grandfather." Alex patted Tyler's arm. "Get back to work. Rick's on his way, he can take us home." He stopped himself from considering the possibility they may not be taking Bella home. Perhaps Tyler was thinking the same thing, for his green-gold eyes took on a distant, faraway look, as if he was struggling to focus. "Appreciate your help."

"Glad to." Tyler enveloped Alex in a bone crushing man hug, oblivious to animals and humans in the vicinity.

Getting his breath back, Alex waved through the window as Tyler jumped up into his truck. As Tyler pulled out, a passing vehicle blared its horn. Tyler clearly hadn't checked his mirrors. Alex wondered if erratic driving was genetically inherited in the Stradman clan. Finding a vacant blue seat, he sat down, fretting about all the work he should be getting on with rather than observing Venice Boulevard's comings and goings. Fifteen minutes later, Rick strode past the windows.

Making a sweeping soap opera style entrance through the clinic's front doors, Rick whipped off his dark glasses. "Where is she?"

Alex was still so mad at Rick for lying about the meeting, yet so relieved he was safe and here to support him, he couldn't immediately speak. After swallowing a few times, he managed to say, "They've taken her through."

"What happened?" Rick sat on a blue plastic chair.

"I went into the house and saw she'd thrown up on the rug. And I mean majorly thrown up."

"She'd vomited?"

"It's what I said, isn't it?"

The straggle-haired lady cradling a cat carrier opposite them shifted uncomfortably.

"What was it like?" Rick asked with incisive eyes.

"What was what like?"

"The vomit."

"Like vomit."

"Duh, but was it chunky? Was it granular? Was there identifiable food in it? Was it fluid?"

"I saw red in it. It looked like blood."

"What shade of red? Bright red like arterial blood, or maroon like dried blood? Was it reddish brown and gritty like coffee grounds? Are you certain it was blood?"

"Oh, for fuck's sake! Forgive me for not calling in *CSI* and getting Marg Helgenberger to come shine her blacklight on it. Bella had thrown up. I thought there was blood in it."

"Ah, so the blood's a possibility rather than fact." Letting a couple of beats pass, Rick asked, "Did you bring some?"

"Some what?"

"Vomit."

"Seriously?" Alex shook his head in bewilderment.

"You could have scooped some of it into a plastic container, the ones we keep under the sink. If you'd brought it along then we'd know for sure if —"

"Your procedural advice comes a tad too late! If you'd been answering your phone, you could've dazzled me with your encyclopedic knowledge of dog vomit when I needed it! I did my best under the circumstances. And I could really do without this stress while I'm trying to get back to work."

Folding his arms across his chest, Rick slumped in the chair. "I know you're upset but don't take it out on me. It's not my fault Bella got sick."

"Lying about where you were this morning's your fault," Alex snarled. "And that has seriously fucking upset me."

"Guys, please control your rage," hissed a woman.

Alex looked up to see the straggle-haired lady, wearing a pink corduroy pinafore dress and pink clogs with white ankle socks, bend towards them.

"Your auras are distressing Molly." The woman poked her finger in the cat carrier to comfort the runny-eyed tortoiseshell peering through the grille.

Rick proffered his palm in apology and muttered to Alex, "Cool it. You're upsetting the cat."

"I don't give a fuck about —"

"Bella Stradman?" Another nurse in teal scrubs, with paperwork in her hand, looked into the waiting area.

"That's us." Rick jumped up.

"Come through ..."

They followed the nurse into the consulting room. Bella was on the black examination table, an IV drip under a bandage attached to her front leg. Alex stroked her paw, knowing only too well what being hooked up to one of those felt like. Bella's tail flapped at his touch. Alex and Rick, responsible and concerned dog parents, stood over their animal as Dr. Amira questioned them about Bella's habits and any other symptoms. She asked if bloody diarrhea had accompanied the vomiting. Rick said her morning poop had appeared normal. Dr. Amira palpated Bella's stomach, which made her whimper. Unable to find any immediate indication of blockages, the doctor explained that the vet technicians had been rehydrating Bella with fluids. With Rick and Alex now present to reassure their dog, Dr. Amira shaved a patch on Bella's neck and drew blood. Alex's head swam as he watched the syringe fill with sticky red liquid. Looking away, he hoped the dizziness would pass. Dr. Amira sent them back outside while she took x-rays.

Alex and Rick waited with folded arms and tight lips, holding their tongues to avoid upsetting sensitive cats. After an hour of checking their phones and trying to get comfortable on the hard seats, the doctor summoned them to the consulting room.

Priscilla, the vet tech, returned Bella to their care. On seeing them, Bella shakily padded to Rick and nuzzled her head into his knee.

"So, what's wrong with her?" Alex asked Dr. Amira.

"The x-rays didn't reveal anything conclusive," said Dr. Amira. "The most likely cause is an allergic or toxic reaction to something she ingested. It could also be an infection or virus."

"Could it be cancer?" Rick asked.

"It's a possibility. I'll call you tomorrow with the bloodwork. Depending on those results we can decide on further investigation. She's had an anti-biotic shot and the front desk will give you more rehydration sachets and meds. Stress can upset their digestion." The doctor switched her focus between Alex and Rick's stormy expressions. "Animals do pick up on tension in the home."

They collected Bella's meds and instructions on how to administer them from a nurse at the front desk. Rick, after momentarily widening his eyes at amount of the bill, settled their account with his credit card. Rick placed Bella on the Prius' rear seat. Alex sat in back with her. Rick drove them home in stony silence. Never fond of being a passenger with Rick at the wheel, he resisted pointing out pedestrians and cyclists behaving randomly so as not to be accused of literally being a backseat driver.

It was late afternoon when they got back to the house. Having spread a blanket on the chaise in the den and settled Bella on it, Rick and Alex faced off in the living room.

Alex released his pent-up frustration. "You seriously pissed me off today!"

"I didn't mean to —"

"What? You didn't mean to lie about the Board meeting? And then have the gall to keep on trying to lie your way out of it when I finally do get hold of you. What's the fuck's going on?"

"There's an issue I need to deal with. I didn't want to stress you out with it too."

"Stop the presses, that didn't work! I'm currently incredibly stressed!"

"Cool it, Al. And don't you yell at me." Rick tipped his head towards Bella, who was resting her face between her paws and watching them from the den with soulful brown eyes.

With a fake smile, Alex continued sweetly, "Where the fuck were you today, darling?"

"When I tell you, promise me you'll stay calm."

Alex laughed bitterly. "I make no guarantees."

"I was at a doctor's appointment in Brentwood."

"A doctor?" A list of terminal illnesses rattled through Alex's head.

"When I say doctor, he's more like a therapist." Rick dropped his eyes.

"And why couldn't you be honest with me about that?"

"One of the multitude of questions I'm grappling with. I truly regret how today went down. I'm sorry I wasn't here to help and I'm sorry I worried you." Chewing his lip, Rick held back tears. "Now could you please stop being so mad at me?" Rick went to the kitchen.

Taking a moment to recalibrate, Alex followed.

Having pulled out the gold dome stopper, Rick poured the last of a bottle of chardonnay. "You're sure Bella didn't eat anything from the trash?"

"The lid was down so I don't see how she could."

"And Manuela hadn't left anything out on the counters or stove top?"

"No. Did Bella pick anything up on your morning walk?"

"Uh huh." A thought struck Rick. Finishing his wine, he pressed the trash can's foot pedal and poked through the tub.

"I told you the lid was down."

"I'm trying to figure out what Bella might have eaten to upset her stomach and make her vomit red. I was wondering what Manuela had done with the beetroot and pineapple shavings. I don't know if either of them's toxic to dogs, but beetroot would account for the dark red color if she'd eaten any." Rick let the trash can's lid drop back down. "Manuela must've put them down the disposal. That rules that out."

Alex recalled the scattered vegetable and fruit peelings around the sink, the trimmings and scraps *he'd* flushed down the disposal. Had Bella reached her head up to the counter and filched some of them? The last thing he needed was an in-depth investigation into Manuela's competence right now, so he refrained from mentioning it.

Opening the fridge, Rick got a fresh bottle of wine. "Oh good, Manuela's fixed dinner." He removed a rectangular casserole covered with plastic wrap.

Alex rubbed Rick's neck as he opened the bottle. "C'mon. Let's take this outside."

Checking in on Bella as they passed through the living room, they crossed the bridge to the meditation garden. Rick reclined on the rattan lounger with tropical print cushions. The bamboo chimes' hollow clang blended with the soft clatter of palm fronds in the breeze.

"You're seeing a therapist then." Alex sat on a wicker chair. "Is this something to do with me?"

"That's exactly why I didn't tell you where I was going. No. This is all about me."

"Has it been going on for a while?"

"Today was my first session."

"Are you unhappy?"

"Not unhappy, more unsettled. Kind of lost. I don't know where I fit in the world anymore."

"What do you mean? You're not lost. You're here with me."

Rick topped up his wine.

"Go on, give me one." Alex tipped his water on the lawn and held out his glass.

"You shouldn't." Rick poured the wine for him anyway. "Maybe 'where' is the wrong word. More like 'why.' I mean, what's my role in life? Back in Venice I was the Ca' dei Venti's gallery director. I controlled our family's interests all over Italy. I made decisions. I took chances. I brokered deals. And I cannot begin to tell you the stress that put me under. Especially when I started divesting assets and tried bringing partners on board to make some financial sense of momma's empire. Boy, the grief I got from all sides on that, especially from her."

"That's why I never thought you'd had to give up anything to come back to me. You told me you were burned out and ready to quit doing what you were doing in Italy anyhow."

"But even though I was stressed out, I had a function." Flopping his head on the recliner, Rick stared at the thickening clouds. "If I'd quit the family business but stayed in Italy, momma would have dealt with it. She'd have been hurt and angry but would have forgiven me in time. But because I quit and instantly left Italy to come live here with you, that devastated her. You know how momma is. Everything's a war. In her eyes you're the invader, she's the ravaged country and I'm the spoils of war. She can't so much as hear your name without vowing to launch a nuclear warhead in your direction. It's insanity. Why should choosing to be with the man I love mean losing my mother?"

"It's not like she's cut you off entirely. You still talk to her on the phone and go visit."

"She hasn't taken my calls for months. And the last time I went home was two years ago and it was beyond depressing. Not the place, I love Venice and of course I loved seeing Patti, but how can I have any kind of relationship with momma when I can't talk about my life with you? I need to act like you don't exist to maintain any semblance of peace with her. And I got lonely over there without you. You'd love Venice, I can't believe you've never been."

"I've never vibed with Europe and the feeling's mutual. My work rarely sells there, and I barely feature in any of their big-name museums or collections. I always had the suspicion your mother threatened to put a hit on anyone in the European art world who got behind me." Alex was expecting Rick to refute this suggestion, but he didn't. "Nothing in the world would get me in the same city as Luisa D'Onofrio. No, not even in the same country as the old witch."

"See?" Rick topped up his glass. "And how do you think that makes me feel?"

"I've never had a beef with Luisa. She started the war. Why can't she just accept you're gay and get over it?"

"I don't think the gay thing's even a part of it anymore. Those years in the eighties, the time she and I were constantly traveling to discover new work and open new galleries, was the happiest time of her life. We went everywhere together. People sometimes mistook us for a married couple."

"Now I know what I'm gonna have nightmares about tonight."

Rick laughed. "When momma's happy she's lovely. She's funny and vivacious and so glamorous. I wish you could see that side of her, it's like being at a non-stop party. When she's that way she attracts people like moths to a flame."

"We know how that ends for the moths."

"Don't be mean. I've lost that side of momma, and I miss it. I guess I'm experiencing a kind of grief." Rick scratched his cheek and sighed. "And, if I'm being brutally honest, I miss the money. That's another part of herself momma cut off from me."

"You didn't get palazzos and country estates, you still walked away with a sizeable pay-off."

"My pay-off was sizeable, but with donations to keep my place on the Conservatory Board, charity galas and general maintenance of my aging face, body and now mind, my money's been only going in one direction for the past seven years and that's out. And I like to pay my way around here."

"Quit worrying about money. My work's always sold well on the West Coast. And Xander Chen's going to open up New York and Asia for me. There's a big opportunity for me, but to make the most of it I need to work. If I don't make art, Chen's got nothing to sell. Maybe this isn't the best time to bring this up, but I spoke with him this morning. He wants to handle all my publicity in the run up to MoMA. To make sure there's no crossover he asked, very nicely, that you not book anything else in for me."

"And that's okay by you?"

"It's only for the next few months. I need to keep Chen on side. And you dedicate too much time to my career as it is. I'm grateful, but you should be putting energy into yours. Maybe you could join an acting workshop or a local theater?"

"Or do Cristina's TV show."

"I was talking about honing your craft."

"You just told me to spend less of my time looking after you and do something for myself. I know you don't like the sound of the show, but it'd be a new direction for me."

Alex realized he'd talked himself into a corner on this. "Whatever's best for you."

Falling dusk tripped the sensor which brought the twinkling strings of fairy lights wound around the trees to life. Rick nudged the hammock and left it swinging as he came to kneel at Alex's feet. "I wish we could go back to the beach house at Sunset Cove. It was all so simple back then."

"Things were never simple between us." Alex smiled and stroked Rick's head.

Rick gave a half-smile in response.

As they crossed the red metal bridge back to the house, the entry phone buzzed. Rather than go in to answer it, Rick put down the empty bottle and glasses on the patio table and opened up the pool door. He poked his head out into the street to see who was there. "Ty, what're you doing here?"

Hearing it was Tyler, Alex waited by the pool house.

"I was worried about Bella, is she okay?" Tyler asked as he entered.

"They treated her and ran some tests," Alex told him. "She's back home and asleep now."

The tap of claws on tile meant Bella was no longer asleep but coming out to see who'd mentioned her name. Upon seeing Tyler, she dropped her head and gamely wagged her curly golden tail as she padded to him.

"She must be feeling better," said Alex with relief.

"I got talking to Sergio about plants and pets," said Tyler. "Moreton Bay Chestnut seeds are toxic for dogs. It's played on my mind all afternoon. That's the tree I brought for you yesterday." Tyler looked around. "Where is it?"

"I moved it across the pool. I didn't see any seeds," said Rick.

"Knowing the way you eat," said Tyler ruffling Bella's curly head, "I'd rather not risk it."

"Do you think that's what made her sick?" Alex asked Rick as Tyler went over the bridge to fetch the plant.

"Maybe ..."

"Okay guys, see you next week," Tyler said from behind the plant's leaves. "Glad Bella's okay." As Tyler was ducking to maneuver the plant through the doorway onto the street, he yelled, "Uncle Al! How's your eye? That crazy vision shit gone now?"

Alex kicked himself for not telling Tyler to keep his mouth shut about that. "Fine. Must have overdone it in the pool!"

"Great. Bye, Ricky!" Tyler bellowed from the street.

In the kitchen, they heard Tyler's truck start up and set off. "What happened to your eye?" Rick casually asked as he diluted Bella's rehydration powder.

"Nothing. Just some weird pop of light in my right eye."

"You told Tyler about it but not me?"

"I know how you obsess over that kind of shit."

Rick heated up the oven and peeled the plastic film from the casserole. "Call the doctor first thing tomorrow. Maybe you should go straight to an eye specialist or —"

"It passed. I lost a whole day of work today. If it happens again, I'll go see someone."

"Up to you."

In the twilight of the living-room, Alex sat listening to Rick prepare dinner and talk to Bella, her claws pattering around the kitchen floor. His little family was home and safe. Then his thoughts drifted to Luisa. He understood Rick's feelings about his mother but was nonetheless relieved that she was out of their orbit and hoped it stayed that way.

    Alex had no taste for fighting, but as long as Luisa was alive the outbreak of another war was always a possibility.

LAYERS

    Building up his laps in the pool each day, Alex felt stronger. He wasn't back to one hundred but managed sixty comfortably. He'd completed three medium size abstracts and the two epic canvases. He'd also been slapping bold washes of color over sheets of lightweight paper. Suki was layering these colored papers onto frames for him to experiment with the idea bubbling in his head.

    Fresh from his post-pool shower, Alex was sitting on their unmade bed toweling his hair when Rick strode in and stood before him. Rick had teamed his ecru pants with a super-tight cranberry merino crewneck which exposed three inches of bare midriff.

    Attempting to pull the sweater's cuffs down to his wrists, Rick let out an exasperated sigh. "I mean, just look!" He spread his arms to model the full effect of the three-quarter length sleeves.

    "Overnight growth spurt?"

    "I'm not big, it's my knitwear that got small!" Rick peeled off the sweater. "I've asked Manuela a million times not to put woolens in the dryer. Cristina, Ellery and Augusta are coming for lunch to celebrate Cristina's appointment to the Board. They'll look like a million dollars and I'll be Raggedy Andy." Rick stomped back to the walk-in.

    "You've plenty more to choose from. And I do mean plenty …" muttered Alex.

    "I hear you!" Rick shouted from the walk-in.

    Alex grabbed his glasses and opened the nightstand's drawer. He dug out the nail clippers. Putting on his glasses and tucking his damp hair behind his ear, he went to cross his right foot over his left knee. His hip wasn't flexible enough. Taking a different tack, he pulled up his right knee but couldn't bend it sufficiently to reach his big toe. "Babe! Need your help."

"If the weather turns chilly Bella can wear it." Rick came back, screwing the shrunken sweater into a ball. He'd changed into a lagoon-blue cotton mock turtle. "What?"

"Can you trim my toenails? My hips aren't loose enough to do it myself."

Taking the clippers, Rick got down on the floor. He looked at Alex's feet. "I've not seen toenails like these since Howard Hughes."

"Less comedy more clipping."

Rick rolled the ottoman from the Eames chair to the bed. Sitting down, he patted his knee. "Right foot."

Alex placed his foot on Rick's knee. Feeling Rick catch his flesh with the clippers he said, a little too brusquely, "Not too short!" From working as a lifeguard, he'd learned the hard way how easily an exposed nail bed can get infected. Because his RA meds suppressed his immune system, he was always super careful about eliminating such risks.

"You've got nice feet. Some men's feet can be so …" Rick turned down the corners of his mouth and shuddered.

"I'm not thrilled about how hairy my toes are getting."

"Other one." Rick dropped Alex's right foot, picked up his left and went back to work. "Not overly hairy, though. You've got long toes. If they were stubby, you'd definitely be in Hobbit territory."

"Something I should be grateful for then."

"Done." Patting Alex's foot, Rick pushed the ottoman back to the Eames chair.

"Thanks." Alex rose to get dressed.

"Wait! Don't move." Rick scrutinized Alex's body from the ankles up. "Take off that towel."

Dropping it, Alex stood naked as Rick traced his fingers over his shoulders and back. "Appreciate the sentiment, but I haven't got time for —"

"I wasn't thinking of that! I'm checking for pre-cancerous lesions."

"Lovely. And?"

"I see something on your cheek." Rick leaned in.

Concerned, Alex moved his face closer. "What?"

"My lips." Rick planted a smacker on Alex's cheek then left to hang the damp towel in the master bath.

Smiling about Rick's funny ways, Alex went to the walk-in. It bothered him that Rick hadn't felt that he could be honest about seeing a therapist, nonetheless he was proud of him for seeking professional help. Sid's confession of Rick's suicide attempts in his troubled youth always lingered at the back of his mind. Fearing the young man climbing the crumbling cliffs of Sunset Cove was a potential jumper was the reason he'd met Rick in the first place. He always wondered if his lifeguard brain, the one programed to rescue with no regard for his own safety, had kicked in that day. Was it that instinct which propelled him to abandon his jog in the surf to climb barefoot over rocks and saltbush to help a young man in potential jeopardy? Rick always insisted he'd ventured up the cliffs in search of a quiet place to admire the view. Alex wasn't convinced. He'd found Rick on the edge of a sheer drop to the rocks below, a perilous location to enjoy a view. How different their lives would be if he'd looked the other way that spring morning in 1974. Would Rick have jumped if he hadn't gone up after him? Whatever the motivation, their life together had been forged by that decision. Grinning about Rick's silly sweetness, Alex steadied himself on a shelf to step into a pair of drawstring hemp pants.

"I'm not nagging, but you will speak with Manuela's son, won't you?"

Pulling on a madras shirt over his head, Alex found Rick watching him from the dressing area. "That sounded like nagging. I'm sure your sweater going in the dryer was an accident. Buy some new ones. My treat." Alex swept his fingers through his hair before tying it back with an elastic off his wrist.

"I don't believe Bella getting sick had anything to do with Tyler's plant. I'm sure Manuela left something out in the kitchen. And what about the night I found her wandering in the street with all our doors wide open? I'm concerned about Manuela's well-being, but I'm also concerned about ours."

"I have to find the best way of broaching her retirement with Jorge. I'll deal with it, okay?" Sensing Rick wanted to push it further, Alex adopted his stern face, slid back the glass door and went outside.

Knowing a line had been drawn in the sand, Rick changed the subject. "*LA Art Quarterly*'s here tomorrow. Now, I'm not interfering, but you should do the interview in the showroom. Your main studio's got too many visual distractions. Are those giant abstracts ready to hang? They'd make a terrific statement with you sitting in front of one of them."

"They're finished but need stretching." These canvases were so large he'd had to spread them on the floor and use squeegees and brushes attached to poles to paint them. He was pleased with the dreamlike orange, peach and yellow swirls, with a bold crimson circle on one of the oversized pieces. Rick was correct, new work on such scale would look dramatic and be a good distraction. He dreaded having his photo taken. "If Kent built a frame this morning, we could stretch one this afternoon. That canvas is a beast, but me and Kent should be able to manage it between us."

"Don't push yourself too hard." Rick wagged his finger. "If you need more hands on deck, give me a shout."

"Gonna bring the girls over to help? Like *The First Wives Club* meets the barn raising in *Witness*?"

"Or you could see if Cayde's around."

"That sounds more plausible." Alex started crossing the bridge, pretending not to notice the construction noise coming from the lot behind when they heard Manuela shout.

"Mr. Rick!" Manuela stuck her head out of the living room door. "The vacuum is not sucking. I think is broken!"

"I'll come take a look!" Shooting a jaundiced eye-roll in Alex's direction, Rick followed Manuela into the house.

Entering the sanctuary of his studio, Alex was relieved to be out the line of fire in any domestic skirmishes. "Morning all."

The staple gun's percussive pops halted as Suki looked up. "Hi."

"Hey, Kent!" Alex yelled. The preppy young black guy hammering wedges in the corners of a freshly stretched blank canvas laid down his mallet, popped out an Earbud and raised his hand in greeting. Suki went back to stapling colored papers over a frame as Alex threaded his way through trolleys laden with brushes, palette knives and pots dripping with turquoise, violet, and yellow vinyl pigments. "You feeling strong?"

Kent rested his hand on the frame. "How strong d'you need me to feel?"

Alex gestured to the giant canvases rolled up on the floor. "*That* strong. I'd like to get one of those hung in the showroom for tomorrow. You up to building a frame?"

"We got the wood, and I ate my Frosties this morning. I can handle it." Kent began selecting lengths of timber, high quality and moisture-resistant wood to prevent warping.

"There's a piece of carpeting up in the showroom, isn't there, Suki?"

"You want me to go up and check?"

"Yeah. And take up the heat-gun and a couple of staplers while you're at it." Alex had designed the multi-vehicle garage block with the intention of using its double-height studio on the second floor as his principal workspace. A compact kitchen and bathroom also were on this level. The top floor housed a roof terrace from which you could see the ocean. The practical aspect that he hadn't taken into consideration on the drawing board was the logistics of getting equipment up to the studio. He thought the external staircase's zigzag design in concrete would look sculptural and cool. It did. But moving materials up and down it was a pain. And on days when his knees ached, the stairs were a literal pain too. Persevering with working up there for a couple of years, he'd given up and moved operations back down to the studio on ground level. He couldn't recall the last time he'd gone up to the roof terrace, he assumed the ocean view was still there. Nowadays he used this space as a showroom and to mount exhibitions for local young artists during *Venice Art Week* and *Open Houses*. He'd met Kent through one such event three years ago. Impressed by the quality of Kent's art-work and amenable personality, Alex had employed him on an ad hoc basis ever since.

      It took himself, Kent and Suki thirty minutes to move the work bench, clamps, saws, mallets, electric drill, electric screwdriver, woodscrews and trimming blades up to the showroom. The last thing they carried up was the artwork itself. Sweat was streaming down Alex's chest and back when they finally heaved the rolled canvas through the kitchenette and into the showroom. Suki had laid out the large carpet rectangle. Summoning his energy, Alex made one last push to lug the canvas across the room. The three of them laid it down. When he stood to full height, a head rush hit. Kent switched on the fans and threw open the balcony windows overlooking the pool.

      Seeing stars, Alex fluffed out his shirt and stepped outside. On the balcony, he inhaled deeply. Across the pool, beneath the patio's peach pergola, two white jacketed men and a girl in a black dress with white collar and apron were laying silverware on a crisp tablecloth. Glancing over the front perimeter wall, he spied a white truck parked in the street. Caterers were obviously involved. Then he saw Rick come out onto the patio carrying a floral arrangement of white lilies which he set down as the table's centerpiece. Preparations were punctuated by Rick's commands of, "Get down, Bella!" as she darted between legs and tried to jump on the table. This 'casual lunch' for Cristina and her friends was clearly a classic Rick-style understatement.

Leaving Kent to get on with building the frame, Alex and Suki went back to the main studio.

Carrying the heavy canvas upstairs had left Alex feeling spacey. Taking on board what Rick said about not overdoing it, he phoned next door to see if Cayde was free to assist with the stretching. Amenable and ever helpful, as the good friend and neighbor he was, Cayde said to give him a shout when needed. The bulk of the morning having been consumed by moving the paraphernalia involved in making art, Alex was thrilled to be getting down to actually making his art.

He examined the frame Suki just finished working on. The last sheet of paper she'd covered it with was a dark maroon. He hadn't specified any order to the colored layers underneath. Alex rolled up his shirt sleeves and lifted the frame. The seven layers of painted watercolor paper gave it a certain heft. He put it on a workbench, with the wrong side facing out. Tilting it, he leaned the top against the wall. "Can you steady it for me?"

Suki braced the piece.

Taking the nail gun, Alex punched a circular pattern of nails in the bottom left corner. He then randomly punched nails into the bottom right. Suki handed him the pliers. He removed some nails from this side but left a few in. Then he stabbed holes in the piece's center with the awl, jiggling it to increase the size and irregularity of the punctures. Upending the frame, Suki braced it again. He swung a hammer at the layered paper's underside. A surprising amount of force was needed to break through the layers. Half an hour later, he'd punctured a variety of holes of varying sizes. Spinning the piece's right side to the front, he secured it to the easel. With the pliers, he pulled through any remaining nails sticking out.

Working from the right side, Alex picked away at the edges of the holes. The ones made with the hammer had large flaps of paper around the wound. Peeling back strips with his thumb and forefinger revealed streaks of the colored papers underneath. "Can you open up some of the smaller holes with the tweezers?" Stepping aside, he watched Suki tear back the maroon paper from a small hole made by the nail gun. Putting on his glasses, he tore strips from the larger holes with the pliers while Suki picked away at the smaller ones.

They worked in companiable silence, the ripping of paper, rumble of construction noise and occasional booming bass from a speeding vehicle on the street outside the only sound. Curly ribbons of painted paper soon littered the floor. Layers of orange, pink, green, black, lemon, and white papers flared from the holes in the maroon top sheet. Alex assessed his work. The fine rips and tears radiating from the small punctures resembled tributaries seen from space. This pleased him. But he really got off on seeing the studio wall through the large holes. He pressed the remote control and the integral blinds whirred down over the skylights. He asked Suki to find the brightest spot lamp. She positioned its tripod behind the piece and turned it on.

"Lower. More to the right. I need glare!" Tucking his glasses into his shirt pocket, Alex directed Suki to keep moving the spot lamp until he got the perfect angle. "Come around here. What do you think?" No light bled through areas with seven intact layers, but the more paper they'd ripped away the more translucent the lower layers became.

Suki bent into the piece on the easel. "Layers beneath layers. Kind of mysterious. Like uncovering the past ..."

"I don't care for the way the paper tendrils droop over the larger holes."

"Could we treat the paper with a stiffener?"

"Let's try that on the next one. This would be great in metal. Imagine the edges of those punctures, sharp, jagged, dangerous?" With faith in his idea growing, neurons and synapses formed chains in Alex's brain. What if he sandwiched photographs in the layers? Or newsprint? Or even pieces of fabric and yarn? Having entered his perfect space where only he and his work existed, he closed his ears to Bella scratching at the studio door. Knowing this space was off limits to her, and how much he hated intrusions while working, he expected Rick to notice and call her back over the pool.

Bella barked.

A wedge of sunlight sliced the studio's paint-stained floor. "Knock, knock," Rick said through a crack in the door. "Do you have a moment?"

"Why?"

"I'd like to bring in Cristina and Lyle to say hi before the others arrive. Can I?"

'NO!' was the word which sprang to mind. "Okay, but make it quick," were the words Alex said. Pressing the remote to draw up the blinds, he turned to find Rick ushering in a man and a woman. Bella snuck in and skittered to him.

"Alex!" The woman strode towards him like she owned the studio.

"Get her out of here!" Alex snapped.

The woman flinched.

"He means the dog. Bella eats anything." Rick grabbed Bella's collar and pushed her outside.

"We had one like that." Giving a relieved smile, the woman said to Alex, "How nice to see you again!"

With her blond upswept hairdo, dangling mother of pearl earrings and aqua, lime and cerise Pucci print midi dress, Alex had no recollection of seeing this Cristina Raban woman ever before, although she moved to greet him like an old friend. Pulling away, Alex raised his hands. "I'm kind of messy."

"Of course. Anyway, hello again." Laughing politely, Cristina blew him an air kiss.

Alex wiped his hands on a rag as Rick steered the man towards him.

"I'd like you to meet Lyle Colquhoun," said Rick. "Lyle this is Alex Morgan, my … my partner in crime."

"Hi." Tossing the rag aside, Alex shook the hand of the silver crop haired guy in a pink Oxford shirt and sunglasses.

"Hi, hi! Honor, truly an honor," stuttered Lyle slipping off his shades. "Privilege, real privilege! Love your work, love it. So, this is the room where it happens. Wow, just wow!"

"Lyle's a huge art lover," said Cristina.

"Lyle's producing Cristina's TV show," said Rick.

The hullaballoo surrounding this 'casual' celebratory lunch of Rick's now made sense.

Lyle's eyes fell on the piece Alex and Suki were working on. "Amazing textures." He studied the multicolor strips radiating from the holes. "Are these rainbows? You going political?"

"Lyle's a vocal advocate for gay rights," added Cristina.

Alex inserted his body between Lyle and the easel. "Work in progress. I'm not sure what it is yet."

Backing off, Lyle laughed awkwardly. "Apologies. Not every day I get to see a great artist at work. Fanboy, or what?" Giving a jazz hands, Lyle put his shades back on.

"Nice to meet you. Don't let me keep you from your lunch." Alex flashed a steely glare at Rick.

Cristina picked up on the vibe. "Yes, we must let you go back to work. Blame me, I forced Rick to interrupt you. I so wanted to say hello again. The last time we met was at that ridiculous photoshoot all those years ago. Everyone wondered who the gorgeous man Rick had in tow was. You were very evasive about his role in your life." Cristina gave Rick a sly grin.

"Mystery solved," Alex replied gruffly. Maybe that was why he found it hard to remember Cristina. He'd blocked out that period around Rick's very public outing.

"We'll get out of your hair. And that's great hair! I'm envious of your talent and your hair! Like a romance novel cover.

Move over Fabio! Whoa, fanboying again!" Lyle did another jazz hands, then nervously stroked the bald spot in his silver crop.

Cristina's fine fingers, adorned with filigree rings and an impressive solitaire diamond above the wedding band, caressed Alex's swollen knuckles. "Haran and I would like very, very much to get to know you better now I've reconnected with Rick."

Cristina's charm offensive blindsided Alex. He couldn't help softening to the piercing eye contact from her lavender eyes framed by dark lashes. If this was acting, she was extremely good. After making some conciliatory noises of farewell as Rick had shown Cristina and Lyle out, Alex struggled to get his head back in gear. This was why he didn't like being interrupted at work. His dreams had lost impetus. Kent coming down to tell him the frame was ready was a welcome distraction from self-doubt. Alex made a quick call to Cayde. Keeping a low-profile, he scurried across the meditation garden. Animated chatter from the other side of the pool indicated the rest of Rick's lunch guests had arrived. Up in the showroom, Kent had unrolled the canvas face down on the carpet.

"What's the big event?" Cayde asked upon entering from the kitchenette. "Some mighty swank vehicles parked out front."

"Rick has some friends over."

"High rollers by the looks of them jalopies. Alrighty, let's get this baby on the wall." Cayde cast his eyes over the giant frame and enormous canvas. He gleefully rubbed his hands. "I see why you needed help!"

Together with Kent and Cayde, Alex lifted the frame and positioned it on the canvas. "Nice work, Kent. Beautifully built. Go grab some lunch. See if Suki wants anything. Here." Fishing in his pocket, Alex handed Kent couple of Andrew Jacksons.

"Want me to get you something?" Kent asked.

"Nah. The memory of the mung bean and kale smoothie I had for breakfast lingers on."

Kent suspiciously tilted his chin. "I never know if you're kidding about that stuff Rick makes you drink."

Shaking his head, Alex raised his eyes. "If only."

Kent left Cayde and Alex to get on with the stretching.

Using the canvas pliers, Cayde tugged the canvas around the frame. Alex punched the first staples in center top. Cayde was a year younger than Alex. With a wiry build and quicksilver energy, he skipped around the canvas like a featherweight boxer. Cayde's paint spattered blue jeans and white t-shirt were so beautifully spattered they could have been designed to look that way. Going to the opposite side of the frame Alex had stapled, Cayde pliered the canvas around. Sunlight created a diamond pattern of shadows from the canvas wrinkling as Cayde stretched it over the frame. "Do we need the heat gun?"

There was a lot of vinyl paint on the canvas. In cooler conditions it may have needed heating to bend around the frame without cracking. Alex mopped his forehead. "I think it's warm enough in here to make it pliable." He feared any more heat may cause him to pass out.

Cayde moved around, stretching the canvas over the frame with the pliers while Alex shot in staples, creating a drum like tension over the piece. Although the canvas was huge, around ninety-six by a hundred and forty-four inches, it didn't take them long to finish the job.

"Let's see this beauty in action!" said Cayde.

Taking a side each, they pivoted it upright and rested it against the wall. Staring at the painting, Cayde squeezed Alex's neck. "You've lost it. Better luck next time."

"You think?"

Cayde playfully slapped Alex's back. "Of course not. It's muted yet extravagant. A crimson ball adrift in a yellow and orange universe. Great stuff." A peal of laughter across the pool caught Cayde's attention. Moving to the windows, he peered over the balcony then gasped in pain and clapped his hand over his eyes.

"What?" Alex asked, concerned Cayde was also having a vision problem.

"Temporarily blinded by the sun glinting off diamonds and gold. What's with the ladies who lunch?"

Standing behind Cayde, Alex stared across the pool. A white jacketed waiter was topping up their champagne flutes. Around the patio table, set with the house's finest china, Cristina, Lyle and two more casually, yet expensively, dressed ladies sat with Rick. All were smiling and laughing, except for the flame-haired lady who had a dour expression. "Rick caught up with this actress he worked with years ago. Well, he never actually got to work with her. She was the co-star of that TV movie he got bounced from when the story about him being gay broke in the press."

"Seem to recall your name getting dragged into that too."

"The news stories made it sound like the shock of discovering Rick's 'sordid lifestyle,' as the scandal sheets so kindly labeled it, was what killed his father. Since I was identified as the owner of the sleazy shack where these lurid gay sex trysts took place, it was unpleasant for me as well."

"Sleazy shack? That was a darned nice little beach house you had at Sunset Cove."

"That kind of journalism never lets the truth stand in the way of a juicy headline. Sid knew about us and was cool. There was no scandal, no-one was harmed. Rick's only crime was being in the public eye and in a relationship with another man. If that story hadn't broken on the day of Sid's funeral, Rick would probably have gone on to be a big TV star."

"If he'd been happy to keep your relationship in the shadows. That was the seventies, remember? When Liberace chose to live alone because he was a confirmed bachelor."

"Anyway, Cristina's given up acting, gotten a wealthy husband and reinvented herself as an art-loving high-society socialite. With Thaddeus's help, Rick's got her a seat on the Conservatory Board. Now he's assembling a power base to oust C.Z. Hulton."

"Good luck with that. Hulton's been around since dinosaurs roamed the tar pits." Cayde moved forward and squinted across the pool. "Who are the others? Conservatory trustees too?"

"Get back." Alex tugged Cayde from the balcony. "Don't let them see we're watching."

"Afraid they'll scatter from the watering hole if they catch our scent?"

"More frightened they may stampede and trample us to death. The guy's a TV producer. Cristina's luring Rick into some reality show about the humdrum lives of Bel Air's rich and idle. Repayment for getting her on the Board."

"A reality show? Like *Laguna Beach* or *The Hills*?"

"Are they on PBS?"

"Leland puts on MTV in the background. Popular culture seeps into your consciousness like ink in blotting paper."

Alex observed the dynamics around the lunch table. Now a different woman was looking sour. Rick raised his glass and made a comment. The whole table burst out laughing in response, including sourpuss. Rick was obviously acting as peacemaker and comedy relief. "This isn't a lunch," muttered Alex, "it's an audition."

Cayde watched over Alex's shoulder. "Will you have to get involved if he does the show?"

"No way! If Rick wants to go down that road to ruin, he'll have to go it alone."

The female laughter and tinkle of glasses drifted across the pool.

No, Alex was not going to be drawn into this adventure of Rick's. Of that he was certain.

THE IMPERFECT PAST

"... that's when my internist said, 'If you don't eliminate dairy, gluten and sugar, you may never have a solid bowel movement again.'" Tiffany sunk in the rattan chair and huddled her gray cardigan around her midriff. "Well, you can imagine how that made me feel ..."

For the past half-hour, Tiffany had been regaling Rick and Alex with her multiplicity of symptoms and equally diverse range of diagnoses from medical practitioners. Around the table on the patio, Alex and Rick had nodded their heads, furrowed their brows and asked appropriate questions, but a suitable response to the prospect of Tiffany's eternal diarrhea eluded them both in the moment.

"... all the signs point to lupus, but the doctors insist my symptoms are stress related. Agreed, I'm under a huge amount of pressure on the show, but how can I avoid that unless I give up my job? And I need to be employed to keep my medical benefits. Plus, I've worked my ass off to get supervising producer credit. And I've got two kids to raise. I need the money."

"Pav pays you alimony, doesn't he?" asked Rick.

"It was a lousy settlement and I fucking hate Pav's guts." Tiffany's cherubic face drooped beneath her ginger-blond curls. She patted her chest. "Darned palpitations."

"But work will ease up once the new season starts shooting, won't it?" asked Rick.

"I doubt it," scoffed Tiffany. "The six episodes we lost to the writers' strike totally screwed our story arcs. And when shooting restarted we were writing on-the-fly, literally throwing pages at the actors as they walked on set. Hasty plot decisions were made, which means we're entering season three with some majorly loose ends. And on top of that, our dearly departed showrunner's season finale painted us into a corner. Word to the wise, if you're going to put a well-loved character in mortal danger for a ratings bump, make sure they're signed for next season. Jed Cavill booked another show during hiatus. It's left us with no choice but to kill off his character in the meth lab explosion."

"Can't you recast? You know, after four episodes with a double in bandages he comes back with a new face." Rick topped up his white wine. "Or put his character in a coma! Jed's new show might tank, and he'll want to come back."

"Jed's fans are gonna desert the show in droves as it is. We don't need to insult the ones who stick around with soap cliches. It's not the eighties anymore, Ricky." Tiffany slurped her kale smoothie.

"Just an idea," said Rick, mildly affronted.

The sky was reddening. Purple shadows crept over the lap pool as the sun sank over Venice Beach. Alex leaned to Rick. "Switch on the heaters, babe."

The dusk timer tripped in as Rick got up to turn on the halogen heaters. Around the compound's perimeter, in the meditation garden across the pool, and on the patio, strings of lights twisted around the trees and the pergola's uprights sparkled into life.

"I forget how pretty your place is at night." Tiffany's pale green-gold eyes sparkled in equal measure to the illuminations. "Before Ty gets back, can I ask you a favor?"

Rick narrowed his eyes. "As long as it's not for a loan."

"I need to overnight in the hospital for some invasive tests. Would you guys have Maddy and Jay sleepover?"

"When?" Rick asked.

"Last weekend of May. Only for one night. Aunt June's not over the bladder surgery and mom's staying on in Omaha. I don't want to ask Pav. It's not his weekend to have them and they hate going to his place when it is. And I can't trust Tyler to look after himself let alone the kids."

Another question was forming on Rick's lips but Alex didn't give him the chance to ask it. "Sure we'll have them."

"But Al, we fly to New York the day after and —"

"It's fine, Tiff. We'll have them," said Alex, oblivious to Rick's pouting.

"Whew, that's a weight off of my mind!" Tiffany's mood lifted. "Now with doom and gloom out of the way, I've got some good news."

"Hooray," muttered Rick.

"In fact, two items of good news. I was manning the picket lines during the writers' strike when I met this other writer and —"

A metallic crash and Manuela's scream from the kitchen halted Tiffany's story.

"What the fuck?" Scraping back his chair, Rick dashed into the living room. Moments later, Bella scampered onto the patio from the entrance hall, an entire roast chicken dangling from her mouth. "Alex, get that off her!" Rick hollered. "Don't let her swallow any bones!"

Fast as he could, Alex tackled Bella. Fighting her frenzied wriggles, he pried her jaws apart. Meanwhile, a fractious interchange erupted between Manuela and Rick in the house. "Pass that platter, hon."

Tipping off the last crudities, Tiffany proffered the plate with both hands.

Wrestling the bird from Bella's mouth, Alex dumped hunks of oily chicken on it. After scooping a detached wing off the terracotta tile, he let go of the dog. Licking her greasy chops, Bella snuffled around for anything he'd missed. He put the platter on the table and hastily shut the doors to the living room and entrance hall before she could dash back inside. Wiping his hands, Alex contemplated the pile of mangled chicken flesh and bones. "A little garnish on top and I'm sure nobody will notice."

Tiffany burst into giggles at his understatement.

When the cares melted from Tiffany's face, Alex saw the same sweet smile of that three-year-old girl he'd first met at Sid's family barbecue in Bel Air all those years ago. "Manuela cooked two chickens. No need to panic."

"Did you get it all off her?" Rick came out, being ultra-careful not to let Bella sneak in. The entrance buzzer sounded. Bella hurtled around the corner of the pool house to the street gate.

"I'll get it." Going to the white door by the pool house, Alex shouted above Bella's barks and whines, "That you, Ty?" Upon hearing Tyler's yelled response, very clearly thanks to his foghorn voice, Alex kept Bella back and opened up.

"Hi." Tyler pushed through the outer door from the sidewalk as a car's headlights sped past on the street.

Alex held Bella's collar, giving Tyler a chance to usher in a neatly put-together guy with trimmed goatee. He was wearing a muscle revealing stretch shirt, closely fitting pants with striped suspenders and carried an overnight bag.

"This is Jack!" Tyler proudly pushed his boyfriend at Alex.

Before Alex had chance to welcome Jack, the smoke alarm's piercing beeps went off inside the house. Bella immediately stopped jumping up at Tyler and raced back along the pool. "We seem to be having some kitchen issues. Hey Tiff, Ty's here! Meet Jack," Alex blurted out as he hurried across the patio. He didn't move fast enough through the living room door and Bella barged in around his knees. On entering the kitchen, acrid smoke caught in his throat. Rick stood on a chair wafting a dish towel under the smoke alarm. The second chicken's charred carcass was unceremoniously dumped in the sink under running water. "What the heck happened?"

Alex asked. Bella skittered in crazy circles, barking just for fun now.

"Manuela thought she'd switched off the oven, but she'd put it up full. She forgot the other chicken was still in it. I sent her to go lie down and take the rest of the night off." The smoke alarm fell silent. "And you can put a sock in it." Rick fixed Bella with a gimlet stare as he got down from the chair. "Why couldn't we have spotted a sweet little abandoned kitten rather than you, you psycho mutt?" Bella gaily wagged her tail in response. Then, on hearing Tyler's voice, she raced back out to the patio. "Ty's here then." Rick surveyed the kitchen mess. "Great first impression we'll make."

"Plan B. Take out?"

"It could take too long. I'll rustle something up. Let me say hi to Ty's gentleman caller then I'll deal with it."

Out on the patio, they found Tyler with his arm around Jack shooing Bella away.

"It's not always this crazy around here." Alex gave Jack an apologetic half-grin.

"It's usually worse! I'm Rick, Tyler's brother." Rick proffered his hand to Jack.

"Technically Ricky's our half-brother," added Tiffany.

"Jack Cornell. Nice to meet y'all." He smiled nervously. "A dog bit me when I was a kid, they kind of scare me."

"Bella's as gentle as a lamb, although she's got the devil in her tonight. I'll shut her in the den to cool off." Grabbing Bella's collar, Rick wrangled her inside.

"And I'm Alex."

"The great artist, Alex Morgan. Tyler's told me all about you. Although he didn't warn me you were so handsome." Jack stared intently into Alex's eyes as he pumped his hand.

"How remiss of you, Ty. Thought I told you that's the first thing you should mention about me to anyone." Although laughing it off, Alex found it an oddly intimate thing for Jack to say on first meeting.

"Introductions done?" asked Rick coming back outside.

"Yeah," said Tyler. "I already gave Jack the lowdown on my famous family. Although Tiff's the only one of us still employed in the heady world of showbiz."

"I'd hardly call supervising producer the height of showbiz glamor." Tiffany modestly dropped her eyes.

"But you work on a hit show." Jack sat at the table.

"You watch *Mothers, Wives and Sisters*?" Tiffany asked, pleasantly surprised.

"Well, my grammy loves it. I watch whenever I go visit," added Jack. "She'll be over the moon when I tell her I met its head writer."

"More than met, honey." Tyler sat next to Jack and stroked his arm. "Shall we tell them?"

"I guess," said Jack. "So long as you're sure?"

"I'm sure." Tyler braced himself. "Tiff, Ricky, Uncle Al, Jack and I feel real comfortable with each other, and both of us want to put down roots, so we've decided to get married as soon as it's legal."

Stunned silence greeted Tyler's announcement.

Tyler shifted nervously.

"Congratulations, great news!" Alex's positive utterances broke the tension. He went around to hug Tyler and then Jack, who returned the hug with fervor and thigh contact.

Tiffany forced a smile.

Rick's eyes fell on the empty glasses. "This calls for champagne."

"Water's fine for me," said Jack.

"Jack doesn't drink alcohol," explained Tyler.

"Oh," said Rick with a startled expression. "You still drink though?" he asked Tyler.

"Sure do."

"Go steady." Jack tapped Tyler's hand. "You've been waking up with those headaches lately."

"Just water, Jack?" Alex checked. "We have juice. Diet Coke? Rick can whip you up a virgin pina colada …"

Rick discreetly patted Alex's shoulder to prevent him offering any more cocktail options he could just 'whip up.'

"Water's fine," said Jack.

"Due to a certain animal's intervention, we've a change of plan for dinner. Hot dog spaghetti okay with everyone?" Rick picked up the platter of chewed chicken.

"Cool! I love Ricky's hot dog spaghetti!" said Tyler.

"Spaghetti with tomato sauce's good for me," said Jack.

"Jack's a vegetarian," Tyler said. "Sorry, I should've told you."

"Gluten and tomato sauce aggravate my hiatus hernia," added Tiffany.

"Not a problem. We've got chick-pea pasta in the larder, and I can put steamed broccoli on it for you," said Rick.

"That would also work for me," said Jack.

"Babe, could you come fix the drinks?" Rick asked Alex as he backed towards the house.

"Tiffany can get you guys up to speed on what's been going down with her," Alex said to the table. Following Rick inside, he glanced over his shoulder to see Tyler and Jack with their heads together and Tiffany scrolling through her BlackBerry.

In the kitchen, Rick hastily opened cans and filled cooking pots with water.

"You think it's worth opening champagne if Jack doesn't drink?" Alex asked.

"Definitely! And put another on ice."

Alex dug a Lalique ice bucket from the island cupboard. "Yeah, gay marriage is cause for celebration."

"Forget gay marriage, I just need a drink."

The refrigerator's dispenser clunked as Alex filled the ice bucket.

"It's very sudden, don't you think? I was under the impression they'd only just met." Rick salted the water and brought up the heat. "And Jack seems so neat and pulled together. Although he's tall, he's kind of dinky. And Tyler's all long haired and floppity. They don't look like they go together at all." Rick frowned as he tipped the different pastas into two pans. "And Jack doesn't like dogs. And he doesn't drink. What on earth can they have in common?"

"Fucking each other could be one thing," Alex pulled a champagne bottle from the refrigerator. "Or is that two things?"

"Alex!" exclaimed Rick.

"What?" Alex cut the foil. "Or playing floodlit tiddlywinks. How does anyone know what makes any relationship tick?"

Clomping into the kitchen, Tiffany brushed past Alex to the fridge. "You might've given me a heads up about this bombshell."

"We told you Tyler had gone to pick up the guy he's been seeing." Rick started chopping onions.

"*Seeing* is different from marrying!" Tiffany snapped open a Diet Coke. "You really mean you'd no idea about this gay marriage business?"

"As much of a surprise to us as it is to you," said Alex.

"I'm in shock." Tiffany fumbled for a glass from the open cabinet. "You know, it'd be much easier if you kept the short glasses in front of the tall ones rather than behind them."

Rick shot Alex an 'I told you so' look between blinking back onion tears. "How come you didn't know, Tiff? What happened to that psychic connection shit twins have?"

"I block out the freaky mess of Tyler's brain." Tiffany poured her Diet Coke. "Has he told mom?"

"How the fuck would I know?" Rick snapped, his eyes streaming. "For all —"

"Here." Tearing off a hunk of bread, Alex stuck it in Rick's mouth, not only to remedy his onion tears but also shut him up. He put the champagne glasses and ice bucket on a tray. "Can you take these, Tiff?"

Mumbling through the bread, Rick set the broccoli to steam and chopped the frankfurters.

"You guys moved the party inside?" Tyler bounded into the kitchen from the living room.

"Have you told mom?" Tiffany instantly asked.

"Not yet. It's kind of a recent development." Tyler reached for a tumbler.

"Marriage isn't something to enter into lightly," said Tiffany darkly.

"You should know, sis. You've done it twice without much success." Tyler filled the tumbler with Evian.

"Trust you to rub that in my face."

"That the reason for the shade? Cause I'm getting married and you can't hold a relationship together?"

"Neither of my marriage failures were my fault. You have no idea how hard my life is! I've got a demanding job, two kids to deal with and feel sick and wiped out all the time. What do you do? Talk to the trees, crash trucks and hang out with West Hollywood hustlers and party boys! And that's only the part of your life we know about."

"You're so freaking judgmental, Tiff! Is it any wonder I don't tell you private stuff? Jack's a musician. He plays flute with two chamber orchestras and spends weekends volunteering for the APLA. He's a beautiful soul," Tyler responded defiantly.

Bella started whining and scratching in the den.

"Tyler, Tiffany, dial it down!" Alex said authoritatively.

"Yeah, bring it down Tiff!" Tyler put Jack's glass of water on the tray with the champagne and carried it outside.

Tiffany sulkily stomped off behind him.

Opening a couple of cans of tomatoes, Rick added them to the onion frying in the skillet.

"You okay in here if I go referee Flossie and Freddie?"

Rick indicated for Alex to remove the bread from his mouth. "Yeah, go. And let Cujo out before she shreds the den."

"What about Jack?"

"Put her on the leash. If Jack's staying for the weekend, he needs to get used to her. This is her home too."

By the time Alex had put on Bella's leash, sprung her from the den and led her onto the patio, Tyler had poured four glasses of champagne. He passed one to Alex.

Carrying a steaming bowl of pasta before him, Rick placed it center of the rattan dining table. Rick accepted a glass of champagne from Tyler. They made a quick toast, Jack clinking his water glass, then Rick went to fetch the rest of dinner.

"Bad luck to toast with water," Tiffany muttered.

They all pretended not to hear.

Once everything was on the table, Rick sat down and served. "Gluten free, vegetarian, low-fat, no additives, alcohol free." He passed plates and bowls around and stuck the tongs in the salads Manuela had prepared. "Everybody happy?"

"Terrific. Thanks, Ricky," said Tiffany.

"Okay, dig in."

Everyone picked up cutlery and began to eat.

"Aren't y'all forgetting something?" asked Jack.

Rick scanned the table. "You need some other seasonings or ketchup?"

"Don't y'all say grace? You know, thank the good Lord?"

All heads pivoted to Alex. His staunch lack of faith and dislike of organized religion was known to all, except Jack apparently. "You're welcome to pray silently but I'm not comfortable with religious utterances in my home."

The atmosphere around the table thickened.

Jack stared at each of them in turn. His expression of shock growing. The last person whose eyes he focused on was Alex. "I'm sorry, but you know what this means …"

Everyone held their breath.

"It means I'm kidding!" Jack and Tyler cracked up like a pair of kids. The sense of relief around the table was so extreme even Tiffany smiled. "Tyler put me up to it. He says you guys kid each other all the time."

"Yeah, it's a real laugh a minute around here," said Rick passing the breadbasket.

Dinner progressed without further drama. Conversation was varied. They spoke about Alex's art and Jack's music. Religion raised its head again when they discussed belief or lack of it. Tiffany mentioned her discussions with the priest who served as the consultant on *Mothers, Wives and Sisters*. The series she worked on was set in an inner-city convent and centered on a nun torn between her faith and her loyalty to her drug-dealer brother.

Once they'd finished eating, Rick cleared the table and dropped by Manuela's apartment to check in on her. Returning to the table with a pot of freshly brewed coffee, Rick subtly passed Alex his evening meds. Then Rick opened a bottle of red, poured glasses for himself and Tyler and sat down.

With everybody's drinks freshened, Tiffany dragged a tote bag from under the table. "Seeing how my good news got hijacked earlier on, I'll try again. Okay, Tiffany's good news take two." She ceremoniously removed eleven DVD cases and fanned them on the table.

"Is the conversation so dull you want to put on a movie?" Rick asked.

"These are all of dad's movies," Tiffany said proudly.

"There couldn't be a conversation dull enough to warrant putting on one of those," said Rick.

Not rising to Rick's sneer, Tiffany passed the DVD jewel cases around. "They're all burned from the same crappy prints used for the video cassettes. Anyway, dad's work is being reappraised as fine examples of classic Hollywood moviemaking. Criterion's gradually acquiring their rights. They found out I own all dad's papers and memorabilia, because no-one else in the family wanted them ..." Tiffany flung an accusatory glare at Tyler and Rick, "that's why they got in touch with me. They have a couple of his early movies under restoration and were interested in using the material I own for the bonus features. You know, storyboards, shooting schedules, costume designs, notebooks and other behind-the-scenes stuff —"

"They'll pay to use them, won't they?" Rick cut in.

"I want to move into writing and producing in my own right, so I offered them access to everything I own as long as they book me to produce the bonus material for any of dad's movies they release. It'll be a good credit for me, but also give me control to make them a worthy commemoration of dad's work. I've got all of his personal contacts from over the years too. I can get unique insights from actors and crew who worked on his movies for the commentary tracks."

"Better hurry," said Rick. "Dad's movies are pretty old. Most of the people who worked on them are either dead or knocking on heaven's door by now."

"*Tornado!*" Alex picked up one of the DVD cases. "That's a blast from the past."

"Not such a blast as it won't be in CYCLONERAMA." Rick nudged Jack's shoulder. "That was the gimmick dad dreamed up for the movie's roadshow release. A fancy name for the giant wind machines they switched on for the tornado sequences in the big theaters. It's a pity dad never lived to see the popcorn get blown out of the audience's hands."

"Never seen 'em." Tyler pushed the cases away.

"You're telling me Criterion seriously consider dad's work worth going to such lengths?" Rick asked.

"Typical!" snapped Tiffany. "I thought the family would be more supportive. You're always so down on dad, Ricky. He deserves to be remembered and treated with respect, not Sid Stradman the eternal joke as you'd have him."

Rick raised a conciliatory hand. "Sorry. Well done for getting the gig, Tiff."

"*Her Imperfect Past*," Alex read the title from one of the DVDs. Putting on his glasses, he studied the black-and-white photos on the cover insert. "Is this …?"

Rick glanced at the box. "It is."

"That's the first one to come out on Blu-ray. The release is timed to coincide with its sixtieth anniversary. It's being hailed as an overlooked classic noir," said Tiffany.

"Momma's one and only Hollywood movie. May I?" Taking the DVD, Rick's eyes misted as he studied the pictures.

Alex hadn't pushed for information on how the therapy was going but knew Rick's ambivalent feelings towards his mother were a major area he wanted to work on.

"*Her Imperfect Past*'s notorious for the drubbing the critics gave it. When the movie flopped, the studio used Luisa's pregnancy as an excuse to cancel her contract. The press then slammed her as well. To give her the chance to tell her side of the story, I thought it'd be fitting if Luisa recorded the commentary track. Do you think she'd do it, Ricky?"

Rick's jaw twitched. "Momma's still bitter with Hollywood for snubbing her. And she's never forgiven dad for being unfaithful after the movie bombed. Any commentary of hers may not be glowing testament you'd care for."

"Good or bad, your mother's firsthand account of the making of that movie, and her feelings about the aftermath, would be an invaluable contribution to movie history. And delivering a coup like that wouldn't do my career any harm either. Would you ask her for me?"

"Momma and I aren't in a good place. I can't," said Rick.

Visibly deflated, Tiffany looked ready to cry.

Seeing the effect his words had on his sister, Rick softened. "I'm not prepared to ask momma, but I'll put you in touch with Patti. Talk to her, see if she'll ask momma the next time she visits." Rick noticed Jack's puzzled expression. "My mother had a fall in Milan before Christmas. Marble floors and new shoes are a dangerous combination, especially when you're eighty-six but insist on wearing three-inch heels. She'd gone to recuperate at the Venice house but couldn't cope with the stairs. My daughter moved her to a nearby nursing home until she's well enough to come home."

"You have a daughter?" Jack asked in surprise.

"Tyler didn't get you up to speed on every single detail of our family then?" Rick laughed.

"Only so many hours in a day." Tyler grinned.

"If momma does say yes, you know she won't be able to travel to do the recording," Rick said to Tiffany. "She can't rustle up enough gypsies and undead to move her casket these days."

"I'll find a way to record the track over there," said Tiffany. "I really want to make this happen."

"Like I said, I'll put you in touch with Patti. You'll have to take it from there." Rick poured the last of the red into his and Tyler's glasses.

Alex wished Tyler and Rick had shown more enthusiasm for Tiffany's project. He also hoped any lingering resentment Luisa had for Sid and the bad blood between her and Rick wouldn't make her reject Tiffany's proposition out of hand. He recalled Tiffany saying earlier about the fellow writer she'd met on the picket lines. Allowing the roar of a jet coming in to LAX to diminish, he asked, "You had two pieces of good news, Tiff. What's the other?"

Tiffany picked up her bag, fished out her car keys and shot a sour glance at Tyler. "It's to do with my work, nothing anyone here would be interested in. Gotta run, I'll tell you some other time." After hasty goodbyes, a somewhat cool embrace with Tyler, and an even cooler one with Jack, Tiffany departed. She left the DVDs behind in the hope Rick may soften his opinion of their father's work having rewatched them.

"Guess I'd better walk Bella." Rick drained his glass.

"You haven't stopped running around tonight, Ricky. I'll take her," Tyler said with a slur. He patted his knee. Bella, her leash dragging on the floor, shimmied to him under the table. "Coming, Jack?"

Jack shied from Bella as she brushed by. "I don't think so. I'll take a shower before turning in."

Rick dashed into the house and dashed out again. "Poop bags!" he declared, stuffing them in Tyler's pocket. "And take care around the boardwalk. The Friday night rabble rousers and party hards can turn nasty if you catch their eye the wrong way. And don't *buy* anything."

Tyler took Bella out through the street door by the pool house and Rick went to tidy the kitchen, leaving Alex and Jack at the table.

"Incredible place you got here," said Jack.

"I sold a lot of paintings in the seventies. And they bought me this." Alex waved his hand around. "Actually, this lot and the one next door were joined when Cayde and I bought them. We had a hippie artist commune going on for a while but divided the lots in the late eighties. Now he's got his studio complex next door and I have here. Come. Let me show you around."

Walking Jack along the pool, they passed the master bedroom's glass sliding doors. "This rear section, with the master suite, second bedroom, walk-ins, laundry and study, used to be one of the original houses." Alex showed Jack around the corner to the secluded rear deck. He flicked on the amber spotlights which cast seductive shadows through the ferns and palm leaves. "Hot tub and pool shower. That door there, that leads straight to our master bath. If you need to shower you could take it out here and jump in the hot tub or take a midnight swim. Though the pool may be a little cool."

"The cold doesn't sound tempting. And I'm not a great swimmer."

"Stick with the hot tub then." Alex patted the door to a compact weatherboard shack set between the lap pool's end and rear perimeter wall. "This cubby's functioned as office, gym and yoga studio in the past. Now we use it as a store for my old surf boards. There's a set of weights in it if you and Ty fancy pumping some iron." Walking Jack back along the pool, they glimpsed Rick moving about inside as he secured the house for the night. "This area," Alex gestured to the pergola covered patio, "used to be the walkway between the two bungalows at the front and the one at the back. I converted one into the pool house and the other one's now the living room, kitchen, and dining room. I had the entrance hall and gallery built to link the living and bedroom areas. The other two shacks across the alley got remodeled into a guest house, which we call the small house, and Manuela's apartment." Alex swept back his hair then slipped his hand inside his shirt to scratch his chest. "I had such a blast painting the buildings different colors, switching rooms around and playing with the spaces over the years. I accept this house doesn't follow the logic of most homes, we got rooms going off rooms without walls or doors, and the rear of the house is a total labyrinth, but that's what I love about it."

"You talk about the house like it was a piece of your art. That's moving."

"Guess it is a piece of my art. An assemblage." Alex took another look at the kingdom he'd built, savoring the rush of satisfaction from Jack's observation. Opening the door to the pool house's kitchen, he placed his hand on Jack's shoulder to usher him into the bohemian interior with chalky green paintwork and oatmeal furnishings. "Fresh towels are in the closet by the bathroom. There's a TV and small lounge around the corner. And that's the bed." Alex laughed. "I guess the bed didn't need any explanation. Make yourself at home."

"Will do." Jack dropped his striped suspenders and unbuttoned his shirt. "Tyler calls you Uncle Al, but you're not related to him, are you?" Jack fanned his shirt fronts to reveal the silky brown hair covering his well-defined chest.

"When Rick came back into my life, his family came too. Ty was going through a rough patch back then. The modeling and acting work had dried up and he'd lost direction. Rick and I helped him get back on track, put him through an arboriculture course at UCLA and other practical training. Then we loaned him some seed money to set up the landscaping business. I tell him to call me Al or Alex, but he and Tiff have got used to the Uncle part."

"I see," said Jack.

A heady wave of Jack's patchouli-based cologne mixed with his sweat swept over Alex. "Ty knows how to fire up the hot tub."

Jack kicked off his shoes, unzipped his pants and pulled them down. "You'll be joining us?"

"Um, er ..." Alex mumbled. "What?"

"In the hot tub." Jack looked at Alex from under hooded eyes as he kicked off his pants.

"Er, why?"

"I didn't pack any swim trunks. I can keep my shorts on if you and Rick are shy. Ty and me are pretty casual with our bodies, not all men are cool that way."

"We're cool, but I thought we'd go straight to bed." Alex gulped. "I mean, I don't think Rick will be up for a hot tub. You, you and Ty ... you feel free to use the tub and pool, well, you know, any way you like."

"Will do." Jack stripped his shirt from his biceps and tossed it on the bed. "Thanks for dinner." Wearing only his cream ribbed jock, Jack wrapped his arms around Alex.

Feeling Jack's bare torso press against his chest and his packet against his thigh, Alex tensed. Unable to read Jack, he refrained from hugging him in return. Instead settling for a couple of avuncular pats on his muscled back. "Yeah, night. See you in the morning."

Unable to decide if Jack was uninhibited or hot to trot, Alex went back to the house. Since Tyler and Jack were getting married, Alex ruled out the latter. He took it as a compliment that Jack felt relaxed enough to be natural around him. The kitchen was in shipshape condition, Rick had done an excellent job of cleaning up. Headed towards bed, Alex heard the TV was on in the den. He went through the living room to find out what Rick could be watching so late at night.

Beyond the den's double doors, the only illumination came from the black-and-white movie on the screen. In a startling close-up, Luisa D'Onofrio's pale face and black eyes filled the forty-two-inch plasma. Her throaty voice, with its slight accent, came through the speakers …

"I don't object to being followed by the police. But I hate small time private detectives pussyfooting after me. I'm a woman with a past, I accept that. And I accept men like you take one look at me and think, 'Once a spy, always a spy. How can anyone ever trust her again?'"

The white glare of Luisa's face lit Rick's profile, then his face also faded to black as the shot moved off her.

"Ready for bed?"

"Yeah." Rick clicked the remote and tossed it on the chaise.

"Powerful stuff." Alex stroked Rick's back as he walked him back through the kitchen. "Why didn't she become a star?"

"Maybe because she was foreign, or she played a dangerous woman too well, or her perfectionism was perceived as difficult and demanding. Perhaps she was just unlucky."

As they crossed the entrance hall, Bella padded around from the pool house and looked in through the double doors. They let her in, then Alex locked up. "What on earth did you put that movie on for at this time of night?"

"Maybe it's getting older, or talking through my feelings with Dr. Susskind, but I've been missing momma. I keep remembering the way she was when I was young rather than later on."

Alex lingered in the walk-in's doorway, watching Rick get undressed.

"When I was around three, I got scared of going to bed. I don't remember why, but something made me afraid momma was going to die in the night. If I stayed awake, I thought nothing bad would happen to her. But I'd always fall asleep. Then I'd wake up convinced she was dead and I was all alone. I'd scream the house down, terrified no-one would come. But momma always came. She'd be wearing some stupidly elaborate nightgown and robe, peach satin trimmed with feathers or the like, and smelling of jasmine. She'd stroke my hair and promise to be there in the morning and stay till I fell asleep." Stepping out of his underwear, Rick tossed it in the laundry hamper. "That's the momma I'm remembering." Rick shivered and rubbed his bare arms. Slipping off his watch, ring and silver necklace, he handed them to Alex. "Put these away for me?" Rick went to use the bathroom.

Opening the drawer in Rick's nightstand, Alex dropped his jewelry into the red velvet box he kept his watches and various other chains and rings in. Alex fingered the carved soapstone eternity pendant he'd given Rick on the cliffs of Sunset Cove just before he left for Italy. Rick had kept it safe for all these years. Lost in thought, Alex stripped off his shirt, pants and undershorts and tossed them over the Eames chair. He was fiddling to take off his stacked leather wristbands when he heard men's laughter. Tyler suddenly darted past the windows, naked. Hastily crossing the room, Alex was reaching to pull the gauze curtains across the windows when Jack sauntered past.

Casually nude, two white towels tucked under his left arm, Jack paused, only a sheet of glass separating their naked bodies. Jack's eyes connected with Alex's.

Instinctively, Alex sucked in his gut.

Jack didn't drop his eyes, just tipped his head, gave a little salute then ambled on to the rear deck.

Alex rapidly dropped the bamboo blinds and swept the rest of the curtains across the windows.

"What's with Fort Knox?" Rick asked, coming in from the bathroom.

Letting go of his gut and rubbing his chest, Alex felt his heart thumping. "Ty and Jack are using the hot tub."

"At this time of night?" After a couple of pumps of lotion, Rick massaged it into his hands as he got into bed. "I thought Tyler would have more consideration. He knows how sound from the rear deck travels at night." Rick pulled up the covers.

"Don't blame Ty. I suggested the hot tub to Jack."

"You? Why?"

"Being a good host. Making him feel welcome." Alex went to the bathroom. As he stood brushing his teeth, Ty and Jack's laughter and splashing filtered through the door to the rear deck. Putting on Luisa's movie had brought down Rick's mood. Maybe he should've suggested they all have a late-night drink in the hot tub to wind down. Visualizing this, Alex was surprised it was giving him a semi. He willed it away to pee. Coming to bed, he switched off his beside lamp and slipped under the covers.

Bella padded in, went to her bed by the fireplace, turned a couple of circles and flopped.

Wanting to comfort Rick, Alex rolled over and held him.

Tyler and Jack's laughter morphed into the gasps and grunts of male lovemaking.

Rick's body stiffened. "How am I meant to get to sleep listening to my brother fuck his boyfriend?"

"Husband to be. Does thinking about Jack that way make it any better?"

"No. Put a pillow over my face."

The guttural groans and male moans from the roiling hot tub intensified.

Aroused again, Alex slid his hand down Rick's stomach. He traced his finger down the dip in his groin.

"What're you doing?" Rick mumbled as Alex swirled his fingers around his cock.

"Birds do it, bees do it, even educated fleas do it ..." Alex threw back the covers and mounted Rick.

"Not now, Al. I'm tired." Rick pushed Alex off, turned on his side and pulled the sheets over his head.

Lying in the dark, listening to Jack and Tyler's gasps and sighs, Alex wished he were doing the same thing with Rick. They still had sex regularly, but it was more like having dinner, walking the dog or brushing their teeth than wild and hot. Had they lost the passion, the kind of passion Jack and Tyler had by the sound of it? Yes, he wished he and Rick were in the hot tub having uninhibited wild sex. Of course, not with Tyler and Jack there too because that would be terribly wrong.

Wouldn't it?

QUESTIONING

"All four of you on stage here tonight were born and raised in other parts of the country. What brought you to California? Why LA?"

"Mom died when I was twelve. After that, my father used to beat me. Sometimes he had a reason. I hadn't taken out the garbage, or got bad grades, or was playing records too loud. Sometimes he didn't. I liked art and poetry. I read books. Maybe Pop was trying to knock those soft things out of me. And, although denying it to myself, I liked boys. Maybe he guessed and was trying to knock that out of me too. My older sister had left home by then. Pop loved Myrna ... *really* loved her. 'Thick as thieves' is how Mom described them. I told Myrna that Pop was hitting me. The beatings were getting more frequent and more violent. She said if Pop did slap me, it was only to keep me in line. He told her I had a wayward streak and was liable to fall into bad ways without discipline. I never mentioned it to her again. What was the point? I kept trying to love Pop, to understand him, even forgive him. But one night his rage was off the scale. He whipped off his belt and beat me with it. The buckle hit my eye. Cut me real bad, took a chunk out my brow. I still got the dent, see? I was crying, begging him to stop, blinded by blood and tears. I was sixteen, wondering what I could've done to deserve such violence. Fathers are meant to protect their kids. That night was the end. I vowed never to let him hurt me that way again. Nothing and no-one would make me cry. I locked my door. I didn't let Pop within six feet of me. I slept with a baseball bat under my bed. I swept yards, mowed lawns, took any job I could. And as soon as I'd saved the fare, I bought a ticket on a Trailways Bus, left Dayton behind and never looked back. Mom's mom,

Dora, lived in LA. I'd only met her once, the time she came to Mom's funeral. I liked her. Dora liked me. She looked at my drawings. She read me her favorite poems. She held my hand as Mom's casket went into the ground. My mother, her daughter ... gone. My family didn't care for Dora. Her name was rarely mentioned. But if it should slip out, I'd hear whispers of what made her so unpalatable. She'd been an actress, she'd left her husband, she lived in a house on the beach, she painted, she had love affairs of *every* kind, she lived for pleasure. Pop warned me to keep away from her. She was immoral, a danger to my soul. But she was the only human in the world I could turn to. She was family, blood family. So one night, when I'd got off that dusty silver bus and used my thumb to get me to Sunset Cove, I scuffed down the track to the beach. I knocked on her door, hoping she'd recognize the scared skinny kid with all his worldly possessions in a canvas holdall. There was no plan B if she turned me away. But the moment she set eyes on me she opened her arms. "Pudding!" she gasped with real warmth, "you look plum tuckered. Come on in and let's fix you something to eat. Now, not that I'm not over the moon to see you, but what the dickens are you doing here?"

    Alex knew this was the answer he should have given.
    The truth.
    However, the Duchamp Stage's auditorium in the Santa Monica Performing Arts Center, sharing a platform with fellow artists Rod Marciniak, Allen Swaine and Cayde Faulkner for the *California Icons of Art* Q and A, didn't seem a fitting place for such a confession. "The light," was the answer Alex gave when his turn came.

    "Yeah," Cayde agreed. "Maybe the light's what attracted all us boys from the farm towns, industrial cities and colorless Midwest who wanted to be artists. We got off the trains, the buses, the beat-up rentals, and the West Coast light smashed our muted lives into Technicolor."

"We saw ourselves as the next Ruschas, Al Bengstons, Keinholzes and Bells." The lighting grid's lamps flared off Allen's steel rimmed glasses as he turned to Cayde for confirmation. "They were our art heroes, our role models."

"But you don't get to be those names by parking your butts on their warm bar stools at Barney's Beanery." Rod's watery eyes glinted. "Although we did plenty of that, but you gotta put in the work. Practice your craft. And we did. The LA art scene was open. There was a lack of rules. A willingness to experiment. A freedom to fail. An audience that allowed themselves to be shocked." Rod directed a challenging gaze out at this audience. "Open minds. That's attractive to young artists. A lot of exciting art went down here in the seventies. Also a ton of crap! Some big names got made that shouldn't have been, and some real talent fell by the wayside …"

Alex wondered if Rod was thinking of Hank and Kaori. If there were any justice those artists should be sitting here tonight, Scotty too. They'd all studied art together then gone on to share studios, galleries and living spaces. Along with Rod, Allen (known by his nickname Scoop back in the day) and Cayde, Scotty, Hank and Kaori had been more than friends, they'd been his family. Hank made sculptures from car parts and industrial waste, commenting on America's love affair with oil and its willingness to sacrifice community for corporate profit. And Kaori's outrageous performance art, like setting cardboard planes full of paper dolls on fire and creating smoke sculptures, was challenging and dangerously beautiful. But it's tough making money from smoke sculptures. And the Beverly Hills matrons and well-heeled industrialist collectors of the mid-seventies hadn't been tempted to shell out big bucks on political art - art which told them they were capitalist scum. Hank and Kaori had had kids, a whole bunch of kids, then got married. Needing to make a regular living, they'd traded LA's Technicolor art scene for the earth tones of auto repair shops and high school teaching in Oregon. Alex made a mental note to email them when he got the chance.

"What was being a young artist like in LA in the seventies?"

"Like being hungry a lot of the time," Rod said dourly.

"We were always on the lookout for cheap places to live and work. Preferably big spaces." Cayde spread his arms for emphasis. "Where we could do both."

Lainie Adler, the LA arts writer acting as the evening's moderator, shuffled her cue cards. "Sounds like things were lean in your early years. How did you all keep going before your art started selling?"

"We had jobs." Alex swept his hand through his hair and lolled back in his seat. The last few weeks had been spattered with the interviews Rick had lined up before Chen ordered him to back off. The relentless barrage of questions from *Art Forum*, *Architectural Digest*, *Painters and Painting*, *Art Daily*, *Art Monthly*, *Art Every Hundred Yearly*, was grating on him. What's to say? You stretch a canvas and paint something on it. Sometimes you like it, sometimes it sucks. And he'd no interest in becoming an art 'personality.' That's just a way to label you. Depending on how truthful he was being, what label would get stuck on him for posterity? The Rheumatoid Arthritis Painter? The Abused Child Painter? The Feels Guilty Because His Wife Died and He Immediately Replaced Her with His First Love Painter? The Gay Painter Who Maybe Isn't as Comfortable with Being Gay as He Thinks Painter? Rod loved the sound of his own voice and thought his opinion the only one worth having. Alex was happy to take a back seat and let Rod do the talking.

"You worked and found time to make art?" Lainie gave an inquisitive shake of her silver bobbed hair and antique gold drop earrings as she looked among the four men. "How did you do that?"

"By taking any job we could that would fit around making art. We did some random stuff." Allen looked to Alex to take the ball and run with this.

Remaining silent, Alex folded his arms.

Cayde took the pass. "Alex worked as a lifeguard and deckhand. And Rod, you were a stunt guy in the movies, correct?" Cayde shot Rod a sidelong glance.

"When you're young and fit you can make a buck doing a ton of dumb shit!" Rod confirmed with his customary gruffness.

"Spraying surfboards, skateboards, custom paint jobs on motorbikes and cars. I painted signs for stores," added Cayde.

"Some of us even got suckered into disreputable professions like the teaching of art." Rod directed one of his super-white non-humorous grins to Allen.

"Anything to pay the rent," came Allen's retort.

Lainie wetted down her Paloma Picasso red lips. "The lifestyle your cohort of artists became associated with, the surfing, the motorcycles, the cars, the drugs, the jazz —"

"The chicks!" For the first time that evening Rod's pale eyes sparkled with genuine delight. A giggle, albeit a nervous one, rippled through the auditorium. "The chicks were also a major part of our lifestyle."

Allen and Cayde chuckled conspiratorially.

Alex smiled wanly. Looking into the second row of the auditorium, he saw Scotty and Rick exchanging whispers, Scotty's lips pursed in disapproval.

Not reading the mood in the room, Rod carried on elaborating about the mini-skirts, long hair and braless beauty of the art groupies who'd hung around their scene. Tension in the audience ratcheted up a notch as Rod tossed the word 'chick' around a few more times, Lainie's scarlet lips tightening with each mention.

Alex wondered if Rod slipped the word 'pussy' into the conversation, either accidentally or to stir the pot, he'd get booed off stage. Still, Rod was speaking honestly. Would he speak as candidly about his sexual attractions? Alex thought back to a few weekends ago. Jack was staying in the pool house with Tyler while he did the yardwork ...

Alex had woken up super early. Dreamlike music mingled with the mournful clang of the wind chimes. Leaving Rick snoring, though he insisted he *never* snored, Alex had got out of bed. Quickly wriggling into a lime Speedo for his morning swim, also to avoid any further inadvertent nude encounters with their houseguests, Alex had rolled up the blinds and cautiously drawn back the gauze curtains. Jack, an indigo batik sarong slung around his hips, stood amidst the foxtail ferns and pink bromeliads of the meditation garden. The music was coming from his flute. Running on from a legato piece, Jack segued into a trippy rippling riff. The notes tumbling from Jack's flute conjured images of cascading water. Wondering which classical composer had penned such a charming piece, Alex grabbed his goggles and swim cap and went out to the pool.

Jack's eyes were closed while he played, lost in his music, swaying with feeling, oblivious to Alex's presence. While he tucked his hair into the swim cap, Alex studied Jack. His deft fingerwork and delicate breath were delightful, counterpointing his sinewy arms and tough guy cropped hair. Alex swished his goggles in the pool and pulled them on. Stepping to the pool's edge, the lyrics to the tune Jack was playing, lyrics about living out of these waters, popped into his head.

Splash!

For the first ten laps Alex couldn't stop laughing about having mistaken 'A Part of your World' from *The Little Mermaid* for some classical shiz. By the time he'd finished his sixty-five laps and climbed out of the pool, everyone was awake. Tyler, his ginger blond hair restrained into a loose manbun, stood atop a ladder in the meditation garden, taking down the lights from the trees he was about to prune. Toweling himself off, he watched Tyler and Jack at work. Tyler, in camo shorts, khaki neckerchief and chunky boots, was stripped to the waist. Jack was at the bottom of the ladder taking the strings of lights, his loosely knotted sarong slipping farther down with each movement. Tyler's muscles were nicely defined, but in a different manner to Jack's. Tyler's muscles had a long, lean quality. His chest was wide and flat with a scattering of freckles and an inverted V of ginger hair across his pecs up to his Adam's apple. Jack's chest was proudly bulbous with silky brown hair swirling over its tanned curves and round his nipples. Alex allowed himself to take pleasure watching the two men's bodies in movement.

He hoped he wasn't feeling lust.

No, he ruled out lust as the motivation to savor Tyler and Jack's bodies. They were healthy, fit, virile men. Traits Alex felt slipping away in himself. He'd not been vain when he was young, spending zero time in front of mirrors, being photographed, or placing himself on pedestals to be admired. Perhaps these were pangs of regret from not celebrating his own male beauty and openly sharing it while he had the chance.

The bedroom door slid open. Poking his head out, Rick saw Tyler topless, Jack's sarong revealing his butt crack and Alex posed in his skimpy trunks. "Is anyone around here putting on clothes today?" Rick tutted. "It's like a Sunday afternoon at George Cukor's."

Another moment during that weekend stuck in Alex's mind. He'd been giving Jack a tour of the house. They were standing shoulder to shoulder in the rear wing's gallery, all walnut wood and violet orchids. *The Boy on the Beach*, Alex's painting of Rick from the summer of '74 was hung here, along with framed pencil sketches of Rick's face and assorted other male nude studies of his. Erotic. Not graphic.

"You have a major retrospective coming up, haven't you?" Jack's eyes lingered on the nudes.

"Correct."

"This is stunning work. There's a quality beyond the drawing. How do I describe it?" Jack took a moment to select the right word. "A yearning. And this body of work isn't in your retrospective?"

"I'm not known for portraiture or life drawing. This aspect of my work would be confusing. I didn't tell the curatorial team about them. And these drawings and paintings have never been shown, so they didn't ask."

"Aha," Jack had said with a knowing nod …

Rod and Allen's laughter, the audience's uncomfortable silence in response to something Rod must have said, and Lainie's shuffling of the cue cards stopped Alex pondering what Jack had meant by that 'Aha.' Alex snapped himself back into the here and now on the Duchamp stage.

"Alex, Cayde, Allen, you're well-established local artists with homes and studios in Venice Beach. And Rod, you were also a local here until a few years ago. What is it about this area that's earned such loyalty from you?" Lainie relaxed, sensing Rod was unlikely to invoke feminist insurrection on this topic.

"The reason we wound up here in the first-place comes back to your earlier question, Lainie. We were broke and Dogtown was cheap," said Allen with a grin.

"Rents in Venice were low back then. Free even." Cayde waved his hands for emphasis. "The amusement arcades had gone, the oil had gone, no-one wanted to be here. Vacant storefronts and deserted factories were manna for us starving artists."

"And any other poor sons of bitches who were on the skids," said Rod. "This place was edgy. The old Ocean Park was junkie heaven, remember?"

"Surfer heaven too." Alex was happy to speak out on this topic. "Shooting the Cove was one heck of a ride."

"The Cove?" queried Lainie.

"The name locals gave the burned-out pier's pilings." Alex felt a pang of nostalgia for the rainbow slick of oil on the water and the surf crashing around the blackened pillars jutting from the sea. "Riding a wave through the Cove tested your surfing chops. If you didn't read the water and hit those piles you were in big trouble. Guys got smashed up bad, killed even."

"And crossing the Zephyrs or Dogtown Boys was also bad for your health!" Allen added with a chuckle.

"The area could be sketchy, but we dug that. So when we achieved a modicum of success and had the means to buy property, we bought into the place we felt comfortable. Property was cheap in the early eighties. And I have to point out," added Cayde with a chuckle, "even great success in those days didn't equate to the mega-bucks *some* artists make today."

Cayde, Allen and Alex all looked to Rod. Recent multimillion-dollar sales of his work were the stuff of modern legend.

Rod placed his hand on his chest and bowed his head.

"But guys like us wouldn't have moved to Beverly Hills even if we had the dough. That's where our buyers lived. We were committed to communal living and kicking against the establishment. We saw buying property as an opportunity to create supportive communities and affordable studio space for fellow artists. The house and home aspects were secondary …"

As Cayde waxed lyrical about their dreams of artists' communes and mutual support networks, Alex looked down at Rick in the audience. The discontented expression which kept creeping onto his face was back again. Telling Rick to step back from having a guiding hand in his career had hit just when he was struggling with his role in life. He'd compensated by showing more enthusiasm for Rick signing to do Cristina's dumb reality show than he felt. Once the exciting flurry of agent's meetings, negotiating fees, signing contracts and multiple trips to Saks and Neiman Marcus to freshen his wardrobe was over, Rick's enthusiasm for *The Belles of Bel Air* had waned. After completing his first two-day shooting block, Rick realized he had an extremely minor role in proceedings. Alex remembered that night when they'd been lounging in the den …

"It's like the only reason I'm on the show is to play Cristina's gay best friend," Rick had said as they watched CNN's coverage of the presidential election primaries.

"But you signed to do a reality show. And that's what you are, isn't it? The show's called *The Belles of Bel Air*. You knew from the outset the women would take center stage."

"I suggested *The Beaux and Belles of Bel Air*."

"That really rolls of the tongue." Alex shook his head. "The show's Cristina's vanity project, it's not about you."

Rick sighed and petted Bella's head on his lap. "You're right, as usual. If this doesn't revive my career I'll have to resign myself to playing guest corpse on crummy procedurals. Guess I should stop bitching, pick up the paycheck and get used to playing second fiddle. Seems that's the only role in life I'm destined for anyway."

Was feeling second best the only thing playing on Rick's mind? Alex kept finding the *Her Imperfect Past* disc in the DVD player. Rick must be watching it late at night ... in secret. Whether from talking through his mother issues in therapy, or Tiffany wanting her to do the DVD commentary, Luisa was back in the forefront of Rick's mind and exerting her unsettling effect on their relationship, as usual.

Alex dragged his attention away from Rick and back onto Lainie and the guys under the Duchamp Stage's bright lights. He'd had it to the back teeth with questions. What was the vacuous woman blathering on about now?

Lainie read her next cue card. "New York was considered the epicenter of the American art world in the nineties. Were any of you tempted to move there?"

"Nah. The surf's better here." Alex's off-the-cuff quip got a hearty laugh. He smiled bashfully in response.

"The light in New York's too harsh," said Allen.

"Us Los Angeles artists were too incoherent for New York. We weren't slick and sellable enough. The East Coast considered their style and taste superior to the land of movie stars and entertainment moguls." Cayde extended an apologetic hand to the audience. "My opinion. Funny thing, New York of the sixties looked exactly like the old movies, movies shot on sets and backlots in Hollywood. It was like Hollywood knew how New York should look better than New York."

"I prefer Universal's backlot Paris to the real one," said Rod. "Universal's Paris is more authentic."

"Easier to get around and they speak American," said Alex. That got another good laugh. He'd found his role for the evening, joker in the pack.

Lainie tittered along with the rest of the audience.

Alex saw Rick's frown had gone. That quip made him laugh. He was relieved. He hated seeing Rick unhappy, especially if he was the cause of it. He wondered if Rod's comment about backlots reminded Rick of when he had featured roles on prime time shows. While the other guys carried on answering Lainie's irritating questions, Alex smiled at the memory of the time Rick had been shooting *McMillan and Wife* and he'd been inveigled into driving him to Universal. He'd taken his field easel and paints to kill time. Doing plein air studies around the backlot had been a blast. That was when he'd met Rosemarie Harrington, the woman who'd suddenly appeared by Mockingbird Square and stood watching him work. When she admired his watercolor and offered to buy it, he felt so embarrassed about taking money for his work he'd gifted it to her. Being a total hayseed around the entertainment industry, he had zero idea she was a faded movie star making her comeback. Rosemarie was one of his first champions and had invested heavily in his early paintings. He considered her one of his oldest and dearest friends. Last Sunday, he and Rick had invited Thaddeus Boudreaux to come along when they visited her …

They'd driven up Beverly Crest's winding roads to collect Thaddeus from his elegant Wedgewood Blue faux Regency mansion. Unable to resist any opportunity to entertain and share his home's exquisite décor and breathtaking views, Thaddeus had insisted they come in for Mai Tais served by his white jacketed houseman, Cedric. Since he was driving, Alex vehemently insisted that his drink be made virgin.

"It's been so long since I had love in my life, I suspect I'm being made virgin too!" Thaddeus laughed merrily as they clinked glasses. "Chin, chin!"

Thaddeus had the gift of making the simplest event into a party. Tongues loosened by the Mai Tais, Thaddeus and Rick spent the drive to Rosemarie's assisted living facility dreaming up increasingly elaborate schemes to remove C.Z. Hulton from chair of the LA Conservatory of Modern Art's Board.

"We're overthinking this," said Thaddeus tartly, "we haven't even tried throwing a glass of water over her."

"I'll put it on the next meeting's agenda," said Rick.

"Okay, so C.Z Hulton's old and set in her ways. You two should watch out, you could be accused of ageism." Alex checked his rear view preparing to turn into the mock Tudor estate.

Thaddeus's good humor plummeted. "Hulton's the one with the problem! For the past twenty-one years I've generously and loyally loaned my entire art collection to LACoMA. And I've served on its Board for twelve years. I don't want groveling thanks when I walk in the building, but I would like some respect. That woman is unable to get her head around the fact a black man, such as myself, can be wealthy, collect art and be a benefactor. She dismisses my opinions, patronizes me, and her knuckles whiten around her purse whenever we're alone together. The last eight years with her at the helm have been extremely unpleasant. One more humiliation and I'm liable to walk and take my collection with me."

"I know, Thaddeus," said Rick. "But we've got Cristina on our side now. We'll get Hulton out. Don't do anything rash. The museum needs your voice, not just your collection."

Following the sudden explosion of tension in the car, Alex was relieved to be in Rosemarie's presence. Even at ninety she exuded a serenity and grace which brought out the best in everyone. An old friend of Thaddeus's, she received the late flowering jonquils he gave her as graciously as accepting an Oscar. Although it was a luxury retirement home, the damask drapes, crystal chandeliers and lavish floral arrangements couldn't disguise the grassy, musty aroma of senior living facilities.

    Greeting Alex last, Rosemarie's frail arthritic fingers gripped his stronger less distorted arthritic fingers. "Isn't it wonderful?" Her dark eyes danced with delight. "After all these years of fighting for equality, gay marriage is a reality in California!" Rosemarie blinked back tears. Both her son and daughter had been gay, she'd lost one to suicide and one to cancer. Rosemarie held one of Rick's hands too and looked between him and Alex. "When are you two going to tie the knot?"

    "Oh, we have partnership agreements and legal things in place." Alex removed his hand from Rosemarie's.

    "Marriage is more than that." Rosemarie smacked Alex's hand like he was a naughty child.

    "We've been showing up every day for seven years on a voluntary basis and still happily do so. We don't need a piece of paper to bind us, do we?" Alex looked to Rick for confirmation.

    "We're fine as we are," Rick had said.

    Dragging his mind back into the Santa Monica Performing Arts Center, Alex tried to glimpse Cayde's watch to see how much longer he had to endure this torture. But Cayde was flinging his arms around like Liza Minnelli on her third encore of 'New York, New York.' Alex chuckled to himself. Living with Rick all these years had truly altered his frame of reference.

    "Large scale works by Koons and Murakami are selling for staggeringly high prices. Giant balloon dogs and the like. In your wisdom and maturity, what do you make of artists such as these?" Lainie sat back, smiling like she'd thrown a match into a box of fireworks.

"It's all about finance." Cayde threw his hand in the air for emphasis. "Works on that scale are beyond painting a picture or making a sculpture. Industrial fabrication's needed."

"Would the artists pay for that?" Lainie asked innocently.

All the men guffawed. Alex included.

"Not if they can help it! They'd look to a gallery or dealer for backing. Art's a whole different ballgame to when we started out. Again, we had no money. We used car sprays and offcuts from hardware stores," said Allen.

Lainie pressed on. "But do you think the kind of art I'm talking about is *good* art?"

"You'd need to consult an art dealer on that," said Rod.

Just when Alex was paying attention again, he wished he weren't. Finance and fabrication were two touchy subjects. He had mixed feelings about Xander Chen's visit to his studio. Alex could still see Chen in the second-floor showroom, with his spiky hair and aggressively tailored navy suit, worn *Miami Vice* style with rolled up sleeves. Chen had been staring at the two giant canvases …

"Big paintings are hard to sell. My Fifth Avenue clients can't get them in the elevators to their apartments. And big pieces are too costly to ship and show at art fairs on spec." Chen had wandered to and fro, glancing perfunctorily at each of the two huge canvases before his restless gaze had searched for something else to look at.

Chen's reaction had disappointed Alex. He'd only remarked on how difficult the paintings would be to sell, nothing about the quality of the work or even if he liked them.

Back in Alex's ground level studio, Chen was enthusiastic about his mid-size abstracts. "These are good. Now this work looks like you." Chen nodded as Kent wheeled each abstract forward on their mobile display mounts, actually garment rails on castors. Alex preferred this method of showing work to taking paintings from stacks and putting them on easels. "No red ones?" Chen looked around hopefully.

Alex scratched his stubble. "I think I've explored that as much as I can. Here's something new I'm working on. I'm really excited about it." Alex was pleased at the way Chen sat forward expectantly as he drew down the blinds. Suki turned on the portable spot lamp. Chen winced and shielded his eyes. Kent rolled the first 'hole' piece between Chen and the lamp. Alex was in love with this layering technique, each iteration producing more depth and complexity depending on the materials used. Light through the holes projected spots over Chen's sharkskin suit.

Kent wheeled the next five 'hole' pieces forward.

"Different," was Chen's only comment.

"I'd like to explore this idea in metal as well. Freestanding monolithic pieces. Each with a different finish. Gold, silver, bronze. Enameled in flesh tones too, brown, tan, pink. Then have holes and slashes ripped and punched in them. Sharp, vicious, dangerous. I've experimented on a small scale. To produce them on the size I envisage I'd need to have them fabricated. I've got a foundry who can do it. They quoted me roughly eight thousand dollars per piece —"

"Sounds reasonable. Show them to me when they're done," had been Chen's last words before he went over to Suki to discuss the handling and shipping of the five of Alex's abstracts being consigned to him for sale.

Things hadn't been much more positive when he'd visited Neroli Copley in her downtown LA gallery.

"I'll never sell to Mariah Greely again!" Neroli popped another tab of nicotine gum into her mouth, her steely gray eyes wide and unblinking beneath her widescreen forehead framed by unforgiving dark bangs. "Last August she purchased your *Sphere 4* from me, vowing she'd treasure it forever. Flipping it at auction less than nine months later is very bad form. That's pop stars for you."

"Her last album bombed. Maybe she needs the money?"

"Alex, dear, we *all* need the money. She should have come to me to handle the resale. She's being greedy, banking that your MoMA show will increase your desirability. But there are no guarantees at auction. If *Sphere 4* achieves a good price, that's nice. Although neither you nor I will profit from a secondary sale. But what if it has a bad day at work, doesn't reach its reserve and gets withdrawn? That would be extremely detrimental to your selling prices in the primary market. And that *is* something which affects us both. *Sphere 4*'s a wonderful piece of work, and I've no doubt in its value, but the market's jittery." Neroli stared through the black frames of her gallery's industrial windows towards the construction project across the street. "That old flour mill's been vacant for over ten years. But soon it'll house thirty thousand square feet of space for the Los Angeles outpost of the Konrad Avery Gallery. Branches in New York, London, Paris, Shanghai and Seoul." Neroli clicked her nicotine gum. "I like the sound of your new work, but I can't offer backing. My gallery's contributed thirty thousand dollars for the catering of your MoMA opening as it is. I'm afraid I can't compete with these big new players." Neroli interweaved her fingers under her chin. "I regret I can't help financially but persevere with the metal pieces then let's talk again. I think you're headed in an exciting new direction with them."

    Neroli's enthusiasm had fired Alex up.

    Estimating he'd need around a hundred thousand dollars for materials and the foundry work, Alex booked a session in Santa Monica with Bryan Gervis, his CPA, business manager and financial guru. Bryan had formed the trust which owned the Venice property and also set up the companies into which Alex's sales and commissions got paid, which in turn paid him a salary. Alex's plan for Manuela's retirement was to buy her an apartment near her son and elderly sister. He didn't want to discuss it with Jorge until the finance was solid. Alex figured a nice place down the coast should come in around four hundred thousand. He hadn't been paying attention to profit and loss sheets while he'd been sick but figured he was good for that.

"Do you want to raise a loan against the house?" Bryan had asked, ruffling his thinning black hair and loosening his tie.

Alex studied the printouts Bryan pushed across the desk.

"Something wrong?" asked Bryan on seeing Alex's puzzled expression.

"I thought my liquid assets had more liquid."

"You have the finest medical insurance money can buy. And I mean that, it's extremely expensive. And you still have deductibles and medications to handle on top. Your investment pot took a massive hit in January. I advise you not to touch that, just pray it bounces back. Property tax on your Venice compound's running at thirty-five thousand per annum. Then you have staff salaries and benefits to cover. You send two thousand dollars to your sister every month. In the past two years you've had big expenses and moderate sales, but you do have massive equity in your property. You can afford to pay for the fabrication of your new work outright, and that would be a tax efficient expense. But as for buying the maid's retirement apartment, I advise you to release equity from your property rather than drain your liquid reserves."

Alex had felt really dumb on the drive home. He'd been reassuring Rick not to worry about money when his own financial picture wasn't as rosy as he thought. They were by no means poor, but the financial drain of his healthcare was depressing, and that expense was never going to lessen. No doubt about it, he needed to carry on working and make some big sales to maintain their current standard of living. If he'd just drifted off into a depressing area, coming back to the tail end of the Q and A wasn't much better …

Sitting up straight, Alex forced himself to pay attention.

Lainie had gone into a quick-fire round. "In one word, how would you describe yourself?"

Cayde: "Practical."

Allen: "Myopic."

Rod: "Virile!"

Alex paused. This hadn't been a fun evening, it involved far too much introspection. "Stoic," was the word he dredged up. He should have said, "Conflicted."

Lainie: "Which of you is the better artist?"

This was a hot potato. The men exchanged glances.

"We don't think that way," Cayde answered on behalf of them all. "Art isn't a competition."

Lainie asked, "What do you dream about?"

Cayde: "Hawaii."

Allen: "My wife."

Rod: "Chicks." His politically incorrect answer elicited a reluctant laugh from the audience.

Alex used that laughter to cover thinking about what he should say. Last night he'd dreamed about Rick. It had been a strange dream. Jack also figured in it. Alex couldn't recall the details, but he'd woken up with a solid erection. His honest answer should have been 'sex with men,' but instead he said, "Being twenty-nine again."

"Final question." Lainie tapped her cards into a neat pile. "Why are you here?"

Rod answered with a glib, "Because you invited me."

"The open bar," joked Allen.

"Best offer I got on a Friday night," said Cayde.

Going last, Alex stared out into the auditorium. It reminded him of the old days when he gave talks at universities and art colleges. All those eager young eyes fixed expectantly on you, like you were about to give them the answer to everything they ever needed to know, that your words would solve the puzzle of their life. When in fact you were still trying to solve the puzzle yourself. Alex's eyes fell on Rick, who'd come into his life at a time when he doubted his artistic talent and was on the verge of quitting. Rick had believed in him, pushed him and introduced him to the clientele who'd made his career. He thought of his grandma Dora, she'd given him a home, forged his moral compass and made him the man he was today. He thought of Danielle, who had been his friend and companion, who'd given him everything and never asked for anything in return.

Why was he here?

"Love," said Alex.

It was the only truly honest answer he'd given all night.

VISIONS

"Cute attempt to stowaway, but you gotta stay home." Rick shooed Bella from the open suitcase on the bed. "She threw up a little food again this morning. I wonder if she's eating too fast, you should wear this on Tuesday."

Rick's aptitude for changing subject mid-sentence caught Alex off-guard. He looked up from packing underwear, electronic chargers and medication in his carry-on. Rick was holding up an intensely crimson formal jacket. Rick had insisted it was *fabulous* when they dropped by Versace one afternoon and he'd been coerced into trying it on. "I dunno. It's kind of showy."

"You wore it to the Murakami opening last year. I still smell your Acqua di Parma on it." Rick buried his nose in the jacket. "You looked so handsome. Every eye in the room was on you."

"Yeah, I felt like I was upstaging Murakami."

"This is *your* opening night, you're entitled to upstage. Your outfit should shout your name to the world."

"How about I get one of my paintings printed on silk then have a jacket tailored from it? My signature could be emblazoned across the back. That way even from behind I'd be identifiable."

"Could we get that done in two days?"

"Do you know me at all? Would I really do that?"

Dropping his eyes, Rick slipped the red jacket off the hanger. "I'll pack it anyway. What are you wearing for the *Vanity Fair* interview?"

"Dunno. Xander mentioned a stylist."

"We should take a couple of your denim shirts. You look super sexy in the one with the appliquéd embroidery. And I'll throw in one of your paint-splashed work shirts in case they want an 'the artist didn't have time to change from his studio' look."

"Why not pack a wet paintbrush to stick behind my ear too? Chen's running the publicity. And I doubt sexy tops his list for promoting me to his client base."

"It should be. Sex sells."

"This is art, not showbiz."

"Everything's showbiz when it comes to selling. Anyway, don't let Chen bully you into wearing something you're not comfortable with."

"Don't worry, I won't." Alex was tempted to add, 'I'll leave the bullying me into wearing something I'm uncomfortable with up to you,' but resisted. Rick's nose was out of joint enough with Chen requesting he be kept clear of all interview proceedings on the basis of not confusing the message. Frankly, he couldn't care less what he wore as long as satin, ruffles and Ascots weren't involved. He shuddered to see Rick piling more shirts and pants in the case. "Do you really need to pack so much? We're only away a few days."

"Chen's townhouse soiree's the night after MoMA," said Rick making another foray to the walk-in. "And Cristina and Ellery will be in town. They're coming to your opening. We're meeting up for drinks and dinner!"

Rick shouted this breaking news from the walk-in, meaning Alex didn't have to disguise his groan of frustration. "Must we? I don't know Ellery, and I barely know Cristina. I'm terrible at small talk with those society women. I've got nothing in common with them."

"You might find you do if you get to know them better. At least my friends are coming to your opening which is more than can be said of your pals!"

"It's a lot to expect the guys to fly cross-country just for me," said Alex rationally. But he'd had to hide his disappointment at the post Q and A dinner in Santa Monica when Rod, Cayde and Allen had all come up with lame excuses why they couldn't get to NYC. Scotty had been the only one at the table who expressed any overt enthusiasm for his retrospective's gala opening. She loudly regretted she couldn't be there, but the forty-thousand-dollar birthday party she was organizing for a five-year-old in Laurel Canyon was the same night. Although he'd been friends with the guys for years, Alex sometimes wondered how seriously they took him as an artist. He always felt like the underdog who'd made his name through luck rather than talent. Cayde hadn't allowed anyone to answer Lainie's 'who's the better artist?' question at the Q and A. Rod was definitely the most successful in terms of selling price, Allen the most original and Cayde the most prolific. Would any of them have mentioned his name in *any* category if pushed?

"You could wear this!" Rick marched into the bedroom with a garment carrier. Unzipping it, he swished out the white jacket from Giorgio Beverly Hills he'd bought for Alex shortly after moving into his beach house. "It's in mint condition."

"I told you at the time I'd never wear a white jacket unless I was selling ice cream on the boardwalk."

"You've hung on to it for over thirty years all the same."

"Gee, look how wide those lapels are. And see that nipped in waist. The seventies were wild."

"Put it on."

"No way. Let's donate it to the Smithsonian."

"Please?" Rick cajoled with his puppy dog look. "Surely you owe me the satisfaction of seeing you wear it at least once."

Alex wasn't going to let Rick's doe-eyes get to him and feel like the fatted calf if he couldn't fasten the waist button. "I'll add a codicil to my will that I be buried in it."

"In that case, I hope I never get to see you in it." Zipping up the garment bag, Rick returned it to the walk-in.

"Wanna come for a ride, girl?" In response, Bella padded to Alex and rubbed her golden head into his knee.

Rick reappeared with another armful of hangers.

"If we end up taking three checked-in bags you'll be hauling 'em all off the carousel yourself, bucko. Okay, I'm going to pick up the kids." Bella went and flopped back by the fireplace. "I was going to take Bella. Seems she'd rather stay with you."

"I must've tired her out on her morning walk. Drive safe."

Alex gave Rick a kiss, happy for a couple of hours on the road to Toluca Lake and back, well out of reach of any more of Rick's fashion stylings.

* * *

The spell of unseasonably high temperatures and strong winds in the middle of May had passed. Now, at the end of the month, the weather had cooled and low cloud diffused the sun. While he drove, it struck Alex how the style and color of vehicles defined an era. The optimistic gas guzzling Pontiacs and Lincoln Continentals in Cherokee Red and Pale Turquoise of the '60s, the hedonistic Mustangs and Camaros in Citrus Green and Grabber Orange of the '70s, and the imposing Dodges and Chryslers in Nightwatch Blue and Mocha Brown of the '80s all had had their corners knocked off. They'd evolved into the homogenous fuel-efficient convoy of dull white, gray, black and silver lookalikes rolling along the 101 on an equally dull day.

Alex glimpsed his face and hair in the rear-view mirror. In his lifeguard and sailing years he could have been lumped into the Tom Selleck category, only his own wavy brown hair had been below shoulder length. How many more years could he carry off his latter-day surfer dude look without coming across as a sad relic? Maybe he already did and no-one had the guts to tell him. Checking his mirrors to take the off-ramp, he noted more silver hairs creeping in amongst the graphite ones. His Tom Selleck days were long gone. He was headed into Willie Nelson territory.

Wondering if he could pick up work as a Santa lookalike if his hair and beard turned completely white, Alex navigated the pleasant tree-lined streets of the villagey neighborhood. Pulling up outside a white stucco villa, he'd barely got out and started lifting the Cherokee Grand Jeep's powered tailgate before Tiffany bustled through her black wrought iron gates.

"Toothbrushes, PJs, Nintendo charger, Jay's asthma inhaler, more of his books, and cream for Maddy's rash," said Tiffany slinging the kids' bags in the Jeep's rear. "This is Maddy's favorite CD. I warn you she'll sing along, loudly, and Celine Dion she ain't." Tiffany handed him a Disney Princess compilation disc. "You're good to go. Don't think I've forgotten anything."

"You have missed a couple of things," said Alex as the Jeep's tailgate latched shut.

Panic flashed across Tiffany's green-gold eyes. "What?"

"The two kids I'm collecting."

"Forgive. I've been fasting since last night for the diagnostics." Tiffany turned to the house. "Maddy, Jay! Uncle Alex is here!" She leaned to him. "Stick to the story I got a night shoot, okay? I don't want to worry them about hospital stuff."

"Cool. I'll get them back tomorrow around six?"

"Great. The hospital's got your contact details. They'll let you know if anything turns up which could mean a change of plan. Maddy's been super clingy of late. If she wakes in the night let her cry it out. Jay will sleep through, no problem. But don't let him read under the covers or you'll never get him up. Anyway, Rick knows how to handle them ..." Tiffany's voice trailed off.

A freckle faced nine-year-old boy with a pudding bowl cut, Harry Potter style glasses and low-slung gangster-chic pants, and a five-year-old girl with corkscrew ginger curls wearing pink dungarees and carrying a pink backpack tumbled out of the house.

"Hi there! You guys ready to roll?" Alex called.

Maddy skipped down the red brick driveway between the neatly trimmed parkway. "Uncle Alex!"

Alex creakily kneeled to hug her. With one arm around Maddy, he turned to Jay. "Howdy, pardner." Alex rubbed his chin in contemplation of Jay's half-mast pants. "Back at the ranch we're gonna find you a belt to hold up them dang pants."

Jay shook his pudding bowl hair. "You've done that joke before, Uncle Alex."

"Yeah, well everyone needs writers." Alex grunted as he got to his feet. He opened the SUV's rear door. Looking from one kid to the other, and adopting a Clouseau style French accent, he said, "We 'ave none of ze, 'ow you say, bathroom breaks on ze freeway, so speek now or forever 'old your piss." This managed a grin from Jay and pursed lips from Tiffany. "Gold and Diamond members take your seats." He took Maddy's backpack as she and Jay clambered in the Jeep. "Don't worry. We'll take good care of them."

Tiffany forced a smile and waved to the kids. "Be good. Don't break anything expensive!"

In the mirror, Alex watched Tiffany's waving hand recede into the green treed distance as he drove off.

Traffic flowed smoothly on the 101. Before long they were back over the hill. Fountain was as quiet as Alex had hoped. Apart from a traffic snarl around road repairs on La Cienega the journey had been plain sailing. Bored with her Nintendo, Maddy asked him to put on her Disney CD. Sat in traffic waiting for the crosswalk pedestrians to clear, the store to his right with PSYCHIC on its blue canopy caught Alex's eye. He was amazed there could be enough weak minds willing to believe that bullshit to keep such places in business. As the intro to 'Beauty and the Beast' played, they got a green. Traffic in front moved.

He accelerated along with the vehicles surrounding him. Pressing the gas and swinging the wheel onto Route 66, he couldn't see clearly. Wondering if the windshield had got schmutzed, he moved his head to look around the smear. The jazzy patch in his vision moved too. Shit. A waterfalling hole had opened up in his right field of vision. He had a vehicle hard on his tail. Slamming on the brakes wasn't an option. The possibility of entirely losing his vision terrified him. He kept on making the turn, doing his utmost to look around the distortion. From his right, a dark-haired woman darted onto the crosswalk. He caught a flash of her hand flailing to the car. He knew the woman. It was Danielle!

"Fuck!" Alex swerved left.

A blare of a horns jarred outside.

Expecting the sickening thud of a body hitting the sidewalk and the crunch of metal, Alex was surprised the only things he heard were Maddy's outraged gasp and Disney strings. He was on Santa Monica, safely in the traffic flow. He had to blink a few times before he could breathe again. The hole in his vision had cleared, leaving a faint shimmering ring. "Everyone okay in back?"

"You said the bad word!" exclaimed Maddy.

"I know, sorry." That scare rattled his heart. To have a vision problem in dense traffic was bad enough, but for the woman he'd narrowly missed to resemble Danielle was beyond freaky. "Can you see her? Did the woman make it across okay?"

"What woman?" asked Jay.

"Crazy lady who stepped out against the light." Over his shoulder, Alex found Jay checking behind them.

"I only saw the silver Buick that pulled out from the liquor store without looking," replied Jay. "If you hadn't swerved, he'd have hit us for sure."

Alex struggled to compute what had just gone down. The blare of horns must have been for the Buick rather than his evasive maneuver. He'd seen no vehicle coming from his right, only Danielle's lookalike with the outstretched hand. But if the hole in his right vision had hidden the Buick, how could he have seen the woman? And Jay hadn't seen anyone on the crosswalk at all.

"If that car had hit us, would we all be dead now?" Maddy asked matter-of-factly.

"No, honey. This Jeep's built like a tank. We may have gotten shaken up, but we'd have been fine," Alex lied. "Erase the bad word I said from your memory banks."

Leaving the near miss behind them, Maddy sang along to her Disney CD, loudly, and Jay played on his Nintendo with his headphones on. Alex wondered if he ought to go straight to an eye clinic, but as the problem had pretty much cleared that seemed extreme. With his New York opening only days away, an optometrist's appointment could surely wait till they got back to LA?

Flicking the remote to raise the door, Alex drove into his garage's safe harbor. It darkened as the motor's hum lowered the door. "Go on in and say hi to Rick. I'll bring your bags." The kids clambered out. They were leaving by the side door when he yelled, "Be careful around the pool!" Leaning on the Jeep, he checked his racing heartrate. When his pulse had slowed sufficiently, he carried the kids' bags over the pool bridge. Rick and Jay were at the patio table. Rick was writing in a greetings card. Jay had his nose in his book. "Where's Maddy?"

"With Manuela in the kitchen. Sign this." Rick pushed the card and pen to Alex.

"Whose birthday?" Alex grunted with annoyance upon reading the name inside.

"Myrna's your sister. She was extremely concerned when you were sick."

"Probably worried her monthly checks would dry up." Alex dutifully signed the card.

"Would 'love, Alex' have killed you?" Rick blew on the wet ink.

Tossing a 'don't push your luck' expression Rick's way, Alex said to Jay, "We've made up the study for you." He tapped Jay's knapsack to Rick's shoulder. "Wanna take him through?"

Rick slipped the card in its envelope. "Let's get you checked in. That must be a good book, you can't put it down. What's it called?"

Jay finished the line he was reading before placing his bookmark. "*The Mysterious Benedict Society*. It may be the finest book ever written."

Jay delivered this opinion so profoundly Alex and Rick struggled not to laugh. Not to mock him but because of his sweet earnestness.

"What?" Rick asked in equally serious measure. "Even better than The Hardy Boys in *Whatever Happened at Midnight*?"

Jay wrinkled his freckled nose. "Is that a new book?"

"No, it's a very, very, very, *very* old book from when Uncle Rick was a boy." Alex picked up Maddy's pink backpack and overnighter.

"It's not that old," Rick huffed as he took Jay to the house's rear wing. "You make it sound like it was written with a quill on parchment."

In the kitchen, Alex found Manuela at the counter folding a napkin. Maddy sat on a tall stool with a napkin of her own, copying. Bella sat expectantly on the floor, her curly tail swishing from side to side, staring up at them both.

"*Ahora, nosotras hacemos dos alas …*" Manuela made two final folds for the wings, placed the napkin on the counter and announced, "*Un cisne*!"

"Wanna put your things in your room?" Alex called to Maddy.

"But we're making swans," Maddy said petulantly.

"We do more later. I teach you how to make a rose." Manuela patted Maddy's hand. "What time you wish to eat, Mr. Alex?"

"Round seven's fine. Come Bella, out!" Due to the unfortunate incident of the cremated chicken in the night, Bella was banned from the kitchen when Manuela was preparing food alone. Having shut the dog outside, Alex led Maddy to the guest bedroom decorated in soft greens and pinks.

The kids had visited the house before, but this was the first time they'd stayed over. The house's rear wing had lots of doors, concealed storage spaces and utilities. Alex and Rick took their time to make sure both kids knew the location of the bathrooms, light switches, and where to go if an earthquake struck. Once toothbrushes had been installed in mugs in the half-bath and PJs under pillows on beds, they regrouped in the entrance hall. "Wanna hit the beach before dinner?" Alex let Bella in, put on her leash and they headed out through the roller gate onto the street.

    Warning the kids to beware of vehicles on the road, and bikers, joggers, skaters and skateboarders on the boardwalk, Rick held Maddy's hand, Alex put Jay in charge of Bella, and they strolled down Brooks Avenue towards the beach.

    The palm trees, colorful boardwalk chaos and clack of skateboard wheels hitting concrete warmed Alex's heart. Finding a bench under the green umbrellas on the sand's edge, he kicked off his sandals. "You guys coming to touch the ocean?" He had a vision of bringing Jay down here with a couple of boards in a few years' time and teaching him to surf. As far as Rick was concerned beaches were purely for lounging on.

    Maddy eagerly undid her pink sneakers.

    Jay pulled back. "I don't like sand."

    "Dogs aren't allowed on the beach, so you hang on the boardwalk with Rick and Bella." Alex thought it odd for a kid not to like sand but didn't say anything. That pipe dream of passing on his surfing tips to this protégé was quickly dispelled.

    Maddy trotted towards the rolling surf. The tide was on the turn with a salty breeze coming in off the Pacific. Slipping the elastic from his wrist to tie back his hair and stop it blowing in his face, Alex scooted around beachgoers to catch up with her. Sand under his bare feet always felt like coming home. After rolling up Maddy's dungarees and his own pants, they wandered along the surf's edge. Maddy breaking off to chase gulls and gaily twirl in the sun with outspread arms. A handful of surfers were bobbing near the breakwater ready for the incoming tide. Maybe Jay's lack of enthusiasm for the beach was for the best. Dudes over sixty looked kinda tragic on boards, and Alex wondered if his surfer's muscle memory was still there anyway. Maybe he just needed to accept that part of his life was over.

"You missed the picking up poop portion of the outing," said Rick when they met back up on the boardwalk.

"I don't like to deprive you of the pleasure. Besides, you do it so well." Alex took his sandals from Rick.

"Yew," Jay added with disgust. "It was yucky."

"Yeah, we really must get her digestion checked out when we're back," said Rick as he helped Maddy fasten her sneakers.

Colorful arrays of original paintings, the woman who engraved your name on a grain of rice, t-shirt stalls, hippie badge sellers, henna tattooists and tarot readers plied their trade in shop fronts and higgledy-piggledy stalls, while street performers punctuated the boardwalk hubbub. Birdie, one of the beach's homeless regulars, sat cross-legged under a palm. Her possessions in three checkered storage bags sat by her side and a hand-written sign saying 'BAD ADVICE - $2' was propped up in front.

"Yo, Birdie." Alex fished in his pocket. "If I ever give up painting, what job should I take instead?"

Birdie squinted up from under her orange Day-Glo visor, chewed her wrinkled lip, then declared, "Fire-eater!"

They all laughed.

Alex handed Maddy a couple of bills and whispered for her to pop them in Birdie's cup.

"Thanks darlin'." Birdie smiled at Maddy and gave a raspy laugh. "If you need bad advice then I'm your woman. Look where it's got me!"

Alex, Rick, Bella and the kids ambled along the boardwalk. Turning to head home, they passed Zofia's stall. Using a blowtorch to melt wax crayons on canvas was her method of making art. The results, weird panels of swirls, drips and lumps, were displayed on stands and easels.

"*Hola*, Alex!" Zofia shouted.

Rick and the kids carried on while Alex paused to admire Zofia's latest creations. There was something angry about her work, especially a couple of new pieces she'd made from red and black crayons. He wished he hadn't looked at them. The tortured, dark wax stirred the memory of that hellish death dream he'd had in the hospital.

"You like?" Zofia toyed with her shell necklace.

"Intense. How's business?"

"Selling art becomes harder here every day. Too many stalls with plastic crap from China, pah." Giving a disdainful glance at her neighboring souvenir stall, Zofia told Alex about a proposal to empower the police to rule on what is and isn't art, thus allowing them to close stalls selling mass produced goods to prioritize space for local artists.

As Alex listened intently to Zofia, he grew aware of the woman with rainbow braids on the psychic stall opposite staring at him. Her gaze made him uncomfortable. Agreeing the proposal sounded like it would help local artists, Alex prised himself from Zofia's clutches. Weaving through sightseers to catch up with Rick and the kids, Alex felt someone tap his shoulder. He wheeled around.

"Excuse me." It was the woman from the psychic stall.

"Sorry, I haven't got time …"

"Alex?"

He was shocked. How could this stranger know his name? She must have overheard Zofia call out to him. "Nice touch using my name but —"

"You're a painter."

"I'm not interested in phony psychic crap." Alex's voice rose. "Pick on some other sucker."

Rick, Jay and Maddy had pushed through the crowd and now stood right behind him. "I thought we'd lost you." Rick was hanging on to Maddy's hand. Jay was holding Bella, who was trying to leg him over with her leash. Rick looked between Alex's angry face and the rainbow-braided psychic's puzzled expression. "Everything okay?"

"Fine, let's go." Alex took Bella's leash.

The braid lady calmed Alex. "I know you —"

"No, you do not! Back off, lady!"

The kids regarded Alex nervously.

"I was at Cal State with you. It's me, Jane. Jane Zalando."

Alex wavered, instantly feeling foolish for overreacting. "Hey." He racked his brain to place her. Nothing was coming. "How're things?"

"It's my second week here. You live nearby?"

"Um, yeah." Alex vaguely motioned to his left. "You?"

"Silver Lake. Some coincidence running into you, huh?"

"Yeah. Look, we gotta get going ..." Alex edged away.

"Just wanted to say hi." Jane looked at Rick, Maddy, Jay and Bella, who in turn were regarding Alex with disquiet. Smiling at Alex, Jane said, "You have a beautiful family."

Her words struck Alex's heart. "They're not mine ..." His world stopped revolving.

Jane looked at him, *really* looked at him.

Alex shuddered.

Jane's countenance changed, almost to shock, like she'd seen something alarming inside him. "Good to see you." Jane broke away.

The boardwalk's noise and bustle faded back in as Alex walked on with Rick and the kids. After only taking a few steps, he regretted how badly that encounter had ended. "Give me a minute," he mumbled to Rick. Working his way back through the shuffling tourists, he went up to Jane's stall. "I acted like a jerk. You caught me off guard, sorry."

Jane nodded.

"Maybe we can catch up some other time?"

"Cool."

"Er, back there," said Alex. "It felt like you wanted to tell me something."

"It's not my place to tell you anything. Not unless you ask me."

Should he, or shouldn't he? "Okay, I'm asking."

Jane shuffled her tarot cards then held them out.

"I haven't got long." Alex instantly wished he hadn't made this connection.

"Pick one."

Hating himself for his curiosity, Alex did so.

Jane laid the card face up on her table.

The Hanged Man.

Alex shied away, that didn't look good.

"Don't panic. I already knew what I needed to tell you. This makes it professional.

"Need to tell me?"

Jane looked through Alex, like she saw someone behind him. "You won't move on until you let him go."

"Uncle Alex?"

He felt a tug on his sleeve.

"Uncle Rick says we need to go home," said Jay.

Farther down the boardwalk, Alex saw Rick giving him an irritated glare while he held on to Maddy and Bella.

"Let go of who?" Alex asked Jane.

"You'll know," said Jane cryptically.

"Al! Come on!" yelled Rick agitatedly.

"I have to go." Alex pointed to Rick.

Jane nodded, then shuffled The Hanged Man into the pack.

"Why'd you go back to her? You hate that psychic stuff." Rick asked as they walked home.

"She recognized me, but I didn't remember her. I was rude. I needed to apologize."

"Why did you take the card?" asked Jay.

"To be polite," said Alex.

Back home, Manuela had laid the table for dinner on the patio. Rick put on a Harry Potter DVD in the den for Jay and

Maddy kept Manuela to her promise of a napkin folding masterclass.

Once Maddy had learned how to fold a rose, a fan and a crown, Alex told Manuela to take the rest of the weekend off. Distractedly, Manuela untied her apron and hung it up. She stroked Maddy's hair before leaving for her apartment. Alex sent Maddy to wash her hands and yelled to Jay to turn off the TV and do the same ready for dinner.

Rick came in to fix the kids' drinks. "Where's Manuela?"

"She looked beat. I told her to take the rest of the weekend off." He noticed Rick's jaw twitch. "She's prepared dinner. All you need to do is serve it."

"If I'd known you were giving Manuela the night off, I'd have suggested we eat inside."

"Why?"

"Because it's easier for me than bringing everything in and out to the patio. I wouldn't mind relaxing as well. Too late now. Take out their juice and water and get them to the table."

Keeping Bella by his ankles to stop her from getting under Rick's feet, Alex entertained the kids while Rick made five trips to the kitchen and back to bring out the enchiladas, tostados, tortilla chips, guacamole and salads.

The kids adored Manuela's meal.

Rick cleared the serving platters, bowls, plates and cutlery. He then made three more trips to bring out the dessert, blueberries with dairy-free frozen yogurt topped with granola and more drinks. Once Rick had cleared away the dessert dishes, they played Jenga around the table. Alex was terrible at this and kept knocking down the pile. This resulted in Bella running off with any blocks that fell on the ground and Rick chasing her to retrieve them. The dusk timer tripped in the illuminations. Rick walked Maddy around to enjoy the twinkling lights in the trees. He then took her inside to get ready for bed while Alex played Scrabble with Jay. At nine, Rick discretely brought out Alex's evening meds. Just after nine-thirty, Rick declared Jay's bedtime, issuing a stern lights-out for ten-thirty with *no* flashlight reading.

Both kids safely tucked up and everything cleared away, Rick opened the wine and poured himself an exceptionally large chardonnay. "I wish you'd discuss things with me before making decisions."

"Huh?"

"Like giving Manuela the night off. Even telling Tiffany we'd have the kids tonight. Let alone all that schmoozing with your boardwalk cronies leaving me to deal with the kids and the dog. You really do act like a one-man band at times."

"That's rich coming from you. How about making dinner dates in New York with people I don't want to socialize with? Taking a part on a TV show you know I didn't want you to do. And how quickly you forget lying to me about seeing Dr. Susskind."

Rick didn't respond. He sipped his wine. "When do you plan on speaking with Jorge about Manuela's retirement?"

"Soon."

"I wish you'd hurry up."

"Can't you hire in extra help for now?"

"I tried, remember? Every time the agency sends a temp Manuela's obstructive. Either she won't tell them where things are or tells them wrong or picks some niggly fault and they never come back. And our household appliances are taking a real beating. She keeps saying our vacuum cleaner's broken. The last time it happened I checked the hose. She'd sucked up two of Bella's chew toys and a pair of my silk briefs."

Alex and Rick looked deeply into each other's eyes.

Then they burst out laughing at the ridiculousness of it all.

"Seriously, it's like living with a malfunctioning Stepford Wife," Rick chuckled.

"Good job we don't keep hamsters." Standing behind Rick, Alex kneaded his shoulders. "Manuela means well. I'll sort it out. Give me time, babe."

The encounter with Jane and the Manuela situation occupied Alex's mind as he gave Bella her last walk of the day. A noisy party with loud music and raucous voices was taking place in the studio apartments across the street. Back home, he locked up the house, finishing with the glazed front door to the decked passage between the houses. Hearing the muffled music's thump from across the road, he checked if lights were on in Danielle's rooms upstairs in the small house. Did he hope there were?

They were dark.

A lone bulb burned behind Manuela's kitchen blind.

Passing the study, Alex peeked round the door. Jay was asleep with no sign of a flashlight under the covers. Leaving the study door ajar, he cut through the storage and walk-in to the master bath. He used the john, brushed and Waterpiked his teeth, washed his face then stripped off his clothes. Rick had drawn the gauze curtains and was reading in bed when Alex slipped in beside him. "I hope Tiffany's okay."

"Me too." Rick closed his book. "Imagine if it's like one of those Lifetime movies where she dies and we end up having to raise the second generation of no-neck monsters."

"We'd manage. They're sweet kids. Though I'm never playing Scrabble with Jay again. The kid wiped the board with me."

"I've done my share of child rearing. Patti was enough, thank you very much. *Buona notte.*" Rick turned out his light.

Alex pondered what kind of father he'd have made. He'd nearly involved the kids in a car crash, said 'fuck' in front of them and let them witness him lose his temper with an innocent tarot reader who turned out to be an old acquaintance. Not exactly a stunning display of parental suitability.

The sound of crying roused Alex from a dream about footsteps and shadows in the passageway between the houses.

Rolling over, he saw Rick's head was raised from the pillow. "Maddy's woken up."

They gave it a couple of minutes.

A child cried out, "Mom!"

"That's not Maddy, that's Jay," said Rick.

They lay still, hoping he'd quieten down.

Jay's crying grew louder.

Rick got out of bed.

"What are you doing?" Alex sat up.

"Going to him."

"Tiffany said to let them cry it out."

Jay's sobs echoed down the corridor.

"He'll wake Maddy. He may be going into an asthma attack." Pulling on a pair of shorts and a t-shirt, Rick went to investigate.

Fully conscious now, Alex heard Rick's voice down the corridor calming Jay. But it sounded like Jay was becoming more distressed.

A moment later, Rick came back in their bedroom. "Put on some clothes. I'm bringing him in."

Fast as he could, Alex fished out a pair of lounge pants and a tank from the credenza and pulled them on. He dimmed the bedside lamp.

"Calm down, it's okay, everything's okay," said Rick soothingly as he brought Jay, in his Harry Potter pajamas, into the bedroom.

"Sit with Alex. I've got your inhaler." Rick guided Jay to the bed.

The kid was shivering fit to bust and couldn't catch his breath. Alex rubbed Jay's shoulders while Rick guided the inhaler to his mouth. Rick gave him two puffs, then waited. Jay's breathing calmed. Once Jay's respiration eased, he began crying again.

"Jay, shh. We're here, you're safe." Rick sat on the other side of Jay. They did their best to reassure him, but the boy was terribly upset. Rick and Alex looked at each other, wondering what to try next. Then Rick had an idea. "I'm looking for a book to read. What was the one you said was so good this afternoon?"

Jay took an easy breath before stammering, "*The M … M …. Mysterious Benedict Society.*"

"Can you tell me what it's about?"

Jay had to calm down enough to inhale so he could speak. "There are these four children, and they're super-smart. And there are all these puzzles and clues they have to solve. You see they need to save the world from …"

In the golden glow of the dimmed lamp, Alex watched Rick listen intently to Jay recounting the story. As he lost himself in the plot, Jay's tears dried and his trembling abated.

"It sounds good. I'll have to read it so we can have a proper book club discussion," said Rick. "That's better. Ready to go back to bed?"

Jay's lip quivered. "No. I'm scared."

Alex was concerned there may be a piece of art or sculpture in the study they'd gotten used to seeing but may frighten a kid in the dark. "What're you scared of?"

"Mommy," said Jay.

"Why are you scared of your mommy?" Rick asked.

"I'm scared m… m… mommy's going to die," stammered Jay.

"Your mom's not going to die. She's young. You don't need to worry about that," said Rick.

"But she's sick. And I know I'm not meant to know, but she's gone to the hospital. People die in hospitals."

"Sometimes they do, but most people who go to the hospital get well again. Remember when Uncle Alex had to go to the hospital because his heart wasn't working properly? He didn't die, did he? The doctors and nurses fixed him up and look at him now. Good as new."

Jay looked to Alex for confirmation.

"All working fine." He tapped his chest.

This information reassured Jay.

"What's happening?" Maddy stood in the doorway, rubbing her eyes with one hand and clutching Flopsie bunny in her other.

"Jay had a nightmare," said Rick. "Go back to bed."

"I don't want to," said Maddy.

Rick stifled an annoyed sigh. "It's three in the morning, Maddy. We all need some sleep."

"I don't want to go back to that room. The lady will look at me," murmured Maddy.

"What lady?"

"The dark lady outside the window," said Maddy.

"That'll be Manuela on her nighttime wanderings," grumbled Rick. "Okay. Executive decision." Rick threw back the sheets. "I for one would like to get more than seventeen minutes sleep tonight. If this is the only way to achieve it, so be it. Hop in."

With a sense of disbelief, Jay and Maddy gratefully clambered into the middle of the bed.

Alex and Rick positioned themselves on the edges. "See. Security guards on either side," said Rick as he pulled up the covers.

A clatter of claws along the hallway. A moment later, Bella raced in and hurled herself on the bed in a Fosbury Flop.

"And a guard dog!" Rick laughed. "This is nuts! Shall we call for Manuela as well?"

Jay giggled.

"Now can everybody shut up and go to sleep?" Rick barked in mock annoyance.

Alex killed the bedside light.

Ten minutes later all was peaceful. The hum of the pool's filter pump, the soft breaths of two sleeping kids and Bella snuffling away were the only sounds in the bedroom.

"Nice work, kiddo," Alex whispered to Rick.

"Night babe," Rick whispered back. "Tiffany'll probably kill me for doing this, but I'm too tired to give a fuck. Love you."

Alex drifted to the other world of sleep, thinking how contentment may enter your life in such unexpected moments.

NEW YORK'S BURNING

Alex and Rick silently slunk out of bed at six-forty-five and tiptoed around. Due to the disturbance in the night, they left the blinds down and let the kids sleep in.

Rick walked Bella while Alex took his morning swim. Taking his shower on the rear deck, he used the door into the master bath, then cut through the walk-in, storage closets and laundry to get to the kitchen.

Rick had laid the ingredients, well back from the edge of the counter and covered, for his supposedly anti-inflammatory morning shake. Blueberries, mango and spinach blended with apple cider vinegar, honey and weird seeds soaked in water resembling frogspawn was today's special. Taking advantage of Rick walking the dog, Alex made a cup of instant coffee to line his stomach for the healthful assault. Sipping the coffee, he thought about yesterday. Thinking he'd seen Danielle when he nearly had the crash, Jane's unnerving psychic message and Maddy saying she'd seen a dark lady looking through her window bothered him on many levels. He didn't believe in life after death. But what if it believed in him? Was the possibility of a person's essence carrying on for eternity a comforting prospect or an alarming one? A lot depended on whose essence it was. He drained his cup, washed it out and put it back so Rick wouldn't get on his back about having coffee.

Leaving the house, Alex crossed the passage and tapped on Manuela's door. "Manuela, you awake?"

After the shuffling of feet, the door opened a crack and Manuela peered through. "Mr. Alex, you need something?"

"No, no. Did you sleep okay? I mean, last night, did you take a walk?"

"Why do you ask, Mr. Alex?"

"Something disturbed the kids."

Manuela tightened her pink nylon housecoat's collar. "The children, they are all right?"

"They're fine." He glanced at the double doors between the houses. "We're pretty secure behind these walls, but I had to put my mind at rest we didn't have an intruder. You didn't hear anything unusual, did you?"

"Nothing unusual."

"And you didn't go out?"

Confusion crossed Manuela's face. "Not out. No."

"Maddy must have had a bad dream." Alex casually looked over Manuela's shoulder. Piles of newspapers and magazines lay around her living-room. Dirty dishes and pots sat on her galley kitchen's drainer. A pan of cabbage and beans simmered on her stovetop.

"Is that all, Mr. Alex?"

"Your son hasn't visited for a while. How is he?"

"Jorge travels for his work." Manuela smiled proudly. "My boy is a very busy man."

"Why don't you go visit him?"

"Rancho del Rey is a long way away. Too far to go there and back in one day."

"Take time off. A vacation. As long as you like. We'd keep you on salary."

"But the house needs me. I could not leave it alone."

"Rick's here. And we can find someone to cover your work. I'm touched by your devotion, but you could do with a rest and —"

"Does Mr. Rick want me to go? He was so mad at me about the chickens. But Missy Bella she so quick. I tell him I pay for the chickens. And then he get mad I buy the wrong honey. I tell him I go back to the store to get the one he want for you. I try to do things how Mr. Rick like, but he say so many things and —"

"This isn't about that. And Mr. Rick … Rick doesn't want you to go away. Neither of us wants you to go away. We've been together so long you've become a part of this house. Like one of the walls that hold it up. But you can't keep carrying that load. And it would be wrong of me to let you. I'm not saying it should happen tomorrow, but we need to find a way for you to finish working and enjoy living."

Manuela raised her eyes to the addition they'd built onto the small house in the mid-nineties, the upstairs rooms where Danielle had spent her final year. "If I am not here, who will watch over her?"

"Danielle's not there. Only her things."

Manuela looked confused. "Yes, her things …"

Behind Manuela, Alex saw steam rising in her kitchen.

"You'd better get that …" he pointed inside.

"Is that all, Mr. Alex?"

"Yeah." Alex stood outside Manuela's closed door, kicking himself for handling this in a ham-fisted manner. He cursed himself for leaving Danielle's rooms as they were for so long. The luxury of too much space had allowed him not to face up to things sooner. But if it hadn't been Manuela looking through Maddy's window last night, could it be that an echo of Danielle lingered here? No, he ruled out giving headroom to such fantastical thoughts, that way madness lies. The moment he set foot through the front door, he heard Rick hit the dreaded blender.

"Morning all," Alex said overly brightly, strolling into the kitchen. Bella padded to him with a floppy tail wag. Maddy and Jay were at the counter eating their granola, Jay chattering with Rick, and Maddy watching cartoons. The next thing Alex knew was one of Rick's gray frothy concoctions being thrust into his hand. The kids watched him chug it down with gleeful horror. "Congratulations to the chef. Up to its usual level of disgusting." He handed the beaker to Rick. "Can you come outside? I need you to look at a lizard by the pool. I think it's sick."

"Can we see?" Maddy got down from her stool.

Judging by Alex's tone that he didn't want to discuss a sick lizard, Rick told Maddy, "No. Finish your breakfast." Rick accompanied Alex to the patio.

"I just had a word with Manuela."

"Did you tell her not to prowl around in the dead of night?"

"I don't think she was."

"Did she say she didn't go out?"

"Yes."

"Not that that means anything. She may have gone out and forgotten. Look, I love Manuela as much as you —"

"No, you don't."

"Manuela adored Danielle. She puts the pots where Danielle used to put them, arranges the furniture how Danielle used to like it and spends more time cleaning upstairs in the small house than she does in here. It's as if I don't exist to her."

"That's not true. Manuela tries to please you, but she said you confuse her —"

"Confuse her? How?"

"With your whims and dislikes. I mean, why are you getting mad at her for buying the wrong honey?"

"All I said was that she should buy the organic honey brand with the bee with a halo if she gets any. And I never even asked her to go to Whole Foods in the first place."

"And she's still upset about how you yelled at her over the burned chicken."

"If we hadn't been around she could have set the house on fire! And what about when I came home to find she'd gone out and left the house wide open? What if she'd done the same thing last night and an intruder got in? You live under the delusion that Venice Beach is a folksy idyll populated by socially aware artists, pacifist poets and third generation hippies, but there's a reason Anjelica wouldn't move into Windward unless Robert built a fifteen-foot wall around their house! You and Cayde laugh about him fishing bullet casings out of his swimming pool like it was some kind of joke!"

"That was years ago when they first moved into Indiana Avenue."

"A guy was beaten to death and dumped on the sand three blocks from here! That was last month! What if some beach crazy had gotten in last night and something happened to the kids? And before you imply I have a grudge against Manuela, haven't you noticed me checking in on her, taking her meals and doing her fucking job most of the time!"

The ferocity of Rick's tirade startled Alex. "It wasn't my intention to upset you."

"Well, you have! This stupid house is a ramshackle mess of entrances and doors and rooms that aren't rooms. I'm constantly walking in circles looking for you or Manuela or Bella. And what about when we have three stories of that monstrosity overlooking us?" Rick pointed at the ominous dark uprights, cranes and wooden frames poking above the rear perimeter wall's razor wire. "Jack and Tyler won't be able to wander around like Adam and Steve in the Garden of Eden then."

Rick's words wounded Alex so deeply it took him a moment to respond. "I'd no idea you felt that way."

"Let's face it, this is *your* house not *our* house ..."

"Where's the sick lizard?" Maddy trotted from the living-room door, Jay trailing behind.

Rick rearranged his frown into a smile. "Uncle Alex must have been mistaken. Maybe the lizard wasn't sick, only asleep. Now what do guys you want to do? Shall we drive Bella to the dog beach?" Maddy was up for this, but Jay wrinkled his nose. "How about a walk around the canals with a stop for Wiffle-waffles at the marina?"

This suggestion was greeted with enthusiasm by both child parties, although Alex suspected the Wiffle-waffles were the big-ticket item.

"Are you sure the lizard was sleeping?" asked Maddy. "What if it is sick and doesn't have a mommy?"

The potentially poorly lizard having captured the kids' imagination, Rick issued a warning to keep away from the pool and left them to search the planters and bushes while he cleared the breakfast dishes.

Holding his tongue until they were out of earshot, Alex said, "Of course this is your house too."

"Every piece of furniture, the drapes, the lamps, the rugs, the scatter cushions, the Navajo throws, the art ..." Rick waved his hand at the Warholesque silk screen of Danielle over the mantel, "... everything in here was chosen by you or Danielle. If there's a ghost in this house, it's me and not her."

Alex froze. Why did Rick mention a ghost? "Don't talk crazy. You can change anything you ..."

Rick was staring at the TV in the kitchen, the cereal bowls in one hand. He raised his empty hand to stop Alex speaking. Putting down the bowls, he raised the volume.

"... dumping thick black smoke into the air. New York is on fire ..." A red helicopter dropped water over vivid orange flames raging from smashed windows and licking around blackened buildings. "Courthouse Square, the King Kong attraction and a video storage vault have been destroyed ..."

Footage of helicopters flying through smoke and angles on burning buildings were accompanied by a firefighter's voiceover, "We have a third alarm fire in the backlot. There have been multiple explosions from gas cylinders in the city blocks and chapels ..." A crucifix crashed down from the toppling steeple of a blazing church.

Jay and Maddy raced into the kitchen, Jay's hands were cupped together. "Is this it?"

"Shh, one moment." Rick was glued to the TV.

"Officials say the fire broke out before dawn on a soundstage at Universal Studios..."

"Uncle Alex, is this the sick lizard?" Maddy pestered.

Jay opened his hands.

"No, honey. Put him back where you found him."

"Is the sick one bigger?" asked Jay.

"Smaller," lied Alex.

The kids ran back to continue their search.

"Some fire." Rick flicked off the TV. "Kind of sad watching Courthouse Square burn down even if it isn't real." After rinsing the cereal bowls, Rick angrily opened and shut a few cabinet doors. He began muttering in Italian as he noisily rearranged the cupboards.

The kids rushed in with another potentially sick lizard. Guessing the hunt would not be satisfactorily completed until the reptile in question was located, Alex comprised his integrity and made a false identification of the creature in Jay's cupped hands. He took the kids to the study to find a suitable box. They punched holes in its lid, Maddy wrote 'lizard hospital' on its side and the patient was confined for observation. The lizard was left to convalesce in the coolness of the bookcase behind the dining room table.

Dispatching the kids to double-check they'd packed everything to avoid a last-minute rush, Alex sensed it was time to dump water on the fire with Rick. He pulled Rick close. "I broached the idea of finishing work with Manuela. I'll talk with Jorge, but I want the finances secured before I make a firm offer about buying a place for her near him. And if you're so unhappy with this house, you should've mentioned it before."

Relaxing into Alex's arms, Rick sighed. "Talking to Dr. Susskind's made me focus on areas I hadn't thought about up to now. Visiting Cristina's place, so clean and elegant, marble floors, chandeliers and gold fixtures, brought it home to me. I never thought I wanted a house like that, but maybe I do."

"But it's Bel Air. You couldn't walk the dog wearing sweats with unwashed hair there. Wouldn't you miss the beach?"

"The ocean's near to us but we can't see it. All our windows look at another part of the house or a cinder block wall.

Covering it with foliage made the front wall look less stalag-like, but it's still kind of claustrophobic."

"You want to move? But what about my studio and showroom? I need a place to work."

"Couldn't we buy a house someplace else to live and you come here to work? How about Malibu? That's not too long a drive. And we don't have to buy a house. Maybe we could lease?"

Holding Rick in his arms, dollar signs whirled behind Alex's eyes. The rift with Luisa meant Rick no longer had big bucks in the bank, so purchasing a new property would rest solely on his shoulders. And as recently discovered, his funds were lower than expected - certainly not Malibu beach house territory. This unexpected Sunday morning conversation was making his temples throb.

Having gathered up their toys and books and dumped their bags in the entrance hall, Maddy and Jay raced back into the kitchen.

Rick pulled away from Alex's arms.

"Why don't I take the kids out and you can drive them home? The pool house is ready for Ty to come dog sit and we're packed for New York. Take a swim or a hot tub. Or do some yoga." Alex's right eye was functioning normally, but he'd rather not drive until he'd had it fully checked out, especially with the kids on board.

Rick went along with this suggestion, which was a relief. Bella didn't come running when he rattled her leash, so Alex just took Maddy and Jay. After a stressful start to the day, he enjoyed ambling around the canals. The kids liked watching the ducks and spring ducklings swimming around. Alex explained the plaque with a quote from Albert Schweitzer, 'Until he extends the circle of his compassion to all living things, man will not himself find peace.' An avian virus broke out in '93. County health officials decreed that all the ducks and geese in the canals should be killed to stop migrating birds spreading the disease. Local residents shocked by such brutality, however, had tried to frustrate the cull by scaring the birds away from the game wardens. Some locals even going so far as to shelter ducks in their homes since they didn't believe the virus was as deadly as health officials made out. The residents didn't succeed in saving all the birds though, so they paid for this plaque dedicated to the memory of the five hundred and nineteen slaughtered ducks and geese to ensure the 'kill' wasn't forgotten.

As expected, the stop for Wiffle-waffles at the marina was the outing's highlight. Alex savored a sneaky black coffee to soothe the heartache of watching all the yachts he wouldn't be sailing today bob at their moorings.

Back at the ranch, the relaxation had lifted Rick's mood. An internet check showed the 101 was running slow due to the fire in the valley. Discretely checking Tiffany had been discharged and was on her way home, Rick told the kids they needed to hit the road earlier than planned to allow for delays.

"Aren't you driving us home, Uncle Alex?" Jay asked.

"I got stuff to do here. And Rick wants to say hi to his sister," said Alex.

"Let's go say goodbye to Manuela. You can thank her for making us such a fantastic dinner." Rick opened the front door and ushered the kids over the passageway.

Alex felt bad for thinking so poorly of Rick in his relationship with Manuela. After cuddles and kisses with Maddy, and manly pats on the back and mock jaw punches to Jay, Alex slammed the Cherokee Jeep's rear doors and waved goodbye to two far happier children than arrived yesterday.

Planning to chill by the pool until Tyler showed up, Alex remembered the falsely imprisoned lizard. He carried the 'hospital' box to the deck, lifted the lid and released the captive.

A lifeless body fell out.

✶ ✶ ✶

Alex had always disliked plane travel. Being up in the air was not in his DNA. Even business class, courtesy of Xander Chen, didn't soften the grind of removing shoes and belts, emptying pockets, going through body pat-downs, x-ray machines and bag checks. Any remaining vestige in the joy of travel had been thoroughly knocked out of him by the time they made it to the SkyClub Lounge. 'Delta flight 324 to JFK. Now Boarding,' immediately flashed up on the screens.

Going down the jetway, Alex and Rick turned left then settled into their seats. Rick accepted the square-jawed male flight attendant's offer of a welcome glass of something white and sparkling. Alex figured Rick's being continually shunted between Luisa and Sid over the Atlantic as a kid was why he seemed so at home on planes. Rick's simple yet sophisticated style of dress and his cool, collected manner screamed class. If by some horrible twist of fate Rick were seated in coach, he was the guy who'd be upgraded. Whereas, in his battered blue jeans, corduroy safari jacket and stacked leather wristbands, combined with his long hair and morning stubble, Alex knew he'd be a prime candidate for a downgrade in any seating stand-off. Sitting beside Rick as they prepared for take-off, it struck Alex they were definitely not one of those male couples who mirrored each other's style. In fact, they rarely appeared to be dressed for the same event.

The plane's doors closed. The cabin crew performed the safety demonstration then strapped in. The clunking and rattling as the plane trundled to the runway ended in a moment of quietude. The 767's engines roared into life, blasting them into the sky. Breaking through haze and smog, intense sunlight flooded the cabin. Alex drew down his window shade. "Did you tell Tiffany that Jay knew she was in the hospital?" He asked, picking at his fruit cup once breakfast was served.

"I did. And I told her to dial down the hypochondria cause it's freaking the poor kid out."

"You don't know it's hypochondria for sure."

"What about the night of the Emmy awards when she thought she'd had a stroke? Turned out that one of her false eyelashes had come unglued. She's had every test under the sun and the doctors can't find anything wrong. I think she's depressed. I said she should go see Dr. Susskind."

"According to you we should all be seeing Dr. Susskind. Is the guy giving you group discount?"

"Tiffany gets so stressed about everything. Patti hasn't got back to her about whether momma's deigned to do the DVD commentary. She asked me to chase her up."

"And?"

"No way!" Rick buttered a warm croissant. "I fully support Tiff's condemnation of dad's work, but I'm steering well clear of wrangling momma into taking part."

"Commemoration," corrected Alex.

"Whatever. The DVD release is scheduled for November. That audio track needs to be in the can by August to make it on the disc."

"Sounds like it's a no from Luisa then. Does Tiff have an alternative?"

"An assistant director and the dialog coach are still alive. Neither of their reminisces promise for juicy bonus material. I understand why Tiffany wants momma to do it, but I refuse to get involved. And Tiffany's stressed enough doing her own TV show. Producing another project which gives her even more stress is insanity. And of course, I'm public enemy number one because I'm doing a reality TV show, killing scripted drama and robbing screenwriters of an income."

"She has a point."

"Why pay top dollar for writers when you can get a bunch of num-nuts to make fools of themselves for nothing? Look at those clowns supposedly proving their business acumen to Trump on *The Apprentice*?"

"The celebration of stupidity's going to get our country into big trouble one of these days," muttered Alex.

Rick put on his headphones to watch Hudson and McConaughey in *Fool's Gold* accompanied by a Bloody Mary.

Alex donned his eye mask and dozed.

Due to congestion, the plane made several bumpy circuits before getting a slot. Coming down to earth, Manhattan's towers appeared – with two significantly missing landmarks.

NYC.

The grass was brown, the tarmac gray, the sky ochre, the traffic into the city dense. Dented trucks, dusty minibuses and slick limos jockeyed for position over the potholes and cracked asphalt thumping beneath their tires.

The flight delay, waiting for their bags, a confusion in finding their driver and heavy traffic meant it was after 6.30 p.m. by the time they'd checked into the Carlyle. Rick hurriedly unpacked, hung jackets and pants to let the wrinkles drop then stripped off. Alex watched his mature, yet still pert, buttocks with their fading tan line disappear into the palatial bathroom.

Kicking off his sneakers and liner socks, Alex kneaded his toes in the rug. He pulled off his shirt, fluffed out his chest hair and stretched his lats and trapezius. As he decanted his carry-on into drawers and the credenza, he tried to figure out what time he should take his evening meds. Beyond the treetops of Central Park and tiered towers and colonnaded lanterns of the San Remo, the sun was sinking in the west. It would be mid-afternoon back home. Alex imagined light from that ball of gas in the sky falling on Bella and Tyler. Feeling homesick, he flopped on the bed. How could sitting on a plane for six hours be so insanely tiring?

Lying there, Alex contemplated a hot shower followed by cocktails in the gilded warmth of Bemelmans bar downstairs, ordering room service, then canoodling with Rick. Loosening his belt and undoing his jeans, he conjured an image of Rick fresh from the shower, all warm and moist, ready to be tongued, probed and willingly violated. He'd made sure to stow the lube in his carry-on. Heck, maybe Rick would be in the mood for a flip flop? Masterfully dominating and penetrating him in return. The room had a big mirror opposite the bed. A little light bondage could be fun, especially in the refined elegance of this classic hotel. Watching primly perfect Rick lose control and get down and dirty always turned him on. And being fucked doggy style while hog tied and ball-gagged would certainly stop him wittering on about Bel Air mansions and Manuela's retirement. Fantasizing about delicious and increasingly sordid ways they could tease, tantalize and defile each other, he slipped his hand into his shorts to savor his hardness. Creating gay porno scenarios with voyeuristic bellmen wielding nipple clamps and dildos bringing them both to eye-popping climaxes, Alex's erotic dreamworld was interrupted by the phone's shrill ring. He hoped Rick would pick up in the bathroom, but the phone's red light kept insistently flashing. Alex picked up. "Y'ello?"

"Rick!" announced a confident woman's voice.

"Alex."

"You two sound alike!"

Alex wondered who this loon could be. He and Rick didn't sound anything alike.

"Rick said you were getting in tonight. I wanted to be the first with a supper invitation … I am the first, aren't I?"

"Who is this?"

"It's me."

"Who?"

"Cristina! We caught up last month in your studio."

Alex kicked himself for answering.

Rick emerged from the bathroom in a pair of white hotel slippers and toweling his hair. "Who?" Rick silently asked.

Alex covered the mouthpiece. "The artist formerly known as Tina Mason."

Rick hurled himself across the coverlet to snatch the handset. "Cristina, hi! Sorry, Alex was half asleep. We had an early start out of LA …"

Rick carried on the conversation while Alex made his imagined sex play a reality. He ran his hands up and down Rick's damp inner thighs, nibbled at his neck and cupped his bubble butt. But Rick swatted him off. Seeing his ardor was no match for Rick's new gal pal, Alex departed to the shower.

Planning to wash his hair in the morning, Alex tied it high to keep it out of the shower jets. The luxurious soap smelled of honeysuckle and myrrh. Lathering up his body with the sensual scent, he resisted the urge to have a wank under the hot water. He couldn't be bothered to shave, besides Rick liked his bristly stubble brushing his balls and butt. Massaging the hotel's oily moisturizer into his chest and shoulders, Alex came back into the bedroom, erect and primed for action.

Rick had on a pair of dressy taupe pants and was fastening cufflinks in his tailored shirt. "The car's on its way."

"What car?" Going to the nightstand, Alex picked up the stacked leather wristbands he was partial to wearing.

"Cristina and Harun have invited us out for dinner."

"Uh?" Alex stood naked in in front of Rick. "Give me a hand?"

Taking the leather bands, Rick fastened the straps.

Alex pressed his swollen cock into Rick's thigh as he did. "I thought we could fool around."

Rick planted a kiss on Alex's fuzzy cheek. "I want to eat."

"I got a piece of meat you can chow on." Alex jiggled his hard-on by its root muscles.

"We can have dinner, get back here for a creamy dessert and it still won't be eight in LA. The night's young. And Cristina's arranged for a limo to take us downtown and back. She's discovered a trendy new Lower East Side restaurant."

"Trendy means noisy." Alex detested New York restaurants' penchant for bare wood and polished surfaces which amplified the screeches of hyped diners.

"We won't be long."

Wishing he'd gagged and box tied Rick before answering the phone, Alex let out a frustrated sigh. He pulled on fresh underwear, loose linen pants and an Aztec print shirt. The Carlyle's white-gloved elevator operator ferried them downstairs. They passed through the black lacquer and gilt lobby with mustard velvet chairs, through the revolving door and onto the street. The hot city air slapped Alex's face like a musty washcloth. The oily body lotion was a mistake, he broke sweat crossing the sidewalk. Luckily, the limo's air conditioning was terrific. "What the heck am I going to talk to them about?"

"The weather. If Montana and South Dakota are going to give Obama the Democrat nomination. We spend so much time with our limited circle of friends and family it'll be nice to have some new adult conversation."

Alex wasn't convinced. The ride down Second Avenue towards the Bowery under a deepening cobalt sky was a stop start affair. His foreboding about the evening deepened as the limo drew up outside an unprepossessing establishment set between a defunct PC repair shop and a derelict lot being used for parking. The limo driver said he'd hang out nearby till they were ready to leave. Alex was determined to keep his wait as brief as possible.

Steeling himself for a barrage of noise and brittle Bel Air trophy wives, Alex was pleasantly surprised by the restaurant's brick walls, red velvet curtains, wooden bookshelves and seductive candlelight. The restaurant was busy, but not crazy busy, with a cozy hum of conversation and Depeche Mode playing at a pleasant volume. A hostess guided them to a circular corner table surrounded by a dark leather button-back banquette.

Cristina broke into a genuine smile and rose to welcome them. She was wearing a mid-thigh emerald-green halter dress with bejeweled collar and dangling emerald earrings. The man with her, in a dove gray suit, airbrush perfect olive skin and black eyes like pools of petroleum, rose in greeting too. Cristina introduced her husband, Dr. Harun Raban, then they all shuffled into the banquette. The server took their drink orders. Harun advised them he had a bottle of Dom Perignon on ice. Rick kicked off with a dirty martini. Alex felt dehydrated from the flight and stuck with mineral water. The initial conversation was the inconsequential chitchat of people who don't know each other well.

"Ellery let us into the secret of this hot new restaurant. It's popular with celebrities," Cristina confided. "It's off the radar so still very exclusive."

Harun surveyed the room. "Newly fashionable New York restaurants resemble exotic desert plants. You have to catch them on the rare spectacular night they're in full bloom, for they'll have wilted and be a mere memory by tomorrow."

"It's a stroke of fortune we're in town for your show. Harun spends a week every year at New York Presbyterian doing facial reconstruction for children with birth defects or who've suffered accidents," said Cristina. "All pro bono, of course. Morgan Stanley sponsor his hospital."

"Today I operated on a little girl who'd fallen onto a barbecue. The final one of four surgeries." Harun launched into the delicacies of taking flesh from other parts of the body to fashion new lips and eyelids and the delicacy of joining nerves and blood vessels. His passion for the subject led to increasingly graphic descriptions of cutting into noses, opening sinus cavities, pulling back cheeks and sawing through jaws. Noting Harun's passion for detail was turning everybody green, Cristina deftly changed topic.

Cristina and Harun were perfectly pleasant. While not the evening he'd had in mind, it wasn't as bad as Alex envisaged.

They ordered food. The champagne was opened. Harun toasted Alex's show and his representation by Xander Chen.

As Alex sipped the champagne, his stomach flipped. Looking after the kids, chatting with Tyler at dinner last night, numbing himself to the discomfort of air travel and indulging in sexual fantasies he was unlikely to ever act out had all been successful strategies to distract from his retrospective's imminent opening. Throughout the meal, his mind kept imagining what tomorrow night would be like. A night dedicated to him. His stomach flipped again. As coffee arrived, Harun's pager beeped. He took his cell outside to call the hospital. Ready to make their way back to the Carlyle, Rick left in search of the men's room.

"Thank you for coming. I wondered if you'd find a reason to back out. I detect you're not overly fond of me," Cristina said once they were alone.

"I apologize if I gave that impression. Rick adores high society events and Hollywood razzmatazz. It's the world he was raised in. I'm a poor kid from Ohio. I feel like a fraud at those black-tie galas. Like any second someone's gonna tap me on the shoulder, say I got invited by mistake and throw me out."

"I was born in Astoria to a Greek father and Jewish mother. Mama and Pa worked themselves to death and still died dirt poor. The day I turned sixteen, I decided that wasn't going to happen to Teena Aida Baros. My real name." Cristina gave him a knowing smile. "I didn't have the smarts, but I had looks, a talent to entertain and blind ambition burning a hole in my guts. I always knew that I wanted to be rich and famous. I'm halfway there, I'm rich." The candlelight glittered in Cristina's emerald earrings. "I'm having another attempt at the fame part."

"You're not tempted to relax and just enjoy being rich?"

"My last little chick flew the nest for college last fall. I've played devoted wife and mother for twenty-four years and found myself in need of a new role. Harun and I adore art and have been amateur collectors for years. Getting more involved in that world seemed a natural progression. I have years of serving on charity boards and organizing fundraisers. I imagined LA's museums would be falling over each other to have Cristina Raban on their board. But apparently I was still Teena Aida Baros from Astoria to them. I admit I manipulated my reacquaintance with Rick as a means of getting on the Conservatory Board. Like I said, when I want something I'm *extremely* focused."

"I admire your honesty."

"And seeing how you live in Venice Beach, I've got another confession. Harun and I vote Republican."

Cristina's candor made Alex laugh.

"We even threw a fundraiser for McCain. There, I've given you even more reasons to dislike me. But I'm not a bad person, Alex. And I'm not proud of how I acted when they dropped Rick from *The Brad and Carol Mysteries*. I should have spoken up and walked off the show. But my then manager, and also husband, convinced me it would be career suicide and wouldn't change the network's mind anyway. Rick's a good actor, much better than I ever was. That's why I'm hoping I can become a personality. I called in some favors to get Rick on *The Belles of Bel Air* to thank him for pushing me on the Board. And this exposure might give his career the shot in the arm it needs ..."

"This restaurant's so dark I could hardly find my way back to the table. Where's Harun?"

"Still on his call," said Cristina.

Rick fished out his wallet. "We'll settle the check."

Cristina vigorously insisted that since they made the invitation she and Harun were paying. Alex was relieved. He wondered if Rick had forgotten the bottle of Dom on the tab. They made their farewells to Cristina at the table. Running into Harun coming back inside, they said goodbye and thanks on their way out. Stepping onto the sidewalk, they realized the limo driver must have found a parking place to keep an eye on the restaurant's entrance, as within moments he'd pulled up and flashed his lights.

"They're nice, aren't they?" Rick asked as they headed uptown on FDR Drive.

"Nice enough. For Republicans."

"What?"

"Cristina did a PR job on me while you were in the bathroom. Confessing her sins and applauding her strengths. I find it hard to believe she's the same girl from that photoshoot."

"Because she's so sophisticated and stylish?"

"No, because she looks nothing like she did then."

"She's married to a cosmetic surgeon. Cristina's face is in the 'based on an original idea' category. Actually, Harun thinks I could use a little Botox —"

"Do *not* go down that road! You're gorgeous as you are. And her accent and the words she uses, where did they come from? Not from Queens, that's for sure."

"Why are you so anti-Cristina?"

"She's overplaying the benevolent lady of the manor. The heart of Lady Macbeth beats beneath her Dolce and Gabbana."

"I'm not naïve. I know when I'm being played. And I know how to play the game in return."

Getting closer to the Upper East Side, and also to tomorrow, Alex's heart began banging hard in his chest. Maybe it was from the glass of champagne. The banks of coldly lit lonely windows in monolithic apartment blocks depressed him. He imagined an alternative version of himself living in one of those towers, old and alone, shuffling around a cramped studio apartment. A version of himself who'd surrendered to Pop and let himself be shoehorned into society's norms, who hadn't picked up a pencil and a paintbrush to splash his dreams over canvas and paper. A life of dreams which would all be on display tomorrow. Alex's head swam. He broke out in a sweat and shivered in the car's AC. He slumped forward, thinking he may vomit.

"Are you okay?"

"I'm dizzy. Can this guy pull over? I need some air."

Rick leaned forward and spoke with the driver. "He's taking us up to Gracie Mansion," Rick said, leaning back.

"It's fourteen blocks back to the Carlyle from there."

"We got him for the night. He'll wait."

Getting out of the limo, Alex and Rick walked through the small park surrounding the Mayor of New York's residence. Letting a dog walker and some late-night joggers pass by on the riverside path, Alex sat on a metal bench to restore his equilibrium. An East River wind ruffled the bushes, swirling odors of sage, soil and dog pee into the damp air.

"What happened back there?" Rick asked.

"My heart was banging and I felt weird. I thought I was having another attack." Alex rested his face in his hands, then swept them through his hair. "Tomorrow there's an entire show at MoMA dedicated to me. How ironic if I died the night before and never got to experience it. Never got to know how it felt."

Rick stroked Alex's shoulder. "Your heart's fine. You're fine."

Getting up, Alex walked to the iron railings. He stared into the splintered reflections of city lights on the inky river. Vortexes of tidal waters on their way back and forth to the Atlantic made this a perilous stretch. "What a thrill it'd be to get in a yacht, raise the sails and feel that tide ripping beneath us. And not on a slack tide. I'd wait till it was racing in. That's when we'd shoot that mass of water as it forced its way into that narrow channel. Hit a cross current at that speed and our boat would get smashed to pieces." Alex slipped his arm around Rick's waist. "But I'd make sure to skipper my boat right. Can you imagine me at the helm and all that power, all that thrust beneath you?" Alex pressed his mouth to Rick's ear. "Would you trust me to sail you through Hell's Gate?"

"Sounds more exciting than a Circle Line cruise."

Alex laughed, but Rick had given a flippant answer.

He didn't say yes.

The driver dropped them off at the Carlyle.

The liveried elevator operator ferried them upstairs.

They were both tired.

Alex took his evening meds.

Rick turned on the TV.

Alex thought about tomorrow at MoMA.
He'd arrived. He'd made it. He was a name.
Alex Morgan was finally a star!
They cuddled, but neither got aroused.
Regretting not having jerked off in the shower, Alex fell asleep.

I WANT TO BELIEVE

An aura of calm filled the Carlyle suite's elegant living room. Ysabel Marchand, Xander Chen's personal assistant and artist liaison for his NYC gallery, had furnished an array of fragrant lilies, a tray of French pastries and a steaming pot of coffee. Once she'd introduced Thom Hannay, the fresh-faced journalist with floppy hair and incisive eyes, to Alex, Ysabel poured the coffee. She withdrew on her three-inch heels. Perching on a white leather chair in the far corner, she donned her pearl framed glasses, crossed her legs, and scrolled through her iPhone. Thom chatted while preparing his notepad and voice memo. With inconsequential conversation about New York traffic, the presidential election and if global warming was responsible for unseasonably warm weather on both coasts over, Thom got down to business …

"Your career spans more than three decades, your work hangs in every well-respected gallery and collection in the country, and you have a major retrospective opening tonight at the Museum of Modern Art, yet from among your cohort of fellow artists – LA's supercool golden-boys of the mid-seventies – you're the least well known. Has keeping the real Alex Morgan, the man behind the artist, away from the spotlight been a deliberate ploy?"

"I wouldn't say deliberate. I'm a shy guy at heart. I like to think my work does the talking for me …" The interview progressed effortlessly. Alex felt comfortable answering Thom's questions about artists who'd influenced his work, what he learned and didn't learn at art school and the source of his inspiration. "… the majority of my work results from accidents."

Thom furrowed his brow.

"Not like spilling pots of paint. I mean, I'll start with an idea, a direction, and something unexpected happens. A passing cloud alters a shadow, or I run out of a pigment and need to improvise, or an unexpected vision hits my eye and sends me off on a tangent. I enjoy dreaming and exploring as much as creating. Getting yourself into trouble and finding ways to get out of it's part of the thrill."

"What do you mean, getting yourself into trouble?"

"Like when you're pushing a piece in the wrong direction, or it's not turning out as expected. That's when you need the skill to pull it back or take drastic action to save it. Or accept you can't save it. That's when you need the guts to let go and grab the razor blades."

Thom looked concerned.

"I don't mean to slit your wrists. No, to scrape off the paint, get back to bare canvas and start over. Not wasting time on saving things that can't be saved can take a lifetime to learn."

"Your work explores a fascination with light, space, and surface. Would you say I'm correct?"

"Definitely. Light is everything. Without surface there'd be nothing to reflect the light. And without space there'd be nowhere for the light and surface to exist …" Pleased with the way the interview was going, and he didn't sound like a complete dodo bird, Alex relaxed.

Thom pressed on with more questions about art. Then, after a pause, changed tack. "That's Alex Morgan the artist. What about Alex Morgan the man? You were diagnosed with rheumatoid arthritis in your early thirties."

Thinking the interview had been going far too smoothly, Alex folded his arms. "Correct."

"And you suffered a heart attack earlier this year. Have those issues affected your work or working practices?"

"Naturally. But I adapt. I change."

"In what way?"

"I don't care to speak about that part of my life. I don't want my weaknesses to define me. When someone looks at a painting of mine, does it matter if I was in pain when I made it?"

"You see illness as a weakness?"

"Perhaps weakness is the wrong word. Limitation may be better. I don't believe you need to know everything about an artist to appreciate their work. In fact, knowing too much about an artist places a barrier between the painting and the spectator. If I were to say, 'I'm a staunch Republican' - I'm not by the way, don't print that! - would you then see my work as 'Republican' art? Would you search for clues and undertones in it? Would you start seeing things in my work that weren't there because of your belief of my beliefs?"

"You live with another man. Is there a conflict between the rugged lifestyle and the all-American male image projected by your peers and your homosexuality? Do you also consider that a weakness?"

Flicking off her phone, Ysabel unfurled her long legs and stalked over.

Alex casually raked his fingers through his freshly washed hair with an apologetic laugh. "The two can co-exist quite happily, can't they? I don't go out my way to —"

"Thom, sorry to interrupt, the photographer's on his way up. You got everything you need?" Ysabel slipped her phone into the jacket pocket of her pinstripe skirt suit.

Thom flipped his notepad shut and clicked off the voice recorder. He locked eyes with Ysabel. "Got it." Standing, he reached out to shake hands with Alex. "I'll be in LA later this summer. I'd be interested in seeing you at work. We could talk more if you like?"

Alex felt the heat of Thom's thumb on his knuckles. "Sure." He immediately wondered why he'd said this. Politeness would be his ruination. Further conversation was cut short when Ysabel intervened to usher Thom out. Bringing the photographer and stylist in, she had a brief pow-wow with them. He needn't have worried about outlandish fashion choices. Within moments they settled on him wearing a black linen shirt. The photographer set up by the windows while he went to change.

      The photographer shot him gazing out blankly over Central Park. Alex never knew what expression to wear for the camera. That's why he liked having a piece of his art behind him or a dog at his ankles, anything other than only him to look at. When he'd attended openings with Danielle, because she was beautiful and a TV star, she'd always been the focus of photographs, he was just a prop. When he and Rick attended events together these days neither of them was noteworthy enough in their own right to merit red-carpet photo treatment. In any media coverage they'd either be bookending Neroli Copley or an adjunct to a leading light of LACMA, LACoMA, MOCA or some other acronym with art inside. Would that change once Rick was back on TV? Would he start being recognized again? And how would he feel being the prop in the couple if Rick were to become a star? Deep in thought, Alex forgot the camera whirring away.

      "Terrific." The photographer grinned and lowered his camera.

      Amazed at how painless that was, Alex remained by the window while the photographer and stylist packed up. The park's treetops resembled heads of broccoli. His joints needed oiling. A walk would have to replace his morning swim. A spear of light bouncing off a West Side windowpane caught his eye. Realizing Ysabel was speaking to him, he turned.

      "... I'll meet you down in the lobby here at five-thirty. Xander will handle the introductions and blue-carpet publicity at MoMA. Welcome drinks will be hosted in the sculpture garden. The Pavilion's formal opening is six forty-five. Guests will then move to the main exhibition in the fifth-floor galleries. The buffet and further drinks will be served up there and ..."

      Having committed the salient detail to memory – lobby 5.30 p.m. – Alex dropped his wallet and phone in his messenger bag and took the elevator down. Rick had left the hotel at ten. He never visited New York without paying his respects at Ground Zero. Because Ysabel wasn't certain how long the interview and photoshoot would last, Rick planned to visit the Guggenheim and lunch with Cristina and Ellery before returning to the Carlyle.

Alex crossed Madison Avenue and walked the block to Central Park. In light of the East Side crane collapse earlier this year, he skirted widely around the construction site on the corner of 76th St. With only four hours to go until his big night, he wasn't prepared to risk a building crashing down on his head. The early morning drizzle had cleared. Watery sunlight was drying the streets and sidewalks to a paler shade of gray. Getting his sluggish hips and knees moving, he power walked down Fifth Avenue then turned into the park.

Passing by youngish couples holding hands, oldish couples dozing on benches and nannies wheeling strollers, he stumbled upon the model boat pond. Leaning on its rock wall, he watched the radio-controlled yachts' white sails wheeling across the water. He wished Maddy and Jay were here. It'd be fun to rent a couple of toy yachts and teach them how to pretend to sail. This solitary walk amongst strangers was making him melancholy. He felt out of step with this city's rhythm.

Ambling back to the hotel, he glimpsed reflections of himself in the plate glass windows on Madison Avenue. New York's unforgiving light wasn't doing him or his clothes any favors. He looked colorless. And shabby. And old. Pausing, he considered his image framed by the Chase Bank's bright blue octagon logo. He'd worn his hair just below shoulder length for as long as he could remember.

What the fuck.

Back at the Carlyle, Alex requested the concierge to direct him to the barbershop.

* * *

"I leave you alone for five minutes and look what you go and do to yourself!"

"It's not like I hacked off my hair with the kitchen scissors."

"Was this Chen's idea?"

"All mine," said Alex proudly.

Rick's x-ray blue eyes with black saucer pupils did another full circuit. "But why?"

"I looked like a flower child gone to seed. No more having to tie my hair back to keep it out my eyes. Yay!"

Rick blinked back tears.

"What're you getting upset for?"

"I loved your hair."

"I still got it ... just less."

Rick's hand snaked out. He wound a chestnut coil with a few strands of graphite framing Alex's temple around his finger, then ran his hand through the springy curls down to the back of his head and caressed the swirls in his nape. "It is kind of nice to see the back of your neck."

"Is it pale?" Alex clapped his hand behind his head. "Do I need to fake tan the back of my neck for the opening?"

Smiling in spite of himself, Rick batted Alex's shoulder. "I recall a time when I had to fight you to get an inch cut off your hair."

"Are you proud of how much I've changed?"

"I shouldn't have overreacted." Rick slipped off his shoes. "It was like walking in the room and finding a different man here." Padding across the suite, Rick flung himself on the bed.

"How was it downtown?" Crawling onto the bed, Alex lay beside Rick.

"Heartbreaking. Reading all the names and remembering again." Rick blinked back tears. "They say time heals ..."

"You don't need to go every time you visit New York."

Rick nestled his head between Alex's jaw and chest. "I do."

"Ysabel wants us in the lobby at five-thirty."
"We got a couple of hours then."
"Good lunch with the girls?"
"We should have eaten before the Guggenheim."
"Why?" Alex asked into Rick's hair.
"We caught the last days of the Guo-Chiang retrospective. The show was titled, *I Want to Believe*. He'd filled the Guggenheim's atrium with seven Ford Taurus's, real cars not fiberglass shells, all suspended from the roof at different angles like they'd exploded from the sky. And they had light tubes shooting out of them, like fireworks. The audio guide said the piece spoke of how destruction was necessary for creation, how the dead are swept away so new life can grow, how our universe was formed in a catastrophic collision of matter. Great in theory. But what if you're the ones getting destroyed in the process of creation? Then he had stuffed tigers shot through with bloody arrows and ninety-nine stuffed wolves racing up the Guggenheim's ramp, all hurling themselves towards a glass wall. The pack madly chasing an unattainable goal, their futile quest ending in inevitable death. I picked the wrong day to go see that show, it hit too many raw nerves."
"The power of art."
"We should have gone to Bergdorf's." Rick toyed with Alex's hair. "It makes you look younger."
"Not a day over sixty." Alex rolled over, got on top and pressed Rick into the bed. Roughly, he kissed him.
"How'd your interview go?" Rick pushed him off.
Unzipping Rick's fly, Alex slipped his hand in. "Okay at first. Then Thom, that was the guy doing the piece, started probing more. Think he was angling for a big exposé. A revelation of the man behind the artist." Alex undid the waistband of Rick's pants.
"Why are you doing this now?"
"Because I didn't get to do it last night."
"I'm not in the mood."

"I wasn't in the mood for dinner with the Rabans." Alex manhandled Rick onto his stomach. "But I got into it." Kneeling over him, Alex dragged down Rick's pants and underwear and slung them aside. "And we should be celebrating my opening." He fondled Rick's buttocks.

"Celebrating my opening will have to wait till I've showered."

Alex grunted in frustration. "At least a hand job?"

"Oh, all right." Turning over, Rick undid Alex's shirt and peeled it apart. He tugged off his own striped cotton crew over his head and lay naked on the bed.

Alex shucked off his jeans and boxers. With his shirt dangling open, he mounted Rick then ground their erections together. "And I was in the mood to do some real dirty stuff last night."

"Dirtier than a Princeton rub?" Arching his back, Rick squirmed beneath Alex.

"Much dirtier, unspeakably dirtier. I planned to tie you to the bedhead and fuck you raw."

Rick tilted his head back. "How'd you plan on doing that? It's a padded headboard attached to the wall."

Alex rolled off, flipped Rick face down and mounted him again. Clasping Rick's thighs between his own, he slid his cock up and down between Rick's buttocks. Supporting his upper body on one arm, he cupped Rick's chin and stuck his thumb in his mouth. "I'd have found a way. I just wanted you totally in my power to do with as I desired."

Rick murmured something indecipherable.

Withdrawing his hand from Rick's mouth, Alex supported his upper body with both arms and humped Rick's butt crack, growing in vigor until he climaxed with a moaning shudder, feeling his cum spurt in the v at the small of Rick's back then he fell aside with a gasp.

Getting up, Rick spread Alex's shirt to fully expose his chest then shimmied up the bed to straddle his ribcage. "Okay, so that's what you did to me. What did I get to do to you?" He rubbed his cock in the silvery mat between Alex's pectorals.

Alex clutched Rick's buttocks. "You tied me up too. Then you forced me to look at brochures of real estate listings in Bel Air."

"Now you're turning me on! More dirty talk like that please." Pressing Alex's arms above his head, Rick massaged his cock up and down his furry solar plexus.

"Kiss me."

Releasing Alex's hands, Rick slid down to lock lips with a deep, probing kiss.

"What did you have with so much garlic in it?" Alex asked as Rick broke away.

"Must've been in the quinoa bowl." Rick shuffled up to straddle Alex again. On all fours, he ground his cock up and down Alex's chest. Rising onto his knees, he jacked himself off, bringing himself to orgasm while Alex cupped his balls. Rick grunted as gobs of white spunk spurted into the salt and pepper hair covering Alex's upper chest and collar bone. Spent, he slid down until their faces were level. They kissed again. He patted Alex's cheek. "Happy opening night."

Grabbing a wadge of tissues off the nightstand, Alex mopped his chest. Being careful not to drip cum on the Carlyle's soft furnishings, he slapped Rick's butt as they headed to the shower.

Washed and dried, they dressed for the evening.

Rick selected a pair of ivory pants and a shell-pink shirt with tiny ruffles on either side of the button stand.

Matching his outfit to his new sophisticated hairstyle, Alex teamed a pair of smart dark denim jeans with a fish print t-shirt which had a gold 'Save the Oceans' logo.

Rick fastened his gold watch's clasp. Opening his jewelry roll, he slipped on a gold ring with a black onyx stone. Then he lifted out the eternity pendant. Rather than a rough cord, Rick now wore the carved stone pendant on a slim gold chain.

How well Alex recalled the moment on the cliffs of Sunset Cove when, instead of a ring, he'd given Rick this silly little surfing pendant along with a vow to love him forever. Odd how a trinket could elicit such deep emotion from the memory of that distant summer. "Who'd have believed when I was down to my last red cent, doubting if I'd sell another painting and wondering if I should give up trying to be an artist altogether, that one day I'd be deemed worthy of a MoMA retrospective?"

"Me." With a smile, Rick patted the eternity symbol resting on his tanned chest. "Now, what jacket are you wearing?"

Alex dithered, then selected the crimson Versace from the rail. Slipping it on, he checked himself in the mirror. "So?"

"Perfect."

Alex grinned at his reflection. He looked good. No, he didn't. He looked terrific! Turning from the full-length mirror, that sharp glint of reflected West Side light dazzled his eye again. He put the jacket back on the hanger. He misjudged hooking the hanger on the closet rail and it fell to the floor.

Picking up the jacket, Rick brushed it off.

Alex blinked, expecting the dark spot in his eye would clear. But it didn't. He sat and covered his eyes with his palms. The glint of light couldn't have been a reflection, the sun was setting over the West Side. Maybe he'd accidentally looked at the sun? "Crap. That thing in my eye's back."

"Like in the studio a few months ago?"

"Yeah. It happened again when I was driving the kids home on Saturday. It was freaky for a moment but cleared."

"Why didn't you say something then?"

"It went away so I figured it wasn't serious."

"You should've got it checked out right away."

"You were stressing out about having the kids the night before we left as it was. I didn't think leaving you alone to deal with them would've gone down well. I planned on visiting the optometrist when we got back to LA. Maybe something got in it when I was in the park. Can you take a look?"

Rick parted Alex's eyelids. "It's bloodshot, but I don't see anything obvious. Oh, Alex! We need to be in the lobby in thirty minutes. This is typical of you. You always think problems will magically vanish. See what happens when you leave everything until tomorrow?"

"Go easy on me, will ya? I didn't do it on purpose." Alex moved his eyes around. The weird blank spot with a jazzy halo moved in tandem with them. Seriously wondering if he should miss the opening and go straight to the hospital, the next thing he knew Rick had darted into the suite's living room.

Returning with his phone clasped to his ear, "Hey, Cristina," Rick said urgently. "Sorry to interrupt you getting ready, but we got an emergency and could do with some medical advice from Harun —"

"My eye's the problem," hissed Alex. "I don't need a facelift!"

Ignoring Alex's protestations, Rick filled in Cristina. Ending the call, Rick declared, "Harun's jumping in a cab."

After increasingly terse interchanges between the two of them, twenty minutes later Harun stood in their suite.

Alex recoiled as Harun's flashlight glared in his eye.

"You had a heart attack earlier this year?" Harun asked.

"Yes, but only a minor one," interjected Rick.

"My vocal cords are functioning," Alex snapped. "The doctor said the blockage could've been caused by a side effect of my RA meds. He's put me on something different now."

"Is this injury recent?

Alex flinched as Harun's index finger probed the dent Pop's belt buckle left on his brow. "Not recent. Why?"

"Trauma around the eye can lead to a detached retina." Harun examined the scar. "A little filler would completely hide this." Harun studied Alex's face. "And laser resurfacing would substantially help your sun damage and —"

Getting Harun back on track, Alex asked, "Thanks, but do I need to go to the ER?"

"When are you due back in LA?"

"End of the week," said Rick.

Alex shot a warning glance to stop answering on his behalf.

"Ophthalmology's not my field of expertise, which makes this an off the record personal opinion. But taking your complex underlying conditions into account, I recommend you get back to LA as soon as possible and consult with your primary care physician."

"It can be fixed though, can't it?"

"The longer you leave seeking treatment the more likely your sight could suffer irreparable damage. Or worse …"

"Worse?" Rick asked.

"A vein in your eye may be blocked by a clot or could have ruptured. Other small clots may be forming. Or this one might move, possibly resulting in a stroke or another heart attack."

"We need to get you to the ER!" Rick's voice was hoarse with tension. "You could have a stroke!"

Rick's stress level was rising so alarmingly he'd be the one having the stroke at this rate. Alex raised his hand to stop the hysteria. "This problem's been coming and going for weeks, a few more hours won't make a difference. I'll leave word with the concierge to get us on the first flight out tomorrow. We'll be back in LA by noon."

Harun agreed with this course of action.

Rick was still agitated. "But what about Chen's party for you tomorrow?"

"Xander will understand. Thanks for coming. I'd appreciate you keeping this between us," Alex said to Harun.

Assuring Alex that he and Cristina wouldn't breathe a word, Harun raced back to The Pierre.

"It's already five-thirty." Rick snatched the Versace jacket off the rail and hustled Alex into it. Rick threw on his own jacket, a Gucci copper brocade with satin trim. "You are going to be okay, aren't you?"

"Yeah, it's not so bad now." Alex waved his hand in front of his eyes. The jazzy blank hole was still there. They'd barely set foot in the hallway when Rick darted back into the room. "What now?" This was so typically Rick, taking hours to get ready, hassling him to hurry up, then wasting time at the last minute.

Rick handed him a pair of dark glasses. "There'll be flash photography, wear these."

"I am not showing up at my gala opening night looking like Roy Orbison!"

With wounded eyes, Rick dropped the dark glasses on the console table inside the door.

"Please don't let this dominate the evening."

"I'm worried about you."

"Don't be. I can deal with myself. Enjoy the night and don't fuss around me every second. It makes me tense."

The white-gloved operator greeted them courteously as they entered the paneled elevator with a small leather bench. On the journey down twenty stories, Alex wondered if anyone ever sat on that bench. The elevator's doors opened into the Carlyle's black lacquer lobby with its potted palms and glossy dark floors.

Ysabel snapped up from a mustard velvet chair and launched herself towards them. "The limo's outside, where …?" Ysabel's voice trailed off. "What happened to your hair?"

"I cut it," said Alex.

"Heavens … you're late." Ysabel's voice dripped with accusation. She hustled them to the revolving door.

Out on the humid street, the Carlyle's uniformed doorman held open the limo's door. Ysabel and Rick climbed in.

"Alex!" shouted a woman.

Steadying himself on the limo's roof, Alex tilted his head to use his left eye, for he couldn't see who called from his right. Dressed in black tapered pants, low heeled pumps and an olive swing back silk jacket, Neroli Copley hurried from the hotel. "My flight got delayed. I nearly didn't make it."

"Do you need a cab, ma'am?" the doorman asked Neroli.

"Yes," said Neroli.

"There's room in the limo, you can ride down with us," Alex said without hesitation.

"As long as you're sure?" Neroli glanced at Ysabel as she ducked past her into the car.

"Yeah, it's fine," said Alex, unaware of Ysabel's disgruntled expression which spoke volumes about how not fine letting Neroli ride along was. The limo driver pulled out. No-one spoke. It dawned on Alex that Ysabel hadn't met Rick and maybe didn't know Neroli personally. "Ysabel Marchand, this is Neroli Copley. She represents my work in LA. And Rick Stradman, my … um …" Alex hesitated how to introduce Rick. 'Partner' was the word he usually chose, but that sounded like a business arrangement on the heels of Neroli's introduction. 'Lover?' too casual. 'Life partner,' too clinical. Alex settled on, "My rock. I wouldn't be where I am without Rick." Alex realized that sounded like he was slighting Neroli. "And Neroli too, of course, I've been with her over twenty years. She's believed in me all the way …" Alex thought that sounded like he was testing Xander Chen's belief in him.

Silently acknowledging Neroli with a cool dip of her pointed chin, Ysabel slipped on her glasses and studied her iPhone.

Under the impression he'd offended everyone in the limo except the driver, Alex decided it was safer to keep shtum.

Ysabel checked her phone every fifteen seconds, scowling at the traffic and drumming her French manicure on the limo's walnut trim.

"Are many of your clients are coming tonight?" Rick asked Neroli to break the awkward silence.

"The Gustavsons, Rhonda Bigelow, Tate …" Neroli stopped mid-sentence. "And a few others who may be in town."

From the edge of his sightline, Alex noticed Ysabel had stopped scrolling on her phone, only to resume once Neroli stopped naming names. Although art dealers didn't openly admit they were in competition with each other, they were. The dealer who makes the sale makes the commission. He guessed Neroli didn't want to give away her client base while she still had it.

The crawling traffic made heavy going of the twenty-block journey. It was six twenty-five when the limo drew up alongside the crowded West 53rd St. sidewalk out front of the Museum of Modern Art.

"One second." Unfurling her legs and heels, Ysabel got out.

From his good side Alex watched Ysabel, her horizontal striped black and white dress creating a strobing effect in his blind spot, in deep discussion with Xander Chen. Ysabel flashed an agitated glance at the limo. Returning, she opened the rear door. "The museum wants to get the VIP arrival underway." She beckoned Alex. "Xander will escort you in."

"You guys get out," Alex said to Neroli and Rick.

Ysabel's palm stopped them. "We're tight on time. They want you on the blue carpet immediately, Alex."

He looked questioningly at Rick.

"Go, do what you need to do. We'll catch up."

Alex spun on the limos' leather seat as much as he could to set foot on the ground. Cameras and eyes pivoted towards him.

Ysabel stepped aside to allow Xander Chen, with his spiky hair and sharkskin suit, and a security guard, with a curly cord up his sleeve and an earpiece in his ear, to escort Alex from the limo.

Steadying himself on the door frame, Alex declined the security guard's offer of a helping hand. The last thing he wanted was to look like a feeble old man in the photos. Ducking his head out of the vehicle, Alex summoned his energy to draw himself up to his full seventy-three inches.

Chen did a double take. "What happened to your hair?"

"Felt like a change." Alex hoped 'what happened to your hair?' wasn't going to be this evening's mantra.

Two other security guards held back pedestrian traffic and onlookers. Chen shepherded Alex to the roped off blue carpet leading into the square recess of the museum's entrance. A phalanx of upright surfboards in glossy blues, reds, yellows and pinks, and blue banners with *'West Coast Light – A Meditation on the Work of Alex Morgan'* lined the walkway into the gallery.

The jazzy hole in his vision was extremely disorientating. Alex couldn't make out anything happening on his far right. Chen's cool hands maneuvered him into position under a hot spotlight. Lenses focused on his face. He hoped his right eye didn't appear as lazy as it felt. Figuring Rick would catch up with him at any second, a masculine hand slapped down on his shoulder. Laughter and applause erupted from the sidewalk crowd. They obviously recognized the man who'd rocked up. Alex turned. "What the fuck?"

"Didn't think we'd let you hog all this limelight to yourself, did ya?" Flash bulbs glinted off Rod's super-white teeth.

To his even greater surprise, Alex found Allen and Cayde patting him on the back. "You told me at the Q and A you couldn't make it?"

"Know what?" Allen smirked. "We lied!"

"Xander arranged everything for us." Cayde jerked his thumb towards Chen, who pressed his palms together and bowed his head. "The seventies bad boys reunited!" Locker room backslapping, ribald laughter and in-jokes ensued as cameras moved in to capture the men's larking around.

"What's with the hair? You trying to make us look like a bunch of old farts?" joked Rod.

A woman's face emerged from Alex's blind spot and planted her lips on his right cheek. "Congratulations. Have a wonderful night!"

Like a ventriloquist's dummy, Alex had to lean back and pivot his head to see who it was. "Claudia, hi." He returned the kiss to Allen's wife, a fitness trainer twenty years younger than Allen. Her spaghetti strap chiffon dress revealed gleaming shoulders and taut upper arms. Brooke, Cayde's diminutive wife, and Rod's current Russian model girlfriend, whom Alex had met twice but couldn't recall her name, closed in around him. All of them congratulating him and passing comment on his hair. Once his famous friends and their glamorous wives and escorts had gone into the museum, Chen introduced more guests, most likely clients or people he'd like to be his clients. Lining them up for photos with Alex, the sidewalk onlookers' excitement level rose with each battery of flashes on each big name. "Yoko Ono … Mary-Kate and Ashley Olsen … Dasha Zhukova and Roman Abramovich … Ramin Salsali …" Alex exchanged words he couldn't remember with the dizzying roll call of stellar names. He didn't know who some of them were, but they all knew who he was. Far out. A high-profile sale to any of these big names would only send his career one way …

Up!

It was incredible, he was *A NAME* too!

Rhaven Williams, the museum's chief curator, sidled up alongside. After shaking hands, he guided him inside.

"I've lost track of Rick," Alex shouted to Chen over the blue carpet hubbub. "Do you know where he got to?"

Chen regarded Alex blankly.

"Rick, my partner," Alex then said to Rhaven, "he should be photographed here with me."

Blue jacketed staff on either side of the glass doors were hurriedly checking off the list as security guards hustled ticketed guests from the sidewalk into the museum.

"The press pack must have cut him off. I'll have security prioritize getting him through," said Rhaven distractedly.

"But I want photos with him here."

"There'll be more press and photo opportunities inside." Rhaven insistently pushed Alex forward.

"That's not the same ..."

"I understand," Rhaven said close to Alex's ear, "but we must perform the Pavilion's opening ceremony while there's an hour or more of daylight. Your contract stipulates the monochromes be viewed solely in natural light. An entire structure's been custom built to house them. You arrived late. Any more delay will skew the schedule. Please, come through."

Alex wanted to put his foot down and insist on a blue carpet moment for Rick, but the quiet desperation in Rhaven's voice, combined with the fact that he had been late to arrive, stopped him from protesting. He allowed Rhaven to shuffle him through the buzzy throng milling around the museum's columned foyer.

Stepping out into the open-air sculpture garden, Alex was greeted by champagne-sipping guests grouped on the marble terraces surrounding lily ponds and bubbling low fountains. On the flat bridge crossing one of the water features, a girl in a crocheted vest was singing 'Make it With You,' accompanying herself on the guitar. A décor seating area of bean bag chairs on a green shag pile carpet had been set up at the base of a twenty-five-foot-high sculpture of an obelisk balanced precariously on the point of a pyramid. Guests weren't availing themselves of the bean bag chairs, instead contemplating them with bemusement as if they were an exhibit in themselves.

... hey, have you ever tried, really reaching out for the other side?

Trying to take it all in with his limited vision, he got his first glimpse of the large windowless graphite cube dominating the sculpture garden's northeastern corner. This was the Pavilion, designed and constructed expressly for his retrospective. As Rhaven inexorably propelled him to the platform with spotlights and a microphone, Alex regretted how easily he'd allowed Ysabel to separate him from Rick.

Rhaven raised his eyes to the evening sky. "The light's perfect." He indicated for Alex to get up on the platform.

Now able to see above the crowd with his good eye, Alex spotted Rick's sandy hair and copper jacket at the back of the audience. He was with Cristina and another woman whom he guessed was Ellery Pritzker.

"Good evening." Rhaven's deep voice echoed off sculptures. Conversation died, amplifying the horns, sirens, and rumble of NYC traffic. "Welcome to *West Coast Light*, an unprecedented gathering of the works of Alex Morgan, with over fifty paintings and drawings collated from all phases of his career. Our museum is proud to host the world debut of this major retrospective. And even prouder that the artist, Alex Morgan, is with us tonight for the opening of this celebration, or should I say *meditation*, of his work. On behalf of the museum, I'd like to thank Neroli Copley, The Harrington Collection, The Huntington Museum, The Norton Simon Foundation and The Geffen Contemporary Gallery for the generous loans which have made this exhibition possible. Thanks too to The Martin Luce Foundation, Xander Chen Gallery and Eli and Corinne Hass for additional funding. It's fitting that as the sun sinks in the west, we on the east coast should have our first sight of the Pavilion. This magnificent temporary structure, sponsored by Lehman Brothers, was constructed expressly for this exhibition. This is so the paintings inside may be viewed in ambient light. Please savor this unique opportunity to experience these works as the artist intended." Applause followed. Lowering the microphone, Rhaven asked Alex, "Would you care to speak?"

To speak or not to speak? Alex didn't particularly want to, he wasn't lying when he'd told Thom he was a shy guy, but this would give him the chance to restore Rick to his side. "Yeah, I'll say a few words." Alex accepted the microphone. "Hi." He let a wailing siren pass by over the wall on West 54th St. "Thanks to Rhaven and his team for assembling this show with such care and genuine love. I thought retrospectives like this only happened to artists after they were dead. I'm hoping you guys don't know something I don't." Alex dipped his head at the ensuing laughter. "As an artist you sometimes come up a with great style or a piece or a collection that catches fire and gathers momentum with galleries and buyers. You suddenly find everyone wanting more from you. Everyone wants an original, but one that's the same and recognizable. But I've never been good at doing the same thing over and over. Even with my hair. See, after all these years I've even managed to switch that up." He ruffled his shorter hair with another shy grin. "I guess what I'm trying to say is, my feeling about art and life is having the courage to keep taking risks and hopefully bring your audience along with you. Sometimes the risk pays off, sometimes it doesn't. That's why I want to seize this moment to call over the man who believed in me at a time when no-one else did. And I want him at my side to share this momentous opening as, honestly, I wouldn't be standing here today without him. Please, let Rick Stradman through to join me."

Alex extended his hand to the assembled guests.

Faces turned and looked behind them to see the man Alex spoke of. The crowd parted with expectation and applause.

Alex squinted over the audience's heads. Rick wasn't at the back anymore. Behind the atrium's glass windows, a TV camera crew with mobile spotlight and boom mic were at work. Through his vision distortion, Alex perceived Cristina's blond up-do and Rick's copper jacket under the lights. Rick must have gone inside the gallery before hearing the end of his speech.

The applause petered out.

An embarrassed murmur passed across lips.

Alex remained standing alone, feeling foolish.

Rhaven beckoned for a guard to go find Rick, but the moment had passed. "Hey," Alex spoke into the mic, "guess he found out where the buffet is and wanted to be first in line. Anyway, even though he's not standing here, he's in here." Alex tapped his chest. "Likewise, to all those people who've supported me and believed in me, and also to the ones who haven't, I wouldn't be where I am today without you. Thanks for coming. It means a lot to me." Stepping back, Alex allowed Rhaven to finish up.

The rope guarding the entrance to the Pavilion was removed and Rhaven led Alex into the dark windowless cube to experience his own work.

ROCK BREAKS SCISSORS

The drops to dilate his pupils combined with the high intensity light used to examine his retinas rendered Alex blind. His entire world consisted of purple spots and zigzags. He sat back from the contraption, apparently called a slit lamp, he'd been peering into.

"I need to inject a fluorescein dye to highlight the veins in your eyes," said Dr. Kastani. "Relax while we prepare the injection."

Relaxing was the last thing on Alex's mind. He ought to be in Xander Chen's Upper East Side townhouse, mingling with Wall Street titans, jet set private collectors, rock stars and stellar artists, not in the Eye Institute at Keck Medicine back in LA.

Twenty-four hours ago he was winding up his impromptu speech and calling for Rick to join him. Pre-publicity for *The Belles of Bel Air* must've kicked in. A news crew interviewing celebrity guests had spotted Cristina and Ellery in the crowd. Having gathered enough soundbites from the Olsen Twins, Steve Martin and Jay-Z, the crew swooped and dragged these reality TV stars of tomorrow inside the museum's atrium for some camera time. Rick had gotten swept along with the tide.

Here and now, in the darkened examination room, Alex heard Dr. Kastani entering notes on his computer. But in his mind he was back at MoMA, it was this time yesterday and Rhaven Williams had just escorted him into the Pavilion for first sight of his *MonoChromantics I - XV* in situ ...

"How'd we do? You happy?" Rhaven had asked.

Floating walls concealed the entrance and exit on opposing corners. The sole illumination inside the matt black interior came from New York's gold-gray dusk filtering through the cube's translucent ceiling.

Twelve of his paintings – all six-foot square panels dating back to the mid-90s – were hung in threes on each wall. He'd done fifteen of these monochromes. Two owners declined the loan and one's ownership couldn't be traced. The pieces MoMA's curatorial team had assembled here were predominantly dark hues - moss green, inky blue, rich purple and the like. One panel, however, was Alex's signature red - a vicious, viscous crimson - and another an eye-popping citrus lemon.

"I'm honored, it's more than I could have hoped for." The diffused overhead light reflecting off the pieces hung on matt black walls gave the illusion of light radiating through them, like stained glass windows. "May I have a moment alone?"

"We need to start moving guests through so we can get them up to the main exhibit."

"I understand. But I may never get to see these paintings like this again." Heck, if his eye problem was serious, Alex figured that he may never see them again full stop.

"Five minutes," Rhaven conceded, then he dissolved into the darkness behind a black wall masking off an attendant's seat and the exit.

Alex couldn't put a number on the days and weeks he'd invested in these pieces, nor put a price on the vast quantity of paints and brushes he'd used to make them. It had taken months of experimentation to perfect the finishing technique. He'd blended microscopic glass beads into the same pigment as the base layer and overpainted once with this. Then he'd overpainted with uneven coats of matt, gloss, and satin lacquer. These virtually invisible layers lent a mysterious dimension to all the pieces, but to the darker works in Payne's Gray and Ultimate Black in particular. A layer of low cloud must have been passing over Manhattan. Diffused by the milky roof, the evening light's subtle shift created watermark patterns in the single-color pieces.

Alone with his paintings, Alex studied his work. The citrus lemon panel spoke to him. The memory of its birth made him smile. Staring into it, a visual echo of his hand working pigment into the board filled the blank spot in his vision. The air thickened with a yellow summer sun's heat. A half-remembered scent drifted by. Lily-of-the-valley and freesia. Had someone entered? Alex turned. A woman dressed in a blue skirt suit and white hat appeared in the blurry hole in his vision. The scent was the perfume Mom used to wear. Alex's head swam. Mom's face came towards his eye with wistful longing. Then, in a pulse of purple spots, grandma Dora's face overlaid Mom's. The floor wobbled beneath his feet. Dora's gentle eyes crinkled into a proud smile which transfigured her face into Danielle's, a beach wind tossing her hair. Danielle's loving eyes momentarily connected with his, then she looked through him towards a distant unseen horizon. What was going on? Swallowing hard, Alex fought for tangibles to ground himself. But there was nothing in here to hang on to except black walls, his paintings, an unstable floor and ghosts.

Alex kneaded his eyes to erase the women he'd loved. Daring to open his eyes again, the red panel confronted him. Staring into its glistening crimson vortexes, Alex willed himself into the present, willed himself to see the life he had now. An image formed in the maelstrom of red whorls. Through his blind spot, Alex watched himself finishing work in his studio at the day's end. On the other side of the pool, Rick was turning on lamps inside the house. A golden puppy ran past his ankles. How could there be a dog in the Pavilion? Especially one whose black nose they'd spotted peeping from a trembling brown carton dumped on Venice Boulevard. Alex had slammed on the brakes, Rick hurtled out and dodged traffic to make sure they hadn't imagined what they'd seen. Ashen faced, Rick carried the soiled box to the SUV. They peeled back the carton's flaps and saw two dead puppies with matted golden fur and a mewling live one …

At the recollection of the dead puppies, nausea rose in Alex's thorax. He fought to see the reflective tape on the inky floor marking the exit. Thinking he'd found it, he followed the silvery line. Shit! He slammed into a solid wall. How could he be lost? The Pavilion was a fucking cube, not a maze! He blindly felt his way along the wall. Touching a painting's edge, he snatched back his hand, he didn't want to damage his own work. In the muted light, the pure black panel filled his eyes. Its luminescent surface, rippling like a night sea, lured him in. With his sanity slipping away like the floor, a man emerged from the sea mist in the porthole of his blind spot. He recognized the man as Pop. His father raised his hand. From years of conditioning, Alex instinctively flinched. But Pop looked so lonely as he plaintively raised his other hand. Alex felt the urge to reach out in turn to give comfort. But just as he was about to, Pop's expression changed. His plaintive, outstretched fingers curled into fists, anger transfigured Pop's face into somebody else's. This phantom now wore Alex's own face as a mask. He was staring at himself, gray and angry and old and alone, a ghost of his future self.

This was like the terrifying waking dream in the hospital, only his time he was conscious, trapped in a black box with invisible exits and dead faces. Any longer in here and his heart would stop. He couldn't escape, he needed to scream for help!

"Sir?"

Alex licked his lips and wiped his damp palms on his pants. Don't throw up, not in here. *Please, don't throw up in the Pavilion built by MoMA to house your work.* "What?"

"May I start allowing guests in?"

The vague blank in Alex's vision shifted. The lonely, angry man wearing his own face transformed into a blue jacketed museum attendant. "Uh, yeah."

"Do you need help getting to the fifth floor?"

"No, thanks." Getting himself together, Alex followed the shining silver tape line leading to EXIT written in reflective lettering on the matt black floor ...

"Ah," Alex gasped. The cold dab of an alcohol pad on his skin jerked Alex from his memory of panic. He was back in the Eye Institute's examination room.

"Sharp scratch. One, two, three," said the nurse inserting a cannula into his arm.

The needle penetrated Alex's flesh.

"You may feel nausea as the dye goes in. It should pass," said Dr. Kastani. "Eyes wide open, Mr. Morgan. Any major discomfort, shout out. Bring your head forward. That's it."

Alex rested his chin on the white plastic ledge and pressed his forehead into the slit-lamp's restraint.

"Dye, please," said Dr. Kastani.

Nothing happened.

Then fire coursed through his veins, burning around his fingers, his legs, his stomach, his chest. Straining to keep his eyes open, the white light became a jaundiced yellow as his heart pumped dyed blood around his brain. The intense light hit his optic nerve. Alex recoiled.

"Wide open," intoned Dr. Kastani.

To negate his nervous system's involuntary reactions, Alex left his body in the examination room and let his mind return to last night at MoMA ...

Hoping he didn't look as shell-shocked as he felt, Alex had shakily emerged from the Pavilion. Out on the marble terraces, fresh air and open sky had come as a blessed relief. He couldn't spot Rick among the guests drifting towards the line for the Pavilion. Rhaven wasn't around either. Or Ysabel. Or Chen. Adrift and alone at his own opening night and feeling like he was taking a bad trip from a batch of tainted weed, he made his way to the elevators.

A smattering of applause marked his entrance to the fifth-floor gallery hosting the bulk of his exhibit. Servers with trays of drinks threaded through guests. The reality of these hallowed halls being dedicated entirely to his art hit home. People were flipping pages in the glossy brochures, discussing his technique, explaining his work to each other.

"There you are. I was about to send out a search party!" Glass of wine in hand, Rick rushed up.

"Thought you may have stuck around downstairs."

"I didn't want to get caught in line for the Pavilion and miss you up here."

"Why didn't you stay until I finished my speech? I called for you to join me."

"I know, Neroli told me. Sorry. I wasn't expecting you to do something like that."

Alex unwisely accepted a glass of white wine. "Why not?"

"This evening's about you, not me. And you seemed to be getting along quite happily without me on the blue carpet."

"Chen's rush to start the arrival publicity was only because we were late. It was unfortunate you got caught on the wrong side of the press pack."

"Allen and Cayde's wives and Rod's paramour got through," said Rick.

More guests spilled from the elevator bank, the gallery chatter grew louder.

An elegantly dressed man speaking with Chen and Ysabel attracted Alex's attention. The blur in Alex's eye covered the man's face. From nothingness, Pop's face lurched towards him.

Alex swigged down the sharp wine. His hand went to his temple. What was happening? Forcing himself to look in Pop's direction again, he'd turned back into the hedge fund manager in a charcoal suit talking with Chen. "Can I get a Chivas on the rocks?" Alex asked the waiter.

The server's smile wavered.

"If you don't have Chivas, any will do." Alex deposited his empty wine glass on the tray.

"We have a red, if you don't care for white wine, sir."

"They're only serving wine, juice and water up here," Rick softly advised.

The server moved away.

"Where's Neroli?" muttered Alex. "Need to let her know thirty thousand dollars doesn't stretch to hard liquor nowadays."

"Darling, you're scowling. Ellery's with Cristina and Harun. Let me take you over, she's dying to meet you." Rick reached for Alex's arm.

Alex shook off Rick's hand. Back with Chen, Pop's judgmental dead eyes were on him again. Pop's face grew enormous, coming towards him through the magnifying lens in the hole of his sight. A film of perspiration bloomed on Alex's chest. Was he having a stroke? The shapes and faces looming in his blind spot were becoming stranger.

"Man of the hour!" Rod swaggered up to Alex. "How does it feel having all this hoopla in honor of yourself?"

"It'd be a helluva lot better if I could get a real drink."

"He's pissed because he wants a whiskey and they're only serving wine up here," Rick explained to Rod.

"That all? Leave it with me." Rod departed with intent.

"You shouldn't be drinking at all with your eye trouble," said Rick. "Think of your heart, and your blood pressure, and —"

"I want a drink, okay? For fuck's sake, I'm a grown man. I don't need a nursemaid!"

Rick stepped back and held his hands in surrender. "I'll go mingle. See if there's anyone in the art world here who still remembers me."

Being watched by faces of the living and the dead was creeping Alex out. Slouching off to a quiet corner, he couldn't help overhearing snatches of conversation …

"His sense of color's faultless …"

"Muted, yet bold …"

"Derivative …"

"His early works are his strongest …"

"So versatile!"

"If you stare at a blank piece of paper for long enough you eventually see something —"

"Here you go." Rod handed Alex a glass with ice and a generous measure of whiskey.

"You send Neroli to the liquor store?" Alex downed a slug.

"Slipped the bartender a fifty."

Warmth entered Alex's chest.

"Ask for Fernando when you need a refill. Just relax, tonight isn't about you anymore. You've done your work." Rod had gestured to the artsy guests, critics, dealers, collectors and media stars milling around the white walls and pale wood floors. "This is their party now. You can't change your work. It's a done deal. What you give them next's the only thing that counts ..."

"Nearly done," Dr. Kastani's voice from behind the slit lamp jogged Alex back into the Eye Institute's examination room. "Feeling all right?"

"Hot and itchy."

"That's the dye. Your skin may turn yellow. Your pee definitely will!" Dr. Kastani said with a merry chuckle.

After the cobalt white-blue band of light moved up and down Alex's right eye for another five minutes, the examination concluded. Dr. Kastani departed. Letting a further ten minutes elapse, the nurse steered Alex down the shiny corridor with pistachio green walls and into the consulting room.

Shards of late afternoon sun slanting through the blinds stung Alex's eyes. Taking a seat before Dr. Kastani's desk, Alex noticed a blurry patchwork of medical degrees, qualifications and awards on his wall. Well, he assumed that's what they were. Between the dilating eyedrops, yellow dye and jazzy spot in his vision, they could be the collected works of Margaret Keane for all he knew.

Dr. Kastani looked up from his computer. "You have a blockage in one of the veins in your right eye. Fluid has spilled onto the retina, which in turn's caused the macula to swell, resulting in your vision loss."

"Is it permanent?"

"Hopefully not. It could clear by itself given time."

"How much time?"

"Hard to say. You've had this problem for a while?"

"On and off for the past couple of months. So if I just wait it'll go away?"

"The longer you have disruption to the blood supply and edema, the greater the risk of permanent vision loss."

"Has that already happened?"

"I can't tell you for sure."

"What're my options?"

"You could do nothing and hope it clears. Some people learn to live with the impairment. But it might not. Given your profession, I understand you may not be willing to risk that. There are treatments we could try if that's the course you wish to take."

"What do they involve?" Alex listened as Dr. Kastani detailed various procedures. After a few minutes of consideration, he opted for an injection to reduce the swelling. Fearing permanent vision loss, he asked if he could have the treatment as soon as possible. The doctor said it could be done on this visit if he were prepared to wait. Wanting to get it over with, Alex agreed.

With his fuzzy yellow vision, Alex cautiously made his way to the front desk. Now the eye examination was over, he could switch to worrying about how Rick was getting on with Bella at the animal clinic. Expecting to find Scotty in the waiting area, he was instantly annoyed to find she wasn't there. He was about to get out his phone when the guy manning the front desk called, "Your wife's gone down to grab a coffee."

Alex suppressed an ironic smile at the heteronormative assumption. Having politely corrected the state of their relationship, he decided to get some fresh air himself. Leaving his cell number with the front desk, he slipped on the dark glasses Rick had forced on him. Playing blind man's buff on his way to the elevators, he did his best not to bump into patients, walls, or pot plants along the way.

Even wearing sunglasses, the daylight stung. Alex headed towards blurry figures lining up at a black and white zebra striped coffee cart. Arriving at the cart, he found none of the blurry figures belonged to Scotty. Wondering where the fuck she went, he was on his way back inside when some blurry white pants, a pomegranate longline sweater and dangling gold neck chains came swaying his way.

"All done?" Scotty asked.

"Afraid not. As the saying goes, 'I'd rather stick a needle in my eye' is about to come true." Alex's vision was shot, but his sense of smell was spot-on. Despite the breath mint she must've popped, the aroma on her clothes was a dead giveaway. "You've been smoking."

"What do you mean?"

"I smoked for enough years to recognize that smell."

"It's my new cologne."

"Eau de Nicotine?"

"What if I have?"

"How long's this been going on?"

"A while …"

"That explains the cough. Why lie?"

"Admitting you smoke these days is like admitting you worship Satan. No, worshipping Satan's not as bad! That may be considered an alternative religion. All right, my name's Fionnuala Scott and I'm a secret smoker," she whispered.

"Why are you whispering?"

"The bushes may be bugged. Everywhere you turn around here there's a no smoking sign." Approaching the entrance, Scotty stepped aside to let a white coated blurry doctor pass. "I was nearly in Pasadena before I found a place to light up without being arrested. Look, I know it's a terrible thing to do, and I know the risks involved, and I know all the other reasons why no-one should do it, but I enjoy a smoke! I'm suitably ashamed yet defiantly unrepentant. Don't judge me!"

"I'm not. You made me want a cigarette now."

"Rick would kill me if I let you smoke. He's still furious with Rod for getting you drunk last night."

"I've replaced nearly every enjoyable food stuff in my diet with vile smoothies and that hasn't worked out terribly well, has it? Fuck eating broccoli and cutting carbs for the rest of my life, I may as well let rip with rump steaks and whiskey and enjoy what time I have left." His cell phone's vibration removed any temptation of a cigarette. Dr. Kastani was ready to operate.

Back on the fourth floor, Scotty took a seat in the waiting area under strict instruction to stay put. Alex retraced his steps along the pistachio corridor with sliding oak doors.

Lying on the couch in the darkened treatment room, Alex listened to Dr. Kastani outline the procedure. It sounded fine in theory, but the reality was a sharp metal object would soon be penetrating his eyeball. Once his eyelids and surrounding area had been swabbed, Dr. Kastani placed a sheet of material over his eyes and forehead. Claustrophobia descended. Dr. Kastani explained the injection would be given from the side. Lying here, wondering how the 'pressure' on his eye, which he knew to be a needle, would actually feel. More eyedrops were administered. What if this injection didn't work? What if he went completely blind? He'd have to rely on memories of how things used to look. What if he forgot the beauty of the world? What if he forgot Rick's face? He wouldn't be able to work if he couldn't see. How would he earn a living if he couldn't paint?

Waiting for the anesthetic to numb his eye, Alex numbed his mind to more questions by returning to last night. He was back at MoMA, standing before his urban plein airs and backlot watercolors ...

"I can't compete with the multi-nationals and mega-dealers. I have no choice but to sell the gallery," Neroli had said.

"You're getting out of the business?"

"The overheads on my downtown location have become untenable. I don't have a client list like Chen's to ask the prices which could make it work these days. And I've lost nearly all my artists who could warrant even attempting to get into that price bracket." Neroli had looked at his watercolor of the struts and scaffolds holding up one of the backlot buildings at Universal. She finished her drink. "I detest the snobbery that puts down figurative art. Frankly, this is the art most people like to have on their walls. Yumi Mihara did well for you in this period." Walking on with Alex around the gallery, Neroli studied *Homeward Bound*.

This diptych was comprised of two panels, both plein air studies from the same location but painted at two different times. Alex remembered those nights on the scrub covered hillside looking down over the coast highway towards Laguna Beach. Rick had come along and held a flashlight so that he could paint at twilight. Alex downed his fifth whiskey. The vision in his left eye was nearly as blurry as his right now, only without the jazzy blank spot. Servers were bringing around finger food. He declined the shot glass filled with prawns in a pink sauce. "Sorry to hear about your gallery."

"Things change." Neroli waved the tray away. "But listen, I had three rooms blocked out for Jerry Weir's solo show this fall. Now he's gone to Hauser and Wirth I've got nothing to fill that two-month slot. If you want to go down with me in one last hurrah the show's yours. If not, I'll shutter the gallery in September."

Alex wrapped his mind around Neroli's offer. The large metal pieces were underway at the foundry, but he hadn't seen them finished yet. And all twelve would need enameling and over-painting, and he wasn't even sure if he'd like them as yet. And if Chen could get good prices for his new abstracts, he'd be mad to consign them to Neroli. His new 'hole' pieces and the metal sculptures excited him, but Chen had expressed no interest in showing them. What should he do, follow the money or his heart? "Can I think it over?"

"Let me know by the end of the month," Neroli said from under her widescreen dark bangs.

Leaving Neroli, Alex made another trip to Fernando. Cradling his sixth whiskey, he vowed it to be his last. He skulked around the edges of his opening night gala, almost willing people not to approach him in case their face should turn out not to be real.

Three bald Chinese men in business suits by-passed his downtown LA plein air paintings without even looking. A girl with white dreadlocks under a green velvet Boy George hat glanced at *The Cliffs of Mendocino*, the painting on which Rosemarie Harrington made the winning bid at Monica Aigner's charity auction. Letting out a derisive sigh, the girl moved on.

His iconic painting *Marooned on Red* and seven further works from his red series had a good crowd, all making appreciative noises. Squinting woozily over their shoulders, Alex made out that the hanging damage to the pieces on loan from Harrison Wilde had been beautifully restored. Buoyed by this, he turned a corner to find Rick in deep conversation with a very tanned white-haired couple in front of *Zephyrs # 1 – 9*, a collection of mid-career works he'd created from thousands of shreds of painted watercolor paper mounted on canvas.

"... the inspiration for these works were the plover feathers Alex found on the beach," Rick was knowledgably telling the couple. Air flow from passers-by ruffled the shreds of emerald, gray and lilac papers in *Zephyr #3*. Rick's eyes shone warmly upon seeing Alex but cooled when they dropped to the half-empty glass in his hand. "Alex, meet Gerhard and Ilse Kleinman. They're turning a former military bunker in Berlin into a gallery. Five stories of solid concrete walls with only four narrow channels of windows. Doesn't it sound fascinating?"

"We shall live in an apartment on the top floor. It is going to be a big adventure. Please, you must visit us when you are in Berlin," said Gerhard.

Ilse clapped her hands in delight. "We have very much space to fill!"

"Gerhard and Ilse are keen to increase their exposure to American art," said Rick.

Alex smirked. Rick expressed it in a way which made it sound like the Kleinmans wanted to increase their exposure to plutonium.

"Ricardo. It is you?"

A young woman with ultra-long blond hair, an extremely short leather skirt and a husky voice approached their group.

"Ileanna. *Si, si. Salve, salve. Come stai?*" Rick and the young woman slipped into one of those rat-a-tat Italian conversations which sounded like an argument even if the people involved were delighted to see one another. "Alex, this is Ileanna Souter," Rick said in English after the barrage of trills and plosives. "She has a stunning gallery in Rome."

"Had," corrected Ileanna. "Is gone many years ago."

"Hi." Alex struggled to focus through his eye trouble and whiskey. Tipping his head back and sideways to get a good look at Ileanna, he almost dropped his glass. The weird faces springing up in his blind spot were nowhere near as weird as this one. Her long blond hair sprouted from hair plugs, and one face-lift too many must've severed a nerve, for one side of her bronzed face didn't move in tandem with the other.

Ileanna wore a concerned expression, well half of her face did, as she asked Rick, "What is wrong with your mother?"

"I've been asking that for years," said Rick.

"Is not funny, Ricardo. Luisa does not answer my calls. And I have called the institute, but they will not tell me how she is," rasped Ileanna.

"She's fine. I haven't spoken to her for a while."

"Then how do you know she is fine?"

"Patti would've told me if there was anything to worry about." Rick sipped his drink.

"When did you last see her?" asked Ileanna.

Rick vaguely waved his drink and said grandly, "We have major issues to deal with at the LA Conservatory, I'm on their board, and I have filming commitments for a new TV show. I'll probably go visit when she's well again and back home."

"She only expected to be in the care home for a few weeks." Ileanna flicked her blond hair back on both sides. Clutching her pearl encrusted Chanel purse to her bosom, she tapped a wrinkled finger encrusted with gold rings on Rick's lapel. "You are her son! You should know more than *think* your mamma is fine." They exchanged a cool kiss before she moved on.

"Thanks for the advice," Rick said acidly while watching Ileanna's skinny legs totter away. "She used to be a big player in the Italian gallery scene. Maybe she should check herself into the institute as well if she's so worried about momma."

Alex finished his whiskey.

Rick looked accusingly at Alex's empty glass. "We should get back to the hotel and pack."

Alex really wanted another drink. Feeling hideously drunk was preferable to lucidity. "I need to go speak with Chen about tomorrow."

A burst of energetic laughter by *Agua Nexus*, one of his mid- 80s pieces featuring scarlet rings, azure waves and geometric white lines, drew their attention.

"Look, it's the Clutters," said Rick.

Dressed in loose fitting casual wear, the mother, father and daughter of the Klotte family from Maryland were in animated conversation with Neroli. Their down-home attire belied their immense wealth. With their fan-like adoration of art and artists and lack of sophistication, they'd acquired the affectionate nickname of 'The Clutters.' They owned *Agua Nexus* and had come to visit their loan.

"Hi hon!" Charlotte Klotte clasped Alex to her leisure suited bust. "It's wunnerful. All just wunnerful!"

"So happy fer you." Eli Klotte, also small, rotund and in a leisure suit, pumped Alex's hand.

Mia Klotte, their thirty-year-old daughter, gazed up at Alex in silent adoration.

The Clutters' enthusiasm, genuine appreciation and vigorous life force lifted Alex's heart. As they joked and filled him in on their recent collecting exploits, from his left-hand side he spotted Chen looking their way with a disdainful air.

Knowing he had to get this over with, Alex excused himself from the Clutters. Struggling to focus on Chen and not slur his words, Alex said, "Thanks for everything tonight, Xander."

"Your abstracts have been well admired. That's the style you should stick with."

"I'll take that on board. Now, about tomorrow night …"

"I'm glad you brought that up." Chen flicked his eyes to Rick laughing with the Clutters. "I'd prefer you to attend the party alone. Like in art, the effect of the finest painting can be killed if put in a distracting and inappropriate frame."

The vision of Pop's phantom talking with Chen reignited in Alex's head. He wanted to tell Chen he didn't care what kind of frame his picture was in, but maybe he did. "I'm afraid I won't be able to attend at all. I need to get back to LA in the morning."

"You can't be serious?" Chen's eyes flared. "Tomorrow night's event has been planned specifically for you. There are important clients that I need to meet. What can be so urgent to warrant missing that?"

"I've developed a problem with my sight. I'm actually struggling to see you right now."

"Why didn't you tell me? I have contacts at the finest hospitals. Let me call someone."

Alex couldn't read Chen's facial expression. "I have underlying medical conditions that could be in play. It'll be more streamlined to have everyone involved in my medical care in the same place."

"Of course, of course. It's regrettable, but I understand."

Leaving Chen, Alex looked around for Rick. Whiskey, adrenalin and panic made a bad mix. The floor was rolling like a ship at sea.

He spotted Cayde. "I don't know where Rick got to."

"I just saw him headed towards the elevators."

"Can you say bye to Rod and Allen for me? Something's come up. We gotta fly home in the morning."

"Oh, yeah. Hope she's okay." Cayde gave a concerned nod.

"Who?"

"Bella. Tyler dropped by the house for advice just before we left for the airport. He thought she'd thrown up blood."

Alex shook his head in confusion.

"That's the reason you have to get back to LA, isn't it?"

"I didn't know anything was wrong with Bella," said Alex.

"Tyler didn't want to worry you. I figured he must have changed his mind and called you."

"No, it's something else. When do you and Brooke get home?"

"Friday."

"We'll catch up then." Alex's head really was spinning now. He steadied himself on the elevator's wall. Stepping out into the lobby, he couldn't see Rick.

A blue jacketed member of staff approached. "The gentleman's out in the sculpture garden. He asked me to let you know if you were looking for him."

Guessing Rick had gone to look at his works in the Pavilion, even though darkness had fallen, Alex went outside. Through his misty vision, two pale figures floated around the marble terraces, their chiffon dresses fluttering in the breeze. The figures were searching on the floor. From around the base of the giant obelisk, Rick's copper jacket and pink shirt emerged.

Walking with extreme care, so as not to trip and fall into a fountain, Alex made his way across.

Rick was on his knees, patting the green shagpile rug around the bean bags.

"Y'all must be Alex! Hi, I'm Ellery," one of the pale figures said.

"Hi, what's going on?"

With a flash of diamonds around her neck, the other pale figure walked up to him. "Rick realized he was missing his pendant when we said goodbye. He thought he'd have noticed if it had fallen off upstairs. We're helping him look down here," said Cristina.

Losing the eternity pendant after all these years must surely be the pinnacle of a depressing night. Alex's heart sank into the same blackness as his black painting.

"Found it!" Rick announced triumphantly.

"Thank the Lord!" Ellery and Cristina cried with relief.

"The chain snapped," said Rick.

"It must've broken while you were trying to sit on a bean bag!" Cristina laughed.

"That's why it should hang on a cord!" Alex snapped. "I told you that chain wasn't strong enough to hold it safely. And why were you sitting on the bean bags anyway?"

"Goofing for the cameras," said Rick. "We were having fun."

"That pendant's precious. Irreplaceable! If you lose it, you'll never get it back."

Chastened, Rick silently nodded.

"Let's go." Feeling giddy, Alex wavered.

Rick put his hand out to steady him. As he did, the pendant dropped, hitting the ground with a sharp crack.

Cristina bent. "Oh, it's broken."

"It's made of stone," said Rick, "how can it be?

"Guess the way it hit the marble. Look, it's split in two," Cristina placed the two halves of the eternity pendant in Rick's palm …

"You're numb now," said Dr. Kastani.

Back in the Eye Institute's treatment room, Dr. Kastani moved the material to expose Alex's eye. "Remain absolutely still. Look straight ahead. You're about to feel the pressure."

Alex felt no sensation of a needle, just pressure on his eyeball as promised. As the injection went in, he wondered if it would work.

"All done. You won't be able to see properly for the rest of the evening," said Dr. Kastani. "You do have someone to drive you and someone to look after you when you get home, don't you?"

"I do." Alex almost wanted to add, 'For now.' He expected his retrospective's opening gala would be the best night of his life and the beginning of a new chapter in his career.

Instead, last night had been one of the worst ever and felt like all kinds of endings.

APOTHEOSIS

'West Coast Lite.'

With far more pressing items to occupy his mind, Alex wished that headline from *Modern Minerva*'s review of his retrospective didn't keep rankling. He didn't know of the journalist, and it was a niche publication, but it had really gotten to him. *The New York Times* had praised the 'masterful use of color and texture' in his *Zephyrs*, the *Post* had thrilled to 'the melancholic summer light' of his plein air paintings, the *Wall Street Journal* was haunted by the 'hungering simplicity' of his *MonoChromantics*, but *Modern Minerva* saw no such positives. Every time he stood at the easel and put brush to canvas, that review ran through his head …

'Although the curator, the legendary Rhaven Williams in his swansong, has done his utmost to present a comprehensive selection of Morgan's work, the result is confusion rather than clarity. There's no through line, no progression, no revelation, just a lot of different ideas. One would hope to walk away from such an expansive show with an understanding of the artist, but the more one looks at his work the harder it is to see the man behind it – as if Morgan is trying on different cloaks to hide from view. The show feels as though something important has been excluded. We turn corners in the hope of glimpsing the artist, but he turns another corner and disappears. Despite the vast amount of space devoted to this exhibition, plus an additional four hundred square foot purpose-built gallery on ground level, Alex Morgan remains opaque. Occasional glimpses of his brilliance prove as fleeting and frustratingly elusive as the shifting sheens of light creeping across his monochromes. One can't deny the attractiveness of his work, which undoubtedly explains his popularity with the assembled ranks of socialites, celebrity collectors and hedge fund investors at the opening. Morgan, whose aging beach-boy looks, California tan and designer clothes render him easy on the eye, is clearly the 'go-to' man for people who like their artists as superficially attractive as their work.'

The criticism of his work knocked his confidence.

The personal comment hurt his feelings.

Figuring his eye treatment would interfere with his work, he'd given Suki and Kent a couple of weeks off - on full pay of course. His recovery had been swifter than expected and he was back in the studio, although with a red and watery eye, after five days. There were a lot of distracting floaters, like dark watery balloons, drifting around in his vision, but the blank spot was no longer blank. He had three new abstracts, as per Chen's recommendation, underway. The foundry, however, had completed the first of the twelve large metal panels. Anxious to play around with it, he'd taken immediate delivery. Something so enormous existing in his imagination, or in scale model form, was one thing but having this eight-foot tall by three-foot wide metal panel standing before him was another. In a former life it had been manhole covers, sewer pipes and radiators. The furnace's hellfire had reincarnated them into this new being.

Following his sketches and models, the foundry was drilling the panels with cobalt bits, then peeling out the holes with oxy-acetylene torches to create the explosive punctures, rips and slashes he'd designed. If he'd used aluminum he could have done this work himself, but he wanted these pieces to have heft. He got his wish. As Rick had banned him from all lifting while his eye was healing, he'd watched in awe as the combined muscle of Tyler, Jack and two burly guys from the foundry were needed to maneuver this beast into his studio.

Taking a fresh can of Strawflower lacquer, he built up another layer of paint over the panel. The holes and tears had looked like shrapnel bursting from a gray battleship's bulkhead when the piece arrived. Using this pinky yellow paint was his plan to give the iron a human dimension. Allowing the fumes to clear, he tore off his goggles and mask. Stepping back to consider the piece, he thought it worked. The protruding metal spikes and slashes took on a poignancy given a flesh tone, although these flesh wounds' tattered edges were sharp and dangerous.

The ninety-thousand dollars he'd invested to produce the metal panels and the half a million-dollar equity he'd released to purchase Manuela's retirement apartment had left a hole in his finances as jagged as the one in this cast iron panel. His initial phone call with Manuela's son had been stilted. Relations warmed once Alex let him know the funds were in place to buy her a comfortable new home along with a healthy pension pot. A plan was made for Manuela to move down to Rancho del Rey to be near her son and elderly sister. As Alex was so busy, Brian, his business manager, had wired the cash to Jorge so he could quickly purchase a suitable property.

Hanging up his mask and goggles, Alex switched focus between his slick, sellable abstracts and the ragged holes of the layered paper pieces. Which path should he take?

The street-sweeping vehicle doing its Tuesday morning gutter cleanse was emitting its fingernails on chalkboard whine, like a dentist's drill, out front. It blended discordantly with the construction rumble from the lot behind. Distracted by the noise, Alex peeled off his fingerless mitts and latex gloves and tossed them aside.

Leaving the studio, he averted his eyes. He didn't want to see the apartment buildings taking shape above their rear wall. They'd definitely need to erect screening on the main house's roof to prevent the pool from being overlooked. Cayde would need to do the same to protect his little Astroturf putting green's privacy wedged in back of his property. Alex entered the house through the door from the patio into the living room.

As the sweeping vehicle's whine faded, Bella's paws clattered through the kitchen then into the living room. Setting eyes on him, Bella loped his way.

"What you got for me, girl?" Bella had a cleaning sponge dangling from her mouth. Bending, he tried to prise it from her. But she wasn't giving up her swag.

"Bella!" Rick bellowed from the rear of the house.

Alex was reaching for the doggie treats hidden in a jar on the coffee table when Rick raced across the patio from the master suite.

"Get that off her! It's got bleach on it," gasped Rick.

"Give." Alex held out a treat with his right hand. Bella dropped the dripping sponge and he grabbed it with his left.

Rick peeled off a rubber glove and wagged his finger. "You are a very, very naughty dog!"

"Lower your voice. The vet said not to stress her." Alex frowned at Rick's grungy t-shirt and old jeans. "What're you doing?"

"Hosting a cocktail party on the rear deck. I'm serving Pine-Sol martinis." Rick snatched the cleaning sponge. "What the fuck does it look like I'm doing? I'm cleaning the bathrooms."

"Why isn't Manuela doing that?"

"She had a dizzy spell when she was loading the dishwasher. I think she hadn't eaten. I made her some eggs and sent her to lie down. Bella's acting up because I haven't walked her yet. I can't deal with this much longer. You need to do something!"

"I am." Alex threw back his head with a sigh. "But I can't move things forward until Jorge finds a place for Manuela."

"How long will that take?"

"I don't know …"

"Are you pushing? You've made him aware how urgent this is, haven't you?"

"I only laid this on him recently, I don't want to unduly pressure him —"

"Why not? He's got five hundred thousand of your dollars to make this work!"

"I'm doing as much as I can. Stop nagging me, will ya?" Rick had been in a low mood ever since they got back from New York. He hadn't told Rick the money for Manuela's new apartment was borrowed. Every little thing was sending Rick into a downward spiral at the moment, that may send him into a big one. "I'll go walk Bella."

"Why aren't you working?"

"I need a break."

"A break? How much work have you done?"

"Enough."

"Get Suki back in the studio if your eye's okay."

"I gotta get my head around which direction to take my work. I need time to think."

"I worry you're losing impetus."

"Leave me to worry about me. You deal with you."

"I wish I could down tools and have some 'me' time. Today I'm pushing the governing body to address our Board's diversity imbalance, then I've got an appointment with Dr. Susskind. I'm doing my best to keep the house running. And, thanks to you letting Tyler stay on in the pool house, I've now got him and Jack mooning around the place like a pair of rutting stags twenty-four seven."

"The lease on Ty's canyon house was up. And Jack's apartment doesn't have space for Ty's truck and equipment. It's only until they find a place together. It's the least I could do to thank Ty for taking care of Bella when we were away."

"The least *you* could do. Exactly! You never even considered how I felt about it."

"I didn't think it was that big of a deal."

"Nothing's a big deal when it suits you and —"

"Leave the bathrooms. Calm down, get dressed, go do what you need to do. Jeez, Rick, you're getting me down, all you do is moan. You're sucking the joy from this place. Come on Bella. I need to get out of here." Alex stomped through the kitchen to get Bella's leash. As her claws pattered on the terrazzo behind him, he spotted a jar of honey on the counter, a bright pink post-it note was stuck to its lid.

Alex didn't even need to read the note to know what it said, the bee on the honey jar's label didn't have a halo.

* * *

After Bella let off steam with a mad dash around the off-leash park, Alex cooled down with a mooch around the neighborhood. The increase in empty homes with tear down notices attached to their crisscross wire fences dispirited him.

Arriving back at the house, he stared gloomily at the turquoise door set into their foliage covered front wall. About to unlock the door, he hesitated. Bella's brown eyes looked up at him, her ears twitched quizzically, perhaps wondering why they weren't going home. Since it was street cleaning day, the Prius would be in the garage rather than parked out front on the street. This meant it wasn't immediately obvious if Rick had left for his meeting. To avoid any further acrimonious confrontations, he decided to swing by next door and say hi to Cayde. That would kill enough time to make sure Rick was out of the house and well on his way.

Putting the pool door's key in his back pocket, Alex walked Bella past the colorful mural of Venice surfers, skaters, bodybuilders, and local landmarks covering Cayde's front wall. His finger stabbed the buzzer beside the speaker grille and industrial metal door. "Yo, it's Alex. You home?"

The door's latch buzzed open.

Entering Cayde's domain always gave Alex a thrill. The exterior yielded no clue to the expansive complex of workshops and galleries behind its high walls and metal doors. Pigments, canvas, and sawdust scented the air. Cayde's two yapping terriers skittered over the paint-spattered concrete floor. With

Bella's propensity for eating unsuitable items, Alex kept her tightly leashed through the open storage area. A wall of shelves held jars of colorful paints, inks, brushes, and pens - below these were banks of wooden drawers with a working sink on top.

Passing through the two small outer galleries, Alex found Cayde at work in his massive main studio with its sixty-foot skylight. Hammering echoed from the outdoor courtyard.

"Hola, chico!" Cayde wiped his hands on his paint splattered linen shirt then petted Bella. "She okay now?"

"Kind of. She's got recurring hemorrhagic gastroenteritis. But the vet's not sure what's causing it. Could be an allergy, or a virus. Could be nerves, she is kinda crazy. Rick's theory is some sketchy breeder dumped her and the other puppies because of congenital defects."

"For real?"

"Hard to say. But you know Rick, once he gets an idea in his head it becomes irrefutable fact. We're monitoring her, but she seems okay for now."

"That's good. Got time for coffee?"

"You bet."

"Leland, you're needed!" Cayde yelled. "The usual?"

"Terrific."

A crop haired, muscular youth wielding a hammer came through the open doors to the courtyard. The young guy did a double take when he saw Alex's haircut. "Hi, you look different."

"Felt like a change. And I gain two hours a day from not having to sweep my hair from my face every five minutes. Summer break, huh? The old man's keeping you busy, I see."

"Payback for those college fees me and his mom are shelling out. Who'd have thought studying economics would be so expensive?" Cayde took the hammer from his son. "Coffee run. Mochachino and a Cortado. Get what you want." Cayde handed Leland a wad of bills. "As long as it doesn't cost more than two bucks. I'm studying my economics."

"Sure, dad" said Leland with a smile while stuffing the money in his jeans pocket.

"And I want change from that!" Cayde called. "And run, boy!" The terriers chased and yapped on Leland's heels. Cayde shook his silver hair and chuckled once the front door slammed shut and the dogs came skittering back. "Let her off if you like," said Cayde noticing Bella staring enviously at his dogs enjoying their freedom.

"If she eats a masterpiece, don't sue me." Alex unclipped her leash. "You've been busy." Alex stared at all the bold multi-color works hanging on the studio walls, swathes of cerulean, indigo, turquoise and whites swirled in wave like patterns on giant canvases.

"Making the most of having my apprentice back home."

"I thought Leland's future was in big business?"

"Leland's been stretching canvases and mixing paint since he could walk. This is in his blood." Cayde gestured to his work, both hanging and in progress. "I want him to do something crazy before surrendering and going to work for a bank. Hell, neither of us followed a career plan and look where doing crazy shit has got us."

Alex let out a rueful chuckle. "To be sure."

"Maybe Leland can find a way to pull business and art together. Lots of tech companies are moving into the neighborhood. Work like ours with paints and brushes could be archaic one day. Art could turn digital. If you don't like the picture, flip a switch and change it!" Cayde looked deep into Alex's face. "You seem down. Everything okay?"

"I noticed a bunch of teardowns while I was out with Bella. Two lots have been razed between Speedway and Oceanfront. The Ray Bradbury house has gone missing too."

"Guessing Martians didn't take it. That was one heck of a cute house."

"A fine old craftsman. I always imagined Ray behind his battered old Corona tapping out stories of fog and mysterious worlds in there. Guess they'll be replaced by the white cubes new builds favor these days."

"Knock that off. Getting misty over the past's a sure sign of embracing old age. And we've done our fair share of changing the neighborhood over the years."

"You're right. I've gotten into a major funk. I thought my MoMA show was going to make me feel like I'd arrived. Instead, I feel like I don't even know where I'm going. I stupidly read some review in an off-the-wall art mag, essentially calling me a lightweight. It's rattled me."

"It's too blue, it's too red, it's too this, it's too that ... blah, blah, blah." Cayde waved a dismissive hand. "They're all commenting, making observations, responding to something *you* made. If you made nothing, they'd have nothing to say. You shouldn't listen to their criticism, and you shouldn't listen to their applause because they're only clapping themselves. A whole industry's blown up from *talking* about art. I see people going around galleries with audio tours stuck in their ears. Those pigeons don't even look at the art, they're listening to someone tell them about it. Everyone's so scared of being confused or looking dumb that they don't engage. Next thing you know, the museums will issue video players so the public don't even have to look at the art, they can watch it on their phones. Don't be scared, Al. Us artists gotta keep jumping off that cliff every day. Taking risks. Loving the fear."

Cayde's words heartened Alex. "Thanks, man."

The entrance door's opening triggered a volley of barking which Bella joined in with, even though this wasn't her territory. Leland's return with coffee and bear claws set serious talk aside. They all sat out in the sunny courtyard, trying to ignore the construction noise from over the wall. Coffee break over, Cayde sent Leland off to carry out more tasks around the studio. Walking Alex and Bella out, Cayde dumped the coffee cups in the recycling. "You guys going to the Eco Fest on the twenty-eighth?"

"You bet. Rick's leading the drum circle," said Alex drily.

Laughing, Cayde put his glasses back on.

"I'm not sure if we'll make it. Ty's tying the knot with his boyfriend that weekend. We'll probably go celebrate after."

"That's terrific news!"

"Yeah. Jack, Ty's boyfriend, is a musician. He plays the flute, he's a sweet guy."

"Thought I heard music from your place."

"We'll have you and Brooke over for dinner to meet him."

"That'd be nice. Give Tyler our congratulations. Now get back to work, do what you want and fuck what anybody else thinks."

"Well, if I've already blown my career it can't get any worse, can it?"

"That's my boy!" said Cayde.

Leaving Cayde's studio, Alex walked Bella home. Fishing for his key, he noticed an odd burning smell in the air. He opened the street door, then the inner door one and let Bella loose. She raced past the pool house and turned the corner onto the patio. A moment later she scuttled back with her tail down. "What's up, girl?" He wondered if the smoke was blowing over from the construction site at the rear. Maybe they were using tarmacadam? Rick had locked the doors onto the patio. As Alex jiggled the key in the doors to the entrance hall, he saw smoke through their glass panels.

Bella barked agitatedly.

"Shit!" Unlocking the door, he dashed through the entrance hall. Smoke filled the passage between the houses. Shielding his eyes, he opened the front door and looked to his right.

Shattering glass crashed to the decking and crackling orange flames shot from Manuela's kitchen window.

FUMAGE

"Manuela!"

Alex grabbed the nozzle and unwound the hose from the reel in the passageway between the houses. He'd called the emergency in to 911, so the fire trucks should be on their way. As the compound had a high front wall and secure doors, the firefighters wouldn't be able to gain immediate access. Although wanting to get water on the blaze and rescue Manuela, he figured he should open up the front entrance between the houses to avoid any confusion over the fire's location. Dropping the hose to do that first, he realized Bella might dash out if the front entrance were left wide open. Or was trying to put out the flames the first thing he should do? He picked up the hose. Smoke in the passageway stung his eyes. He hoped it didn't fuck up his eye treatment. His mind froze in panic. If this were man overboard or an imminent capsize, he'd instinctively know what to do first. Prioritizing keeping Bella secure, he dropped the hose again, opened the main house's front door and went inside.

Bella did her best to shove past his knees as he wriggled in. Getting under his feet, nearly tripping him over, she careened in circles, barking wildly. Grabbing her collar, he dragged her across the entrance hall, opened the doors to the patio, shoved her outside and shut them. She jumped up, her paws frantically scrabbling at the glass.

Heart thumping in his ears, Alex dashed back to the passageway and slammed the front door to keep smoke out of the house. Pulling his t-shirt over his mouth, he picked up the hose. His clumsy fingers fumbled with the spigot. The water took several long seconds to fill the hose's length. Shielding his eyes, he sprayed water over the flames licking from Manuela's kitchen window. Only five feet separated the houses. He feared flying embers may set the main house on fire. Pivoting, he played the hose over its side wall, roof and around the guest bedroom's window.

A siren's wail let him know the fire truck was closing in. Things were crashing down inside Manuela's quarters. The choking smoke grew denser. Tugging his t-shirt down from his mouth, he yelled, "Manuela!"

No answer.

Covering his mouth and nose again, he hosed her front door. Stepping back, he kicked the door. It didn't budge. He dropped the hose. It bucked and twisted, gushing water everywhere, including over his legs. His waterlogged training shoes squished as he stumbled down the passage. He flung open the double doors between the main house and the small house, squelched past the garbage cans and punched the button to raise the street door. As the metal roller door clanked up, he raced back along the passageway, slipping in sooty water sloshing over the deck. Picking up the hose, he went back to spraying the flames from the kitchen window. The entire side wall could catch alight any second. He wondered if Manuela may have escaped up the external rear stairs linking her apartment to the small house's upper floor. But if she had, she'd have responded to his calls or made her way out by now, wouldn't she?

Slamming doors, yells and walkie-talkie crackles were followed by heavy footfalls of firefighters' boots running onto the property. "Anyone in there?" barked a yellow suited firefighter from under his helmet's brim.

"Our housekeeper." Alex wiped gray sputum from his chin with the back of his hand.

"Stand back, sir," ordered the fireman.

Alex whipped the hose aside, shut off the spigot and flattened himself against the wall. Two more yellow suited firefighters barged past, dragging in a line. Donning breathing equipment, the first guys on the scene stepped aside as the crew's hose shot high-pressure water on the flames in the kitchen window. White steam mixed with acrid black smoke. The firefighters directed their water jet around the entrance door. Turning the water aside, a firefighter in breathing equipment smashed the lock with his ax. He kicked the door. It swung open with a crunch of splintering wood. The firefighters operating the line inched forward, shooting water inside Manuela's quarters.

More firemen arrived on site, cramming into the passageway between the houses.

The yellow suited firefighters in breathing equipment entered Manuela's home. Dreading what they'd find inside, Alex fought back images of Manuela prone on her bed overcome by smoke or lying on the floor charred by flames. Cursing himself for hanging out with Cayde rather than coming straight home, he sheltered in the recess of the main house's entrance.

An anguished scream startled him. Wiping soot from the glass to peer inside, he saw Manuela enter the house from the doors to the patio. She must have come in through the pool door from the street. "Don't let Bella in!" he bellowed. Too late, the crazed, barking dog bulldozed her way past Manuela's legs.

Manuela dropped the brown paper sack she was carrying. It fell to the parquet floor with an explosive smash. She flung the front door open. "*Dios mío!*" she cried, crossing herself.

"Stay inside!" Alex shouted, pushing her back.

But Manuela forced her way past him. "Oh, no. Oh, no!"

Bella's snout poked through the open front door. Alex manhandled her back in and slammed the door, painfully bashing his wrist in the process.

Manuela stumbled through the firefighters.

"That's her. She wasn't in there," Alex shouted to the fire crew while pointing at Manuela.

Manuela jostled her way through the firefighters to the small house's side door.

"Keep back, ma'am!" A firefighter restrained her as she tried to open the door.

"Miss Danielle! She's up there!" Manuela brushed the fireman aside.

Pulling off his sooty mask, a firefighter staggered from Manuela's apartment. "Clean inside!"

"Is there someone in that house?" The firefighter squinted at the upstairs windows while restraining Manuela.

Alex pushed through the mayhem and filthy water. "There's nobody up there."

"She is! I see her!" cried Manuela.

"She gets confused," Alex explained to the firefighter.

"You're certain the house is empty?" the firefighter asked Alex.

"She's up there!" Manuela shouted defiantly. "This is where she belongs. Here, with me, the baby and her things!"

"Danielle's dead! She's gone. They're both gone! And they're never coming back!"

Manuela's body convulsed with grief. "No, no!" Her fingers reached to the fire crew, their heavy boots trampling filthy water in and out of her little home. "This is all I have." She clutched her chest. "It is my life …" About to collapse, Alex supported her.

A firefighter rushed to Manuela's aid. He cupped an oxygen mask over her face. "This lady needs assistance. Get her onto the street."

Another fireman dashed forward to carry Manuela through the chaos.

"We need an ambulance here at the Hampton Drive call-out…" a fireman barked into his shoulder walkie-talkie.

Above the bedlam in the passageway, Bella let out a heartrending howl. Checking she wasn't behind the front door, Alex hurried into the main house, treading foul water into the entrance hall. He couldn't see the dog. Approaching the doors to the patio, something crunched underfoot. He'd stepped on a brown paper sack with a jar of honey inside. The sack was torn, jagged shards of glass mixed with sticky amber liquid were splashed over the parquet.

Outside, Bella lay on her side by the pool, her ribs heaving rapidly. A violent spasm wracked the golden curls on her body. Kneeling beside her, Alex checked her mouth. Honey was smeared around it. Bella coughed. A plume of bright pink froth spluttered from her gullet, a splinter of glass along with it. "Bella, baby, no, no, no …"

Bella struggled for breath. Pink foam dribbled from her lolling mouth.

Preparing to lift her up and rush her to the animal clinic, Alex sensed her energy failing. Tuning out the chaos on the other side of his property, and the wail of another siren, he creakily sat down on the ground beside her. Stroking her soft golden ear, he spoke softly and gently. "It's okay baby, I'm here."

The pool door opened. "Al, what the …"

Alex held up his hand to stop Cayde from speaking.

Cayde looked between him and Bella.

Connecting with Cayde's eyes, Alex shook his head. He knew it was hopeless. He went back to speaking to his dog. "You'll be okay, our good girl. Our beloved little girl."

Cayde trod softly towards Alex and Bella.

Willing the air to become silent and still, Alex carried on rubbing Bella's ear and speaking loving words.

Kneeling beside them, Cayde rested his hand on Alex's shoulder.

The moment came.

The last shuddering breath departed Bella's body.

And although Alex couldn't see her velvet brown eyes, he knew the light behind them had gone out for good.

* * *

A pall of grief hung over the house, as tangible as the smoke willfully clinging to the furnishings and drapes.

Alex had walked through the rest of the day following the fire and Bella's death without being present. He'd watched from over his own shoulder as he and Cayde had carried Bella's body over the pool to his studio and covered her with a plastic sheet. He called Rick to let him know what had happened. Dreading recriminations, accusations and cries of 'I told you so,' once he got over the shock, Rick's quiet acceptance of events was a relief.

Blame wasn't required.

Alex couldn't feel any worse than he did.

While Alex accompanied Manuela to the hospital, Cayde and Leland dropped everything to take care of matters at the house. The fire department needed to ascertain what caused the blaze. Apparently, the police department had shown up. They promptly departed when the source of ignition was unequivocally identified as the pan of rice Manuela had left simmering while she ran an errand. The pan had boiled dry, setting light to the cabinets above. The smoke alarm required by code was fitted and functioning. It must have gone off … only no-one had been around to hear.

Although not voiced, Alex knew Rick carried his own weight of guilt. The sudden remembered errand which led to Manuela's absence was running to the market to replace the wrong brand of honey she'd bought again the day before. Although too late to change anything, Rick called Dr. Amira at the animal clinic. The veterinarian reassured them that even if Bella had swallowed glass, it was unlikely to have had such an immediate and catastrophic effect. The most likely cause of death was an undiagnosed weakness or malformation of the blood vessels in her upper digestive tract which had suddenly and catastrophically ruptured.

Alex stayed with Manuela at the hospital until Jorge arrived. The sudden shock had triggered atrial fibrillation and the doctors wanted to keep her in to monitor it. The damage to her apartment was too great for her to return to her former home anyway. The next day, along with Jorge, Alex picked through her belongings and packed up anything salvageable. Her bedroom and bathroom were relatively unscathed, so at least she had her clothes and familiar personal items. But her living-room, kitchen, and their contents were write-offs. Although polite, Alex detected a simmering hostility from Manuela's son, almost as if his need to determine how best to care for his mother from here on in was a major inconvenience. Eventually Jorge decided when Manuela was discharged from hospital, he'd find an elder care facility in Rancho del Rey where she could recuperate until she was well enough to live independently again.

On hearing the sad news, Thaddeus immediately offered a place on his property to lay Bella to rest. He called the lush leafy spot on the crest his 'Enchanted Hill.' Tyler came along to dig the grave and, as sunset fell, Jack played 'Annie's Song' on his flute. Alex and Rick reverentially placed the wicker basket containing Bella's remains, along with her collar and name tag, into the ground. Thaddeus's white jacketed houseman served Vieux Carré cocktails off a silver tray as the city lights sparkled into life. Tyler filled in the grave while they toasted Bella's life and remembered their unique, loving, if slightly insane, dog.

"This way she'll have playmates on the other side," said Thaddeus as they made their way back to his house, "all my old dogs are buried on the Enchanted Hill. Along with several of my old lovers." Thaddeus looked cheekily over his shoulder at Alex and Rick, savoring Jack and Tyler's shocked expressions since they were not familiar with his wicked sense of humor.

* * *

Although Rick wasn't happy about it, Alex was glad he'd let Tyler stay on in the pool house. He'd been a supportive and reassuring presence over the past week. Rick had been out a lot, not getting back till real late and often in a distant mood if he should make it home for dinner. He was fulfilling his filming commitment on *The Belles of Bel Air*, putting in fourteen-hour workdays on the current filming block. Apparently, these 'workdays' involved Cristina and her friends getting dolled up in designer clothes to attend polo tournaments, jewelry design launches and charity fashion shows while acting like they were mundane occurrences in their daily lives. Some minor slight or incident would occur between the 'friends' at said events and then 'who said what about whom' would be regurgitated and rehashed at the following event. Alex jokingly called the show *Rich People Filling up their Empty Lives.* Well, he said it once. Although Rick wasn't over the moon about the show, he got huffy and defensive should anyone else criticize it.

  Not having Bella to walk freed up a couple of extra hours each day for Alex to stew about his new work. He'd been dabbling with the abstracts, but his heart kept coming back to the layered pieces. Suki was back. The other day he'd had her build one up using pages from supermarket tabloids topped off by a vintage 'Maps to the Stars' tour of Hollywood homes. Once she'd shellacked the papers, laid them on top of each other and let them set, he'd worked a power sander over them. He loved the random, sometimes oddly meaningful, juxtapositions revealed, like when part of a scandal sheet's lurid headline peeped out beside the promise of seeing where Lucille Ball actually lived.

  The foundry had delivered two more of the standing metal pieces. For the past hour, he'd been poised in the studio staring at the one with a single gash down its center. The rip was straight and elegant. It had been opened out from the middle and resembled a vertical eye. Spraying this panel gold would look good, or better yet, covering it in gold leaf would heighten its brutal sensuality. The opened slash invited penetration, yet the edges of its curled-out metal lips promised injury.

Alex heard a growl.

It was his stomach.

Realizing it was past eight o'clock, and he hadn't eaten since lunch, he needed to line his stomach for his evening meds. The master suite's dark windows appeared empty and forlorn in the twilight. Down to the left, a lamp glowed in the pool house's circular bedroom window. Wondering if Tyler and Jack, if he was around, were in the mood for ordering in or hopping over to Martin's on the Beach, Alex crossed the pool bridge.

Hearing flute music, he knew Jack was home. The pool house's side door was ajar. Giving a perfunctory knock, Alex walked in. "Rick's shooting late on *Rich People Filling* …" The words died on his lips. The aroma of weed hit him.

Jack sat on the chair at the foot of the bed, one leg draped over its arm, totally naked.

Mortally embarrassed, Alex turned on his heel so suddenly he smashed his face on the doorframe. "Shit."

Slinging a madras pareo around his hips, Jack rushed over. "You okay?"

Alex rubbed his nose. "Apologies. I shouldn't have barged in on you like that."

"You looking for Ty?"

"I was about to go get something to eat. Wondered if you guys were in the mood for sharing."

"Ty had a heavy day at work. His head was banging when he got home. He just hopped in the shower."

"Come to the house when you're ready. We can order in or go out depending on how Ty feels." Alex's eyes flicked to the joint on the nightstand.

Jack noticed. "You got a problem with that?"

"Oh, no. Just surprised you smoke because you don't drink."

"Alcohol's a manmade toxin. Pot's a natural high. And a natural pain reliever. Makes the music sweeter too."

"Your music's sweet enough as it is. I envy your gift."

"Ty won't be long. Stick around till he's out the shower and see what he feels like." Jack went to the nightstand, picked up the joint and offered it to Alex.

With a half-smile, Alex accepted it between his finger and thumb. Taking a deep drag, he held it … let go. "Haven't done that in a while."

Jack shook his head questioningly.

"I used to. I liked it. Maybe I liked it a little too much." He passed the joint back to Jack.

"Do you play?"

"Eh?"

"An instrument."

"Oh, the guitar, a little back in the day." Alex flexed the misshapen knuckles on his right hand. "I was no good and that's totally out now. I thought the saxophone could be cool once. I had a seductive image of me playing some mellow notes on the beach. A friend had one. I tried but couldn't coax a single note from the wretched thing. So I blew off that idea."

"People think playing a wind instrument's a matter of blowing hard. It's far more nuanced than that. Where the breath comes from and how you support and control it's the hard part. Fingering's pretty straightforward compared to that. Here." Jack put down the joint, picked up his flute and patted the bed. "Give it a try."

Chilled from the hit and Jack's easy presence, Alex sat on the bed.

Jack pressed his tush up against Alex's. "You're right-handed?" Jack passed the flute to Alex and reached around to position his hands on it.

The weight pulled Alex's arms down. "Heavier than it looks."

"Now to warm up your lips." With his right arm around Alex's shoulder supporting the flute, Jack massaged Alex's lips with his left.

Alex giggled.

"Slacken those lips, mister."

Releasing tension from his face, Alex let Jack's finger flap his lips up and down.

"Now hum," ordered Jack.

Alex cracked up as a *bub, bub, bub, bub* sound came out of his mouth around Jack's finger.

"You got nice soft lips. Good! Now the breath." Parting his pareo to move freely, Jack scampered around on the bed to kneel behind Alex.

Alex felt Jack's hands cup his lower rib cage.

"Think about widening down here. Push my hands apart as you breathe in."

Concentrating on his breath, Alex closed his eyes.

"Fill your belly with air. Don't pop your stomach out. Think of the air going down rather than in. Deep down, like you're filling your nuts."

Jack slid his hand in the waistband of Alex's jeans. He pressed his flattened palm into Alex's abdomen and stroked down to his pubes. "Fill yourself wide and deep. A couple more times. In. Out. In. Now for the embouchure. Purse your lips to the mouthpiece. Don't blow over the hole. Breathe over the hole. Visualize your breath caressing the mouthpiece. And out …"

Alex let his breath go. Amazingly, he produced a note.

"Cool!" said Jack in delight.

"Boy, that's a killer! I couldn't keep that up for long." Gasping as he lowered the flute, Alex rolled his shoulder to shake off the ache.

"You get used to it over time." Still kneeling behind him, Jack massaged Alex's right shoulder.

Without the flute in his hands, Alex became ultra-aware of how close Jack's body was.

Jack worked his thumbs deep into Alex's shoulder and neck muscles.

"Ah." Chills and tingles rippled over Alex's body. Jack had magic in his fingers. Surrendering to pleasure, he realized the tingles were spreading to his cock. "Jack, um …" Alex jumped up. Feeling dizzy, he dropped back to the bed and touched his hand to his forehead.

Jack's pareo fell away as he jumped down. Naked, he kneeled at Alex's feet. "Did the deep breathing give you a head rush?"

"Maybe."

"Put your feet up." Jack lifted Alex's feet up so he could lie flat. Then he came and laid beside him, soothingly stroking his arm. "You okay now?"

"Haven't smoked in a while. Yeah, I'm fine."

"Good. Now I've taught you how to blow over the hole, on our next lesson I could show you where to put your fingers." Taking Alex's hand, Jack lifted it and let it hover over his own erect cock. "If you'd like that?"

Alex's head swam. He hadn't intimately touched any man other than Rick for over ten years. "Jack, what about Ty?"

"You're right. We should wait." Jack let go of Alex's hand. "He loves to watch. Hey, feel better for that?"

Alex raised his head, and his hand, to see Tyler emerge from the bathroom, a striped towel around his waist.

Seeing Alex with Jack on the bed, Tyler's mouth moved, but he didn't speak.

"Been giving Alex a music lesson." Jack picked up the spliff. He offered it to Tyler with one hand and patted the bed with the other. "Was telling him a trio can more fun than a duet."

Tyler sleepwalked to the bed.

Alex swung down his legs. "I need to go eat."

Springing up from the bed, Jack closed in. He passed the joint to Tyler, sandwiching Alex between himself and Tyler.

Feeling Jack's naked body pressing up behind him and Tyler's almost naked body pressed up against his front was sending all kinds of conflicting messages through Alex's body.

Tyler took the spliff.

Alex watched Tyler's strawberry lips close around it. He took a drag. Through the towel, Alex felt Tyler growing hard. Alex shuddered as Jack's moist mouth sucked down on the back of his neck. Reaching around, Jack ripped apart his denim shirt's pearl snaps. Momentarily, Alex's bare chest and stomach connected directly with Tyler's. Stepping back, Tyler watched Jack's hands caress Alex's pecs and toy with his nipples.

Never having experienced anything like this before, the overdose of male flesh was too delicious to bear. And this was only the touch of skin, what more delights could be on offer? Alex saw Tyler drinking in Jack's hands on his chest. Lust flashed behind Tyler eyes. Jack's hands trailed down his stomach to unbutton his jeans. Tyler dropped his eyes to watch. Feeling Jack's fingers about to release his aching erection, Alex's resolve was weakening. About to surrender to the moment, he raised his gaze to meet Tyler's. Desire behind his eyes had been replaced by disquiet. Then Tyler's eyes flared at Jack. Suddenly feeling extremely uneasy, Alex extricated himself from the two men. He fastened his jeans. "You guys are high. Go easy on that shit. I'm going to grab a bite at Martin's. I'll be there for a while if you want to come eat."

Picking up his meds from the kitchen and dropping by the master suite for his wallet, Alex beat a hasty retreat. Passing the pool house on his way out, the blinds were lowered and voices raised. Settling into his regular booth on the terrace, Alex wondered if Tyler and Jack would be along, but kind of knew they wouldn't.

All was quiet when he got back from dinner.

The pool house was dark.

Alex showered, with cold water, slipped on a terrycloth robe and got into bed. Preparing to read, he put on his glasses.

But his mind was distracted. Instead, he stuck in his earphones and listened to Fleetwood Mac on his iPod.

Having dozed off, the opening and closing of doors and a far-off rattling in the kitchen woke him. Blinking sleepily, he saw Rick kick off his shoes while unbuttoning his shirt. It was an unnecessary question, the look on Rick's face telegraphed the answer, but he asked it anyway, "Bad day?"

"Thaddeus resigned from the Board. He's withdrawing the loan of his entire collection." Rick tossed his shirt on the ottoman.

Alex got onto his elbow. "What made him do that?"

Rick undid his pants. "The diversity report I persuaded the museum to commission backfired. An internal memo with the input from Hulton and the governing body got leaked. It described Thaddeus as 'minority, ethnic.' No mention of his years as a trustee and collector. I was labeled, 'minority, sexual.' Cristina, because of her Greek and Jewish heritage, checked the 'minority, ethnic' box too. The idiots thought they were proving how diverse our Board is, but instead they insulted half of them. Seven long serving members are walking, leaving Hulton with a WASP majority. Hulton will claim the Conservatory was acting in the interests of equality and I'm the one who put the gun in her hand. I'm quitting too. There's no point in carrying on if no-one wants to listen to me."

Rick stripped off and went to the bathroom. Ten minutes later, he came back massaging night cream into his face.

"Do you know what your problem is?" Alex asked.

"I've got the feeling you're about to tell me."

"You have an uncontrollable urge to manipulate. The world's a more complicated place than it used to be."

Rick got into bed. "Thanks for the sympathy."

"No, I'm sorry how this turned out. Thaddeus is a good man. He deserves better. If the Conservatory's as fucked as it seems, you're probably better off out of it as well."

"How was your evening?" Rick pumped two shots of moisturizer into his palm.

"I swung by the pool house to see if Ty wanted to go eat with me. Jack was there and well, he was doing ... he was doing ..." Alex wondered how to phrase events.

"He was doing ...? Doing what?" Rick asked in irritation. "The Locomotion?"

"Smoking pot."

"Thought I smelled weed, although it's white noise in this neighborhood."

"Anyway, while we waited for Ty to come out of the shower Jack was showing me how to play the flute and he kind of made a move on me. I think he wanted a threesome."

Rick stopped massaging the cream into his hands. He looked at Alex with wide eyes then burst out laughing. "Were you on the wacky baccy too?"

"What's so implausible?" asked Alex, mildly affronted.

"Jack and Ty are seriously hot. And young. And ..."

"And?"

"And we're old. The only reason anyone's interested in our bodies these days is for medical research."

About to state the details of being sandwiched between Jack and Ty to prove that they apparently did seem to have more interest in him than just as a med school cadaver, Alex thought the better of it. "How it seemed to me."

"They're getting married next week." Rick pulled the sheets up to his chin. "If you weren't mistaken and that's what the younger generation believe marriage is all about then I'm disappointed."

"There's that Catholic upbringing of yours again."

"Talking of which, momma's agreed to do the commentary."

"Good news."

Rick didn't respond.

"Isn't it?"

"On one condition."

"Which is?"

"That I go over and supervise the recording."

"And will you?"

"I resent momma using everything a bargaining tool, but Ileanna was right. Momma should have been home months ago. I was angry with Jorge for being so cavalier about Manuela's well-being, but I'm acting exactly the same way with momma. I know Patti's not telling me everything. I really should go."

"What's stopping you then?"

"I'm scared of what I may find." Rick turned out his light. "Would you come with me? I don't want to face this alone. I could do with your support. Please?"

"No way! I loathe flying at the best of times, then being trashed by your mad mother in a foreign country after fifteen hours of airborne purgatory's too much for any man to bear." Alex put out his light.

They lay silently in the dark.

Alex reached out to Rick.

Sniffling, Rick pulled away and turned his back.

Maybe Rick couldn't believe anyone else desired him because he didn't anymore. He'd wanted to be honest and open with Rick, but maybe he should have just gone with the moment, savored a new, erotic experience and lied.

RECTO / VERSO

Rick overslept and was running late in the bathroom.

Alex found it odd being alone in the kitchen at breakfast. He'd always come in from his morning swim to find the place a hive of activity - Bella crunching kibble, Manuela chopping and preparing for lunch or dinner, and Rick's finger poised on the blender ready to froth up one of his godawful health shakes. The morning sun illuminated the art deco stained-glass window above the sink. The rosy glow of red tulips and soft green leaves radiated a wistful melancholy today.

Alex put on the coffee. Taking advantage of Rick's absence to dodge a broccoli and sprouted mung bean smoothie, he fixed himself a bowl of oatmeal with honey and blueberries. When Rick finally did show up, he entered the kitchen with a dramatic sigh. "You gonna be filming late tonight?"

"Nope. Today we have a lunch at Cristina's to chew over some earth-shattering topic like themes for Joli's midsummer ball. Hopefully that's all. Although someone, probably Augusta as she loves stirring shit to hog camera time, is bound to bring up the museum business. Cristina being appointed to the Board's a major storyline. Trust something like a massed resignation to hit while we're shooting. There's a real possibility the museum will go under because of this."

"How inconvenient for reality to intrude on reality TV."

Rick spotted the cup in Alex's hand. "You know what the doctor told you about coffee."

"Only one cup. I needed a lift ..."

Simultaneously, they both looked at the spot where Bella's food and water bowls had sat.

Rick sighed again then foraged in the refrigerator.

Alex drained his cup, rinsed it and set it on the drainer.

Closing the refrigerator, Rick came away with a slice of cold pizza in his hand.

Being a stickler for healthy eating, kicking off the day with leftover pizza was out of character. "Is the museum business the only thing getting you down?"

"Momma played on my mind all night long. I have such mixed feelings about the thought of going home."

"Home?" The way Rick said that so naturally and casually disquieted Alex. "Is that how you still think of Italy?"

"Not the country as such, more the situation. It'd be nice to see Patti again. But going back to the Lido house … the past hangs heavy there."

"I always wonder about people who speak different languages. When you sleep, what language do you dream in?"

"I haven't given it much thought. But then again, I don't dream much these days." Rick went to get his things together.

Alex remained in the kitchen, deep in thought. He needed to make some calls to book contractors to repair the fire damage. The door from the master suite to the patio clacked shut as Rick left for work. Alex wandered around the house. He looked at the paintings and sculptures. A Ken Price Japanese Tree Frog Cup signed on the reverse in pencil, a black-and-white Serge Hambourg photo of the '68 Paris protests, Rod's 'word' painting - the legend *FREEDOM* written in razor wire over a clear blue sky. When Danielle was alive, they'd thrown big parties for the local art community. Alex recalled one such night when Rod had removed the vase of lilies masking his painting, silently depositing it on the floor with an air of disdain.

Going over to his studio, Alex put on his paint splattered glasses and fired up the Mac. As his inbox filled, he considered the 'hole' works in progress. Did they have a right and wrong side? The gashes and tears in the metal panels needed to protrude, tempting the viewer to come close and peer into them yet their sharp edges threatening injury to anyone who did. But how best to show the layered paper ones? Should they dangle freely in the center of the room? Or be hung on windows? Looking *through* them rather than *at* them was their whole point. Scrolling down his inbox, he spotted a message from **F. SCOTT** with the subject: "**Fantastic**!" Intrigued, he clicked and read ...

$1.1 million and u thought it may get bought in! Miss Greely's flip did u 1 big favor @Christies. Call u l8r. Off 2 Encino 2 set up a Sweet 16. Hope a nose job's top of the kid's gift list! xx

Alex chuckled at Scotty's email patois. Given his MoMA show's mixed reviews and Xander Chen's coolness in their wake, he'd eliminated *Sphere 4* going into auction from his consciousness. An internet search confirmed his piece had achieved a surprisingly healthy price. Although the appreciation in his work's value would bolster Christie's and Mariah Greely's bank balances rather than his or Neroli's, he allowed himself a momentary glow of pride that his work was desirable. About to see if he could discover the buyer's identity, a knock on the studio's door distracted him. "Yeah?"

Tyler shifted uneasily on the threshold. "Can you talk?"

"Sure." Alex powered down the Mac.

Tyler, dressed for work in combat shorts, boots, fatigue shirt and neckcloth, his ginger blond hair tied back, tentatively entered the studio. "Uncle Alex, about last night."

Taking off his glasses, Alex rubbed the bridge of his nose. "We were all high. Forget it."

Tyler folded his arms, the pressure of his fingertips making white marks under the golden fuzz on his freckled forearms. "Jack may have been high, but he shouldn't have done what he did. He can be ... easygoing with other guys. I mean, well ... *we* can be easygoing. But he crossed a line. Sorry he put you in an uncomfortable position." Regret clouded Tyler's sweet eyes.

Alex hated seeing the boy upset. "Look, it's okay. Forget it."

"It won't happen again. Um …" Tyler chewed his lip "Jack's gone. I kind of ended everything."

"Oh, Ty." Alex stroked Tyler's back. "That's a shame. How you guys roll in private's none of my business. It seemed like you had a good thing going."

"Hah." Tyler let out a bitter laugh. "Whenever my life's running smoothly I've gotten used to something screwing it up. You know how Jack and me were finding a new place to live together, but now …"

"The pool house is yours. As long as you need. Get to work."

"Ugh," Tyler pouted. "My head's not in a work-space."

"Mine neither. Limitless possibilities and choices usually excite me. Today they overwhelm me. Maybe I made a colossal misjudgment with these babies." Alex went to the gold monolith with the slash down its middle. The flesh toned one with shrapnel protrusions stood beside it.

"I don't understand them, but you can't ignore them. They're intimidating." Tyler fingered a puckered hole in the skin toned panel.

"Careful. Those edges are sharp –"

"Yowzer!" Tyler snatched back his hand and sucked his finger.

"I told you it was sharp!" Alex leaned into him.

Tyler waved his intact finger. "Kidding!"

Alex shook his head in frustrated amusement. "Back when I shared a studio with the guys, on days when the work wasn't flowing we'd grab our boards and hit the surf."

"This feels like one of those days." Tyler mooched around Alex's abstracts. "I've seen your boards in the pool store. Today's gonna hit the mid-eighties. Wanna play hooky?"

"I gotta work."

Tyler's face crumpled like a disappointed kid's. "Aw, I don't have anyone else to do that kind of shit with. Jack didn't like swimming, let alone surfing."

"It's not Rick's scene either," said Alex. "Nah, dudes over sixty look kinda lame on boards."

"You lived on the beach. If anyone's gonna look lame on a board it'll be me! You can coach me. Surfer dude masterclass!"

Alex was still smarting from Bella's death and Manuela's inglorious exit from his house. Tyler was bummed from splitting with Jack. Didn't they both deserve a little R and R? "Fuck it. Think I got a suit you can squeeze that flabby ass of yours into."

"Hey!" Tyler pulled back his chin in insulted outrage.

Alex patted Tyler's tightly muscled butt. "Kidding."

* * *

Alex and Tyler walked their boards down Brooks Avenue, past the corner café's red umbrellas, across the boardwalk and onto the beach. Alex contemplated the surf. "Let's head towards the breakwater." He pointed to the line of rocks jutting into the ocean. "The sand banks up round there. We can pick up some nice rights."

"Huh?"

"When the wave breaks to your right on its way in."

"Told you, masterclass!"

"See if you're still saying that when my knees give out and I'm dragging my dick into shore," said Alex as they trudged across the sand.

A flock of sandpipers were picking around on the shoreline, venturing farther out as the tide receded and scuttling back up the beach as it swooshed in. "They're playing chicken!" said Tyler zipping up his short-john wetsuit.

Tyler's mixed metaphor of sandpipers playing chicken made Alex chuckle. Surfers were bobbing on the waves, but the water wasn't overly crowded.

Tyler secured the board's leash to his ankle.

Alex approached the ocean's edge, a little trepidatious about getting in.

"You cool?" Tyler came up behind.

"Haven't done this in a while," Alex said over his shoulder, checking his own ankle leash was attached okay.

"Me neither. If anyone's gonna look like a grom it'll be me. Let's do this thing. Who hoo!"

Inhaling deeply, Alex watched Tyler's freckled calves splash through the surf. "Here goes nothing," Alex muttered as he followed. After a moment's unsteadiness when feeling the ocean's fresh chill on his skin, he felt relief. His steadfast friend, the sea, was unchanged. Once in deep enough, they got up onto their boards and paddled out.

Sitting on his board, Alex figured floating was his favorite part of surfing. He loved the meditative state of getting in sync with the sea, becoming one with nature, sensing the rhythm of the waves, listening for your gut to tell you when the perfect one was on its way. The waves were mellow this morning, maybe too mellow. He was debating over moving down to the Fisherman's Pier, where larger waves broke but the rip could be fierce, when a barely perceptible change took place in the ocean's color. "Action!"

Hearing Alex's shout, Tyler shot him a thumbs up. Increasingly large white crested rollers broke against the breakwater. Surfers nearest the breakwater paddled out to sea. Tyler was about to follow their lead.

"Hey!"

Tyler flicked water off his hair to look around.

Alex made a 'hold it' gesture. Some Benny paddling to the heart of the lineup would really get them pissed. "Let those guys catch the first set!" The surf was building nicely. "Ride these out!" Alex yelled to Tyler. The guys who'd been waiting the longest could take these waves, they were ankle busters anyway.

Surfers farther out paddled away from the incoming wave's peak, checking over their shoulders as they built up speed. The wave rolled under them. A couple of guys had positioned themselves perfectly, popped up and took the ride. One guy had spent too long in the lineup judging the wave and let it wash under him. Another guy completely misread the wave. That dude's board flipped, royally dumping him.

Allowing the surfers before them to catch the next couple of rides, Alex yelled to Tyler, "Move on up!" The next set of waves would be on them in around five minutes. Getting into position, they paddled around in anticipation. Alex felt promising movement in the water. Staring out to sea confirmed the show was on. He yelled to Tyler, "Get down!"

Tyler looked puzzled.

Alex made a fist, then flattened his hand.

Getting the message, Tyler lay face down on his board.

Blocking out the pain in his shoulders and blinking salt spray from his eyes, Alex paddled his arms to build momentum.

Tyler followed Alex's lead.

Having built up speed, getting into top paddle gear wasn't too much effort. Looking behind him, Alex saw a clean wave headed inland. This was it! His arms flailed faster to match the wave's pace. Tyler, good boy, was matching the wave's pace. The guys who'd been sitting were only just now getting flat on their boards. Since he and Tyler were down and paddling, they were ahead of the game. They'd easily take this wave … if he could pop up in time.

Alex craned his neck. The swell was on his tail. Pressing the full weight of his shoulders and chest into the board, he forced its nose into the wave, paddling for all his might. The board became weightless. Putting his hands under his chest, he got on his toe tips and planked. Would he be limber enough to pop up? Would he have a heart attack? Would be go blind? Fuck it. Only one way to find out.

Alex arched his back and lunged his right foot between his hands. The dude to his left let his weight fall back, his board tipped, flipping the guy off. Keeping low and forward, Alex lifted his hands, driving the board's tip into the wave with his leading foot.

Elation!

He was riding the wave, the wind whistling through his hair. He was seventeen again! Maybe, not seventeen, but a passable thirty-five.

Putting his weight forward, Alex drove his board's nose hard into the wave. Knees bent, as much as they could, he twisted from his hips to trim left.

Disaster!

He lost control, taking a brutal dive into the wave's pit.

Wipeout …

Passing overhead, the tide's rush drove him down. Holding his breath, he wrapped his arms around his head and hoped to heck no-one smashed into him. In the wave's swirling cauldron, his leash wrapped round his leg. He couldn't untangle himself and protect his head at the same time. The following wave caught the board, its tow dragging his leg behind him. Shot through with agonizing pain, afraid he'd dislocated his hip, and still protecting his head, he surfaced for air. Tyler had made it to the shore, doing a little rock dance as he hopped off his board. Blowing snot from his mouth and nose, Alex swam with one arm, supporting himself on the board with his other.

Spotting Alex was in trouble, Tyler unfastened his leash, ditched his own board and came swimming out.

"You okay?" Tyler splashed towards him.

"Banged up my leg." Alex's foot hit bottom. The tide's momentum carried him forward. He stumbled. Tyler's strong arms caught him mid-fall, just before he smashed his jaw on his board. Staggering from the sea, he doubled over to cough up water while Tyler unfastened his leash and took care of the board.

Carrying both boards past the lifeguards' tower while Alex got his breath back, Tyler upended them in the sand by the palms.

Unzipping his suit, and feeling like a total dweeb, Alex limped across the beach. "Good ride?"

"You bet! But this suit of yours is turning me into a hunchback." Tyler wriggled his arms out and rolled down the wetsuit's top. He untied his hair, fluffed it out and leaned on his elbows. "Wanna go again?"

"Give me ten minutes." Alex massaged his painful thigh.

Tyler scratched his ginger-blond chest hair. "That undertow nearly wiped me out too."

"Don't humor the old man. There was no undertow. I fucked up the timing. I'm out of practice."

"Then we should do this every day."

"Let's discuss that with my leg tomorrow," said Alex with a laugh followed by another cough. "There used to be an old pier up there." Alex waved his hand to the right. "The rips and currents around the piles of the old Ocean Park were something else. And if the pylons didn't take you out, the Zephyrs would hurl glass and concrete at any out-of-towners who got in their way."

"Sounds awesome," Tyler exclaimed gleefully.

"It was."

Clasping his hands behind his head, Tyler stretched on the sand. "This is the best day I've had for an age. Totally epic."

"Ty, you don't have to answer this if you don't want to, but last night, you and Jack … is that the kind of thing you often do? You know, with other guys?"

"If the mood hits, why not?"

"But you guys were getting married?"

"We're good together. But Jack needs more."

"And you're okay with that?"

"I thought so."

"I don't want to sound like a fuddy-duddy —"

"Jesus, just saying that makes you sound like one!"

"Okay, a square."

"Even worse! Let go of the seventies. Stop acting like an old man! You're cool."

"You and Jack, you're always … careful when you're with other men?"

"Yeah. We get regularly tested and always play safe."

"Good." Falling silent, they watched the seabirds. "You know, an artist can have a picture nearly perfect and think one more stroke will make it better. But that one extra stroke nearly always ruins a perfect picture."

"Nice allegory, Uncle Al."

"You don't always realize how precious nearly perfect can be until you lose it. Are you sure it's over between you and Jack?"

"I never got jealous before. But seeing him with you was different." Letting go of that thought, Tyler pulled up his suit and wriggled his arms in. "Ready to go again?"

The water was getting busy.

Alex glanced at the lifeguard's tower. A girl and guy in red were raising the yellow flag with the black circle. "Too late. We've been blackballed."

People with boards turned back from the water and surfers started coming ashore.

"That sucks," said Tyler.

Alex nodded in agreement but secretly was hugely relieved.

∗ ∗ ∗

Alex ducked into Kai's surf shop to leave his board, saying Tyler would come pick it up later. The walk home was torture, searing pain in his hip growing more intense with every step. The Prius was parked out front of the house, Rick was home. Alex inelegantly fished the door key from his ankle leash's stash pocket. He let Tyler go on in ahead with one board and limped in behind. "Hi, hi!" Alex called out.

Tyler was taking the board to the pool store when Rick came from the patio. "You left your phone. I wondered where the hell you'd gone." Seeing Alex limping, Rick dashed forward. "What have you done?"

Alex dragged a chair from the table under the pergola. "I took a bad dive. Then my leg got tangled in the leash." Unzipping his suit, Alex struggled to pull it down. "Can you give me a hand?"

Rick helped Alex get his arms out.

"Hi, Ricky." Tyler unzipped his wetsuit as he ambled back from the pool store.

Rick looked from Tyler to Alex and then back again. "What have you two been doing?"

"Uncle Al was giving me a surfing lesson," Tyler said with a goofy grin.

"Why aren't you at work?" Rick asked Tyler.

"We were both having one of those days, so we went to the beach," said Alex.

Rick shook his head at Tyler. "I'm so glad we bought that new truck for you to carry on your business. And how exactly is this helping your career?" Rick asked, turning on Alex.

"Chill, babe." Alex heaved himself up from the chair.

"Don't blame him. It was my idea," said Tyler.

"Oh, I should've guessed seeing how you're the Grand Poobah of bad ideas! He's still getting over a heart attack and eye surgery. And you ..." said Rick directing his ire towards Alex, "and you went along with his idea? What are you two? Dumb and dumber?" Rick stormed into the house.

"Don't be that way." Alex shot Tyler an apologetic shrug then limped off in pursuit of Rick. Entering the kitchen, he found Rick taking the blood pressure cuff from the meds cabinet. "You. Sit!" Rick pointed to a stool.

Alex's tone hardened. "Cool it, Rick."

"We need to check your blood pressure. Have you taken your meds? Let me look at your eye …"

"Stop it! Just fucking stop it!" Alex snatched the blood pressure cuff and hurled it across the kitchen.

From the living room doorway, Tyler looked in apprehensively as the cuff clattered onto the terrazzo.

"What the hell were you doing?" Rick spat at Tyler. "Trying to kill him?"

"No, he was making me feel alive! And don't yell at Ty. I actually had fun today. Which makes a change from the soul crushing cosseting I get from you, treating me like an imbecile or a child all of the time. I'm a man, Rick! A grown man capable of making my own decisions!"

"And what great fucking decisions you make! Thanks to you our housekeeper nearly burned the house down, our dog's dead and you're practically broke! Yeah, I know about the loan for Manuela's new place. How do I compete with that? I'm just the fag longtime companion, worrying about you night and day, sitting by your bedside in the hospital, putting my life second to yours. What was it you called me on your opening night at MoMA? Your rock! Maybe that's what I am, a dead weight dragging you down. Well Ty, if you think he's so fucking wonderful, why don't you try it for a while?" Rick picked the blood pressure cuff up off the floor and shoved it in Tyler's hands. "He's all yours!" Rick marched out of the kitchen.

Alex and Tyler stood in shocked silence.

"Maybe it's not a good idea for me to stay here," murmured Tyler.

"Go shower. I'll calm him down." Limping through the house, Alex found Rick on their bed with his face in his hands. Alex rolled his wetsuit down to his hips. It stuck on his thighs. "Babe, please?"

Uncovering his face, Rick wearily cast his eyes heavenwards and got to his feet. He kneeled to tug the wetsuit down to Alex's ankles. "That's one hell of a bruise." Rick studied the purple band under the hair on Alex's thigh. "Lift." Rick patted Alex's right foot.

Alex rested his hand on Rick's shoulder and raised his knee.

Rick peeled the wetsuit off one foot. "Change."

Alex raised his left foot and let Rick drag off the other leg.

Turning the wetsuit right side out, Rick fluffed it out and went to rinse it under the shower.

"Hey." Naked, his body all salty with ocean, Alex pulled Rick back to him. "I left something out back there."

"What?"

"I'd be eternally lost without you."

"You don't believe in eternity."

"Lost for a very long time then."

"Good." Letting the anger leave his body, Rick dropped the wetsuit and softened into Alex's arms. "I've booked my flight. I'm going to Italy. Tiffany works hard, she deserves someone on her side. I can make sure the DVD recording gets done. And like it or not, I have to go see how momma is."

"You must do what you must do."

"And I think we could do with a break."

"You do?"

"The show's between shooting blocks. And it's actually quite liberating not to be tied down to any more Conservatory Board meetings. I'll only be away a couple of weeks. You won't even notice I'm gone."

Alex stared into the bottomless black pupils of Rick's blue eyes. "I'll notice." Wrapping his arms around Rick, he held him close while feeling their hearts grow farther apart.

✶ ✶ ✶

Once *Sphere 4* achieved a higher-than-expected price at auction, Chen's emails and phone calls resumed. Chen's renewed interest in his work didn't come as a total surprise. Shortly after, Chen sold two of his small abstracts for half a million apiece and Harrison Wilde expressed interest in selling one of the *Red* paintings he'd loaned to MoMA through Chen. Keen to sell more of Alex's original work, Chen dangled the lure of seven figure selling prices and a solo fall show as long as the pieces were abstracts. Preferably red ones. Alex emailed photos of his new metal sculptures and layered pieces.

Chen didn't respond.

Having given Chen a couple of days more, Alex emailed the same photos to Neroli then called her a few hours later. "That offer to be your gallery's final show still on the table?"

"It is. But I warn you, my client Rolodex can't compare to Chen's. Or my asking prices. Especially with experimental work."

"I take that on board. And I still have *carte blanche*? I want to show the metal and layer pieces, but I've got another idea brewing for the third room. One that may shock people."

"Terrific!" Neroli laughed. "I haven't shocked anyone for a long time. Let's give the fuckers something to really talk about."

* * *

The tangible goal of a fall opening for his new solo show at The Copley Gallery inspired Alex to put his nose to the grindstone. While he worked non-stop on the metal sculptures and layered pieces in his main studio, he set Suki and Kent to work in the studio above the garage.

Taking a breather from spraying more of metal panels, Alex pulled off his mask and gloves and crossed the meditation garden. He grunted up the rear staircase with clicking knees. Walking in, he looked around the humid upstairs workspace.

Gessoed boards, blank white canvases and stretched watercolor papers of varying shapes and sizes were propped against walls or on easels, grocery store baskets containing art materials sat in front of each blank media. Alex hung by the kitchenette, lost in the Zen of Suki and Kent fastidiously checking the dimensions of every single canvas and board with metal rulers.

"Delivery!"

Tyler's foghorn bellow from the rear staircase jolted Alex out of his reverie.

Tyler lugged a large cardboard carton into the studio. "Where'd you want this?"

Alex glanced around. Every shelf and surface in the studio was crammed with brand-new paint tubes, brushes, palettes, thinners, gouaches and pastels. "Dump it on the counter. Suki can unpack it later."

Tyler set the box on the galley kitchen's counter and wiped his hands on his camo-shorts. "Anything else I can help with?"

"I don't suppose you know how to work one of these?" Alex held out a pricing gun and a roll of labels.

"Mom forced me to work in a 7-Eleven the summer I turned sixteen, her retribution for catching me smoking pot. I'm skilled in this field." Tyler eased the end of the paper roll through the gun, snapped the label dispenser shut and clicked it a few times to feed the labels. "Good to go."

Alex experimented with the gun by sticking a label on the back of his hand. "Cool, thanks."

Tyler checked the yellow label on Alex's hand. "A dollar ninety-nine. Bargain! I'll take two."

Alex laughed at Tyler's silly sweetness.

"I bought us something in for dinner," said Tyler. "What time are you finishing up?"

"I'll be home in an hour."

"I'll hold you to that. All work and no play makes Alex a dull boy."

Alex smiled as Tyler went downstairs and Suki and Kent got on with the new show. It was nice having the house filled with activity. And being busy and having Tyler around stopped him worrying about how Rick was getting on in a country on the other side of the Atlantic.

✳ ✳ ✳

"*Casa di riposo*. 'House of repose' beats retirement home or elder care facility any old day," Rick said with a wan smile. "But whatever language you say it in, momma hates it all the same."

"And this home's run by nuns you say?" asked Alex.

"It is. And some of them are seriously questioning their faith after dealing with momma for six months. I swear Sister Anastasia's pouring fertilizer on that patch of deadly nightshade in the refectory garden."

"So you're doing the recording tomorrow and you'll be home next week as planned?"

A noise in the background distracted Rick. His face left the frame as he leaned back.

Coming closer to the screen, Alex heard a voice in the background on Rick's end. He couldn't make out all she was saying due to her hushed tones and speaking in Italian, but he knew enough to understand '*dieci minuti*' and '*Papa.*'

"I'm on with Alex," Rick said off camera, "come say hi."

A moment later, a blond woman holding a glass of red wine ducked into the frame. She swept a strand of hair off her face and tucked it behind her ear. She grinned into the laptop camera. "*Buona sera, caro* Alex. *Come stai?*"

"Hi, Patti. I'm *stai*'ing fine this afternoon, *grazie*."

"Why did you not come with Papa? Is too long since I have seen you."

"I'm like vintage wine. I don't travel well."

"Then I must bring my glass to you." Patti sipped her drink and grimaced. "A fine wine will make a change from the one Euro ninety-nine chianti Papa buys by the box."

"I do not buy wine in a box!" Rick interjected.

"The boxes are lighter. For he cannot carry so many bottles from the supermarket on each trip ..."

"Thanks for your contribution, dear. Haven't you something more important to do anywhere else in the house? Say goodnight, Patti."

Patti giggled, light flaring off her long silver earrings. "Papa doesn't like me telling his secrets. *Buona notte*, Alex."

"Night, Patti," Alex said into the computer's camera.

Patti blew him a kiss and disappeared from frame.

Rick cast an annoyed glance after her. "Kids get so sassy once they turn twenty-nine."

"Like I was saying, you're back next week as planned?"

"Sorry, no. The schedule's changed. I hopped into Venice to scope out the studio Tiffany had booked. Some elements of practicality got lost in translation. The studio had a whole load of steps leading up to it. And I don't think we'd get momma in a water taxi to get her over there in the first place. She insists she can walk without a problem but her mobility's extremely poor."

"Oh, I see," Alex said flatly.

"I've discussed options with the studio manager. He's suggested they bring the equipment to her, set up a playback screen and do the recording in the home. Tomorrow, I'm going to ask Head Nun if we can use one of the dayrooms. I've started saying Hail Marys in preparation."

"Bringing equipment over? Sounds expensive. Can Tiffany's budget run to that?"

"Momma's actually all fired up about the project now. Patti's offered financial assistance from the gallery. One benefit of her running momma's empire is easy access to funds. That is something I sorely miss. I might ask momma to reinstate my pocket money while I'm her good books."

"Good books? Things are better between you then?"

"Great at the moment. But that's because she's the focus of my attention for this DVD commentary. She's excited about me doing it with her."

"I thought you were just supervising?"

"I got worried momma might lose concentration and we'd have to do endless takes. I talked it over with Tiffany and we thought it'd be a good idea if I took part in the commentary. I can keep things going if she dries up. Ask questions, steer the topics, jog her memory, that kind of thing. It's turning into a real family project! I kind of feel I'm doing something good for dad at last."

"Actually, Ty's gotten curious about Sid's work. He'd never seen most of his movies We're working our way through that pile of DVDs Tiffany brought over. We watch a movie each night in the den after dinner."

"How sweet," said Rick tartly.

Alex resisted a retort. Being truthful with Rick was sometimes as precarious as lying to him.

Letting an awkward pause pass, Rick asked, "How's your leg?"

"Better."

"And your eye?"

"Fine."

"You're taking your meds on time?"

"Yeah."

"Don't let Tyler wear you out. When the two of you get together you act like a pair of goofballs. It's late and I need to look holier than thou for tomorrow. I need to get some sleep, 'night."

"Yeah, 'night." Alex clicked off the Skype connection and sat in contemplation. The late afternoon's velvet light was falling on the oleanders outside the study window. Echoes from the past blended with construction noise from the lot behind. Although only in Italy for just over a week, the Rick he'd known and loved seemed to be disappearing into the mysterious realm behind those large black pupils again. He shut down the computer.

Standing in the kitchen, he wondered what they could have for dinner. From over the perimeter wall, he heard the roar of Tyler's truck pulling up followed by the garage door raising and lowering. After the clicks and clacks of Tyler coming over from the garage block into the living room, he yelled, "Wanna beer?"

Blinking slowly, like he couldn't focus, Tyler walked in the kitchen. "That'd be great." He dug around in the cabinet with Alex's meds.

"What you looking for?" Alex asked from around the refrigerator's door.

"Got any Tylenol?"

"Should have."

"Found it." Tyler popped a couple in his palm.

"Apologies. Frozen lasagna is the best I can offer for dinner. We'd better go grocery shopping tomorrow." Alex opened the beer and handed Tyler the bottle. "Unless you want to go out to Martin's?"

"Go out and miss the next instalment of our Sid Stradman film festival? Lasagna will be fine." Tyler swallowed the painkillers with his beer. "Let me go shower. Meet you in the front row."

Alex switched the oven on to heat up, put the lasagna tray in the microwave to defrost and opened himself a beer.

Having changed into jersey shorts and a baby blue voile shirt, Tyler joined Alex on the patio for dinner. Conversation with Tyler always flowed without effort. They covered politics, climate change, Alex's work, Tyler's work and cracked each other up with dumb jokes and observations. Tyler cleared the dishes while Alex opened a bottle of red. He poured two glasses then they crashed on the chaise in the den.

Alex flicked on the plasma and the DVD's drawer swallowed the disc of Sid Stradman's 1957 WarnerColor Sci-Fi opus *The City at the End of the Sea*. The evening had turned humid. Barely a hint of breeze wafted into the den.

When the movie's end titles rolled Alex yawned, realizing he'd fallen asleep midway. "What did you think of that?"

"Not one of dad's finest. I'm no judge of acting, but the leading man was so wooden they must have had to spray him for termites."

Alex laughed, gosh Tyler cracked him up. "The special effects were good though."

"For their day."

"Another?" asked Alex picking up the empty wine bottle.

"Nah, I wanna shake off this headache."

"I can offer you a Diet Coke. Or whip you up a wheatgrass, beetroot, coconut, and toad's gonad smoothie?"

"I'll take the Diet Coke."

"Wise move."

Alex brought out a couple of chilled glass bottles and a bowl of ice to the patio.

"Boy, it's hot tonight." Tyler undid his shirt and fluffed it out. Picking up an ice cube, he ran the ice over his forehead, his pink cheeks, his throat and chest. Water trickles left dark blue trails on his shirt.

"Feel like another movie?"

"Nah. Watching too many of dad's movies is like eating too much candy. Feels good at first but leaves you feeling nauseous."

"You sound like Rick talking about your dad. Come on, it's cooler in the garden."

The pool lights rippled under their chins as they crossed the red bridge. Lounging on the recliners beneath the meditation garden's illuminated palms, they sipped their drinks.

"My memories of dad are sort of fuzzy," said Tyler. "What was he really like?"

Alex thought for a moment. "Sid was a true character. He liked putting people on the spot, firing questions at you left, right and center but never listening to the answers. Not that most of Sid's questions needed answers."

"And he knew about you and Rick being together and was cool with it?"

"Sid played dumb, but he got the score pretty early on that we were in love. He ended up being really good to me. He was happy Rick had someone who cared about him. You see, Rick had made …" Alex stopped himself from disclosing Rick's suicide attempts. "Rick had a habit of screwing up. And since he'd fallen out with Luisa at the time and did the opposite of everything his dad told him to, Sid relied on me to keep him on the rails."

"The habit of screwing up must be genetic. Maybe that's why I wreck trucks, fall out of trees and fall in love with the wrong guys."

"We all screw up at times. And look at the positives you've achieved."

"I cut down trees, dig flowerbeds and plant bushes."

"Stop that. You run your own business. You employ people, *legally*. And I know how skilled you are at your job. How could anyone not see? Your work's all around us." Alex gestured to the tended foliage, glorious shrubs and cacti, and perfectly groomed trees. "I watch the way you consider the color of which plants should go next to each other and how their shapes and textures complement each other. I see how you cut back the trees so they grow stronger and in proportion. I mean, I can *feel* you work with them, like you're listening to them and sense what they need to grow. Tyler, my buddy, you're an artist."

Tyler smiled shyly. "You think so?"

"I sure do. Gee, the air's so still and wet. I wonder if we're in for a storm." Alex creakily got up from the recliner. Steadying himself on the metal ladder, he rolled up his pants, sat on the pool's edge and dangled his feet in the water. "That feels so good."

Tyler came and sat down beside Alex. He dangled his feet in the pool.

"I'm proud of you, Ty." Alex playfully sloshed water up against Tyler's calf. "You've grown into a fine man with a kind and loving heart. You may have done some truly dumb shit, but not once have I witnessed you act with malice or anger. I'm sorry it didn't work out with Jack, but you'll meet someone else. You're still so young."

"Thirty-six?"

"And fit, handsome and healthy. Take it from this creaky sixty-two-year-old, enjoy those things while you can. Don't waste your life feeling down, revel in every moment." Alex slung his arm around Tyler's shoulders. "You're just a kid with your whole life ahead of you."

"Maybe I'm too much of a kid. Maybe I'm scared of growing up. Hey, I know what we should do!"

"What?"

"It's hotter than Hell and you got a pool. Let's swim!" Tyler stripped off his shirt. Sweeping up his hair, he tied it into a makeshift manbun with an elastic from his wrist.

"That's a freakin' great idea! I'll grab some trunks."

"Aw, don't be a … what's that word? A fuddy-duddy!" In one swift move, Tyler got up, pulled down his jersey shorts and flung them aside. Boldly naked, his firm thighs and muscled buttocks stepped over Alex and strode to the pool ladder.

Averting his eyes until Tyler was in the water, Alex clambered to his feet. "You can skinny dip, but this fuddy-duddy's going to get his trunks!" Crossing the bridge, Alex saw Tyler's underlit naked body gliding through the water beneath him.

Pulling back the glass sliders, Alex entered the master bedroom. He emptied his pockets into the nightstand tray, then stripped off his pants, boxers and shirt. Opening the credenza's drawer, he selected a funky neon pink Speedo from the drawer. Sitting on the bed to pull it on, he noticed his phone had an alert. Tapping the screen, he saw it was a new text message from Rick.

'Momma wants me to stay with her till after my birthday. You don't need me for anything back there, do you?'

Bleakly, Alex shut off the screen. Luisa was exerting her power over Rick once again, and once again Rick was caving-in to her demands. Tossing the phone aside, Alex felt like punching the wall. He'd never doubted the solidity of their love ... until recently. A shift had taken place in New York at his opening night. His eye problem, the weird disorientation he'd experienced in the Pavilion, visions of ghosts from the past, the lack of satisfaction he'd felt from a celebration of his work, the eternity pendant breaking. Were energies from the other side trying to tell him something?

The Hanged Man.

'You won't move on until you let him go ...'

That stupid message from Jane Zalando, boardwalk psychic, came into his head. Did she mean Rick? Alex kicked himself ... hard. What kind of a fool was he to allow such crap to occupy his mind? But even so, he sensed something needed to change in his life. It wasn't working the way it used to.

"You're missing the pool party!" Breathing hard, a pool towel round his hips, and his chest and arms slick with sweat and water, Tyler rested a muscled arm against the doorway.

"Carry on without me. I'm not in the mood." Realizing he hadn't put his trunks on, Alex tightened his thighs and rested his hands in his lap.

"You've crashed, man. What's gone down?" Tyler untied his damp hair and untangled its ginger blond waves.

"I just saw a message from Rick. Luisa wants him to stay on in Venice." Alex's chin quivered, angry and sad in equal measure. "And he is. I had plans for us to celebrate his birthday here."

"That sucks." Tyler sat on the bed beside Alex, this time it was he who slung his arm around Alex in comfort.

Alex sighed and leaned into Tyler. The air between the two men thickened, the way the sea thickens when a big wave's about to roll in. A hot movement stirred at the base of Alex's spine. Tyler's bare armpit and chest pressing against his naked skin was disconcertingly arousing. Alex's throat constricted as his cock stiffened beneath his palms.

"Sure I can't change your mind about the pool?" Tyler rose to his feet. Dropping his towel, he ran his hands over his thighs, provocatively displaying his nakedness.

"Ty, don't." Alex turned his face away.

"You're down. I'm down. Why not get ourselves up?" Bending forward, Tyler removed Alex's hands and spread his thighs. He gave a lopsided, dreamy grin at Alex's erection jutting from his salt and pepper pubes. He rested his hands on Alex's shoulders. "May I?"

Alex mutely permitted Tyler to place one golden haired freckled knee beside his hip then raise his other leg to straddle him.

Tyler laced his hands behind Alex's head and restrained it. He lowered his face and kissed Alex wetly on the lips.

Unable to resist this delicious man, Alex drove his fingers into Tyler's luscious hair. Grasping Tyler's head, he thirstily returned the kiss. Tyler tasted of Diet Coke and pool water. Breaking apart, Alex rested on his elbows to drink in Tyler's stunning torso. He wished he were a sculptor, Tyler's taut body deserved to be immortalized in marble for eternity to savor. Without willing them to, Alex sat up and allowed his hands to cup Tyler's juicy buttocks.

Tyler tossed back his hair and gasped as Alex clasped his butt to his chest.

Alex shuddered, feeling Tyler's luxurious erection against his stomach, pre-cum oozing from its tip.

Tyler caressed Alex's head and passionately kissed him again. Then he roughly pushed Alex back on the bed and mounted him. Tyler's hands were all over Alex, and his were all over Tyler.

Passion rose in Alex's chest, passion stoked by anger. Fuck Rick. If he didn't want to be here with him, he had another option! A beautiful man who didn't want to nursemaid him, or tell him he was inert, or stupid, or not working hard enough, or how he should dress or wear his hair. Tyler adored him, worshipped him as a mentor, a god! This gorgeous young man would allow him to suck him, fuck him and he would make Tyler pant and moan and beg for more of his cock. Alex seized Tyler's chin, ready to ravish him to buggery. He stared into Tyler's open, trusting, beautiful face.

'*You won't move on until you let him go ...*'

Reality hit.

"Ty, no." Pushing the naked young man away, Alex withdrew from the bed. Going around to bathroom, he slipped on a robe. Coming back into the bedroom he saw Tyler had covered himself with the pool towel.

"But, why not?" Tyler blinked disappointment from his green-gold eyes framed by dark lashes.

"This isn't a casual hook up."

"It could be." Tyler looked deep inside Alex. "I'll take one night. No-one need ever know."

"I find it hard to separate love and sex. I'm too old to try and learn."

"But I thought you did love me."

"That's the problem."

Tyler bit his strawberry pink lip and turned his face. "I get scared. I got a feeling I'm standing on the edge of something. A change is coming. I feel it when I'm alone, this darkness. And it's worse at night. Please, Al. I don't want to be alone tonight."

If Alex were being totally honest with himself, neither did he. "Wait." Leaving Tyler in the bedroom, Alex went to the walk-in and fished out some pajama bottoms. He put on one pair and cast his robe aside. Coming to the bed, he tossed the other pair to Tyler. "Just for tonight." Alex threw back the sheets.

Tyler wriggled into the pajama pants and got in bed.

They reached to the lamps either side of the bed, put out the lights, then Alex cradled Tyler's head on his shoulder and imagined what his life would be like if Rick never ever came back.

UN LUNEDI A VENEZIA

Alex emerged onto the busy concourse.

The opaque glass doors from the arrivals hall slid shut behind him.

This was it, no turning back.

The plane journey had been the usual torture, with the additional torture of a transit thru New York. In the long-haul sector he'd managed some sleep on the Delta flatbed. But it had been that shallow, dry-mouthed kind of sleep and hadn't stopped him feeling exhausted as he rolled his compact carry-on down the humid jet bridge. The line at border control was long and arduous. Filling in the landing card, he'd fudged about where and how long he'd be staying. He did his best not to look shifty. The uniformed officer behind the Perspex screen deposited a retro stamp in his passport and waved him through. With only carry-on, at least he hadn't had to hang around at baggage claim.

Now he needed to work out how to reach his final destination.

A kiosk with the sign 'Speed Boat to Venice' looked the easiest, probably most expensive, option, but he was too wiped out to give a fuck about cost, easy topped his list. He joined the short line. Once he'd gotten to the front, he dredged up some rudimentary Italian to explain where he wanted to go. Hearing his American accent, the stylish lady in angular white framed glasses behind the counter switched to English. As he wasn't headed to a hotel, a lot of gesticulating and pointing at maps went on between her and her colleagues to establish which landing stage he needed. Once that was decided and a price agreed, he handed over his credit card. Cradling the phone between her neck and shoulder, the lady made a call while writing out a pink slip. She hung up, pushed the paper over the counter, then told him to leave the terminal, turn left and follow the signs to the water transport. At the landing stage, he needed to ask for Tommaso who'd match him up with his driver.

Leaving the moderate air-conditioning of the airport terminal behind, Alex dragged his bag into the cauldron-like midday heat. He imagined the water taxi station would be right beside the airport, but the narrow walkway leading to it zigged and zagged across airport service roads and ramps to the car park. Opaque plastic canopies, intended to shelter passengers from the sun, unfortunately also trapped the humidity. The trek seemed interminable, with the added annoyance of bumping into travelers coming in the opposite direction, all intent on kneecapping him with their luggage trolleys. Every time he thought he was nearly there, another blue arrow on a brick wall with a boat cartoon saying '*Trasporti via acqua*' indicated another corner to turn. Tired, sweating, and massively irritated that he couldn't simply jump in a car and be on his way, Alex cursed this godforsaken, primitive, waterlogged city.

With every step lowering his mood, eleven minutes later he arrived at the water taxi dock. A modernization program was underway at the airport. This was a temporary landing stage, which perhaps explained the chaos. Red faced and ill-tempered travelers, all waiting for private taxis or lining up at the yellow cabin by the dock for tickets on the Alilaguna water bus, were fanning themselves with guidebooks, staring at phones and milling around in agitated confusion with oversized rolling cases and heavily laden luggage trolleys.

Tommaso was not immediately visible.

Subjugating his innate American desire for clarity, Alex took several calming breaths. Amidst the chaos, he eventually spotted a guy in khaki shorts and white polo shirt who appeared to have an official duty. The tattoo saying 'Tommaso' on his calf confirmed this to be his man. Circumnavigating an agitated

Japanese family with enough luggage for a world tour, Alex said, "*Buongiorno,*" and proffered his pink chit.

Glancing at the paper, Tommaso scanned the sleek ivory and burled wood boats at the moorings. All the slips were occupied. A knell of doom hit Alex's stomach, he suspected there'd been some colossal continental-style fuck up and now he'd have to trudge back to the kiosk in the terminal. Just as he was about to blow his top, Tommaso spied a classic mahogany Riva limousine hanging back on the choppy water. He held up a finger and said something Alex took to mean 'one minute.'

Getting the lay of the land, Alex realized 'one minute' translated into Italian as 'fifteen minutes.' The Japanese family and *all* their luggage had to be loaded onto the boat in slip four before it could back out. Alex's driver was finally able to pull in. Tommaso beckoned Alex, who was seriously considering lying down and falling asleep on a luggage trolley at this point, and directed him to his boat.

The water taxi driver - golden tan, silver link bracelet and candy pink polo shirt with flipped up collar – slung his rope around a mooring post and reached for Alex's case. With that stowed, the driver gripped Alex's wrist to help him onboard. Legs still stiff from the flight, negotiating his way down the steps onto the boat was an ungainly affair. The driver waggled his fingers with an outstretched palm. About to blow his top at the driver for soliciting a tip before the journey, Alex realized the boatman needed his pink slip. Once he'd handed it over, Alex ducked into the cabin then inelegantly slid his butt sideways along the beige leather bench seat to the open cabin in the stern. Becoming grumpier by the second, Alex decided he detested this city, cursed his impetuous decision to come and confirmed he was correct in having resisted all Rick's attempts to lure him here in the past.

From the stern, Alex suspiciously eyed the manner the Riva's driver was reversing from the slip, one hand casually resting on the wheel and the other waving to fellow drivers. As the boat turned and puttered along the waterway, the cool breeze took the edge off the midday sun searing his face. He hadn't packed sun block or a cap in his messenger bag. The boat traveled parallel to the runway, with reed beds on either side and jets on final descent overhead. The waterway widened into open water and the driver veered to port. The Riva roared forward as the driver opened up the throttle and they bounced over wakes left by other boats.

Squinting across the water, watching other speedboats, limousine taxis and water buses headed to and from the airport, Alex allowed the tension from the flight to dissipate. After sixteen hours in the air he was back on his own element - water. Studying the driver's relaxed technique, Alex figured piloting a powerful boat like this for a living looked fun. They passed a small private island on their left, then the driver let it rip and they were thrillingly racing across the glittering lagoon.

The driver slowed to a crawl to navigate through the island of Murano. The tourists strolling past terracotta and ochre houses, window shopping in the glass factories or eating lunch beneath umbrellas at waterside restaurants reminded Alex of a Disneyland ride. On leaving Murano, the driver opened up the throttle again.

Then, across the hazy water, Alex got his first sight of the red-tiled rooftops, noble bell towers and golden domes shimmering like a mirage in the pellucid blue-gray light.

Venice.

The driver peeled away from the wooden posts marking the waterway to Venice and cut across the lagoon to the Lido. Drawing up alongside a small wooden platform, the driver maneuvered the boat in, slung his rope over a pole, and backed up as close to the wooden steps as he could. Alex had shuffled his butt along the bench seat and was hunched inside the cabin ready to disembark. Ducking his head out, he allowed the driver to help him up the boat's steps. The boat bobbed. He unsteadily grabbed at the wooden post. Somehow, he hauled himself over the moving gap between the boat and the wooden steps. The driver passed up his roller case. Clinging to the wooden post, he leaned forward to take its handle, hoping neither he nor his case ended up in the drink. Alex wondered if he should tip the driver. Rick would instinctively know whether to do that or not, he was a master of discretely slipping the right amount of cash to the right person. It didn't matter. After a perfunctory *arrivederci* the driver had cast off and was speeding away.

      Having spent time with a map on the plane, Alex knew the first thing he needed to do was cross the road in front of him. Dragging his case off the rickety landing stage, and nearly getting taken out by a truck speeding down from the ferry terminal as he stepped out from between the parked cars, he took the second turning on his left. He followed the tree-lined canal past a rustic little trattoria and there it was ...

      An absolutely beautiful home.

Stately.

Imposing.

Classically Italian.

      Raised up and set back from the road, it occupied a corner plot. Constructed from terracotta stone, the house had two lower stories with windows edged in cream Moorish detailing, and a third story with a terrace running around. It also had a basement level accessed by a separate entrance. Red tile covered the roof. On the side facing towards the Adriatic, a square lookout with a red tiled roof jutted high above the chimney pots. Tall hedges protected the grounds, and a regal pair of Cypresses guarded the green wrought iron gates opening onto the street corner. A cream stone path ran between the lawns to a flight of marble steps leading up to a small terrace. An elegant porch shielded the ornate front door.

      Now he'd gotten here, Alex suddenly felt at a loss how to proceed. He hadn't spoken with Rick since their Skype call three days ago. Before leaving for LAX on Sunday morning, he'd sent an email telling Rick not to be concerned but he was going into radio silence to devote his mental power exclusively to the new work. He'd made up an excuse about a family emergency involving his sister in Ohio to explain his sudden departure to Tyler. Since Myrna was highly unlikely to call the house, he felt it to be a safe alibi.

There was no sign of life in the house.

Alex wheeled his case to a shady spot outside a derelict villa beside the local garbage and recycling dumpsters. All he could do now was watch the house and wait. An elderly woman on a bicycle, with an equally elderly wire-haired terrier in the basket on the handlebars, cast a wary glance his way as she cycled past.

Since he never wore a watch, he allowed the sun's position and vast amount of sweat drenching his linen shirt to tell him he'd been lurking by the dumpsters for well over an hour. Dehydrated and needing to take his meds, Alex dragged his case over the bridge straddling the small canal with moored boats and up the dusty street on his right to find someplace to get a drink. Arriving at the sea front, the dull thud of bass music alerted him to an outdoor café on the tree-lined road running parallel to the beach. Although there was only one other customer, the waitress took forever to notice him. When she did come over, he asked for a lemon soda. Ice would've been nice but she struggled to understand his request for lemon soda, he didn't have the energy to describe ice, get misunderstood and end up receiving a plate of raw fish. The waitress bought the can and a glass. The lemon soda was sharp and refreshing. He downed it in one. When the waitress paused from chatting to the guy behind the bar, Alex held up his glass and tapped it to indicate he'd like another.

He thought he'd made it perfectly clear what he wanted, but the girl wended her way through the tables to ask him something in rat-a-tat Italian which he didn't understand. Taking a chance she'd asked if he wanted another, he answered, "*Si.*" After a glacially slow trip to the bar and back, she delivered the second can. He emptied it into his glass and briskly downed it with his pills. Ready to go back and resume his vigil by the dumpsters, he was unsure if the waitress would bring the check to the table and he should pay her, or if she'd bring the check to him and he should pay at the bar, or if he should just go to the bar and pay. He asked the waitress for the check with the universal sign language of writing in the air, but nothing came of that. Due to the lack of interaction, he was ready to walk off and see if that got her attention. In the end he went to the bar. He was sure he'd used the correct word for pay, *pagare*, but the guy behind the counter rested one hand on the coffee machine and narrowed his eyes in confusion like he'd been asked for a Fabergé egg or something. Waving a couple of bills got the message across. The barman searched the tabs, pushed a white cash register receipt over and Alex pushed a five Euro bill back.

Alex suddenly felt very American. Things were so much more straightforward back home.

Keeping to the shady side of the street, he walked back to the small canal and assumed position behind the dumpsters to watch the house some more. The late afternoon crickets' chirruping was pervasive, the vibration of their wings melded with the saturated air and clogged his lungs. The old woman on a bike cycled past. She'd given him a strange look before. She shot him an even more suspicious glance on her return journey. Even her little doggie gave him the side-eye this time.

A moment of not being able to remember who he was, where he was or what day of the week it was overtook him. The out of body panic he'd felt in the hospital and at MoMA threatened to seize him. He couldn't allow that to happen here. Struggling to get his brain in gear, he told himself it was Monday and, judging by the shadows, around five p.m. He'd only left this spot for fifteen minutes to go to the café, so guessed he couldn't have missed anything at the house. A queasy pang of panic gripped his stomach. What if Rick had gone away?

No.

Alex ruled that out. The DVD recording was scheduled for this week, making it highly unlikely he'd be out of town. Fearing he'd pass out if he hung around here any longer, Alex reluctantly decided to go find a hotel and come back tomorrow. Just as he was about to give up, a silver Fiat drove past.

Alex ducked behind the dumpsters.

Passing over the bridge, the car pulled up outside the house on the corner.

Meerkating over the dumpsters, Alex saw the property's green mesh vehicle gate slide open. The Fiat pulled into the driveway and the gate slid shut. The sound of car doors opening was followed by frenzied yapping. Looking at the house, Alex saw two fluffy white toy dogs scramble up the steps to the front door. Then he saw Patti digging into her shoulder purse as she carried two plastic grocery bags up the steps. She was model slim, dressed in a black linen tunic accessorized with a chunky silver chain belt slung around the hips, and oversized Jackie O sunglasses. The dogs fussed around her ankles as she unlocked the door. As soon as it was open, they scampered into the house. Patti followed them inside.

The Fiat had taken Alex by surprise, he wondered if Patti had been alone. Then she came out of the house. Leaning over the balustrade, she said something towards the car. Alex couldn't hear who replied, but Patti laughed in response and came down the steps. The Cypress tree and hedge masked the car. Moments later, Patti reappeared with two more grocery bags which she carried up into the house. The Fiat's door slammed. That's when he saw him ...

Rick.

Wearing loose white pants and a lime green shirt, Rick lugged a large rectangular box with a plastic handle to the house. Resting the box, which looked like it contained a flatscreen TV, on the lowest step to adjust his grip allowed Alex to get a good look at him. His hair had gotten blonder and longer, his arms browner. Having a better hold on the box, Rick hauled it up the steps. Then, as if sensing eyes on him, Rick put down the box, pushed his sunglasses onto his head and looked around. Alex slunk into the shadows. Shrugging it off, Rick carried the box into the house and closed the door.

Okay, this was it.

No point delaying the inevitable.

Alex rolled his bag across the bridge. Resting his case against the wall below the hedge, he pressed the button on the brass intercom beside the double gates. He stepped back so the Cypress tree would hide him.

"*Pronto.*" Patti's voice crackled from the speaker grille.

Alex didn't speak. When the intercom clicked off, he pressed the button again.

Patti's voice came from the speaker again. "*Chi è là?*"

Alex stayed silent.

The buzzer clicked off.

Alex waited thirty seconds before pressing the bell once more, a good long buzz this time. Hooking his messenger bag over his roller case's handle, he moved to stand dead center in the green wrought iron gates. As expected, the front door now opened. But it was Patti, not Rick, who came outside.

Shutting the dogs in, Patti came to the top of the steps, her expression a mixture of concern and annoyance. Then she saw him. Her eyes widened in startled amazement. She was about to speak ...

Alex lifted his finger to his lips. '*Sshh.*' He raised the flat of his hand, his eyes telling her to wait.

Patti understood.

The dogs carried on yapping inside.

Alex leaned to press the buzzer again. He gestured to Patti to move aside, which she did.

The front door opened.

Rick squeezed out.

Seeing Patti motionless, Rick frowned and extended his free hand in a gesture of 'what's going on?'

Patti pointed towards the gates.

Rick's eyes followed Patti's finger.

Alex gripped the green iron scrollwork like a prisoner staring through the bars. His bleary eyes connected with Rick's. A realm of emotions swam through the mind behind the big black pupils in those powder blue eyes. Confusion, disbelief, concern, and then, as Rick broke into the broadest of smiles Alex had ever witnessed on his lips … unadulterated joy!

Rick bounded down the steps, raced down the stone path, unlatched the gates and flung them open. Then he flung his arms around Alex, pulled him close and held him tight. The dogs had gotten out and run to the gate. Rick was sniffling and blinking back tears. The dogs were yapping and jumping up and down in joy even though they didn't know who this new visitor was. Leaning back, Rick clasped Alex's face. "You look terrible."

"Gee, thanks!" Alex said with a laugh.

Rick's fingers brushed a stray curl from Alex's forehead. "I mean tired. And you got a sunburn! Didn't you put your block on? Jesus, what time is it in LA? Have you taken your morning meds?"

"Yeah, all in hand."

Patti hurried down to control the dogs.

"How'd you get here? What's going on? This is insane." Rick's words tumbled over each other. "Have you got any bags?"

Alex pointed to his luggage by the hedge.

"I'll get them." Rick darted into the street.

Patti held the dogs' collars. "Hi, Alex. One moment, then I shall hug you too!"

Rick dragged in Alex's luggage and latched the gates.

Letting go of the dogs, Patti embraced Alex. "I am blessed! The vintage wine has come to me!"

"You're looking well, dear." Alex kissed her.

"You are in Italy now!" Patti clutched Alex's shoulders and vigorously kissed him on both cheeks.

"Steady! Delicate wine here," laughed Alex.

"I'll take these into the house." Patti hesitated at the bottom of the steps. "You are staying with us, aren't you?"

Alex didn't reply.

Patti and Rick exchanged nervous glances.

"We'll see," said Alex. "I need to speak with Rick. Can you give us a couple of minutes?"

"*Va bene*," said Patti solemnly.

Once Patti and the dogs were inside, Rick asked, "What's going on? What are you doing here?"

"You and I need to talk."

"And you couldn't have phoned or Skyped?"

"What I have to say to you shouldn't be said over the phone or the internet. It has to be face to face. That's why I needed to come here. We can't go on as we are. Something needs to change between us." Alex stared deeply into Rick's eyes. "We haven't been working like we did. You feel it too, don't you?"

Rick's head drooped. "It's not you, it's me. I know it's me. You're mad at me all the time. All I want to do is look after you. But when I do too much it's like I'm crowding you, then I do things purely for me and I feel like I'm being selfish. And I don't know where I stand. If I fade into the background, it feels as though I don't support you, but if I push too hard you feel I dominate things …"

"This isn't the time or place to go into it. First, I need to use the john. I mean, I *really* need to use the john. Then I need to shower and lie down for an hour. Then we should get something to eat. Is there someplace around here I can take you to dinner?"

"I can cook while you can catch up with Patti —"

"No. Just the two of us. And someplace nice. Real nice. I don't know how you're going to respond to what I have to say to you. So, either way, I'd like this to be an evening we may both remember pleasantly one day."

"You're scaring me. Can't you just tell me?"

Alex put his finger to Rick's lips. "Later."

"If you say so," Rick reluctantly agreed as he led Alex into the house.

* * *

"The condemned man ate a hearty meal." Rick put down the menu and stared out bleakly over the darkening Adriatic.

"Would you like a drink?"

"God, I would. But my stomach's in knots. Water will be fine."

Coming to their table, a waiter explained the menu. It was all very fancy with charcoal dusts, seaweed foams and the like. Alex was relieved the server spoke really great English. Many ingredients were so off-beat he wouldn't have stood the remotest chance of understanding them in Italian. Rick selected oven baked scallops while Alex went for the truffled chicken.

"Actually, I will have a glass of chardonnay. A small one." Rick handed the menu to the waiter.

"Very good, signor." The waiter bowed his head and moved off.

"Excuse me," Rick called to the waiter.

"Signor?"

"Make that a large glass."

"Of course." The waiter took two steps.

"Hey," Alex called the waiter.

"Signor?"

"Make it a bottle ... save the guy a trip," Alex said to Rick once the waiter left. Alex stared up at the Excelsior Hotel, a very grand but somewhat faded renaissance palace. A mixture of Belle Époque and Moroccan architecture, with an onion shape domed tower. "Nice place. Good choice."

The full moon's milky luminescence glimmered on the inky sea and candles on the tables cast amber light over the hotel's marble dining terrace overlooking the beach. The pianist was playing an extremely laid back, practically comatose, arrangement of 'The More I See You' on a white grand piano.

"The Palazzo del Cinema's across the road. This hotel's popular with the big players during the Film Festival. It's got its own landing stage downstairs so the stars can arrive in total privacy," said Rick.

"Funny how people who spend their lives being looked at for a living should hunger so for privacy."

"Not all the stars look so great without the right lighting."

"And are all the arrangements in place for the DVD recording then?"

"I think so. Nun at the Top's granted permission for us to use the *sala di soggiorno*, that's like the communal living room. Matteo, the studio manager in Venice, is going to have the sound baffles and recording equipment delivered to the institute tomorrow. He'll come over to set everything up on Wednesday morning. The TV in momma's room isn't big enough to use for the monitor. That's why we had to go to Treviso to buy a new one. It's LCD, much lighter than a plasma. We'll put it in momma's room after this. She's always complaining she can't see the one she has at the moment. Not that she thinks there's ever anything worth watching on it."

"How is Luisa? Will she be home soon?"

Before Rick could answer, the sommelier brought the wine. He displayed the label to Alex, who directed him to Rick. Having approved the wine, the sommelier was about to pour a small amount for tasting, but Rick told him to just pour. Alex covered his glass. The sommelier placed the bottle in an ice bucket then removed Alex's glass. "What were you saying?" Rick asked Alex.

"Luisa. When is she coming home?"

"She's not. I had a long talk with her doctor. Her heart's failing. And now her kidneys too. It's not like she's got a sickness that can be cured. Her body's worn out. The nuns want us to keep it from her. That she's dying, I mean. They want her to remain hopeful while they do overtime praying. It's terrible, but when she asks about coming home Patti and I lie to her. We say things like 'soon' and 'we'll see.' The other day she asked me, 'Am I going to die?' and I changed the subject." The candle glow highlighted the moistness in Rick's eyes. "I suppose that's the reason I didn't want to come here. I guessed the situation and didn't want to be truthful with myself about it. I feel bad for momma. She can practically see our house from the window of her cell."

"She's that close?" Alex practically gulped.

"Don't worry, she can't get out. They have electrified fences and armed nuns manning the gates."

Alex shuddered. He may actually have passed her home when he walked to the café. It was a sobering thought, Luisa D'Onofrio so close again after all these years.

"But on the positive side, Patti can easily drop by to visit her. And Bobo and Bebe, momma's dogs, the nuns won't let them into the home, but Patti walks them up there. Momma can look at them from her window and pet them through the fence."

"Can't you get someone to care for Luisa in the house?"

"Patti looked into it, but there are too many steps."

"Tell me about it," grunted Alex. "My knees certainly appreciate being on level ground these days."

"And Patti spends every fall and winter in Milan. She adores nonna Lu, but I couldn't let her give up her life to stay with momma until the end."

"Is that what you're thinking of doing? Staying here with your mother until the end?"

Rick reached for the wine bottle. Before his hand had barely moved, a waiter rushed to fill his glass. "Grazie," said Rick. "Is that why you came? Were you scared I wasn't coming back?"

"It's happened before," said Alex darkly.

"If I didn't come back to LA this time around it wouldn't be because of momma."

"Why would it be then?"

"That depends on what you're going to say to me …"

The food arrived. The waiters arranged a smaller table alongside theirs to serve from. Once their plates were filled, the waiter said, "*Buon appetito*." He gave a bow, a gracious smile, topped up Rick's glass and withdrew.

Alex was starving and dug in without further ado.

Rick toyed with his food.

"Isn't yours good?" Alex asked between mouthfuls.

"I can't eat. I'm truly happy to see you, I never thought I'd have you here with me in Venice. Seeing you out of the blue standing at our gate was the miracle I've prayed for. There's so much I want to show you and places I want to take you. But I don't know if it's going to be that kind of visit."

"You're not happy in the house back home, I mean back in LA, are you?" Alex put down his fork and gulped some water.

"There are many aspects of it I love, but it's not my home. But being here in the Lido house with Patti again, I know this isn't my home anymore either. I don't have a career. I don't have the Board. I'm lost and rootless, a boat that's come adrift."

Alex picked up his fork and began eating again.

"It's Tyler, isn't it?" Rick asked through narrow eyes.

Alex kept eating.

"I see how the two of you are together. You have fun with him. And he's clearly devoted to you," said Rick bleakly.

"Yeah." Alex broke a hunk of bread and wiped his plate with it.

"Go easy on the wheat. Your system will be sluggish from the flight and bread makes you bloat at the best of times."

"I have to admit being with Tyler makes me feel young." Alex finished the bread.

"And I don't?"

Alex blotted his mouth with the linen napkin. "Sometimes you do make me feel like a geriatric."

Rick's eyes welled up. "Your heart attack freaked me out. If I'm not around anymore you have to look after yourself. I mean, be careful with yourself. Going surfing with Tyler? What madness was that? And then flying halfway around the world at the drop of a hat to come here. What if this affects your heart, or your eyes, or …"

"Look I'm here, aren't I? Alive and kicking! Ta dah!"

"And what about your work?"

Alex screwed up his napkin and tossed it on the table. "I have the fall show at The Copley Gallery."

"That's not going to pay the bills. What about your work for Chen?"

"Chen can take what I give him and on my terms. And if he doesn't like that, tough. Neroli's supported me all these years, I owe her one final fling. And she truly believes in me."

"But what about money? Chen can get you the big bucks."

"I want to make my art. The art *I* want to make. I'm not chasing the dollar."

Rick looked dubious.

"I'm seizing up. I need to stretch my legs." Alex pushed back his chair and creakily got to his feet. He slung his messenger bag over his shoulder. "Let's take a walk."

"Are you finished, *signori*?" asked the waiter.

"We'll be back for *dolce* and coffee," Alex told him.

"Dolce?" Rick asked as they walked down the marble staircase to the beach.

"I'm picking up the lingo," said Alex with a smile. His stiff knees struggled with the steps. "Jeez, what is it with this place and stairs?"

"Need a hand?" Rick reached out.

"Yeah, thanks." Alex used the handrail on one side while letting Rick steady him on the other. "That's better," Alex said nearing the bottom when his muscles had loosened up.

They strolled along the paved pathway over the sand which led to a pier jutting out into the sea. Gentle waves washed on the shore. The restaurant's piano echoed down from the terrace. The pianist, amazingly still conscious, had gone into a somnambulist Bacharach medley which had got stuck in the groove of the bridge to 'Close to You.'

"Come on, Alex. Break it to me, this thing you came here to say." Rick stared into the watery darkness as they walked along the pier. Waves splashed against the rocks on either side.

"We've come to the end," said Alex.

"What?"

"Of the pier."

They stood on the circular wooden platform out in the sea.

"Like I said, we can't go on as we are. You broke my heart when you left me back in seventy-four. I had a good life with Danielle, but that would never have happened if you'd stayed with me then."

Rick turned away from Alex. "You're right."

"Everything went wrong in New York. I was bummed when you said you wouldn't trust me to sail you through Hell's Gate. And I was so high on my own importance I let you get pushed aside on the blue carpet. That night, every hurt and loss from the past crept up on me. Having my life's work together in one place made it seem less, not more. And not being able to see properly made me feel weird, like I was hallucinating. I felt sad for the past and scared of the future. The eternity pendant breaking seemed like a bad omen. But having thought about it, I realized what a fool I'd been to have given you that in the first place. A piece of stone on a string with a vow to love you forever. It was a stupid thing for me to have done."

"Alex, stop. You're breaking my heart." Rick stared into the sea wind.

"That's the reason I came here, to stop repeating patterns of the past." While Rick still had his back to him, Alex fished in his bag. Rick was about to turn. "Don't look at me." Alex cursed his clumsy fingers, then found the box. "I've not been fair on you.

I'm through with unsatisfactory gestures. I've always loved you, but I've not given my heart to you without reservation. And I want to. Because you fill my heart. Don't turn around!"

"What are you doing?"

"I need to ask you something." Creakily, Alex got down on one knee and positioned the box in his hand. "Now you can look at me."

Rick pivoted and quizzically stared down into Alex's face.

Alex gazed up at Rick. The wind ruffled his hair, the moon and constellations were his backdrop. "You see, the reason I came to Venice was to ask you, in person, face to face, man to man …"

Alex opened the box and held it out.

"Rick Stradman, will you marry me?"

FOR BETTER OR WORSE

"Did you hear me?" Alex gazed up at Rick who silently stared down at him. "At this point in the proposal it would be helpful if you said something."

Still Rick didn't speak.

"So, would you care to spend the rest of your life hitched to me? Legally obliged to turn up every day, no running out on me ever again."

The only sound came from the surf crashing against the rocks beside the pier.

"My knee's locking up. A simple yes or no will do."

Rick came to life. "I'm in shock, I thought you'd come to break up with me."

"Why'd I do that? I was afraid you're sick of having me around."

"Not at all! I love being with you. Every crazy moment. Even when I'm mad at you I'm happy," Rick said with shiny eyes.

"Terrific. Now we've established that, can you put me out of my misery and answer? Any longer down in this position and we'll need the coastguard to airlift me off."

"Oh, yes. Yes! Of course, I want to marry you!"

Alex took the ring from the box. "Give me your hand then."

Rick extended his hand.

Alex slipped the ring on his finger. The full moon glinted off the polished platinum band edged by two fine brushed bands.

"It fits! How on earth did you get this together?"

Alex tried to stand. Seeing him struggling, Rick bent forward to assist. Dusting off his knees, Alex extended his arms. "Give your old man a kiss, you crazy kid." Alex enfolded Rick in his arms as the waves crashed around them. Their mouths met and explored each other. Making love with Rick had always been wonderful, but there was renewed passion in his embrace and a heartwarming compliance, as if they were melting into each other. As Rick pressed in real close, Alex's cock filled to aching fullness. Through his tailored pants, he felt Rick growing hard. Stepping back, Alex gazed into Rick's eyes. "Jeez, I desperately need to fuck you."

"If you had trouble kneeling, this isn't an ideal location."

"You don't say?" Alex held Rick's arm as they walked back along the pier. Nearing the beach, with its rows of white cabanas shaped like Arabinan tents, Alex grabbed Rick's waist. "How about I tear off your clothes and ravish you right here?" He jokingly pretended to wrestle Rick to the sand. Music from the hotel drifted down. A female vocalist had joined the pianist and was warbling an ultra, ultra-slow arrangement of 'Feelings,' so soporific it should've carried a health warning. "Come on. Dare you." Alex playfully dragged Rick towards the surf.

"I'd prefer to do it without an audience." Rick pulled back.

"Fuddy-duddy," chided Alex with a grin.

Steering Alex back onto the path over the sand, Rick glanced up at the diners on the hotel terrace. "Although they might find two guys making out on the beach more entertaining than this cabaret."

Alex halted at the marble steps up to the terrace. "Jeez, freakin' stairs!"

"We can go in on this level and take the elevator."

After entering by way of the shuttered beach bar and passing through a bijou arcade of boutiques selling expensive resort wear, they took the elevator up one level. As they walked through the double-height atrium lounge, Alex tapped Rick's arm. "Go to the table. I'll ask the bellman to call a cab." Once he'd seen Rick go out to the terrace, Alex delved in his bag for his credit card, approached the front desk and had a word with the young man in horn-rimmed spectacles behind it ...

"Want anything else?" Alex asked, sitting back down at their table on the terrace.

"No. Let's get the check." Rick dreamily contemplated the ring. "Seriously, how long have you been planning this?"

"Totally spur of the moment. I found a ring I know fits in your jewelry box. Then I got Scotty to run to Georg Jensen with it while I was arranging flights and travel documents on Saturday."

"Scotty picked this? She knows about the proposal then?"

"Only one who does. I described exactly the ring I wanted. One I thought you'd like. We can change it if you don't?"

"It's perfect. I can't give you a ring, can I?"

Alex rubbed his knuckles. "Not a great idea with these babies. We can come up with something else. Maybe I could have your face tattooed on my butt?"

"Definite possibility. Placement of the portrait could make or break the success of that idea." Rick's eyes watered with hilarity the more he thought about it. "At least the artist would have a large canvas to work on."

"Imagine," Alex continued deadpan, "having your face on my butt would mean I could sit on it every day."

A snorting laugh burst from Rick. "Stop, people can hear."

They carried on chuckling. "After tonight, you'd better give me the ring back so I can keep it safe till the wedding."

"The wedding." Rick raised his eyes. "May I tell Patti?"

"Sure. We can tell everybody now you've said yes. We need to think about dates and places and who we want to be there."

The candlelight glittered in Rick's eyes. "This is a fitting location for the proposal. We began on a beach, after all."

"Back when I was down to my last red cent, and you forced your way into my beach house."

"I didn't force my way in!"

"C'mon, you'd only been in the place half-an-hour before you decided my spare room was getting a tenant … you!" Alex laughed. "I often wonder, when did you fall in love with me?"

Rick smiled bashfully. "The first moment I set eyes on you. When you climbed barefoot up that cliff to rescue me because you thought I was in danger. Then the edge crumbled and you nearly fell off! It was very funny," Rick chuckled.

"I still can't fathom why I should love someone who found the possibility of my imminent demise quite so amusing."

"I caught you, didn't I? When did you fall in love with me?"

Alex had to think deep.

"You're taking an awful long time."

"It's tough because there were so many moments. I mean, I knew you were gorgeous the first time I noticed you on the beach at Sunset Cove. All dressed in white and beige, so poised, so aloof, yet kind of sad. Having said that, once you moved into the beach house you were a royal pain in the ass. I mean, you could be so totally precious and —"

"Moving on. Cut to the falling in love part."

Alex thought again then slapped the table. "It was the day I took you sailing for your birthday. That was the first time I'd ever confessed to anyone just how bad Pop had beaten me. I'd buried the pain and the shame of it for so long. And when I told you about the night his belt smashed my eye, and how terrified I was and how I wept and bled, and you … you cradled my head and kissed my scar." Alex touched the dent on his eyebrow. "You made me feel safe, and loved, and valued, and that was the moment my heart was hopelessly, irretrievably, profoundly lost to you."

"That long, huh?"

Their eyes connected over the flickering candle.

"Sir?"

Alex tore his eyes away from Rick's to find the young man from the hotel's front desk by their table.

"Everything's taken care of," the reception clerk said.

Alex got up. A waiter darted forward to ease out Rick's chair.

"This way, signori." The reception clerk gestured them to follow.

Having thanked the maître d' and their waiter, Rick caught up with Alex. "We haven't paid."

"Taken care of," Alex said curtly.

The reception clerk guided them to the elevators.

Rick glanced at the revolving door onto the street. "Why are we taking the elevator? Did they call a water taxi? A car's better. There's no place to moor —"

"Chill." Alex cut Rick off. "Grazie, Mauro." The reception clerk passed a key card to Alex, and Alex subtly pressed a folded bill into Mauro's hand, making it appear like a handshake.

"You can find your way?" Mauro asked.

"Yeah, thanks," said Alex.

"Buona notte, signori."

"Get in." Alex ushered Rick into the elevator and hit 6.

"Up?"

The doors closed.

Where they were going dawned on Rick. "This place costs a fortune! Our house is only ten minutes away."

"Jet lag's kicking in. I got no time to waste getting you into bed."

"How'd you check in? They need to register passports."

Alex tapped his shoulder bag. "Had it on me. Apparently, foreigners have to register with the local police, so this gets that over with too." The doors opened with a muted ding. "Move it, boy." Alex hustled Rick down the endless corridor of Moroccan arches and ornate lanterns. Finding the right door, Alex tapped the key card to the panel. He flung the door open, pushed Rick inside and kicked the door shut.

Instantly, Alex tugged Rick's silk shirt out his pants and propelled him across the room. Rick tumbled back onto the huge bed which had been turned down for the night. Alex unbuttoned his own shirt while kicking off his sneakers. "Do yourself," muttered Alex.

"What?"

"Your shirt." Frustrated with fiddling to undo his top button, Alex ripped his own shirt off over his head, undid his belt and rolled his pants and boxers down in one. Kicking his clothes aside he pushed Rick onto the bed and mounted him. Pain shot through his leg. "Shit. I must've done something to my knee on the pier. This isn't a great position for me." Alex rolled onto his back. "Get on top."

Sitting up, Rick wriggled out of his pants and underwear and slung them away. He put one knee up on the bed beside Alex's hips and swung over the other to straddle him.

Alex clasped Rick's hips to restrain them and rubbed his cock against the silk of Rick's dangling balls. Rick eased back a little, leaned forward, placed his hands beside Alex's shoulders and rubbed their moist chests together while grinding their cocks against each other. "Mm, nice." Alex clasped Rick's face to his and thrust his tongue deep in Rick's mouth. Getting up again, Rick shuffled his knees up the bed and, getting onto all fours, rubbed his erection in between Alex's pecs. Alex swirled his tongue around Rick's belly button, then pushed Rick's shoulders away to bite and suck on one of Rick's firm rose pink nipples.

Rick moaned as Alex's teeth tugged his left nipple real hard, then moved to his right. He gasped again as he noticed something on the table by the window. "Oh look, they left champagne."

"I had Mauro send it up," Alex murmured, moving up to nuzzle Rick's neck.

Rick, shuffling his knees up on either side of Alex's chest, raised himself.

Staring up at Rick in adoration, Alex trailed his hands over Rick's stomach, chest, shoulders, and flittered them down his back and over his butt. Wanking Rick with one hand, he slid his other between Rick's thighs to work a finger into his ass.

Rick moaned. Through half-closed eyes, he gasped, "Is it a sea view?"

"Pah huh?"

"This ... ah ... room. The drapes are ... ah ... closed," Rick got out between sighs and moans. "Does it have a sea view?"

"Don't know. Don't fuckin' care." Alex wanked Rick with extra vigor while probing his ass deeper.

"Damn. We don't have lube," moaned Rick.

Alex reached to the nightstand.

"What are you doing?"

"Calling reception." Alex grabbed his messenger bag from the nightstand. "I'm prepared ..." Taking out a travel tube of lube, he tossed it to Rick.

Catching it, Rick unscrewed the top. "You're such a boy scout!"

"Just in case your ring was tight."

Rick poured a dollop in his hand, then swirled it around Alex's rigid cock. He squirted another cool glob onto Alex's hand. Tossing the tube onto the nightstand, Rick raised one leg so Alex could work the lube into his butthole.

Nicely slick and slippery, Alex maneuvered himself up the bed so that he was sitting up against the headboard. Facing him, Rick squatted on his hips and, reaching behind, guided Alex inside him.

Alex supported Rick as he lowered himself. "Ah, wait a moment ..." Rick lifted himself, repositioned Alex's angle of entry, then lowered his weight again.

Alex caught his breath as Rick slid down, eased himself up as a little as Alex's cock hit a moment of resistance in his sphincter, then fully opened up and dropped his hips. Rick's butt swallowed Alex's full length.

Placing his hands on the headboard, Rick raised his haunches in a squat allowing Alex to thrust in and out.

While staring at Rick's elegant profile, his eyes closed and mouth agape, Alex's vision blurred from exhaustion and pleasure.

"Ouch," Rick cried mid-thrust.

"Okay?"

"Cramp in my hip." Keeping Alex inside him, Rick adjusted his position, so he was kneeling rather than squatting.

Unable to fuck with Rick's weight on him, Alex muttered, "It's all down to you now, babe."

Rick bent forward and kissed Alex. Then supporting his weight on his hands, he rode Alex while Alex clasped his buttocks, urging them along to add momentum.

Alex felt himself climaxing. He gazed into Rick's face and widened his eyes. Rick got the message, widening his eyes in return. Rick increased the movement and speed. Alex nodded. His eyes rolled back. His mouth grimaced open. He spasmed into Rick with a grunt, then a moment later felt Rick cumming from his erection's friction against his hairy abdomen. "Come, come, come, babe …"

Rick cried out, his cum squirted onto Alex's stomach.

They continued rocking for a few more moments. Then, spent, Rick eased Alex out of himself and fell aside.

"Kind of hot in here." Alex scratched an itch on his calf.

"I'll check the air con." Rick looked around the room. "They must have air con? Drink?"

"A little."

Rick went into the bathroom. After the toilet flushed and water ran in the bidet he returned with a handful of tissues. "Nice room, but the bathroom's kind of tired."

Taking the tissues, Alex cleaned himself up. Then he creakily got off the bed to have a pee and brush his teeth. Shuffling back into the bedroom, he saw Rick had pulled back the drapes and poured the champagne.

"We do have a sea view. And a balcony!" Rick said in delight.

"I'll take your word for it." Struggling to keep his eyes open, Alex flopped onto the king size bed.

Rick handed Alex a glass and lay beside him.

Putting his arm around Rick, they clinked glasses. "Here's to us," murmured Alex.

"To us." Rick clinked in return.

Alex had two sips, put his glass down and scratched his leg again. He covered himself with a single layer of sheet. "Love you." Alex gave Rick a goodnight kiss.

"Love you too." Rick drank his champagne and admired the ring. "Mr. and Mr. … Who'd have thought. What legal stuff do we need to do? I'll check on the internet. Do you think …"

Alex vaguely heard Rick talking, but the jet lag, sex and two sips of champagne had done him in. Today, he'd set something in motion which would change their lives, for the better or worse, forever.

A distant thought about how Luisa would react to this news flickered through Alex's mind, but he cast it aside, closed his eyes and that was the last thing he knew.

* * *

Alex had stirred in the night with cotton mouth and itchy eyes, he'd thrown off the sheet and sipped some water but still woke up sweaty and dehydrated. A much-needed breeze wafted across his matted chest hair. Scratching the irritating itches on his ankle and calf, he lugged himself out of bed.

Gentle wind rippled the ivory gauze curtains over the door to the balcony, pulling them aside Alex stuck his head out. "Good morning."

Rick, wrapped in a white toweling robe, was lounging on a white wicker recliner. "Sleep well?" he asked seeing Alex.

"You bet." Alex scratched his head, his armpit and then his lower leg.

"You want to get breakfast here or go back to the house?"

"What's the time?"

"Eight-thirty," said Rick.

"Let's take it here. It's paid for."

"Fine, then we can walk home along the beach. I let Patti know we weren't coming home last night. She's going into the gallery this morning. You want to do something today?"

"Nah, I'll take it easy."

"You should. We haven't gone on a vacation for a while."

Now his eyes could focus, Alex admired the view. The sky was clear turquoise, and the Adriatic was sparkling. Out in the distance, big ships were lined up on the horizon, a couple of tankers and a cruise liner. Alex scratched his leg again then dipped his head to see what was irritating him. A rash of angry red bumps dotted his calf and ankle. "Shit!"

Rick jumped from the recliner and bent to look. "Oh, I should've warned you about the mosquitoes …"

"That would've been enormously helpful. Didn't they get you?"

"I think only new blood on the island attracts them."

"This one's a doozy." Alex rubbed one bite which was coming up to a giant bump.

"Scratching makes them worse. Get showered and I'll take care of them."

Feeling more human after soaping his face and letting cool water spray over his body for ten minutes, Alex came back into the bedroom. Rick was dressed and pouring boiling water from the kettle into a cup. Tugging his crumpled shirt back on over his head, he watched Rick dip a teaspoon into the water. Unraveling his underwear from his pants, he sat on the bed to get into it.

"Let me do this before you put on your pants." Rick removed the spoon from the hot water. Kneeling, he pressed the spoon's bowl onto the large bite on Alex's calf.

"Yowzer!"

"Too hot?"

"Just felt like singing."

"This draws out the poison." Leaving the spoon in place for a couple of minutes, Rick removed it.

Alex saw clear fluid suppurating from the bite.

Rick dipped the corner of a towel in the hot water and wiped it clean. "It'll crust over. Don't pick. You don't want the bite to get infected."

The hotel's breakfast was served on the beach bar's terrace looking out over ocean.

"I don't care if coffee is bad for me, I need it. Lots, if I'm going to make it through today without crashing," said Alex as they sat at a table next to the sand.

Rick chose the fruit platter while Alex hemmed and hawed over the other choices. "I really could go for pancakes and syrup." Alex waited for Rick's admonishment.

"Then have them."

Alex glanced around nervously. "Did you get taken over by a pod person in the night?"

Rick smiled. "I just want you to be happy today."

✱ ✱ ✱

"This joint has a pool! If I'd planned it better, I could've brought my trunks and taken my morning swim," said Alex once they'd checked out of the Excelsior and were strolling along the shore.

"There's plenty of sea out there." Rick smiled towards the waves. "We could rent an umbrella and spend the afternoon on the beach if you like?"

"Sounds like a plan."

They passed assorted private beach establishments, each with a different style of beach huts, umbrellas, and sunbeds. The fanciest were those of the Grand Hotel des Bains, where attendants in white uniforms were laying out white towels on the walnut framed rattan sun loungers outside cabanas with coconut fringed roofs behind an empty stretch of sand.

The Hotel Des Bains' private beach gave way to a section of free beach, packed with people who'd brought their own towels to stretch out in the sun after swimming. Passing several blocks of yellow and blue striped umbrellas with blue sunbeds, Rick then steered them left up a white and blue plastic walkway laid over the sand. Alex steadied himself on Rick's shoulder to put on his shoes. They made their way through a buzzing snack bar covered by white tented tops, which resembled one of Madonna's conical bras, then up a ramp, out through the gates, across the tree-lined road and a couple of minutes later were at the house.

Rick unlatched the front gates. They heard the dogs barking inside. "I'll visit momma after lunch to make sure she's all set for tomorrow. She needs to get her brain in gear. I'll call Matteo to find out when the equipment's going to arrive. I can take the new TV up to the home so that'll be there ready as well."

Alex was about to groan about the steps up to the house but found his knees remarkably easier this morning. "Hey, that wasn't so bad."

"Maybe the weather here suits you? Howdy, furballs," Rick greeted Bebe and Bobo whose tails were beating a furious welcome.

"Papa, you're here!" Patti emerged from the darkened rear of the house.

"I thought you were going to be at the gallery this morning?" Rick asked Patti in surprise.

"I was waiting for you. I didn't want to spoil your morning by calling the hotel."

Rick tipped his head suspiciously. "Spoil?"

Twisting her hands together, and with a face of doom, Patti said, "Sister Marta called first thing. It's nonna Lu."

"Oh my God, she hasn't died, has she?" Rick asked in reaction to Patti's solemn tone.

"It's not that." Patti wetted her lips and switched her attention between Alex and Rick. "Nonna Lu didn't come down to dinner last night. The carer went to get her for ready for breakfast this morning, but nonna Lu refused to let her in. They can't get her washed and she hasn't eaten since yesterday lunchtime. Nonna Lu says she wants to be left alone."

"Just because I didn't go see her yesterday she's gone into a full-on Garbo," Rick said with a tut.

Patti shook her head. "It is worse than that. She says she cannot possibly do the recording."

Rick clenched his fists. "God, give me strength!"

Alex spotted the vein in Rick's temple pulsing. "Calm down, babe."

"Calm down? I've arranged the recording engineer, the equipment and had to sweet talk the institute director and a very scary nun into letting us use the dayroom. What I wouldn't give for a day around momma without drama! Why, for fuck's sake, does she have to go and pull this today of all days!"

"She knows Alex is on the island." Patti smiled apologetically at Alex. "And …"

Rick's back stiffened. "And?"

"And she wants nothing more to do with you, Papa. She wants you to leave this house, this island, and go back to America. She never wants to see you again."

Rick rubbed his forehead.

"Should I go talk to her?" Patti asked.

Rick shook his head. "No matter what she says I need to go see her." Allowing a moment's thought to let the news sink in, Rick asked, "Who the hell told her Alex is here?"

"It wasn't me Papa, honest," said Patti.

Rick stroked Patti's arm. "Some loose lipped nun must have blabbed. We should have put momma in a home run by a silent order ... but how could anyone at the institute know about Alex being here?" Rick's mind raced, then he spun round and fixed Alex with a gimlet stare. "The Excelsior registered your passport last night, didn't they?"

"And you think the hotel's front desk has a hotline wired up to a retirement home run by nuns?" Alex replied askance.

Rick twisted his mouth in frustration. "And you came straight to the house from the airport?"

"Yeah."

"You didn't go anywhere or speak to anyone else?" Rick's tone hardened as he zeroed in on Alex.

"Wanna grab a spotlight and shine it in my eyes? Like I said, I came directly here and hung out on that corner!" Alex pointed across the road. "An old woman on a bike, a couple of students throwing bottles in the dumpsters, the cab driver who took us to the Excelsior and a vicious mosquito are the sum total of my interactions on Lido." Alex scratched his leg.

"Don't scratch it," snapped Rick.

Then Alex added, "Oh, and a surly waitress and barman at the café bar when I walked up to get a drink."

Rick's eyes narrowed. "Which café bar?"

"For Pete's sake, I dunno. The one on the traffic circle at the top of the road."

"That's it!" Rick walked around punching his fist into his palm.

Patti and Alex exchanged puzzled glances.

"Now Miss Marple's solved the mystery could she share the denouement?" Alex asked in irritation.

"Momma's room looks out over that roundabout! She's always complaining about music from the bar and smell from the fish truck that parks there. She must have been looking out her window for something to moan about and seen you in the café. This is a disaster. No wonder she's furious with me. She must think I've been hiding you being here from her."

"This is fuckin' ridiculous. I'm through with Luisa's bullshit." Alex strode down the hallway towards the front door.

"Where are you going?" Rick asked.

"To see Luisa and have this out once and for all."

"But Alex, you can't. Wait!"

"The only way to deal with a bully is to stand up to them, something we should have all done to your mother long ago!" And with that, Alex marched down the steps and along the stone path to the front gates, with Rick, Patti and two little dogs chasing after him.

HOW DO YOU SOLVE A PROBLEM LIKE LUISA?

"She must avoid all stress! It's not good for her health," gasped Rick.

The dogs yelped around Alex's ankles as he unlatched the gates. "This insane behavior of hers isn't good for your health. Or mine."

"Let me go reason with her." Rick shooed back the dogs.

"I let things get out of hand this year because I didn't take action soon enough." Alex stepped into the street.

Rick grabbed Alex's arm. "This isn't the time for confrontations."

"I disagree." Alex wriggled free then crossed the road. He strode up the street which cut diagonally towards the beach.

Patti locked the dogs behind the front gates and hurried in pursuit.

Passing several blocks of rectangular gray apartments on the left, Alex noticed gothic windows with green shutters in the rear of the imposing old building to his right. The street ended in the tree lined road running along the seafront. On the other side of the roundabout with the cedar tree was the café bar he'd visited yesterday. The building by his side must be Luisa's retirement home. Following its railings around the corner, he came to a wrought iron gate set between stone pillars with 'Instituto Santa Maria' engraved on a brass plaque.

"Don't do anything rash!" Rick pleaded.

Alex jabbed his finger on the bell and peered through the hedge behind the railings. Three silver haired ladies in wheelchairs, blankets over their knees despite the morning heat, were parked amidst the oleanders in the triangular courtyard. Alex's finger was about to press the buzzer again when a nun shuffled from the reception. Rick having said the institute was run by nuns he'd formed a mental picture of them in black robes and white cornettes. This nun, however, wore a navy polyester skirt, navy drip-dry wimple and beige training shoes.

The nun screwed up her puffy eyes and squinted through the gate's ironwork. "*Che cosa vuoi?*"

"I need to speak with Luisa D'Onofrio. It's urgent." Alex would rather have stated his case in Italian but wasn't prepared to waste time.

"Signora D'Onofrio, *non visitatori*," replied the nun.

"*Mi dispiace*, Sister Marta," said Rick apologetically over Alex's shoulder, "*amico mio* …"

Although he didn't understand much Italian, Alex understood 'my friend' and rounded on Rick. "Time to cut the *amico* crap and get some honesty going on."

"Signora D'Onofrio *non vuole nessun visitatore oggi*," Sister Marta repeated. "*Nessuno*," she added to Rick with flattened palms to emphasize no-one, not even family, was getting in to see Luisa today.

The old women in the courtyard stopped staring into space and peered towards the front gate.

A pair of green shutters on the second floor slammed against the wall. A wrinkled face leaned over the windowsill.

Realizing his fuse was burning fast, Rick pacified Alex. "Come back to the house. Maybe after lunch we can …"

But the red mist was billowing. Alex stalked to the roundabout then switched his gaze between the café bar and the institute. Before he saw the truck selling fish, he smelled it. If Luisa could see the café and smell the fish truck, one of the windows in front of him must be hers. Back at the railings, he cupped his hands to his mouth. "Luisa D'Onofrio! I know you're in there!"

Rick's eyes bulged. "Are you nuts? You can't do this!"

"Can't I? Just watch me. Luisa, I've got news for you!"

Further bangs followed as more green shutters flew open and more wrinkled faces looked down from windows.

"Here's the big news, Luisa! Do you hear me? Does everybody hear me?" Alex waved his arms to attract attention. "I am in love with your son!" Figuring not all the residents may be bilingual, he wracked his brain for the words in Italian. He knew 'I am in love' so shouted, "*Sono innamorato!*" Then he struggled with the word for 'son.' He saw Rick propped up against the railings, clutching his chest like he was about to have a seizure. Patti was doing her darnedest to remain serious but was clearly on the verge of hysterics. Beckoning her, Alex hissed, "Son, remind me of the Italian for son."

"*Figlio*," Patti replied.

"You're not helping!" Rick snapped at her.

"Luisa D'Onofrio, *sono innamorato con tuo figlio!*"

Now every window in the institute except for one had faces hanging from them. Nuns, cleaners, carers, cooks and residents were all staring down. Even customers in the café bar were craning their necks to watch the spectacle. A couple of young guys in lycra shorts cycling past braked and dropped a foot to find out what the crazy American was shouting about.

"And I have asked him to marry me!" Alex bellowed up to the lone pair of closed shutters. He dragged Rick from the railings and draped his arm around his shoulders. "What's Italian for marry?" he whispered to Patti.

"*Sposare*," replied Patti.

"*Mio a lui*," Alex pointed between himself and Rick, "are going to *sposare!*"

The two young guys on bikes whooped and applauded before cycling off.

"Is this what you were about to tell me, Papa?"

"Yeah," muttered Rick. "I hadn't planned on having it announced quite like this."

Keeping hold of Rick, Alex continued, "Hear that, Luisa? I have asked your son to marry me. And he has said yes! And ..."

An extremely flustered Sister Marta came shuffling from the pedestrian gate. "*Venire, venire,*" she said breathlessly approaching Alex, Rick and Patti. "Signora D'Onofrio will see you. *Venire.*"

Rick's face was a mask of disbelief.

They followed Sister Marta through the gate. The nun halted in the courtyard. "*Solo lui.*" Pointing to Alex, she then hustled him inside the main building, leaving Rick and Patti dumbfounded beside the matrons in wheelchairs and statue of the Virgin Mary.

The institute's somber interior was in stark contrast to the sunny morning outside. Sister Marta led Alex down an amber terrazzo corridor which smelled of bleach and cooking. Without speaking, she took him up two flights of stairs. The height of the treads was gentle, and they were covered with a carpet runner held in place by brass rods so the stairs didn't overly stress Alex's knees. Sister Marta paused on an upper landing. After a moment's wheezing, the nun led him down a long hallway covered in faded mustard carpet. Sister Marta stopped outside the door at the end. She knocked. While she listened for a response, another door opened across the hall. Alex caught the eye of the old lady who peeked out. She looked from him to Luisa's door and back again, then shot him a 'better you than me' expression before locking her door. Hearing something from inside the room, Sister Marta opened the door a smidge, said, "*Entrare,*" to Alex and shuffled off as fast as her beige training shoes could carry her.

Girding his loins, Alex pushed the door and crossed the threshold into Luisa's room.

Alex's eyes grew accustomed to the semi-darkness. One wall of the room was occupied by brown wood furniture, two wardrobes and chest of drawers. A floral bedspread with pink frills covered the single bed. A salmon pink porcelain lamp with cream shade and a large clock showing the time, day of the week, month and year on a red digital display sat on the nightstand. A wooden crucifix hung above the brown headboard. On the wall opposite the bed hung a vivid modern abstract painting of swirling lines. And in a chair beside the shuttered window, a cream throw with red poppies draped over her knees, sat Luisa D'Onofrio …

She was excruciatingly thin, a chenille robe clutched around her and sheepskin bootees on her feet. Despite her frailty, fire still blazed in the pin sharp eyes above her chiseled cheekbones. Luisa shifted, glanced towards the crack of light in the shutters and snarled, "How dare you humiliate me in such a way."

"Nice to see you too, Luisa."

"I am certain it is. *Prego*, take pleasure in my circumstance. This is how they make me live now. Go ahead, gloat."

About to respond, Alex checked himself and turned towards the abstract painting instead. "Beautiful."

Luisa grunted in agreement.

"It would benefit from some light. May I?"

Luisa put a wizened hand to her mouth then airily fluttered it. "As you wish."

Alex squeezed behind Luisa's chair. He undid the latch holding the shutters together and threw them aside. Welcome daylight flooded the room, along with the thump of the café's music and, he had to admit, a whiff of fish. Alex admired the painting in daylight. Clearly a piece of fine art, the flowing curves in hues of orange, lilac and lime were as alien to this world of brown as blossom trees on Mars. "I assume this didn't come with the room?"

Luisa gave a bitter laugh. "Is from my private collection. Libby Beuys."

"I'm not acquainted with her work, but I'll surely search it out. Exquisite."

Luisa rubbed her chin then flapped her hand. "You did not come here to admire my art. What is it you want from me?"

"I want you to end the war you declared on me so we can live out our days in peace."

"How can there be peace between us? Yesterday, when I sit here looking from my window, looking at a world which used to be mine, I see a man. This man is older, his hair not as long as it once was and it is going gray, very gray, and he carries more weight, much, much more weight than I recall, but he appears familiar. Then I recognize who this man is and a bomb drops on my world! This man has come to take away the only joy I have left. This man has come to steal my Ricardo. To drive a wedge between me and my son and cast me out —"

"Cut the crap. I can't deal with your bullshit any longer. It's a waste of my life, and it's certainly a waste of yours. Don't you see the strain you put on Rick with your demands and ultimatums? You profess to love him when he does what you want, but it's you who casts him out if he doesn't blindly obey you."

"How dare you speak to me in such —"

"I didn't come to steal Rick. I traveled halfway around the world to be with him because he wants to be here with you."

"Ha," snorted Luisa. "He is only here because he wants something. Wants me to do this recording. A commercial enterprise of some greedy producer to make easy money from selling an old movie of mine. Trading on my name, my past, *my memories* —"

"Rick's getting nothing out of this. Tiffany, Sid's daughter, has got two kids, health problems and works her ass off as head writer on a TV show. She got the gig to produce the special features for the DVD reissue of her dad's movies. She's not making big bucks for doing it either. This project's a labor of love, a way for her to be close to Sid, the father who died when she was three. She asked for your help, and you agreed. Then you added the condition you'd only do it if Rick came. And he came and —"

"And when it is done, when they have taken what they want, I will be of no more use to them and he will leave. Just as he left me before. For you!"

Alex raked his fingers through his hair in frustration. "He told me you wanted him to stay here for his birthday. I wanted him to come home to be with me for it. And I was furious with him for wanting to stay here. But then it hit me that I was being as unfair on him as you. That's why I dropped everything to come here. I'm trying to find a way for us all to be happy. But it's a waste of breath talking to you. Rick will have to break the news to Tiffany that the recording's not gonna happen. It's a pity you're throwing away the chance to leave your footnote on history through spite. I'll tell Rick to call off the photographers and reporters who were coming. And since you don't want to see Rick again, we may as well take the next flight out. Goodbye, Luisa." Alex slowly walked to the door.

"This girl, the daughter of Sid, and … who was the last wife? Is so hard to keep track of the names."

"Letitia," said Alex, his fingers on the door handle.

"So, this girl …"

"Tiffany."

"Tiffany, the child of Sid. She is family."

"Yeah, she's family."

"And after the recording is done, Ricardo will stay?"

"Yeah. And I will too."

"One cannot have everything, I suppose. Have you no work to get back to?"

"I do, but that's not my priority right now."

"Great artists are selfish! They place their art above all else!"

"Maybe I'm not a great artist then. But you already knew that." Alex glanced back at the Libby Beuy's painting then opened the door.

"Photographers, you say?" Luisa swept a strand of lank hair off her face. "Tell Ricardo to be here at one. And on your way out, tell them to send up Dorata. And tell them I need to eat. And tell them I need the hairdresser. And —"

"And to whom should I address these demands?" Alex asked, sensing the tide had turned.

"Some nun or another." Luisa shrugged. "They all look the same to me."

"So this means you'll do the recording?"

"What say do I have in anything? I am clearly powerless." Luisa huffed. "A marriage between two men is not possible."

"Well it's legal and binding in California."

"Is a travesty. A mockery!"

Closing the door with a click, Alex swiveled and marched back into the room. Coming to her chair, he raised his hand.

"Do not strike me!" Luisa recoiled.

Alex rested his hand on the back of her chair, leaned forward, kissed her on both cheeks then stood.

Luisa clutched her throat. "What was that for?"

"Soon you'll be my mother-in-law. I look forward to seeing you tomorrow, and the day after that, and the day after that, and ... well, you get the picture. *Ciao.*" Alex couldn't resist smiling wryly as he left Luisa's room.

"How is she?" Rick asked as Alex came outside.

"Still alive if that's what you mean. She's issued a list of demands. She wants Dorota, something to eat and you to visit her at one o'clock. Oh, and she wants the hairdresser."

"Hairdresser?"

"I told her photographers and reporters will be coming tomorrow. I was improvising to sweeten the pot. Guess you'd better round up some guys with cameras."

"She's agreed to do the recording then?"

Alex nodded.

"How the hell ..." Rick glanced at the statue of the Virgin Mary. "How the heck did you talk her into it?"

"Never mind. Now, while you attend to Lucrezia Borgia's laundry list, I need to change out of this shirt and pants before they walk home by themselves."

"So how'd momma react to the news about us getting married?"

"Over the moon. Can't wait for me to start calling her mom."

✷ ✷ ✷

Once Luisa had consented to do the recording, the remains of yesterday had been consumed by a flurry of preparation. Despite Luisa running them ragged, the staff at the home were relieved she'd come out of isolation and was taking her meals again. Luisa's demand for the visiting hairdresser came too late to fit her in, but Patti had dug around in Luisa's boxes at the house and found a pleated white turban to cover her hair.

Wondering how they were going to deliver on the press photographers Alex had promised, Rick and Patti put their heads together. They decided to go big. Patti phoned her press office at the gallery, the Ca' dei Venti, and told them to issue a press release stating famed cinema star of yesteryear, Luisa D'Onofrio, would be making a rare professional appearance on the Lido. The island's history of hosting the Venice Film Festival, and Luisa being the guest of Umberto Barbaro at its 1946 opening ceremony - the first-year American movies had been readmitted after WW2 - made a good hook. The press release didn't linger on detail that the professional appearance entailed Luisa coming downstairs to make a sound recording in the dayroom of an elder care facility. A couple of Venice newspapers, however, instantly got back to say they'd cover it. And Tele Venezia, the local TV station which occasionally screened Luisa's old Italian movies between commercials for Persian carpets, promised to send a crew. The press coverage wasn't major league but it was something. Matteo and his team had constructed an impressive temporary studio at the institute in one morning. Sound deadening screens and textured foam acoustic baffles surrounded the huge flatscreen TV on which Luisa and Rick were to watch the movie.

So at two o'clock, despite initial protestations that the Instituto Santa Maria was dedicated to God and not entertainment, Sister Marta opened the doors to admit the photographers and reporters. The majority of people at the home were unaware of Luisa's film career. To them she was just another old lady, and in Luisa's case not a very pleasant one. But once gossip spread about why Rick and his American lover were here, people recalled Luisa had once starred in a Hollywood movie.

Intrigued by the TV cameras, spotlights and photographers, residents and staff lined either side of the amber terrazzo corridor and gathered in the reception area for the event. A hushed expectation descended as the rickety elevator rattled down. As its grille clattered back, Alex peered over the stooped silver heads to see Rick help Luisa from the elevator. Wearing the cream dress Rick had selected for her, with a white pashmina fastened by a glittering firework pin on one shoulder, the white turban and starburst diamond earrings, Luisa looked every inch the star. She'd declined the use of a wheelchair, so her procession to the dayroom on Rick's arm was painfully slow. Bursts of applause and small gasps of admiration from the onlookers as she passed by lent the occasion an odd gravitas.

On Rick and Luisa reaching the reception lobby, a volley of flashes erupted. The Tele Venezia reporter, a balding, stooped guy in his mid-seventies himself, pushed his microphone at Luisa and asked about her memories of working in Italian cinema and on *Her Imperfect Past*, her one and only Hollywood movie.

Watching Luisa's eyes and diamonds sparkle to life in the photographers' flash bulbs, and Rick protectively holding his frail mother's arm, Alex found something profoundly moving in this extremely minor event. As Rick helped Luisa to the dayroom, Alex followed at a suitable distance to keep out of her eyeline. His very public declaration of love for Rick and proposal of marriage had sent a ripple of intrigue around the home. Judging by some dismissive glances and whispers behind hands as he made his way through the crowd, Alex could tell several ladies disapproved. But on the flip side many others dipped their eyes and smiled coyly at him, the memory of love and romance rekindled in their hearts no matter whom it was between.

The small press corps followed Luisa and Rick into the dayroom. Having photographed Rick and Luisa take their seats before the microphones and TV monitor, they dissipated.

The exterior shutters were closed to block out any street noise.

Alex slipped into a seat behind the sound desk and Matteo leaned back to pass him a pair of headphones.

Making sure Luisa had enough cushions around her, Rick took his mother's diamond earrings, slipped them in his pocket then helped her put on the headphones. Rick passed Luisa a glycerin throat pastille, then an unknown person killed the dayroom's already dim electric lights.

The room darkened.

Matteo asked Luisa and Rick to say a few words for sound levels while one of his assistants adjusted the boom microphones. Satisfied the technical aspects were in place, Matteo demanded, "*Silenzio totale!*" then hit Play on the DVD machine. The transmitter logo of RKO pictures appeared on the large monitor and the small video screen behind the sound desk's sliders.

The movie, *Her Imperfect Past,* began to unfold.

Tiffany had scripted a brief monologue to lead Rick into the narration. While the main title's lush orchestration played, he explained his connection to the movie – son of Sid Stradman, producer and director, although uncredited as producer due to contractual issues, and Luisa D'Onofrio, the movie's star. Cool light flickered across Luisa's face as she stared intently into the screen. Rick had hardly finished speaking before she cut in to point out this wasn't the title sequence's original music. Howard Hughes had taken over RKO just prior to the movie's release and found the original score too lightweight so asked Roy Webb to compose a darker theme.

Despite Luisa's many failings, Alex conceded she was a consummate professional when it came to work. No-one need have worried about prompting her. In fact, once she got going it was hard to shut her up. Sips of water and more glycerin pastilles were the only respite from her constant flow of comments on hairstyles, makeup, her disagreement with the director over motivations, her dissatisfaction with co-star, Harry Gaunt, and numerous other issues related to the studio's intervention and comprises made for various reasons.

Every so often, Rick consulted Tiffany's outline to steer Luisa in a certain direction or get her back on track if her wanderings down memory lane threatened to get them lost. Seeing Rick and his mother working together, with Rick's assured presentation skills and Luisa delivering the goods on the backstory, Alex realized in the domestic shuffle of cooking, cleaning, walking the dog and arguing over who takes out the garbage, how easy it is to forget the professional work done by one's nearest and dearest.

Alex cut between watching Matteo's small video monitor on the sound desk and dodging his head to look around the sound baffles to glimpse Luisa's flickering white face.

"… he loves her. But if the agents of her government find them together, she knows they will kill them both," Luisa commented on the movie's plot in a hushed voice. "The only way she can keep him safe is to make him hate her. She plans on making him believe she has betrayed him. This is why she conceals the gun. Oh, this scene … ah …" Luisa caught her breath.

Hearing Luisa's gasp through his headphones, Alex bent forward to squint at Matteo's monitor. Having watched the movie again with Rick and Patti last night, Alex knew they'd reached the climactic sequence where Reade, the American agent played by Harry Gaunt, confronts Natalia, played by Luisa, a former spy now working for the Americans, about her true character.

"*You don't believe a woman like me can change, do you*?" said Luisa on-screen in her role of Natalia.

"*You can change your hair, change your accent, change your style …*" said Reade pressing his face close to hers. "*All of them can be diverting for a while.*"

"*But I can't change my true nature. That's what you're saying, isn't it? A woman like me can never be trusted by anyone again. Even a man she loves.*" In the harshly lit close-up, Luisa's pale face and dark eyes dominated the screen.

"*You call this love? I'm merely the highest bidder*," said Reade.

"*I have done many things I regret to serve my father and my country, but I never sold my heart for money. And I never will. How dare you!*" On-screen, Natalia lashed out at Reade.

Luisa's voice came over Alex's headphones. "That line should have read, '*I never sold my body for money*.' The censors would not allow it. This new line made no sense to me. The change made me angry. Although madly in love with Sid at the time, a terrible argument took place between us," Luisa said into the microphone as the scene played on. "I felt nauseous, dizzy. I ran off the set. My period was late. I'd blamed the strict diet and early morning calls for the change in my body. How well I recall the morning we shot this scene. Sid forced his way into my dressing room. He reasoned with me, screamed at me, begged me to return to the set. His movie was behind schedule. If I did not finish the scene, he could lose his job. Although I was sick, what choice did I have? I came back on set. Sid shouted, 'Action!' The blinding lights hit my face. The camera rolled towards me. The celluloid ribbon rattled through the gate, the lens probed my soul, and, in that instant, I sensed the change taking place inside my body was a new life."

By now, Alex, Matteo and the sound assistants were no longer looking at the movie, anyone with direct line of sight to Luisa was riveted on her staring at the on-screen fight taking place between the leading characters.

Luisa narrated the action, "Natalia threatens Reade with the gun. He raises his hand to her. I suddenly had a greater action than portraying a character in a movie. My only desire became to protect the being who had taken root in me. On that first take I was terrified when Harry's fist flew at my face. Harry Gaunt was a clumsy oaf at the best of times. Should one of his blows accidentally connect and I fell, it could end the fragile life within me. On take after take of that close-up, I grew more and more distant from my character. I placed my unborn child's safety above my art. Sid used my best take, but it wasn't good enough. The critics called my lack of commitment in this pivotal scene the movie's fatal flaw. I didn't … how do they say these days? I didn't *nail* the scene. And the reason sits here beside me. My child."

The sound baffles masked his face, but over his headphones Alex heard Rick clear this throat.

"You never told me that before, momma." Rick's voice thickened with emotion. "This movie truly marks my first on-screen appearance."

Luisa let out a small laugh.

"Remind me to update my IMDB page," Rick joked.

The movie's story reached its resolution. Reade had always believed Natalia's heart was true. Guessing her plot, he'd played along to pull his own double cross. Arresting Natalia with her own gun, Reade walks her out of the mansion in plain sight at gunpoint. He's left behind the crucial piece of evidence that will lead to the villain's downfall at the hands of his comrades, who now think it was him who betrayed them to the Americans.

    Rick wrapped up with his closing speech, his voice low and familiar for the microphone. "Many thanks to Matteo Scolare and his team at Suono Sull'Acqua Studios for arranging this recording. Thanks to Tiffany Strezlicki, my sister, who put this project together. Thanks to my father, the late, great Sid Stradman, without whom we'd have been staring at a blank screen for the past two hours. And most of all, thanks to my mother, Luisa D'Onofrio, for taking us behind the scenes today. We hope you've enjoyed this insight into Sid Stradman's 1948 movie, *Her Imperfect Past*. This is Rick Stradman signing off."

    '*The End*'

    The score's last notes died as the final RKO logo rolled.

    Fade to black.

    A couple of beats passed.

    The shutters were opened.

    A gilded shaft of afternoon light illuminated the dust motes whirling in the air.

    Matteo kicked off the applause.

    Then his assistants joined in.

    Taking off his headphones, Alex laid them on the mixing desk. Everyone gathered around Luisa in congratulation. Alex couldn't follow all the Italian chatter, but it must have been praise, for Luisa positively glowed in acceptance. She raised her frail hands to cup Matteo's face as he kissed her on both cheeks.

    Breaking away, Rick came over to Alex.

    "Awesome job, babe," Alex said in Rick's ear. "And you never knew she was pregnant with you while they were shooting?"

    "She always said it happened after the movie wrapped. But you know momma, always some surprise up her sleeve. She's fading. I'll go find a wheelchair."

    "You finish up here. I'll get one." Alex walked off then made a U-turn. "What's the word for wheelchair?"

"*Sedia a rotelle.*"

Repeating it in his head as he went to the reception, instead of Sister Marta, Alex found a smartly suited young woman behind the desk. "Hi, I'm looking for, er ... *io bisogno di una sedia a* ..." The word has already escaped his memory. "*Una sedia con* ..." Alex pantomimed wheels.

"A wheelchair," the woman replied with a smile.

Alex pointed to his nose with one finger like in charades.

"One moment." The woman went out to the courtyard then came back pushing a wheelchair.

"Thanks. It's for ..." Alex pointed to the dayroom.

"Signora D'Onofrio." Emilia tapped her own nose with a finger. "I'm Emilia Ravello, the institute's director."

Alex was momentarily surprised she wasn't a nun. It must've shown on his face.

"The sisters do God's work, I deal with the bureaucracy," Emilia said with a humble laugh.

"I'm Alex Morgan, I'm ..." He stumbled for words.

"The partner of Signora D'Onofrio's son. Your very vocal declaration of love left no-one in doubt of your identity."

"Forgive me. I mean ..." Alex kicked himself for getting tongue tied because of the building's religious connotations. "I don't mean to offend, but I'm not a believer in organized religion."

"I don't get involved in that side of the business." Emilia smiled. "My job is to pay the bills and make sure we don't get sued."

Alex smiled back at Emilia then took the wheelchair.

Matteo and his team had already stacked up the acoustic baffles, packed the mixing desk and microphones into padded metal cases and his assistants were reeling cables onto rolls. The disconnected flatscreen TV sat forlornly on the parquet floor. The movie magic had evaporated, and the dayroom was revealed to be the dowdy brown box it was before. Luisa struggled to remain upright on her chair. Rick was supporting her.

"Here we go." Alex wheeled the chair to them. "You need help getting into it?"

"What's he doing here?" Luisa turned her face from Alex. "I do not need a wheelchair."

"It's a long way to your room, momma," said Rick. "Everyone will be coming down for dinner. And I'm tired. The chair will be quicker."

Luisa raised a shoulder. "If it is easier for you."

Rick helped Luisa to her feet.

Alex pulled the wooden chair from behind her and quickly put the wheelchair in its place.

"Let's get you back upstairs, momma." Rick lowered Luisa into the chair. He pushed her down the amber terrazzo corridor to the elevator.

Alex remained in the lobby watching them go.

Coming up behind him, Emilia asked, "She used to an actress?"

"She did. Thanks for letting them use the room."

"Sister Marta considered it frivolous, but I convinced her otherwise. The sisters look after their physical needs but sometimes forget our ladies had dreams, careers … loves. Spiritual solace wears many guises. There's nothing unnatural about wanting to feel young and vital and having a place in the world again. Or, when you become old, simply being noticed every once in a while."

A loud clang made them both jump.

Alex turned to see a tiny birdlike nun by the brass gong outside the dining room. Drawing back the mallet, the nun gave the gong another solid whack.

"Sister Anastasia," Emilia confided once the resonance had diminished.

The little nun gave the gong a final bang. Sister Anastasia twirled the mallet, blew the end of it like a gun, and grinned at Alex and Emilia. She hung up the mallet then hooked open the refectory's double doors.

Sounds of activity stirred throughout the sleepy building.

"No one's ever late to dinner when Sister Anastasia is on duty." Emilia went back to her office.

Alex watched as elderly ladies emerged from rooms and carefully walked down the stairs. Carers wheeled the ones who weren't mobile from the small elevator and in through the front entrance from the other wing. Some residents smiled politely or said a reserved '*Buona sera*' as they passed.

Alex took a seat in the courtyard beside the statue of the Virgin Mary.

When he finally came outside, Rick's first words were, "She wants to see you."

"Me?"

"In her room. Now."

A knell as resounding as Sister Anastasia's gong shook Alex's heart.

What did Luisa want with him that couldn't wait?

THE WEIGHT OF SOULS

"You want to see me?" Alex stuck close to the door.

Luisa was in her chair by the window. "My voice is tired. Come nearer."

The last thing he needed was another drubbing from Rick's mad mother. But being a peaceful guy, Alex obeyed.

"None of them answer when I ask, even the doctors evade and turn aside. You brandish the truth like a weapon. I have a question. And do not spare my feelings with your answer."

Although he dreaded what was coming, Alex saw no point in beating around the bush. "Shoot."

"Am I dying?"

Of all the questions Luisa could have asked, this one caught him from left field. His attitude softened, his tone with it. "Yeah, you are."

"How ... how long?"

"Six months. A year, at most. Your heart's failing and now your kidneys are too."

"Good news. Not long until you will be rid of me forever."

"You asked for the truth. I didn't say this to hurt you. You've had a long afternoon. You should rest."

"You told me a truth, now I give one to you. This afternoon, as I described how I would have done anything to protect my unborn child, a dark guilt overcame me. I did something which hurt that same child many years ago. Before I take this secret to my grave, it is time to release the weight from my heart." The disco beat of music from the café made a strange underscore to Luisa's revelation. "The news story which blamed his father's discovery of Ricardo's sordid lifestyle for his death, it was I who first gave that story to the press."

"You? But why?"

"I was livid when the producers dropped me from Ricardo's TV show. That part was to be my return to the screen! The role was written for a strong woman, not Rosemarie Harrington's simpering coyness. It was humiliating." Luisa shifted in her chair. "At first I was jealous, my son was to have the Hollywood career denied me. But neither of you believed that career would be denied him too if your relationship became public. I intended the rumors about Ricardo's sexuality to be a warning. But the fuse had been lit. And when Sid died, it burned to the inevitable explosion."

"The breakdown you used to lure Rick into taking you home to Italy, you faked it didn't you?"

"If he had remained with you in America, I never would have got him back. And he never would have a produced an heir without my intervention. Allowing my family's bloodline to die was a risk I dare not take. I have always been aware of Ricardo's weakness for power and money. I gave him both to keep hold of him. This confession gives you the power to destroy me forever in my son's eyes. Go, tell him and be done with me for good." Luisa closed her eyes.

Alex's legs trembled as he walked into the courtyard. "Can we get a drink? I need to sit."

Rick steered Alex over the road to the café bar.

Not a fan of thumping music in noisy bars, Alex actually found the café's lively atmosphere a welcome relief from the institute's decrepitude. They sat at one of the round tables and the same waitress from the other day, a tray tucked under her arm, sashayed through the packed tables.

"Aperol spritz," Rick ordered without hesitation.

"*Due?*" questioned the waitress.

"What are you having?" Rick asked Alex.

Looking at Alex, the waitress greeted him with an amiable, "*Salve! Limonata?*"

Alex was taken aback, not only that she remembered him but also his order. "You got a beer? *Birra?*"

The waitress responded with a flurry of words.

"Bottle or draft." Rick translated.

"Draft."

"*Alla spina, grande.* What did momma want you for?" Rick asked once the waitress had gone to the bar.

"I don't know. She wasn't making sense."

"She seemed pretty on the money this afternoon."

"Can we change the subject? Luisa's dominated proceedings enough for today." The ice-cold beer and relaxed atmosphere refreshed Alex, although the humid evening air was thickening. Thunder rumbled down from the Dolomites as they walked back to the house.

Home from work, Patti walked in and kicked off her heels. Pouring a glass of wine, she sat cross legged on a kitchen chair as Rick prepared dinner and recounted the recording session's success.

With Luisa's revelation churning in his guts, Alex remained silent in the background. Although he couldn't resist commenting when he found a carton of red wine in the fridge's door. "Exhibit A!" he declared, brandishing it. "Mr. I Never Buy Wine By The Box. Red too. Sacrilege."

"I use that for cooking!" Rick replied while Patti giggled.

Leaden clouds brewed overhead as they took their drinks onto the verandah. Learning from itchy experience the local mosquitoes were particularly bloodthirsty at sundown, Alex liberally doused his arms and ankles with repellant. The dogs raced to and fro along the fence yapping at passers-by while Patti regaled Rick and Alex with art gossip and weekend plans. Her boyfriend in Milan was arriving on Friday to spend a few days. "I told Vincenzo I cannot wait for him to meet my parents!"

Alex was about to ask if Giuliana was also coming when he realized by 'parents' Patti meant him and Rick. It was true, soon she'd officially be his stepdaughter. Rick went inside to cook. A warm, fatherly glow settled over Alex as he listened to Patti's excited talk about celebrations for Rick's birthday and the Redentore festival this weekend, casting thoughts of Luisa aside.

"Dinner!" Rick put the steaming pot on the table and dished up.

Patti was in awe of her father's squid ink pasta with shrimp and dug in with gusto.

Alex recoiled from the bowl placed before him, the super fishy fish smell and dark pasta triggering his gag reflex.

"Too fishy?" asked Rick.

"Too black. I don't want to deprive you and Patti." He pushed his bowl across the table. "Enjoy." Excusing himself, he saddled up Bippy and Boppy, as he'd taken to calling Bebe and Bobo, and walked the lapdogs to the local pizzeria to get a takeout.

Increasingly frequent lightning flashes signaled the storm was approaching as he walked back. Most houses and apartments had closed up their shutters in preparation. The few open windows revealed old style televisions flickering over hunched forms in unlit rooms. Bippy and Boppy threw a yappy fit when they ran into an old man walking his black cat on a long leash. Alex restrained the crazy pooches while the cat haughtily strolled past.

Carrying his pizza box in through the front door, Alex unleashed the hounds. They scampered upstairs. He heard Rick winding up awnings and securing shutters around the house. "Babe! Can you bring down my meds?"

"There you go." Rick came out onto the verandah and passed him the pill bottle.

"Where's Patti?" Alex asked between mouthfuls of deliciously meaty pizza diavola.

"Vincenzo called as we finished eating. She went upstairs with her phone and never came down."

Alex felt Rick's eyes boring into him as he devoured the spicy pizza. He swigged his meds with another beer.

"We need to get you back on to a healthier diet. I should go out and buy a blender in the morning. Your nutritional intake will be missing your morning smoothies."

"My nutritional intake may be, but I'm not. Can I take a vacation from the smoothies until we get home?"

"I guess."

"I need to hit the sheets," said Alex finishing his beer. "You coming?"

"Not yet. My mind's too buzzy."

"Don't stay up too late." Alex stroked Rick's head.

Gathering wind swayed the yews and white wisterias surrounding the house.

"Throw your laundry in the hamper," Rick called. "Paola's doing housework tomorrow!"

Alex's weary legs climbed the staircase. The Liberty-style villa was immaculately decorated with tasteful furnishings which complemented its baroque features. There was a lot of scrolled brown wood furniture, however, and too many gilt and ormolu sconces with fussy fringed silk shades for Alex's taste. Overall, the house felt oddly dark and heavy for one in a city of light. Patti had taken over the second-floor's master suite. Luisa's rooms also occupied this floor. Alex imagined her furniture and boxed possessions lurking ominously under dustsheets behind the locked doors. He walked along the third-floor landing to the guest suite, peeled off his pants and tossed his sweaty shirt and underwear in the laundry hamper. After peeing, rinsing his face, and brushing his teeth, he collapsed into bed and fell asleep before closing his eyes.

A thunderclap woke him.

Rick was sleeping soundly at his side … snoring.

Guessing it must be nearly morning, Alex turned his bleary eyes to the digital clock. Its glowing numerals read 12.15. Jet lag had played its jolly little trick. Trying to get back to sleep, he thought about the brief phone conversations he'd had with people he'd lied to about his whereabouts. Most of them now knew the truth about his location and the proposal. Suki had been full of congratulations and, with Kent's help, was getting on with the studio work. Tyler's happiness was muted. Alex felt bad about lying to the kid. Scotty was thrilled, in particular that Rick adored the ring she'd selected. Alex kicked himself for setting his mind in motion. Practical matters crowded in. His work, Luisa, how he and Rick would live when they were married, where they would live, the wedding itself, how, where, who, what, when, why ...? Chains of multiplying concerns revived him to unwanted lucidity.

A sliver of light split the shutters. He counted, one elephant ... two elephant ... thunder. The storm was overhead. A clatter of rain slapped the roof. Then he heard another sound. Crying. He listened harder.

A woman was crying.

Moving slowly so as not to wake Rick, Alex got out of bed. Taking Rick's zebra print silk kimono off the back of the door, he slipped it on. Knotting its red tasseled belt, he closed the door and tip-toed down the landing. The mournful crying, melding with the rainstorm, was coming from the lookout on the roof. Being careful in the dark, he climbed the twisting staircase. Opening the door at the top he found Patti out on the terrace. The wind whipped her hair but the canopy protected her from the rain. "Patti?"

"I did not mean to wake anyone." Clutching her phone to her chest as she turned, Patti wiped her face. Lightning zigzagged across the sky, highlighting his robe's zebra stripes. Patti couldn't mask her surprise at seeing him in such a louche garment.

"First thing that came to hand." Alex bobbed his head in recognition of the incongruity of his chest hair poking from the chichi robe. "It's Rick's. From the Norma Desmond collection."

Patti smiled through her tears.

"What are you doing up here?"

Patti raised her phone. "Vincenzo is not coming."

"That's a shame. Work?"

"Wife." Patti began crying again.

"Oh, Patti." Alex came forward and hugged her.

Patti buried her face in his shoulder. "He keeps telling me the marriage is over and soon he will be free. But …"

Lightning ripped the sky above the churning sea.

"It's tough, honey. And I hate to sound old fashioned, but there's a heck of a lot of other men out there. Sure you want the one who keeps causing you pain?"

"Should falling in love always make life easier?" Patti's green-blue eyes with the black saucer pupils formed like her father's stared questioningly at him. "I love him."

Thunder rattled the house.

"Then I guess you'll have to find a place to hide the pain until it sorts itself out."

"That is when I come up here. Vincenzo is a sailor on a long voyage. I stare out to sea. From up on high I shall be the first to see his ship's mast appear over the horizon. And as soon as I see it, I shall run down to the harbor ready to welcome him home."

"Vincenzo isn't a sailor I take it?"

"Architect." Patti tapped her phone to her heart. "We shall be together. Someday."

"If that's what your heart tells you, then you must trust it." Rain rolled off the lookout's tiled roof. The cloud cover diffused another lightning flash. "Some storm."

"When the air has been hot and humid for days in a row, we always get a storm. Sometimes so fierce they knock down trees and cut off the electricity. But tomorrow the sky will be clear. I can show you around Venice. There are so many galleries and museums you must see. Would you care for that?"

"Maybe later in the week. I need a day of doing nothing to clear my head."

A mist of rain gusted in.

"You are getting wet. We should go inside," said Patti.

"Yeah, and you ought to get some sleep." Alex wiped the fine mist, like sea spray, from his face. "Talk of seafaring's stirred my blood. Know what I'd really like to do? Get out on the water. You've so much of it here."

"Giovanni and Paola live in the basement. Vincenzo has borrowed Giovanni's boat when the vaporetti have been on strike in the past. We could ask Giovanni for you to borrow his boat if you like?"

Alex immediately envisioned himself piloting a classic Riva launch. The idea did appeal. "Do I need to pass a test or something?"

"Not for a boat like Giovanni's. Shall I ask him?"

"If the weather's fine that'd be great."

On hearing the landing's boards creak, Bippy and Boppy came scampering up the stairs. Going down to her bedroom, Patti softly called them back through the balustrade's spindles. But the dogs were intent on scrabbling at the guest room's door.

"They can come in with us," Alex whispered.

In the bedroom, Rick was sleeping like the dead but snoring like the living. In fact, his snoring was louder than the inefficient A/C unit. Alex hung Rick's robe on the door. As soon as he was in bed, the little dogs made Herculean efforts to jump up. Alex rolled on his side, listened to the dying storm and let his imagination drift to fast boats on wide water ...

✲ ✲ ✲

Giovanni proudly threw back Esmerelda's navy tarpaulin.

Alex hoped his face didn't telegraph his disappointment.

Esmerelda being Giovanni's 18-foot boat with a modest 40 hp Mercury outboard motor. The boat was moored on a bend of the canal across from the house.

Once Alex accepted that he wasn't going to be channeling his inner James Bond, cutting across the lagoon in a racy speedboat, he appreciated Esmerelda's Pelican blue hull and the love and attention Giovanni had clearly lavished on the craft.

Patti watched from the concrete path alongside the canal as Giovanni used a mixture of sign language, gesticulation and going 'vroom' and 'eeeee' to demonstrate the throttle and trim controls. Patti translated Giovanni's explanation of the *bricole*, the oak-wood posts jutting from the water which delineated the *canali*, the navigable passages in the lagoon. The lagoon could be deceptive. Some areas, particularly in the north, were only inches deep even at high tide. The bricole had numbers on them showing the water depth so boats didn't accidentally run aground, also the speed limit - 20 kph being the maximum anywhere in the lagoon. Giovanni warned it was an offense to tie up to the bricole, you should always moor to the single poles, *paline*, usually topped by a color, or the metal rings set into walls and pathways by the canals. As with every city, parking was an emotive issue in Venice, and docking your boat in someone else's slip was a complete no-no.

"I'll take good care of Esmerelda," said Alex. "Tell Giovanni I once skippered a forty-two-foot Carter yacht through a Force eight in the Gulf of Mexico."

Giovanni's eyes widened below his bushy eyebrows. He slapped his hand to his cheek and shook his head as Patti translated. Then he nodded enthusiastically, patted Alex's arm, handed him the keys while wishing him a *buona giornata* and patted his arm again for good measure.

"When you go from our canal into the lagoon the gas station is to your left," Patti told Alex as they walked up the concrete steps to the road.

"Cool." Alex folded the map and navigation guide Giovanni gave him.

"Alex, what I told you about last night. Papa and nonna Lu do not know Vincenzo's wife is still in the picture. Could you keep that between us for now?"

"Buongiorno!" a woman called as they entered the house.

"Ciao, Paola!" Patti replied. "Giovanni's wife," Patti explained as the vacuum cleaner started up in the living room. "They work at the hotel around the corner. They have lived in our basement for over twenty years. Instead of paying rent, Giovanni cares for the grounds and Paolo does our housekeeping." Concern crossed Patti's face. "When nonna Lu is no longer alive, I suppose we shall have to sell the house."

"You wouldn't want to keep it?"

Patti picked up her purse. "My ambition, when young, was not being forced to live in Venice as guardian of the Ca' dei Venti. That role fell to me when Papa left."

"Don't you enjoy your work?"

Patti grimaced. "The Ca' dei Venti is over five hundred years old. Every year the bills for repair, renewals, security, staff, cooling in summer, heating in winter, maintenance and restoration of the paintings, insurance, safety, all increase. And when there is *acqua alta* we must move everything from the low levels, and then put everything back and repair the damage when the waters recede. Admission prices cover only a fraction of such costs. Every day is an endless struggle for grants, funding, donations and sponsors. And I have spent seven years of my life doing something I have no desire to do in the name of family duty."

"How'd you see your future then?"

"I would like the simpler life. If nonna Lu left me everything, I would sell it all. Take just enough for my needs and give the rest to charity. Set up a foundation for young artists perhaps." Patti stopped talking when the vacuum cleaner switched off. They heard Rick speak with Paola, then the vacuum started up again. "Don't tell Papa about this either. I do not want him to feel guilty."

Alex had to laugh, now bearing the weight of Patti's family secrets on his shoulders too.

"Buongiorno, my darling girl." Rick bounded into the kitchen, Bippy and Boppy at his heels. He stopped to admire Patti. "You look very smart."

"I do? Is only an old black work dress."

"Well, you look nice. Very *comme il faut*." Rick rinsed the dogs' bowls while they stared up expectantly.

"*Va bene. Andiamo.*" Patti put on a pair of oversized sunglasses. "Enjoy your day on the water."

"Want me to give you a ride to work?" Alex asked.

"I take the vaporetto. A Force eight gale cannot compare with angry gondoliers furious with the Americano in a motorboat who got in their way."

Rick wished Patti goodbye. "Old work dress, my ass," he said, putting down the dogs' food. "Last year's Ferragamo. With Bulgari earrings and Blahnik sandals. Not to mention the Hermès bag. The way she talks anyone would think she dresses from a thrift shop."

Alex mused on interpretations of 'the simple life' as he went to check the weather and tides on the Mac in the study.

"What's this about a day on the water?" Rick brought his coffee in and peered over Alex's shoulder.

"'I must go down to the seas again, for the call of the running tide is a wild call and a clear call that may not be denied.'" Alex grinned. "'And all I ask is a tall ship and a star to steer her by.'"

✷ ✷ ✷

"A tall ship and a star?" Rick asked sarcastically as Alex chugged the boat to the filling station. "This crate's more like a bathtub with a sewing machine motor on the back."

"Shh. You'll hurt Esmerelda's feelings. Apparently, you need a license to drive anything over forty horsepower. And as I don't relish rowing you around the lagoon this is the best I can offer." Alex slung the rope around a red topped pole. He dropped a couple of fenders and reversed the boat in close, being careful not to trap his fingers as the line tightened. He hitched her up securely and squinted at the pumps. "Is there an attendant?"

"Not anymore, it's all self-serve these days."

"Hop out and pass down the nozzle then."

Rick climbed onto the filling station's lower platform.

"Pump on your left. Senza pb!" Alex called as he killed the motor. Fishing in the cockpit for a rag, he found one and clambered out. Creakily kneeling, he removed the fuel cap.

Rick went up the steps to street level, unhooked the gas nozzle and handed it down. "Al! Could you handle one of those?"

Alex turned his head. The white mountain of an MSC cruise liner was passing, a tug guiding it through the deepest part of the lagoon to dock in Venice. Its turbines rumbled the fragile waters. Inserting the nozzle, Alex pumped the gas. "Not my style. Computers sail those ships, not sailors." Being careful he didn't overfill and drip fuel, not only dangerous but bad for marine life, Alex rocked the boat. Leaning his ear to the tank, he gave one last squeeze. Hearing he was at the right level, he shut off the fuel.

"Guess I get to go pay now?" Rick took the nozzle.

"First mate's duty. Got cash?"

"Yeah." Rick hung up the nozzle and crossed the road to the kiosk beside the gas pumps for land vehicles.

Alex wiped the boat's side, replaced the fuel cap and clambered back on board. The boat was an older model, which was ideal as he was familiar with classic dial displays rather than the digital ones on new high-tech boats.

"All done." Rick skipped down the steps and gripped Alex's wrist to get on board.

"Full attention for the safety drill." Going into captain mode, Alex ran through the rudiments of the controls in case he became incapacitated, pointed out the fire extinguisher, life buoy and reminded Rick to hang on to the boat with one hand when moving around.

"Aye, aye, captain. Now for my safety drill." He dug in the bag on the rear seat. "Hold out your hands." Removing Alex's sunglasses, Rick squirted sunblock in his palms. "Don't get it in your eyes," he commanded as Alex rubbed it on his nose and forehead.

"Gee, you're a swell mom."

"And don't let the sun catch the back of your neck." Rick flipped up Alex's blue and white striped polo shirt's collar.

"That's why the boat drivers do that! I figured it was a fashion statement," said Alex facetiously. As Rick put the sunglasses back on his face and rubbed a stray blob of sunblock in his cheek, Alex became aware of two older men by the pumps staring down at them. The big one muttered an aside to his pal, a ferret faced runt, who sniggered in response. "I thought we'd head up to Torcello." Alex pulled away from Rick. "Sound good?"

"Cool."

Conscious of the two men watching him, Alex fumbled untying the mooring line. He heard them laugh. "Bring in the fenders, babe." Checking over his shoulder for oncoming water traffic, Alex started the motor. Pulling out and swinging around, he glanced up. The big guy casually spat on the floor in their direction. The ferret faced one muttered something audible over their motor. "Sweet of your old boyfriends to drop by."

Rick glanced behind him as the boat picked up speed. "Yeah, a real pair of cuties. One of them rides around on a beat-up motorbike like king of the hill. The other's a minor official on the beach patrol."

"What was that he said?"

Rick put on his sunglasses and swept his hair off his face. "*Frocio*. Nasty slang for queers, pansies, you get the drift."

Patti was correct about the storm clearing the air. Apart from a scattering of fluffy white clouds, the sky was a perfect azure. Helming a boat again, even one as modest as Esmerelda, brought deep joy to Alex's heart. Concentrating on unfamiliar waters was a good distraction from that unpleasant experience at the filling station. Funny, no matter how successful or accomplished you may feel, an incident like that slapped you right back down to earth to make you feel like nothing. And, on a dark street, encounters with nasty bigots like that could lead to physical violence rather than just name calling.

Alex kept one hand on the wheel and rested the other on the throttle as he guided the boat up the Lido's inner coastline. The car ferry had just pulled into the terminal, its engines kicking up spiral currents. Having negotiated that tricky backwash, Alex carried on until the top of the island tapered away. He opened the throttle and trimmed up. The bow rose, the steering lightened and Esmerelda skimmed over the vast expanse of open water.

Leaning forward, Rick pointed out the industrial landmass in the middle of the San Nicolo inlet to their right. "They built that island for the MOSE flood defenses," he yelled above the wind. "The plan is to raise barriers that block off the inlets to stop tidal surges into the lagoon. The project's billions over budget and years behind schedule! And no-one even knows if it will work if it's ever finished!"

Alex suddenly didn't feel so bad about the money he'd put into his new metal sculptures.

A pang of envy hit Alex as they passed three stately white 22-foot yachts motoring out to the Adriatic. Approaching Treporti, the northern top of the mainland, bricole with 20 kph signs began appearing and water traffic increased. Other vessels were buzzing all around. Family boats, delivery boats, garbage boats, ambulance boats, boats of every shape and kind. There were navigational rules, but Alex suspected they were rather fluid in these parts. And he doubted any craft, including his own, stuck to the 20 kph speed limit unless they'd broken down and were being towed. Having burned off the last stray clouds, the midday sun was beating down with a vengeance.

"If I were a steak I'd be overdone by now," said Rick.

"Put up the bimini. Know how?"

"I'll figure it." Rick clambered to the stern.

Alex checked Rick was following the 'one hand for you and one for the boat' rule. He was proud to see his boy taking due care. Anchoring the rods into the docks in the stern, Rick raised the canopy then clipped its front to the cockpit shield. "Nice work. Anyone would have you marked as an old salt," he said as Rick sat back down beside him in the shade.

"Doing my best. I hear if anyone on this ship steps out of line the captain whips down their pants to give them a good spanking."

"And sometimes the captain does that just for fun," said Alex with a sly laugh.

Signs of habitation increased on the mainland to their right and large islands on their left. The waterways and inlets were dotted with people fishing from small vessels at anchor. On portside, Alex spotted a leaning bell tower above the rooftops. "Is that Burano we're coming to?"

"Yeah. Let's stop. You should see its colored houses. They're real pretty."

Slowing, Alex glanced down the first canal they passed. Its bridges were low and the boats moored beneath them were variations on flat-bottomed skiffs. The last thing he wanted was to go down one of those and get Esmerelda stuck under a bridge. "Look for someplace we can dock on the perimeter." He puttered on for a while, then Rick pointed to a deck with tables and umbrellas which had slips out front. Alex brought the boat around. Slinging his rope around a post, he restrained the boat and let Rick hop ashore to check they were okay to stop.

Moments later, Rick popped out of the café to give him the thumbs up.

Rick was sitting at a table on the deck by the time he'd moored and gone up to join him. Putting on his glasses to study the marine charts, Alex downed a couple of lemon sodas while Rick imbibed his first spritz of the day. The café's proprietress said they could leave the boat, so, after settling the check and making a bathroom pit-stop, they strolled around the island.

Freshly washed sheets baking in the midday sun scented the air. Everywhere Alex looked heavily laden washing lines were hung outside the colored houses or strung across narrow streets. Some clothes lines appeared to have every garment in the house neatly pegged out on them. The laundry outside one peppermint house with a pink and white striped awning amused them, the threadbare sheets were practically translucent.

"You know," said Rick, "the word for laundry, *bucato*, comes from when the washboard's ridges used to wear out the fabric. It literally means holes."

This fact charmed Alex as he studied the canal's rippling reflections of multi-colored *bucato* on the washing lines flapping in the wind. It resonated with his layered works. The little island's purple, fuchsia, yellow, orange, turquoise and countless other hues of home were a visual delight.

"The fishermen used to paint their houses a different color to guide themselves home late at night or in a fog," Rick explained on their way back to the mooring as they passed lace shops and smallholdings growing produce. "I believe people still have to apply to the government to check they don't have the same color as someone else's house."

Untying the boat ready to get underway, Alex saw the body of water across to Torcello was busy. "Stow the bimini. I need to keep my eyes peeled getting over there."

It was a wise move.

A double-decker water bus, limousine taxis, small private boats, and even a group of kayakers were jockeying for position around the inlet to Torcello's central canal. Alex stood at the helm, resting one arm on the windshield as the boat swayed in the wash of the water bus mooring at the outer dock. Alex had no-one behind him, so he let the water taxis and another private boat go on ahead. Then he allowed the kayakers to pass before gently following them in.

Torcello's central canal, edged on either side in red brick, ran between overgrown fields. Graceful trees with feathery pink leaves and dark bracken bushes rose up on their right. A gaggle of tourists, rushing to catch the ferry which had just docked, scuttled down the pedestrian footpath on their left. Alex put-put-putted through the island, amazed at how truly deserted it was. A square bell tower loomed in the distance. Another canal joined from their right and a couple of seemingly private houses sprung up on their left. Alex looked questioningly at Rick, wondering if he'd taken a wrong turn as the island was *so* deserted.

"Keep going," said Rick.

Alex moved into the center of the canal to pass beneath the strange bridge coming up. Covered in scaffolding while being restored, the bridge had no side rails or balusters. "Is it meant to be that way?"

"Yeah. The Ponte del Diavolo. Many ancient bridges didn't have sides. Having gotten through the Black Death I guess falling off a bridge didn't seem so big of a deal."

A taverna and a couple of bed-and-breakfast establishments appeared behind the pathway on their left. Window boxes with scarlet geraniums and cascading fuchsia florets lent charm to their run-down appearance.

"You can stop anywhere now," said Rick.

Moored to the single poles lining the canal's left bank, small boats bobbed in Esmerelda's wash. The Riva limousines were dropping their passengers on the sharp bend in the canal outside a yellow taverna with a green awning. Seeing a space, Alex slowed and brought the boat in. He tied off, stern and aft, leaving enough movement for the tide. Raising the outboard, he checked the prop for leaves. It was clean. Rick then helped him off the boat and steadied him up the steps onto the pathway. They hastily stepped aside to prevent getting mown down by an officious female guide in a red jacket. She strode determinedly along the footpath carrying a raised white flag, her jittery tour group struggling to match her pace.

Alex and Rick wandered over the bridge crossing the canal into a gravel covered square lined with cypress trees. The ancient churches and bell tower were up ahead.

"Torcello. The name is formed by our Italian words for 'Tower' and 'Sky'!" the red jacketed tour guide announced to her group as Alex and Rick caught up with them. "After the fall of the Roman empire, this was the first island in the lagoon to be settled by peoples fleeing the barbarian invasion of the mainland."

"Is this it?" asked Alex surveying the ruins.

"What did you expect? Caesar's Palace?"

Not a fan of organized religion, Alex allowed Rick to pay the admission fee at a kiosk.

"Torcello was once the commercial capital of Venice but over time the island turned to swamp. Malaria, plagues and other epidemics killed off much of the population. The island's buildings were dismantled and recycled to build a new city in a more favorable part of the lagoon ..." The tour guide's voice faded out as she led her group towards the basilica.

Alex trailed behind Rick, finding interest in the medieval structures' architectural and decorative elements rather than their sacred heritage.

"That's Venice. A city built on mud," Rick said as they entered the Church of Santa Fosca's arched portico.

The coolness inside the church came as a welcome relief from the midday heat. A woman with a black shawl over her bowed head sat in the pews before the altar and wooden crucifix.

Rick read the plaque by the entrance out loud, "The church was dedicated to house the relics of the virgin martyr

Santa Fosca of Ravenna, who along with her nurse, Santa Maura, were killed in two hundred and fifty A.D. for refusing to renounce their faith under the persecution of Roman Emperor Decius." On their way out, he slipped some cash in the collection box.

They caught up with the tour group inside the cathedral of the Santa Maria Assunta.

"The lowest level in this depiction of The Last Judgement shows a number of scenes ..." The guide was pointing out details in the giant mosaic with her white flag. A tourist raised her camera to take a photo. A hatchet-faced female security guard stepped forward and loudly rapped the 'No Photography' sign. "Please, no photos!" The tour guide gave an apologetic nod to the guard then went back to the mosaic. "In the center, we see the Virgin Mary, Archangel Michael and the Devil weighing souls. On their left are the Blessed in Paradise, to their right are the damned souls suffering the torments of Hell ..."

Alex and Rick moved to the apse. A huge, but simple, rendering of the Virgin Mary holding the Christ Child stared down from the shimmering gold mosaic dome with depictions of the twelve apostles arranged below.

"This cathedral's ancient origins date back to the seventh century ..." Walking past them, the tour guide continued her commentary.

"Wanna go up the bell tower?" Rick asked Alex.

"Is there an elevator?"

"Sure, they installed one midway through the twelfth century. Of course, the donkey that powers it may be on lunch."

"You're a joker. Show your captain some respect."

"Or else?"

"You know the answer." Alex subtly patted Rick's butt. "Enough history, I'm hungry."

Back outside, they trailed across the dusty square to the yellow taverna with Locando Cipriani written on its green awning. Since they had not made a *prenotazione*, the patron regretfully shook his head. If the signori could wait one hour, though, he would find them a table. Hearing boisterous laughter and raucous voices from an Australian tour group out back, they decided to find someplace more subdued with a table right now.

Crossing the bridge, they followed an irregular stone path around the canal's bend. It led to an old farmhouse which had been converted into a ristorante. The interior dining room's dark beams and checkerboard floor would be cozy in winter but felt claustrophobic on a summer's day. Thankfully, the place had a delightful terrace in the rear. Surrounded by cultivated flower gardens warmed by rose and jasmine fragrances, Alex and Rick were seated at the single table under a vine covered pergola. A formal and profoundly serious Italian waiter took their order.

"You put some cash in the collection box back there," said Alex to Rick. "That the Catholic coming out in you?"

"From experience of looking after the Ca' dei Venti, I know how much old buildings cost to maintain."

"But these are churches. Surely the Vatican could sell a few trinkets on eBay to help out?"

Rick gave a sardonic laugh. "You'd think."

The waiter served their drinks. Alex had another lemon soda while Rick had a mezzo carafe of prosecco.

"That tour guide was very instructive. So which side of the mosaic are you on? Blessed in the garden or torments of Hell," asked Alex pouring his soda.

"Torments of Hell, for sure." Rick filled his glass with prosecco. "To get my marriage annulled I had to stand before the Vatican Board and declare myself a deceptive raging homo. They share information like that with the Big Guy."

"Isn't annulment just the Catholic version of divorce?"

"Divorce is a legal end to marriage. Annulment means the union wasn't genuine or fulfilled, essentially it means the marriage never took place at all."

"Does that make Patti …?"

"Illegitimate? The religious machinery is complicated and full of double talk. So even though technically we weren't married when she was born, Patti's spiritual standing is okay with the church. She can still go to the good place."

"And Giuliana?"

"There's room in the garden for Giuliana too."

"I was always under the impression you two separated right after Patti was born."

"We did. But pressure was exerted to glue us back together. We managed to maintain the illusion until Patti turned fifteen. That's when I got a new personal assistant, Francesco, and Giuliana fell in love with the notary dealing with the summer house she'd bought on Lake Garda. Giuliana wanted to get married again, in church. That's when her father got dragged into things. He was still clinging to the hope she'd give him a grandson. At her age that really would've been a miraculous conception. Anyway, the only way she could move on without blame was for me to take the fall. If I hadn't thrown myself on the sword I'd be part of Padua's autostrada extension by now. No-one goes against Aldo Pessina."

"So you, er, never consummated the marriage?"

"Giuliana's a lovely woman but …" Rick shuddered. "Patti's a miracle of medical science."

"You never told me all of this. Well, not in so much detail."

"Giuliana and I made a deal to keep our parents happy. Giuliana wasn't beautiful. Aldo feared she'd become an old maid. He got a large investment for his failing construction company from momma, and momma got an end to gossip about my private life and an heir. The annulment was the most humiliating experience of my life. Not as public as having my name splashed all over the scandal sheets. 'Was Discovery of Rick Stradman's Sordid Lifestyle to Blame for Father's Death?' Not as humiliating as that but definitely a close second."

The conversation assumed a lighter tone as they ate. Rick had John Dory with salad and Alex the gnocchi with chicken ragu.

Lunch finished, check settled, Alex was keen to explore some more. When they got back to the boat, Alex put his hands on his hips and laughed. The tide had dropped. Esmerelda now sat two and a half feet below the canal's edge. In his youth, Alex would have hopped down with no issue. As it was, he needed to creakily lower himself on the bankside then dangle his legs over while Rick steadied him onto the boat. "Jeez, what a cronk. If the guys from the old days could see me now." Alex chortled as he dusted off his butt and brought in the fenders.

Instead of retracing his route down the canal, Alex took the sharp left ahead which made it look like a dead end. He brought the boat out on the other side of Torcello. They'd only motored a short way when he sensed from the water's surface movement and disappearance of the bricole that the lagoon rapidly turned to mud. This area may be navigable in a flat-bottomed boat but Esmerelda needed to turn around. Alex raised his sunglasses to squint at an empty island on the horizon, like a single green brushstroke dividing the sea and sky.

This side of the island was far quieter than the other, with herons and egrets lazing in the reed-beds. "I should've used the bathroom back there. Pit-stop." Going as far up a shady creek as he dared without running aground, Alex found a tree to sling his rope around. The bank dropped away sharply enough for him to scramble ashore. Reeds covered the uneven ground. Despite a few stumbles, he found a spot in the bushes to pee. Getting back to the boat, he saw Rick had raised the bimini, undone his shirt and was lounging on the grassy bank. Alex creakily got down beside him, flopped on his back and let his eyes be filled with blue. "This is my church. The sky, the water, the trees, the soil." He reached for Rick's hand. "You."

They both lay staring up at the sky.

"I should've told you last night why Luisa called me to her room," said Alex. "She asked me if she was dying."

"What did you tell her?"

"The truth. Sorry if I did the wrong thing."

Rick sighed. "I suppose it's only right she know. When we first met I told you my mother was dead, I was so angry with her all the time back then. But now she really is dying I'm afraid of losing her. I know she's difficult, and God knows we've had some terrible spats, but she's my mother. And I love her."

Alex kept his eyes fixed on the sky. "And since I'm in my church, the church of nature, I've another confession. The night before I came here something happened between Ty and me."

"Oh."

"It was a hot night. Ty suggested we take a swim. He stripped off and jumped in, buck naked. Anyway, I went in to get my trunks and he, well, he got out of the pool, followed me into the bedroom and …"

"And?"

"I'd just picked up your message saying Luisa wanted you to stay here and you were going to. I felt down about Bella and Manuela, and you not coming back home. He hugged me, to comfort me, and then, in a moment of weakness, we kissed."

"You kissed?"

"You know how Ty is, he's a very tactile guy. But I stopped it right there, at one kiss. He seemed so sad, and kind of lost. I didn't want him to feel rejected, so I gave him some PJ pants, put some on as well and let him spend the night. Ty looks like a man but he's a boy at heart. I really do love you, but that night part of me was still unsure of how you felt about me. And that's why I had to come here like I did, in secret, with no warning. I needed to know how you'd look at me with no preparation, no calculation. Like we were meeting for the first time. And when I stood at your gates, and your eyes fell on me and you ran to me, that's when I knew you love me. Truly, honestly love me."

"Why were you unsure about how I felt?"

"When things go wrong you run away, you shut off your emotions and disappear inside yourself. Intimacy isn't just about sex, it's about sharing the shames and doubts and hurts and humiliations along with the awards and triumphs and successes. I haven't been entirely honest with you or myself. I found it so hard to let Danielle go because I know she loved me more than I loved her. I just hope I didn't make her unhappy."

"Danielle was a strong woman with a mind of her own. I knew her. Remember she was my friend before yours. If Danielle weren't happy she wouldn't have stayed with you. And when she got sick were you ever not there for her? Did you ever let her be alone or frightened?"

Alex shook his head and blinked water from his eyes.

"Danielle!" Rick called into the blue sky. "Thank you for looking after Alex for all those years when I couldn't! I love you! We love you."

A gust of wind rustled the linden trees.

"See, Danielle's cool," said Rick.

"I wish I could believe that."

"Why can't you?"

"Because if there is God and spirit and all that, why's there so much unhappiness and cruelty and inequality and pain in the world? How can I believe in a force that lets babies die and planes crash, and the good in life be punished and the evil get rich?"

"If all we ever saw was blue sky and beauty we wouldn't even notice them." Rolling on his side, Rick snapped off a reed and traced its tip down Alex's cheek.

Alex laughed as Rick tickled his neck with the reed. Rolling onto his side, he got up on his elbow. "I have the new show coming up. I need to get to back to LA. I want you with me."

"I'm not sure I can leave momma …"

"We'll come back in fall. And we'll stay as long as you need so you can be with Luisa at the end."

"We?" Rick dropped the reed. "But you hate Venice, hate Italy, hate Europe! You're willing to come back?"

"When you began seeing Dr. Susskind you told me you didn't know where you belong. Well, I do. You belong with me. And I belong with you. The location's irrelevant." Alex sat up and scooped a handful of creek water. He let it dribble through his fingers. "Maybe I could get my boat license and buy a speedboat. A proper one." Alex waved apologetically towards the little blue boat bobbing beside the bank. "Sorry, Esmerelda. Who knows, I may even speak decent Italian with a little practice."

"Just talk loud and fast and wave your arms around and you'll fit in like a local."

"You'll come home with me to LA then?"

"Name the day. I'm not looking forward to breaking this to momma, though. We've found a new understanding over the last few days."

"Why not let me tell her, then?" Alex leaned on his knee to stand then helped Rick up. "She and I seem to have found a new understanding over the last few days too."

Having taken another pee in the bushes, Alex untied Esmerelda and motored around the island's eastern shore. Then he took a westerly route through the other islands. As soon as they'd passed through Mazzorbo the whole world became sky and water. Following the bricole, Alex assumed his place in the stream of taxis, barges and vaporetti headed towards Venice.

Cutting across the lagoon and turning into the Lido canal, the one they'd only left a few hours ago, Alex felt like he'd traveled to another world and back. Lightness filled his heart. Chatting with Rick as they secured Esmerelda, he hadn't a care in the world. They climbed the steps from the canal and crossed the road to the house.

Bippy and Boppy were bouncing up and down and barking crazily at the gate. They welcomed Rick and Alex as if they'd been gone for years.

"Patti must have come home early." Seeing the front door was ajar, Rick pushed it open.

A sense of encroaching doom gripped Alex. Boxes and packing cartons were strewn around the hallway, their brown tape ripped open, clothes and jewelry tumbling from them.

"Patti! You home?" Rick yelled nervously.

Alex guessed Rick was thinking the same thing he was. They'd been robbed.

"Up here!" Patti called back. "Papa, *aiuti mi*!"

"Shit!" Rick raced upstairs.

Alex followed, his blood pressure ratcheting up with every step. On the second-floor landing, the gilt framed double doors to Luisa's rooms were flung open. Going in after Rick, Alex found an extremely agitated Patti amongst more hastily opened packing boxes. She was showing Rick a large straw hat with one hand and a white hat with a massively wide brim with her other.

They were having one of their quickfire Italian conversations, the type which Alex could never tell was about something of world importance or a discussion of where to eat. "Turn on the subtitles! American here struggling to follow the plot."

"It's momma."

"Oh, no …" Alex prepared to receive the news Luisa had died.

Rick tapped the white hat with the big brim. "That's the one. She bought it on the via Condotti because it looked like the one Sophia Loren wore in *Arabesque*. Oh, God! My hair needs cutting! And they really have to do this on Saturday?"

Patti nodded.

"Rick?" asked Alex, unable to work out what was going on.

"Come downstairs. I'll fix us a drink."

"You said I shouldn't drink."

"Believe me," said Rick, "you'll need one when I pass on this piece of news. It's a humdinger!"

NEOREALISM

Rick downed a large glass of soave while quickly explaining the reason behind the panicked ransacking of Luisa's boxes. He refilled his drink and raced back upstairs to Patti.

Processing this new information, Alex carried his beer out to the verandah, amazed at how his rash promise of publicity to lure Luisa into going ahead with the recording had initiated this unexpected chain of events.

The Ca' dei Venti's press release about Luisa's 'professional' appearance had gone out to their regular mailing list. This included all the mainstream newspapers, magazines and broadcast media as well as the small fry. There'd been no expectation of interest from the big players. It came as a total surprise when the arts desk of the *Corriere Della Sera*, one of Italy's oldest daily papers, had got back to them this morning. The paper was preparing a feature series on the upcoming 65th Venice Film Festival. The release's angle on Luisa's attendance of the 1946 edition's opening ceremony, her small role in Rossellini's *Paisà*, which was awarded the Festival's ANICA cup that year, and her family residence being on the Lido had piqued their arts editor's interest.

While he and Rick had been enjoying a reflective day on the lagoon, Patti's day had been consumed by back and forth conversations with the arts editor, who had back and forth conversations with Luisa, who then had more back and forth phone calls with their cinema correspondent and chief critic Ettore Zorzi, who, by the time Rick and Alex arrived home, had escalated the minor story into a major feature with photos by Elio Toscani.

Not having been party to the conversations, Patti had no idea how Luisa had spun a puff piece about her presence at the 1946 Film Festival into a glossy romp about three-generations of her family's involvement in the Venice art world. But no matter how, Luisa had made Rick and Patti integral to the article. Chiara Bonelli, the newspaper's photo editor, deemed the Lido di Venezia's elegantly faded Grand Hotel des Bains to be the ideal backdrop. Toscani's photo setup was to be on the hotel's private beach, the location that Aschenbach, played by Dirk Bogarde in the movie, had met his pathetic and lonely end in Visconti's *Death in Venice*. Zorzi's spin was to have Luisa D'Onofrio, alive and kicking, surrounded by her loving family on the exact same beach with the upbeat strapline 'Life in Venice!'

The motivation behind Patti's frantic search for extravagant hats and jewelry was to disguise any visible deficiency in Luisa's health. Hearing more boxes being ripped open upstairs, an uneasy feeling crept over Alex. Like Luisa, he too was aware of Rick's weakness for wealth and power. Fame also featured on that list. He wondered if Luisa's insistence on Rick's inclusion in the article was to prevent him from immediately leaving for the USA once he knew she was the one who'd leaked his homosexuality to the press in '74. Wanting to make it abundantly clear Rick's imminent return to LA was non-negotiable, Alex put down his beer. Patti and Rick were so engrossed in their quest to fill Luisa's accessory list he wouldn't be missed for a while.

Gearing up for a fight, Alex trotted up to the Instituto Santa Maria. The Italian words he'd been dredging up to persuade Sister Marta to grant him access were unnecessary. Emilia was on the reception desk and waved him up with a smile. Saving his knees, he used the rickety elevator. The TV could be heard through Luisa's partially open door. He knocked. "Luisa?"

"Who is there?"

"Alex."

After a long moment she said, "Come."

The brightness of Luisa's room startled him. The shutters were flung open, the drapes pulled back. The large flatscreen TV had been installed and a grainy Italian movie was playing on it. Luisa sat propped up on her bed, rummaging through a box of photos. A heady scent drew his attention to the spectacular array of pink lilies in an equally spectacular Venetian glass vase.

Peering over her glasses, Luisa saw him admiring the flowers. "They arrived this morning with a note from Sid's girl."

"I told you, Tiffany's a good kid."

"If you speak with her, please let her know they were gratefully received."

"I'll tell her when I get back to LA next week. I'm taking Rick with me."

"Next week? Were no sooner flights available? I expected Ricardo would wish to be free of me as soon as you had told him what I'd done."

Picking up the remote, Alex turned down the TV sound. "I haven't told him."

"Why not? Do you want money to keep my secret?"

"A woman who loves her son as much as you love Rick wouldn't be capable of doing what you claim to have done. Another woman leaked that story. A different woman. It's time we left that woman behind and moved on. Rick and I have things to do in LA, but we'll come back in fall. Bribes, coercion and manipulation aren't necessary to keep him with you. He loves you. He *wants* to be with you. If you want Rick to know what you told me, you'll have to tell him yourself. I'd rather you be a thorn in my side for however long we have left than hurt him like that."

Luisa tapped the arm of her glasses to her lips then pulled a photo from the box. She held it out to him.

Coming to the bed, Alex took the photo.

"Bergamo. Nineteen thirty-five. A noble family on their summer estate."

Expecting to see top hats, long gowns, and stiff poses, Alex was surprised to find a casual snapshot taken beside a lake.

The balding man in the center wore an open necked shirt with cravat, the blond woman to his left, a belted floral dress. The woman's arm was linked with a laughing young girl's. The man's arm held a youth possessed of intense eyes and chiseled features.

"My father, Barone Ludovico di Durazzo, my mamma Maria and my brother Vittorio. As a girl, mine was a carefree life. I was pampered, indulged and allowed to playact on stage … with the provision I use my mother's family name for my work. Vittorio bore the weight of carrying the Durazzo name into the future. But war held a different plan for him. A Nazi bullet ended Vittorio's life in nineteen forty-three." Luisa wagged a bony finger at Alex. "No-one should judge. Every day was a battle to survive, for the rich and the poor. Allegiances changed. Heroes became traitors overnight and vice versa. Deals were brokered. Compromises made. And so the war comes to an end. The once carefree girl now carries the burden of a great many cares through a broken country. She gets caught up in a new war. A war between duty to her family and her dreams." Luisa picked out another photograph and passed it to Alex. "Rome. December nineteen forty-six. American producer searching Italy for a new star discovers local actress."

In this photograph Alex saw Sid, with jet-black hair and a double-breasted pinstripe suit, peering through his viewfinder at a doe-eyed Luisa.

"Cinecittà Studios had been commandeered to house refugees. Poles, Jews, Russians, Roma gypsies, all those who had escaped the death camps, lost their homes, their families, their dignity. Those stateless people, all living amongst the movie sets, backdrops and props. The Americans had to use a bombed-out warehouse to make their screen tests. The producer chooses one girl from hundreds and takes her to Hollywood to become his star." Delving in the box, Luisa proffered another photograph.

Alex accepted it.

"Los Angeles. Nineteen forty-nine. The actress's debut movie has been released. American critics label her too cold, too wooden. Too *foreign*. The studio denounces her as box office poison. Her contract is cancelled. She is cancelled. The producer, now her husband, tires of her and searches for a new star. The woman in the photograph realizes she too is a stranger in a strange land, another displaced person living amongst backdrops and props while her parents are dying in another country. But there is one thing she may salvage from the ruins, a son to take home to Italy. The precious soul she felt take root one dawn on a soundstage. She has not totally failed. Her father may die fulfilled. His bloodline will continue."

Without his glasses, Alex needed to stretch his arm and tilt his head back to see clearly. This photo revealed a more mature Luisa, her eyes haunted by disappointment and bitterness. She was cradling a blond-haired baby. Witnessing her past and learning her story, Alex began to comprehend the complex motivations behind Luisa's actions. He mourned the loss of that carefree young girl who once laughed beside a lake. He returned the photo.

"In my ambition and anger and fear, I forgot to be gentle with the child in this picture." Luisa pushed the photograph back at him. "He is in your care now."

"I'll do my best, Luisa. Look, despite what's happened between us in the past, I hope we can …" Realizing the TV screen had captured her attention, Alex stopped speaking.

"It is me." Luisa clasped a hand to her mouth. "Sound, sound. Alex, quickly!"

Alex picked up the remote and raised the volume.

The screen's bottom right corner had the Tele Venezia logo. The old movie had finished and local news was on. The video footage of Luisa making her entrance to the recording session played on-screen. Alex couldn't follow the language but stood beside the bed to watch with Luisa. The news item cut from the reporter's interview with her outside the dayroom to a clip from a faded black-and-white Italian movie. It took him a moment to recognize one of the girls dancing around the hangdog-faced comic actor wearing a crown was a young Luisa.

"*Senza una Donna*! This is mine!" Luisa was beaming, so delighted to see the movie clip she patted his arm.

The sonorous clang of Sister Anastasia beating the dinner gong reverberated through the institute.

Alex slipped the photograph in his pocket, walked to the door and said goodbye.

Luisa flapped her hand in his direction without looking, unable to take her eyes from the TV screen, lost in the happiness of a moving image of herself from the past.

* * *

Alex restrained the dogs, two bundles of primped and fluffed white fur styled by Yelena at the grooming parlor earlier this morning, in the suite's bedroom. There was enough mayhem going on in the adjoining living room without them joining in.

The Grand Hotel des Bains' sea view rooms had the downside of catching the morning sun's full force. The shutters to the ones comprising this top floor suite, with honey parquet floors, Murano glass chandeliers and swagged drapes, had been closed and the elderly A/C turned up full prior to their arrival. Within half-an-hour of the three-person styling team, along with racks of clothes, blow dryers and makeup brushes, Ettore Zorzi - the *Corriere Della Sera*'s arts & culture correspondent - Rick, Patti, Luisa, Luisa's private nurse, Alex himself and Bippy and Boppy being packed into the suite, however, the ancient cooling system had given up the ghost and stopped even trying. When the temperature hit twenty-eight degrees, they put the air con out of its misery and flung open the windows.

The Adriatic breeze wasn't having much success in cooling things down either. The dogs' pink tongues were lolling from their mouths. Alex spotted a fancy porcelain bowl on the credenza. Wiping it out, he poured some of his mineral water in it and set it on the floor.

Rick darted in from the adjoining room. "Is this a good look?" Fastening the buttons of a flashy lime, ivory and black silk shirt, he slipped on a pair of sunglasses with gold Medusa studs.

"For a Miami drug lord, it's a winner. Could the makeup girl give you a gold tooth as well?"

"Hmm. Maybe it is a little over the top," Rick conceded while unbuttoning the shirt as he ducked back to the other room.

Alex swigged from the mineral water bottle and rubbed his eyes. From relaxing in the peace and quiet of a deserted island only two days ago, things had snowballed into the three-ring circus which always accompanied even the simplest of events associated with Rick's family. His mineral water bottle was empty and Bippy and Boppy's tongues were still hanging out. Wondering how much longer they were going to take getting ready for the photoshoot, Alex tied the dogs' leashes around the leg of an art nouveau chiffonier and ventured into the suite's living-room.

Patti sat in the makeup chair having cake-eyeliner applied. Her hair had been braided into a coil and styled into a twisted up-do. Luisa was lying on a chaise by the open windows. Ettore, the journalist, sat beside her scribbling in his notebook as she spoke. The private nurse, in a starched white uniform, held a battery powered fan to Luisa's face to prevent her perfectly applied tan foundation from melting, while the hair stylist scraped Luisa's dyed caramel hair into a severe side part.

Alex waved at Rick.

"What?" Rick asked, distractedly slipping his tanned arms into an ice-blue shirt. His sandy hair had been blow-dried and a subtle sheen of foundation smoothed the fine lines on his face, making him look thirty years younger.

"I'm taking the dogs downstairs," said Alex. They needed to cool off and it would get him out of this madhouse.

"Alex, do I hear Alex?" Luisa broke away from Ettore and squinted gummily through her false eyelashes.

"Don't panic, Luisa. I was just going," Alex replied, expecting his presence was about to rile her up.

"What do you mean, going?" Luisa retorted. "Stay!"

"This shirt's better, isn't it?" Rick asked, rolling up the sleeves as he came to Alex.

"Yeah, you look terrific in that one, babe," Alex replied.

The fashion stylist, a tiny man dressed entirely in black topped off by a black beret and nose stud, clasped his hands together and bowed his head in thanks of the praise.

"Papa, Alex, you like?" Patti, now out of the makeup chair, twirled to show off her sleeveless candy pink trapeze dress while fixing a pair of black and white op-art danglers to her ears.

"Beautiful," gasped Rick. "Momma, look at Patti!"

"… the allies had commandeered the Palazzo del Cinema on Lido, so the films were screened in the Cinema San Marco …" Luisa spoke to Ettore as the hairstylist jabbed more pins in her hair, "… a little tight …" Luisa said as an aside to the hairdresser before going back to Ettore, "… of course, this was not tradition but …"

The dogs started yapping in the bedroom.

"The dogs are overheating," Alex said to Rick.

"*Dov'è il cappello?*" snapped the hairdresser.

"*Il cappello?*" the stylist vaguely looked around.

"I brought the hat!" Rick scuttled across the room.

"… remember, I was little more than a girl and to be working with Rossellini was an honor as well as a challenge …" Luisa went on to Ettore.

"*Qui, qui,*" Rick shoved the white hat with satellite dish brim at the hairstylist.

The dogs' yapping ratcheted up an octave.

"These earrings are too much." Patti checked herself in the mirror. "*Penso solo bianco*," she said to the stylist.

"… this was many years before Rossellini met Bergman and …" Luisa carried on to Ettore as the hairstylist experimented positioning the hat on her.

"Bebe, Bobo, *silenzio*!" Rick yelled into the other room.

"*Gli orecchini in oro* …" Luisa snaked her hand to the stylist while speaking to Ettore, "… Maria Michi was heartbreaking. *C*ara Maria. *Paisà* was raw. There were no working movie studios. Rossellini filmed on ruins with a hand-held camera. He used real soldiers. *Real* people. No glamor, no soft focus, a new realism in Italian cinema …"

Ettore scribbled furiously to keep up.

"Let me take the dogs …" Alex inched to the door.

"*Piace*?" The stylist offered Luisa a pair of gold button earrings.

"*Bene, bene*," Luisa said in response.

The suite's main door opened. A stressed woman peeped around. "*Scuse*. Ettore, Toscani's set up on the beach." Then she asked the stylist, "*Quanto tempo ci vorrà*?"

"*Dieci minuti. S*olo Alex *da fare adesso*," replied the stylist.

Hearing his name, Alex's ears pricked up. The stylist was sizing him up as Rick and Patti checked themselves in the mirror.

"Get everyone down to the beach," Chiara, the shoot's coordinator, firmly told the styling team.

The whining dogs sounded distressed.

"Chiara, *tesora*!" Luisa bellowed in a surprisingly powerful voice. "Take Bebe and Bobo downstairs. Give them water!"

This duty was obviously beneath Chiara but wanting to move things along she grudgingly took care of the dogs.

"… the past, art should *never* look to the past," Luisa intoned to Ettore. "Art is made in the present, and artists must constantly change with the times to remain relevant …"

"Signor, *per piacere*," the makeup artist beckoned Alex.

"I don't understand," muttered Alex.

"A little makeup to cover the sunburn on your nose is all," said the makeup artist guiding him to her chair.

The hairstylist rubbed some product between his palms then tousled Alex's hair. "*Bei capelli.*"

"Is good?" The stylist held up an ecru shirt.

"I still don't understand ..." Alex murmured as dark tan concealer got sponged on his nose and cheeks. Confused, he looked to Rick and Patti for enlightenment, but they simply looked at each other, equally baffled.

Luisa squinted across at the ecru shirt and said decisively, "*Forte. Marrone!*"

The stylist swept a bitter chocolate silk shirt off the rail.

"*Si, si,*" Luisa barked at the stylist, then went back to Ettore, "... the world shapes the artist. And artists shape the world by reflecting their vision of the world back to the viewer ..."

"Signor, you try?" The stylist proffered the shirt to Alex.

Alex looked to Rick, whose grimace in response said, 'just go with it.' So, still with no idea why he was involved, Alex unbuttoned his own shirt while the hairdresser twiddled curls on his forehead.

* * *

The tunnel beneath the busy road running from the hotel's basement opened directly onto the Hotel des Bains' private beach and buffet bar. The nurse had helped Luisa into a wheelchair to bring her down. Once the nurse had rolled Luisa past the bleach club's ritzy sun loungers and raffia topped cabanas, one of the red-vested lifeguards carried Luisa to the white canvas director's chair set up on the sand. Shielding her from the sun with a parasol, the nurse arranged pillows to keep Luisa comfortable ... also upright.

The photographer, Elio Toscani, was shooting from a low angle so he could have the Grand Hotel's castle-like façade rising behind Luisa. Down on the sand, Elio, clad in cargo shorts, desert boots and fatigue shirt, shouted directions to his team about positions for the light reflectors as he lined up the shot. The hairstylist carried the oversized white hat on set, then adjusted it on Luisa's head. He clipped the gold earrings to her ears. A mirror was brought for Luisa to approve her appearance.

Feeling like he'd slipped into a Fellini movie, Alex stood barefoot on the sand, his unfastened silk shirt billowing in the wind. Chiara carried Bippy and Boppy into shot and deposited them, rather gracelessly, onto Luisa's lap, clearly glad to be rid of dog-sitting duty. Rick and Patti sheltered from the sun in a cabana the styling team had commandeered.

Toscani shouted for everyone not required in shot to clear. Checking his viewfinder, he snapped at Chiara to remove some unattractive hotel guests on sun loungers from the frame. He allowed the two tanned young men in skimpy trunks and a taut girl in a crocheted bikini to remain. The hairstylist and nurse withdrew. Toscani issued directions in Italian. Luisa summoned the fiery light behind her eyes. Connecting with Toscani's camera, she smiled and posed like a pro.

"*Forza della natura.*"

Alex glanced at his side to find Ettore Zorzi had joined him. "Sorry, my Italian's a little rusty."

"That woman, she is a force of nature." Ettore gave Luisa an admiring nod. "Such passion in her public life." Ettore chuckled lasciviously and nudged Alex's elbow. "Also in her private life ..."

The reason Luisa's story had so appealed to Ettore dawned on Alex.

"I had not heard her name for years. I feared she may be dead. But no, look at her. Luisa D'Onofrio, as dazzling as ever!"

Alex had to agree. With her immaculately made-up face punctuated by the gold earrings and framed by the hat's huge white brim, a white pashmina draped around her shoulders and two fluffy white dogs with perfect black noses and pink tongues on her lap, Luisa D'Onofrio was the epitome of glamor. Toscani got plenty of coverage on Luisa. Then he bellowed at Chiara to get Rick and Patti on set. The nurse shaded Luisa with the parasol as the makeup artist leaned under the hat to blot shine from Luisa's forehead and cheeks.

Toscani directed Patti to kneel on Luisa's right. He wanted Rick leaning on the chair's left arm, both with their backs to Luisa. Rick couldn't rest his weight on the chair, so an assistant brought in a stool which they angled so Rick could give the illusion he was leaning on the chair. The stylist tailored Rick's shirt to his waist with bulldog clips and Patti's shoulder straps were kept in place by double-sided tape. Luisa rested a loving hand on Patti's shoulder and, following some stage management to negotiate the big hat, Rick rested his hand protectively on his mother's shoulder.

Everyone cleared.

Toscani shot again.

"Sensational!" Ettore gasped.

The insanity of an elderly woman in a giant hat with two toy dogs on her lap, Rick in his ice-blue linen shirt with blow-dried hair and Patti's intricately knotted hairstyle with retro 60's makeup and stunning pink dress, all artificially posed as if they'd wandered onto the beach for a casual afternoon, raised the photo's composition into surreal territory.

"The son, Ricardo, lives in Los Angeles, has great influence in the art world and is filming a new show for American television?" Ettore checked his notes with Alex.

"That's right."

"And the grand-daughter, Patrizia, studied fine art in Florence, has degrees in art restoration and curation and maintains Luisa's art collection and her gallery in Venice."

"Correct."

"And you? What role do you play in Luisa's life?"

Alex was saved from fumbling for a reply.

"She wants you in now." Chiara clasped Alex's arm and dragged him into the shot.

Ettore followed behind with his note pad.

"*Là dietro.*" Toscani positioned Alex behind Luisa on the opposite side to Rick. "*Buttoni, buttoni!*" The photographer flapped his hand at Alex's open shirt. "Close. Close!"

As Alex fastened his shirt buttons, the hair stylist dodged in to twist a few Roman curls around his temples. Alex became aware that Luisa was speaking to Ettore.

"… he is Alex Morgan. An extremely well-respected modern artist … in America. He is most successful … over there."

Ettore scribbled in his pad and Toscani's assistants angled the reflectors to light Alex.

Alex exchanged glances behind Luisa's hat with Rick, both unsure of what was coming next.

"… over the years he has been extremely good to my son. There is great love between them. And I am pleased to announce that on their return to California they are to be married."

All activity froze on set.

Ettore's pen hovered in mid-air.

Even Bippy and Boppy looked up at Luisa with cocked heads and a 'say what?' expression on their faces.

"Art and artists must embrace the modern! And I still consider myself an artist. This is my family. My very *modern* family," Luisa declared.

Ettore finished scribbling in his pad with a flourish.

The hairstylist and lighting assistants cleared the shot.

Luisa pulled herself to full regal height in her chair.

And Toscani moved in to click away with his camera.

✶ ✶ ✶

"Don't look now," hissed Rick.

Of course, Patti and Alex immediately turned to look.

"I said, don't look now!" Rick snapped as Esmerelda swayed on the dark water. "His boat's drifted again. He's pulling up the anchor for another try. Poor guy will be even more nervous if he knows he's being watched."

Patti reached into the cooler for the prosecco. She refilled their plastic glasses. "Happy sixtieth, Papa!"

"Let's not mention numbers," said Rick.

"Happy birthday, babe." Alex tapped his plastic glass to Rick's.

"Did you spend a nice afternoon with nonna Lu?" Patti asked.

"Once I'd gotten over the shock of that stunt she pulled at the photoshoot. Momma couldn't just call me and Alex to her room and say, 'I'm happy for you and give you my blessing.' No, she has to announce our marriage in the national press, reinventing herself as the poster girl for gay equality." Rick sighed and sipped his prosecco.

Alex had to admit Luisa's public declaration of their relationship had also taken him by surprise. He hoped it signified a true change of heart on her part, not just switching sides in the face of defeat. "But apart from that," said Alex, "how was she?"

"Weak. She put on a brave face for the shoot. When I helped her to the chair in her room, I felt fluid building up on her chest. She hadn't taken her diuretic this morning because of being out. I sat with her while she went through the family photos. I suppose they'll all end up coming to you," Rick said to Patti. "Must say, I've got zero idea who half of the people in them are. I guess that's all our fate, ending up in photographs as a face no-one remembers."

"He's not setting the anchor," Alex remarked sagely, watching the guy with boat trouble. "He thinks just the weight of it will do the trick."

"Can't you go tell him? This is his fifth attempt. Why doesn't he tie up alongside someone else's boat?" Rick steadied himself on the gunwale as several small launches jostled through the inky water to find space to tie up or anchor in St. Mark's Basin.

"The boat he is in, all sleek and polished, I do not think he is from around here. Perhaps he does not speak Italian well enough to ask?" Patti remarked.

"Look, he's got his boat back in position to try again," said Rick.

Making no pretense not to look now, they all turned to watch the man on the fancy yacht prepare to drop anchor.

Music from the five-piece band on a barge floating around the moored vessels mingled with lapping waves in the night air. Referees' whistles and shouts in the dark came from police launches directing traffic around the zone designated for boats to watch the Redentore fireworks.

"You care for *sarde in saor*?" Patti took a plastic food container from the cooler.

"Say what?" asked Alex.

"Sardines in onion. I'll take some," said Rick.

"Alex?" asked Patti, filling up Rick's bowl.

"Passarino." Alex shuddered at the thought, glad he'd gotten a takeout pizza before they set off at sunset from the Lido towards Punta della Doggana. "I'd like to give Giovanni something for letting me borrow Esmerelda again."

"Is okay," said Patti. "He and Paola are working the Redentore party at the hotel tonight. They wouldn't be using her to come watch the fireworks anyway."

"I'd still like to give him something." Alex patted her hull; he'd become quite enamored of the little boat. And Esmerelda looked very festive tonight, all dressed up in the paper garlands and balloons Rick and Patti had strung around her in honor of the Festa del Redentore, a classical Venetian event celebrating the end of the great plague in 1576.

"Ciao, Patrizia!" a girl shouted from an oncoming boat.

Patti peered into the mass of bobbing craft on the lagoon. When Patti spotted who'd called to her, Esmerelda swayed, rippling the boats she was tethered to as Patti clambered to the prow.

"Always hang on to the boat with one hand, Patti!" Alex warned when he saw her wobble on her way.

"Mia! *Come stai?*" Taking Alex's advice, Patti leaned out over the water and waved with one hand to a young woman on the flat-bottomed barge festooned with lanterns. The barge carried a full-sized dining table surrounded by family members, wineglasses in hands, all sitting on chairs. "It's the Bassani's," Patti explained, turning back to Rick and Alex. "I was at school with Mia." A rat-a-tat conversation took place between Patti and Mia. The conversation over the water growing louder as the Bassani's family barge moved on, finishing with Patti yelling, "*Si, ho due papà! Devono essere sposati*!" Whoops and hollers issued from Mia's family at the news Patti was to have two fathers as they raised their glasses and the Bassani's barge blended into the sea of boats.

"Take six." As he ate, Rick watched the guy in the swish boat swing the hook once more. "Okay, here he goes."

Splash.

Splash!

"Shit." Esmerelda rocked as Rick stood. "He's fallen in!"

The boats tied together rocked as everyone in them rose to gawk at the yacht with a man overboard.

"Fuck! Is the guy okay?" Alex leaned on the windshield.

"Is fine, someone on his boat is pulling him in," said Patti.

Rick stroked Alex's arm. "Hold your horses, darling. No need to dive in after him."

Splashing and raised voices were followed by applause and cheers as the anchor man was hauled back onboard.

"We should take a photo." Patti dug in her bag.

"Of him?" asked Rick through a mouthful of food.

"Of us, Papa!" Patti got her digital camera. "Get together."

Rick and Alex moved close to each other. Rick ran his tongue around his teeth, wiped his mouth and smiled.

The flash went off as Patti snapped. "Family photo. We need one with all three." Patti moved to them and held the camera for a selfie. "*Un secondo.*" She clicked again then turned the camera to check its LCD screen. "Is good!" Patti passed the camera for Rick to see. The ring of his cell phone distracted him.

"What did you bring that for?" Alex detested electronic devices interrupting real-live events.

"In case we got lost at sea," Rick pithily replied fishing in his pocket for his phone.

"See?" Patti showed the photo to Alex.

The camera's screen was tiny. He put on his glasses. The image was magical. Patti in the center, her long blond hair falling in ringlets from the photoshoot's hair style, Rick's super-white smile against his tan and his sandy graying hair fluttering in the night air, and himself … a fuzz of stubble on his strong jaw, hint of mustache on his upper lip, a pinpoint of light in his olive-hazel eyes, a tinge of silver in the Roman curls framing his forehead. In the background, a flotilla of boats decorated with garlands, lanterns and people making merry. And rising behind them, the spires, domes and belltowers of Venice and twinkling stars of the night sky.

"I have some pictures of Mama on here if you would like to see?" Patti scrolled through the photos.

"It's Jack," said Rick checking his phone.

"Jack?" Alex frowned. "How'd he get your number?"

"Dunno."

"See Papa? This is Mama and Silvano when I visited Garda in the spring." Patti showed the photo to Rick.

Rick did a double take when he saw the picture. He took the camera from Patti and turned it around like he was looking for more of the photo. "Wow, did you need some kind of special lens to take this?"

"You know Mama always eats when she is happy," Patti said.

"She must be freakin' ecstatic," commented Rick as he passed the camera to Alex.

Alex studied the photo. No doubt about it, Giuliana, dressed in a vivid Pucci print caftan, did fill the entire frame. But then again, she did look extremely happy, so that was more important. "What's up with Jack?" Alex asked seeing Rick growing concerned.

Rick put his phone away. "Tyler's had an accident in his truck."

"Not again," said Alex. "Is he okay?"

"Think so. I'll call Jack when we're back at the house."

Whoosh!

The first rocket shot into the sky.

Bang!

The rocket exploded in a ball of shimmering stars.

The stars tumbled to earth.

Cries of delight and excitement rose from the boats.

More explosions.

Applause and screams of wonder from the boats.

A volley of firepower.

Gunpowder erupted into red, green, and white balls of fire glittering, glimmering, flashing in the black sky.

Alex stared up, allowing the millions of specks of brilliant light above Venice to consume his retinas.

The joyous explosions were magnificent, glorious, celebratory. The plague was over.

Life had overcome death!

But Alex suddenly realized not all of the colors in his eyes were fireworks.

Flashing purple spots were blanking out the vision in the lower quadrant of his right eye.

THIN AIR

Chasing the sunset, the 747's engines blasted four white contrails behind its wings.

The twenty seats inside the bubble of its upper deck were arranged in a ying-yang pattern, aisle seats facing the direction of travel and window seats facing backwards. The plane took off just after 3.30 p.m. London time, estimated arrival LA 7.30 p.m. local, an extended flight duration due to headwinds. After doing a bar service, Leo, one of the two upper deck flight attendants, served afternoon tea and refilled everyone's drinks. The window blinds were lowered, blanking out the saturated turquoise sky, the lights dimmed, and the plane entered an endless twilight.

The upstairs cabin was hushed and intimate like a private jet. Although detesting flying, Alex had to admit it was the nicest environment he'd flown in, although his knees didn't appreciate the steep and narrow staircase to get up to it. Their sudden return to the USA meant a return to the worries about his finances, his new show, his ongoing eyesight issue, and Tyler. While the other passengers relaxed with a movie, dozed, or kept their alcohol levels topped up, in seat 62B Alex twisted, fidgeted, shifted, stretched and anything else he could do to fall asleep on the flatbed. But slumber was elusive. Instead, he kept clicking on the flight information channel. Two hours in and the yellow plane graphic seemed to only have just started crossing the Atlantic. Rick had downed his customary quota of champagne. Glancing at seat 62A, kitty corner to him, this proved more effective than popping an Ambien. Rick was reclined under a blanket, eye-masked, slack jawed and snoring lightly. Willing the plane to move faster, Alex flicked between the flight information and movie channels. Unable to sleep or lose himself in Patrick Dempsey's problems in *Made of Honor*, Alex mulled over the events of the last couple of days. Constantly aware of the shimmering patch in his right eye, he recalled the moment when he realized his vision was on the fritz again. Rick and Patti were screaming and clapping at the fireworks' spectacular finale. Hoping against hope the purple spots would clear, he'd repeatedly blinked his eyes …

"Best Redentore fireworks in years," Patti had said while delving into the cool bag.

"Amazing how the city council can't fund public toilets yet can blast a hundred thousand Euros in the air to celebrate the end of a plague four hundred years ago," Rick had retorted.

"Watermelon?" Patti offered the platter of red slices. People in the other boats were also rounding off their evening with watermelon.

"I'm fine, thanks." Alex unhitched the knots restraining Esmerelda to their neighboring boat. The craft rocked as vessels around them raised anchor and untethered themselves. The basin rapidly became a churning maelstrom of thumping motors and red and green sidelights as boats scattered in every direction. "Patti, Rick, put on your lifejackets."

"Lifejackets?" Rick asked, watermelon juice dribbling down his chin.

"There are strangers to the area out here tonight. And a lot of them have been drinking. Better to be safe than sorry. Secure the cabin. I want to get underway." As Rick and Patti packed up the plastic plates and glasses, Alex started Esmerelda. He flinched as an unlit skiff with an outboard glided from his blind spot on starboard. He wondered if he should ask Rick to take the wheel. But as Rick wasn't the most spatially aware driver in a car, asking him to navigate through maritime mayhem on choppy water wasn't the wisest move. '*C'mon, man,*' Alex gave himself a talking to, '*if Nelson got through Waterloo with one eye, you can do this.*' Going into a Zen zone, he used the sounds on the water and his sense of the currents beneath Esmerelda's hull to bolster his picture of marine activity since he couldn't trust his eyes alone. He recoiled from a dark figure walking towards him on the water. The image resolved itself into a sailboat's mast. Odd faces and brick like patterns emerged from the dark water, making it hard to know what was real and not real.

Taking it slow and ultra-cautiously, Alex negotiated his way through the undisciplined boats. Rick and Patti clearly had faith in him and were relaxed enough in back. Both were wearing their lifejackets as instructed. If he should fail in his captain's duty of care and allow another boat to run into them or, worse, he run into it, they'd be safe. He also had a duty of care to Esmerelda. The thought of damaging Giovanni's pride and joy weighed heavily on his heart. The Lido filling station and streetlights on the bridge over their canal appeared across the lagoon. Alex casually asked Rick to shine the flashlight to illuminate the way to their mooring spot. With Rick and Patti's assistance, he got the boat tied up and covered. It was after 1.30 a.m. when his wobbly knees climbed the concrete steps. As they crossed the road to the house, clusters of unsteady youngsters were straggling to the beach for a night-time swim and more drinks while waiting for the sunrise.

Hearing the key in the door, Bippy and Boppy came hurtling downstairs. Still in a party mood, Patti and Rick carried the bags to the kitchen. Alex closed the front door and leaned against it. He heard the pop of Rick opening a fresh bottle of prosecco.

"Jack, slow down. Say again?" Rick emerged from the kitchen, phone in one hand and prosecco in the other. He held the bottle to Alex with a questioning expression.

As they'd been couped up since early evening, Patti put the dogs' leashes on. Alex stepped aside to let her take them out. He declined a drink. Rick's happy mood deflated as he returned to the kitchen listening to Jack. Going to the living room, Alex dropped to the peach brocade sofa with scrolled wooden arms. Five minutes later, Rick came in. "What's up with Jack?"

"He's at the hospital with Tyler."

"The hospital? What the fuck's Ty done to his truck this time?"

"It wasn't his fault. He was on his way to a job and got caught up in a multi-vehicle pile-up on the 405. He managed to avoid running into anything, but when the highway patrol got to him he was acting confused. He hadn't hit his head but they had the paramedics check him over anyhow. They found his pupils were unevenly dilated and rushed him to UCLA with a suspected whiplash concussion. The ER couldn't reach Letitia or Tiffany. Tyler was getting distressed about being alone. Because we weren't around either he got them to call Jack. And Jack dropped everything to go be with him. Letitia's at the hospital now. The doctors are keeping him in for observation but aren't unduly concerned."

"That was kind of Jack to let us know." Alex rested his hand on Rick's knee. "Now give me your word you won't panic when I tell you this."

Rick's back stiffened.

"Either I've developed a new blockage or the inflammation from the old one's back."

"Oh, shit. Did it just happen?"

"It came on while we were out on the water. It's worse than New York. Half my vision's distorted. I mean, it's like you're not even sitting there."

"Was that the reason for the lifejackets?"

"I didn't want to scare you and Patti, but I was afraid I might not be able to get us home in one piece."

Rick set his glass on the side table and put his arms around Alex. "You should have said something."

"It was a tricky situation out there. I couldn't have expected you or Patti to deal with it. Anyway, we made it. This isn't how I wanted your birthday to end. Sorry, babe."

"It's not your fault. No-one gave me a card with numbers on it and I had you and momma in the same room without bloodshed. Gifts don't come better than that. I had a good day."

"I need to get back to LA and see Dr. Kastani. I understand if you want to stay on here with Luisa."

"No, I'll come with you. You can't travel alone like this." Rick picked up his drink. "I'll change our flights tomorrow. Rather, today. Don't worry, we'll get you back, and I'm sure it'll all be okay."

Patti was understandably disappointed by the curtailment of their stay. After rising early, Rick spent several hours on the phone making new travel arrangements. He'd flown in on a British Airways flexible fare, so changing his booking was relatively simple. But as Alex had flown in on Delta, and it wasn't a partner airline, they had to swallow the cost of a new ticket on BA for him. "I thought we were economizing," Alex commented when Rick told him the Club fare cost.

"We are." Rick arched an eyebrow. "We're not in First, are we?"

With everything in place to fly back, Rick raced to the little supermarket around the corner before it closed at noon. He wanted to make a memorable last supper for Patti. In the afternoon he paid a final visit to Luisa. Alex feared she'd revert to form and throw a spanner in the works to keep Rick in Italy. When Rick returned from the institute, however, he was subdued but the trip was still on.

In the early evening, Rick laid the table on the verandah with the house's best linens, glassware and china. The wine flowed as he laid out a small banquet. Despite the change of plan, the three of them sat around the table and laughed as they relived the madness of the events leading up to yesterday's photoshoot. Rick was about to serve dinner when his phone rang inside the house.

Alex shot him a warning glance.

"I should take it. It may be the airline," said Rick.

Taking her father's place, Patti dished up Alex's tagliatelle and peas.

Alex was digging in the breadbasket when Rick returned.

"Tell me all the planes are cancelled and you have no choice but to remain here with me," said Patti brightly.

Rick gave a half-smile. "That was Letitia. Tyler doesn't have a concussion, he's got a meningioma. The doctors suspect the tumor's been silently growing for years. The whiplash put extra pressure on his brain which is why he suddenly started showing symptoms. They're doing more tests."

"Shit." Alex put down the bread, his appetite ebbing away.

On Monday morning, waiting for the water taxi to pick them up on the same landing stage he'd been dropped off less than a week ago, Alex's heart was awash with emotions. He'd always railed against coming to Venice, constantly refusing invitations to Biennale events or anything else to do with the art world here because of Luisa's presence. He regretted the pleasures he'd missed out on from not having had the guts to face her before now. He'd learned so much over the last few days.

He could recognize the different types of local boats, the *mascareta* was a lightweight sandolo, the elegant *pupparinos* and *caorlinas* were the boats rowed at sunset by young men practicing for the races. Now he knew the classic Venetian dialect didn't use the double consonants of mainstream Italian, hence Rick being Ricardo, rather than Riccardo. And he'd grown to feel warmly about the people too. Giovanni dabbed his eye with a red handkerchief when Alex pressed two fifty Euro bills into his palm to thank him for the loan of Esmerelda, then patted his cheek like he was an eight-year-old boy. Even Carla and Luca, the waitress and barman at the café where he'd had his first lemon soda and walked the dogs to each morning for his secret espresso, were sad to see him go. They bade him farewell in Italian, which he understood. And on that last morning, as he turned to walk the dogs back to the house, he spotted Luisa in her window at the institute. He hesitantly waved across the roundabout. Luisa met his eye. Raising a bony hand, her pinched fingers tapped her forehead, then her chest … the wind blew the gauze curtain across her window. When the curtain dropped away she'd melted into the darkness of her room. The Cedar tree on the roundabout rippled in his eye. He wondered if he'd really seen Luisa or just imagined it.

For a man who never cried, hot tears sprung all too easily from Alex's eyes as he kissed Patti goodbye. Rick helped him bridge the moving gap between the landing stage and the water taxi. From the open cabin in the stern, he gazed back at the shore, fixing the part of his eyes that still worked on Patti's waving hand. She evaporated as his vision's negative space swallowed her. His heart pounded. The black hole in his sight was growing, sucking everything from view. The Lido, the lagoon, the waterbuses, all were swirling down into the black drain-hole in his eye. He'd flung his hand out to hang on to Rick, afraid it wasn't his vision disappearing into nothingness but himself. He'd turned to the seat beside him but Rick's face had gone. Rick had gone! He'd lost him forever, as he always feared he would. A giant water monster rose from the lagoon. A tentacle slithered over the taxi's side. The muscular wet limb snaked around his chest. It lifted him out of his seat and dragged him overboard. He'd let out an anguished cry, "Rick! Help! Save me!" But no-one came. And he was falling, being dragged down into dark water. He screamed in terror, "Mom …!"

A gut-wrenching judder and the *ping!* of the seatbelt sign jerked Alex awake. He blinked groggily. "What's up?"

Rick was sitting bolt upright. "Turbulence."

The yellow plane on the TV screen was crossing the top of Newfoundland. The cabin air felt chill. Alex put his seat up and pushed back the screen.

Panicked activity filled the cabin as the crew hastily ensured everyone was belted in and loose items stowed.

The plane dropped.

The female flight attendant hurled herself into the jump seat across the cabin and buckled up.

"Fasten your seatbelts, boys," Leo, the other flight attendant, said with a twinkle as he swept away Rick's empty glass, "it's going to be a bumpy night." Steadying himself on the overhead lockers, he rushed to his crew seat by the galley.

Alex knew what he didn't like about flying.

This.

The 747 juddered like a jeep with shot suspension speeding over potholes.

"We've hit the headwinds," said Rick.

"I know, but —" Alex's neck snapped back. The upper deck passengers emitted a collective gasp. The seatbelt dug in his stomach as the plane fell away. He bumped back into his seat with a meaty thud. "I don't like this."

"Sailing on rough water wouldn't scare you."

"I can see and feel water and I'd be in control. Air's invisible. You just have to have faith it's there."

The plane bounced and lurched.

"Keep calm. It'll pass."

Alex felt Rick stroking his hand. The altitude fluctuations were making him nauseous. He imagined how it would feel if the plane fell from the sky. "I didn't used to be afraid of death." He closed his eyes. "Just accepted it was the end."

"Babe, we're not going to die."

"We are. One day."

The plane rattled and dropped.

"In the hospital, after the heart attack, I'm sure my heart stopped. I had this dream, a dream of being out of my body and seeing death. Only it didn't feel like a dream, it felt real. And the place I went to was frightening and lonely. It's made me scared of that place on the other side."

"I think momma is too. When I held her hand and said goodbye, something had changed in her. She didn't manipulate.

She didn't criticize. There was a kind of acceptance, like the fight had gone out —"

The plane juddered. Everyone took a sharp intake of breath. Although they were on the upper deck, the engines' roar went up a notch.

Alex swallowed to clear his ears.

"She wanted me to look at the photos again, like she was reliving the past. I only really remember nonna Maria from them. She was very down to earth. A worker. Papa Ludo's family thought he'd married beneath him. Guess that's why he was devastated when momma married dad. Sid Stradman, the son of vaudeville performers, and an American to boot. Then she came home divorced. Once I overheard nonna telling a neighbor that papa Ludo died of shame."

"Shame?"

"Momma made no secret of having men in her life. This was Italy, remember, a Catholic country where old ladies sit on benches and gossip. I'm not sure momma can receive the Last Rites, or even if she'd want to. I never imagined having to consider these questions. I blamed momma for the problems between us, but I'm to blame too. I hid myself from her. I didn't want her to be ashamed of me. And that made me into a liar …"

The plane vibrated like it was being shaken in a snow globe. Overhead lockers, the stowed tray tables, the bottles in the bar carts and people's teeth rattled in tandem.

Alex gripped Rick's hand, ready for the oxygen masks to drop. "Since the heart attack, I keep seeing things. Faces, images, ghosts. If I see Mom, or Danielle or Dora, they're nice, comforting even. Other times, like if it's Pop, they frighten me. Part of me wants to believe something of us lingers on, but I can't bring myself to. But then the idea of living all this life for nothing, that all we've learned and experienced is just lost, is unbearable. Do you believe there's something more to our existence than the few years we walk on earth?"

"I do." Rick squeezed Alex's hand. "And if it gives you comfort to believe people you've loved who are gone can hear you and know you think of them, maybe even help in time of need, does it matter if it's true or not?"

Alex closed his eyes, praying the shaking would cease.
The plane must have climbed above the rough air.
The engines' roar softened.
Five minutes of uninterrupted smooth flight passed.
The tension in the cabin relaxed.
Reclining his seat, Alex stretched his legs.
"It was probably the drugs," Rick said out of the blue.
"What drugs?"
"The drugs they were giving you for the heart attack. They must have given you those dark thoughts in the hospital. Drugs like that depress the system. Think of how many people you got out of trouble when you were a lifeguard. You saved lives. You'd be first in line for wings if that's how the deal works."

The female flight attendant unstrapped herself and went to the galley.

Ping!

The seatbelt sign went off.

"Those wings better come with flying lessons then." Alex laughed diffidently. "Forget my crazy talk. Turbulence freaks me out." But Rick wasn't listening, Alex saw him peering over his shoulder towards the galley. "What're you looking for?"

"Trying to see if Margo Channing's restarted cabin service. I need another champagne. We're not even over America yet."

Alex smiled as Rick pushed his call button.

* * *

Alex hadn't wanted to leave LA in the first place and expected to be overjoyed about getting home. But opening up the street door and dragging their luggage in while Rick paid the cab didn't fill him with joy. The contractors had repaired the damage to Manuela's former quarters and given the sides of both houses a fresh coat of paint. They'd done a good job and cleared away their crap. Everywhere was clean, tidy … and empty.

Carrying their shoulder bags in through the double doors between the houses, Rick glanced up at the small house's upstairs windows. "Where'd the drapes go?"

Alex unlocked the front door. "I had the movers clear out the place. They've put Danielle's things in storage. I'll see if her brother would like anything, then we should have an estate sale and give the proceeds to her favorite charity."

"Oh, Alex," Rick said sadly as they walked in the house.

The entrance hall smelled musty.

No wagging tails.

No Manuela in the kitchen.

No Tyler's foghorn voice booming from the pool.

"I figured it'd be easier if they took everything away when I wasn't here to see," said Alex.

Rick wheeled their roller cases to the closets behind the master suite.

Alex went around switching on lamps and put on some music to bring the place to life. A half-eaten bowl of granola and cup of cold coffee sat on the kitchen counter. Tyler must've been halfway through breakfast before dashing off to work. Opening the door from the living room, through the study's window over the patio he saw Rick powering up the Mac. Alex walked to the pool. The apartment buildings on the lot behind had shot up while they were away, peering over their perimeter wall like a nosy neighbor. He contemplated crossing the bridge to check on his studios but couldn't face work quite yet.

In the other Venice, the one on the other side of the Atlantic, it would be early morning. If he were there right now he'd be walking the dogs to the cafe for his early morning espresso. He sensed movement behind him. He turned to see someone emerge from the pool house. His heart leaped, Ty must have been discharged and come home! On closer inspection, the figure became a random reflection from the pool lights. The purple patch in his eye was behaving differently now, moving in kaleidoscopic waterfall patterns. It was actually rather pretty. Maybe regular injections to keep this eye problem at bay were to become an unwelcome addition to his already heavily accessorized medical routine. Which reminded him, time for his meds. He slipped through the bedroom's sliding doors to get his pills. Unzipping his messenger bag, he heard Rick in the study. Hearing Tiffany, he realized they must be on Skype. He went to find out what was going on.

"… I can't leave the kids alone but I should be with him."

"Your mom's at the hospital," said Rick.

"I know it's bad, Ricky. I feel it. We're twins. You think that's what's wrong with me? That I've got a brain tumor like Tyler?" On-screen, tears streamed from Tiffany's eyes.

"You're making yourself hysterical and that won't help anyone," Rick said to the camera. "Get some sleep. You need to stay strong for Maddy and Jay. I'll catch up with you in the morning." Rick closed the chat window.

"What's happened to Ty?"

Rick swiveled around in the chair. "He had a series of seizures. The neck injury's caused bleeding from the tumor."

"Oh, shit." Alex steadied himself on the door frame. "Should we go to the hospital?"

Rick picked up his phone. "Let me call Letitia. I've lost track of what time of day it's meant to be anywhere in the world, but I've the feeling we should be asleep. You look beat. And you need to be up early so we can get you to the eye clinic. Go to bed." Rick scrolled through his phone. "Guess that explains it."

"Explains what?"

"Tyler's crazy behavior. I always said something was out of whack in that boy's head."

Leaving Rick, Alex prepared for bed. Maybe totaling trucks and falling out of trees were due to sensory issues the tumor was exerting on Tyler's perception. Looking back, he recalled moments where Tyler's eyes didn't seem to be focusing properly. But would operating on his brain remove Tyler's off-the-wall comments, his unashamed passion, his goofy lopsided smile – were they the result of something foreign in his head too?

Drying his face, Alex fingered Tyler's ikat hair elastic on the bathroom shelf left from the night he slept over. Alex pictured the vibrant, larger than life young man who'd laid beside him, now lying in the hospital attached to monitors and tubes. Getting into their own bed was a wonderful relief. Alex pulled up the covers and willed himself to remain awake until Rick came in from the bathroom. "What did Letitia say?"

Rick climbed into bed. "They'll operate in the morning."

"There's no alternative?"

"The tumor's growing. Even if he comes out of this episode okay the same thing could happen again. Only worse because the tumor would be bigger. Tyler can't make the decision himself, but Letitia knows he wouldn't want to live with a timebomb in his head. She's given consent on his behalf. If the operation's a success he'll be able to lead a normal life."

"And if it fails?"

"Someone on a waiting list gets a new heart." Reaching out, Rick turned off his bedside lamp.

MEMENTO MORI

"Non-attendance will result in a charge."

"I understand," said Alex. "Something unavoidable came up. Family emergency."

"The longer you delay treatment, the greater the possibility of permanent vision loss," the Eye Institute's receptionist said over the phone.

"I'll come in as soon as I can."

"Without an appointment you may have a long wait time, but the doctors will do their best to see you as an emergency. I strongly advise you get here as soon as you can."

Alex hung up the call. He felt Rick's eyes boring into him from the hospital's waiting area where he was sitting with Letitia and Tiffany. Setting his phone to silent, Alex rejoined the family on the button-back vinyl sofas.

"You don't need to stay, Alex. You should've gone to your eye doctor appointment. I'll call as soon as we know anything." Letitia stared earnestly up at him.

"I feel better being here with you and Tiffany. Can I get you a coffee or something?" The purple rings under Letitia's eyes concerned Alex. The woman clearly hadn't slept in days.

"I'm good, thanks honey." Fatigue riddled Letitia's voice.

"Hey, they got a state-of-the-art eye casualty here." Rick fluttered an information pamphlet for the newly opened Ronald Reagan UCLA Medical Center in Alex's direction.

"Dr. Kastani has my medical history and scans. I'd rather wait to go see him than start from scratch with someone new. And my eyeball isn't dangling on my cheek or got a nail in it. An injection solved the problem last time." Alex settled down beside

Tiffany. "The doc will give me another shot and everything'll be fine."

"Yew." Tiffany grimaced. "The doctor stuck a needle in your eye?"

"Duh. Where'd you think he'd stick it?" Rick looked at her gone out. "Into his butt?"

"Pipe down, you two. I'm tense enough without this bickering," Letitia snapped.

"Sorry." Rick shuffled in his seat.

Letitia cupped her hands over her face. Taking a few cleansing breaths, she rubbed her eyes. "No, I'm sorry. I shouldn't have snapped. I miss Tyler joining in with the bickering. You're all grown adults but when the three of you get together you act like kids."

"I was never a kid with the two of them," scoffed Rick. "There are twenty-three years between us."

"How true," said Tiffany. "Did you arrange to be out of the country on your birthday to divert attention from turning sixty?"

"If you recall, Tiff, my being out of the country was due to having to wrangle momma in front of a microphone on your behalf."

Letitia stifled a smile. "It was kind of you to help Tiffany with that. Belated happy birthday. Did you have a nice day?"

"Great, thanks. And Tiff, dial-down any mention of the 'S' word and me around TV industry people." Rick flicked his eyes around like the waiting area might be bugged. "I'm not ready to be cast in grandpa roles yet."

"You look nowhere near sixty. You've always been a kid at heart, Ricky. Oh my, where does the time go?" Letitia checked the clock. The hands sat on 2.05 p.m. "He's been in surgery over five hours."

"I'll go see what's happening." Tiffany got up.

Letitia restrained her. "They'll page as soon as he's out. The longer he's in though, the more I'm afraid there'll be complications."

"What kind of complications, mom?"

"Even if they excise the tumor the hemorrhage could've caused brain damage." Letitia looked at each in turn. "Tiffany, Ricky, Alex, we need to prepare ourselves for the fact that even if Tyler pulls through, he may not be the same Tyler we know. There could be mental impairment, he may be paralyzed, or …" Letitia dug in her purse, "or he may never wake up at all."

Tiffany's mind was rolling. "What about his hair? Will they have shaved his head?"

Letitia pulled out a Kleenex. "They planned to go in behind his ear." She huddled her olive cardigan around her and dabbed her eyes. "But I don't know."

Talk of Tyler losing his luxurious hair distressed them more than any other aspect of his illness discussed so far.

"Oh, Jack's here." Brightening, Letitia stuffed her tissue up her sleeve and got up to greet him.

"How's he doing?" asked Jack striding past the gift shop.

"Still in surgery."

Jack enfolded Letitia in a comforting hug. "Hi," he said to Tiffany. She smiled wanly in response. Jack was wearing one of his super tight shirts with striped suspenders. He dipped his head to Alex and Rick. "Hear congratulations are in order. Tyler told me you guys are getting married."

"Thanks. Only took thirty-four years," Alex said with an awkward laugh. The last time they'd met Jack was nude and his hand was on his dick. "I need coffee." Alex slapped his thighs and stood. "Anybody else?"

"Get me one if you're going to the cafeteria," said Rick. "But make this your last. You've had two this morning."

"I'll take a chamomile tea with honey," said Tiffany. "Make sure the honey's organic."

Letitia waved away Alex's offer.

"And a muffin," Rick added. "Banana walnut. Low-fat."

"Oh, I'll have a four-piece maki set from the Grab 'n' Go sushi bar," said Tiffany.

"No, blueberry," said Rick. "Heavy on the blueberries."

"That everything?" Alex asked, sincerely hoping it was.

"I'll give you a hand," said Jack.

The cafeteria's shiny floors, reflective chrome legs of the chairs and tables and people perambulating with trays severely tested Alex's faltering eyesight. The signposting was poor. He peered around to determine the different food stations. Locating the sushi bar, he stepped forward. "Apologies, my bad." Alex walked into the attendant with a cleaning cart hidden by the jazzy spot on his right side. "Got a little problem with my vision," he explained to Jack as the attendant moved on.

"Lucky I came along." Gripping Alex's belt, Jack guided him to the sushi bar. "Sorry if I embarrassed you the other week," Jack said as they waited in line. "Tyler lost it with me afterwards. I misread the situation."

"Taking a flute lesson from you while wearing nothing but a sarong and smoking pot probably sent the wrong vibe. I'm from a different generation to you and Ty. I've got no experience of casual encounters."

"You lived through the sixties. Those were the days of swinging, free love and rolling naked in Jell-O, weren't they?"

"For some." Alex grabbed a tray. "It still wasn't that easy for men like us to be open. Chicks burning their bras got more interest than guys burning their jocks. Anyway, an over the hill, dried up old man like me wouldn't expect a fit guy like you to even notice me ..." Aware of people close by in line, Alex dropped his voice, "... in a sexual way. I regret acting naïvely and stirring up trouble between you guys."

"There was more to it than that. Other issues had been brewing. Tyler was having problems with my work."

"Your music?"

"That's a hobby. No, my real job. The sex work —"

"What may I get you?" asked the sushi station server.

At the front of the line, Alex fumbled resting the tray on the counter. "Um, a four-piece California roll." As the assistant got his order, Alex asked in a whisper, "Sex work?"

"Adult movies, nude modeling, exotic dance."

The server passed over the sushi box. Alex steadied his hands as he lifted the tray. "Ty never mentioned that."

Holding Alex's elbow, Jack steered him to the next station. "Tyler had toyed with getting into the adult movie scene, so I figured he was cool. I have contacts who could've gotten him work. Tyler has the talent and zero inhibitions. I mean, he can do it anywhere with anyone, and there's a market for his hippie surfer look. He could've made good money. Now for The Sweet Spot."

Alex was baffled.

"Rick's muffin."

The Sweet Spot had no line. "Banana walnut." Alex said to the counter assistant while pointing at the trays. "Low-fat."

"Uh huh," Jack interjected. "Blueberry."

"Sorry. Blueberry."

"That one." Jack pointed to a muffin.

"How would your work have fit in with you guys getting married?" Alex watched the server bag the muffin.

"Plenty of couples work in the adult industry. Drinks?" Jack rested his hand on the small of Alex's back. "You really do need that coffee. You're shaking."

"Right." Alex allowed Jack to push him around. "But doesn't that put a lot of pressure on a relationship?"

Hooking his thumbs in his pockets, Jack rested his hip on the beverage station's counter. "Not really, you got your professional life and personal life. I adore Tyler and only want the best for him, but I couldn't limit myself to *only* him. And the way you kept on watching me and Tyler necking and making out around the pool got me to thinking you guys were open too. It would be weird being with Rick and Tyler together, but I figured you and Tyler could play while I had fun with Rick."

"What are you having?"

The beverage server's question caught Alex off guard.

"Mister? To drink?"

"Er … two coffees. Black. And one chamomile tea with honey. Organic honey… Anything for you, Jack?"

"Nah, I'm good. But after Tyler lost it with me, I knew our relationship couldn't work that way anymore. He'd fallen in love, you see. Deep love, the kind that can't share." Jack watched the beverage server put the drinks on Alex's tray.

"That's why you split, then? Ty wanted you to give up the work and be exclusive."

Jack unhooked his thumbs. "Not me. I'll carry, you pay." Jack took the tray to the cashier's desk.

Alex fiddled for cash in his pocket. "If not you, then, who'd Tyler fallen so deeply in love with?"

"You," said Jack.

Alex's hand was so unsteady that the cashier gave him a strange look as he paid. "Keep the change."

In the waiting area, Rick stashed his phone as he saw Alex and Jack return. "Where'd you go to? That took forever."

"One coffee and one blueberry muffin. Low-fat. Heavily fruited. I picked it special for you." With a sly grin, Jack handed Rick his drink and bakery bag. "I got a feel for how you like 'em."

The way Jack said that to Rick made Alex feel uncomfortable. "And sushi and one chamomile tea with honey." Alex handed Tiffany her order. "Any news?"

"Only that Ellery's furious with Cristina," said Rick.

Stirring her tea, Tiffany shot Rick a withering glance.

Alex blew on his coffee. "I meant about Tyler."

"Still in surgery," said Letitia wearily.

"Reality TV people make a drama over anything." About to open the soy sauce, Tiffany asked, "Is this low sodium?"

"Yeah," said Jack confidently.

Not convinced, Tiffany set the sauce aside.

"Okay, spill. What's the big deal with Cristina?" Alex was happy for anything other than Jack and Tyler's sex life to occupy his mind.

"A story broke on *Radar Online*. You know how Ellery's husband has an investment company, apparently two of his clients went to withdraw their funds and found there ain't no money there to withdraw."

"Let me guess. Cristina and Harun are the clients," said Alex.

"Correct! Ellery's accused Cristina of leaking the story and blackening her husband's good name. It's ugly. And —"

Bleep! Bleep! Bleep!

Everyone jumped as the pager went off.

Letitia scurried to the duty nurses station beside the information desk.

Alex, Rick, Jack and Tiffany watched intently for any clue as to the information she was receiving ...

* * *

High-rise buildings and tall trees cast afternoon shade over the grassy yard with inlaid gravestones.

Tucked away in a secluded part of Westwood, the resting places of a veritable *Who's Who* of Hollywood lay behind the memorial park's walls. A few tourists wandered around, exchanging words and taking photographs whenever they stumbled across a familiar name.

Alex, Rick, Jack, Tiffany and Letitia gathered around the grave.

Getting to her knees, Letitia brushed a wayward leaf off the plaque and trailed her fingers over the inscription.

Sidney Abraham Stradman
1912 – 1974

Letitia laid the spray of yellow roses by Sid's name. "Hey darlin'," she spoke out loud. "Hope you can hear me. Our boy needs help from your side."

The dappled shadows over the stones combined with the kaleidoscope effect in his right eye were making Alex woozy. Being in the memorial park reignited memories of the dark days in the wake of Sid's funeral. Coming here feeling raw and off kilter after Tyler came out of surgery maybe wasn't the best idea. But since the doctors predicted it would be several hours before Tyler regained consciousness, *if* he did, taking a break from the hospital seemed like a good idea at the time. Realizing the cemetery was close by, Letitia wanted to visit Sid. On their way here they'd passed a flower shop filled with yellow roses. Being Sid's favorite flower, Letitia had rushed in to buy twelve. Needing to get the disorientating shadows out of his eyeline, and also let Letitia converse with her dead spouse without his skepticism impinging, Alex subtly withdrew. Being careful not to tread on any plaques, he picked his way to the road around the yard.

"Last time we were here, helicopters were buzzing the place and news crews were chasing me. All desperately hoping I'd admit that the shock of discovering I was gay was what killed my father. Surreal being here again, isn't it?"

Alex found Rick had followed him. "Sure is."

"Remember how momma whacked that cameraman with her purse? She was so furious with the press that day. But she was mad at me too. And bitter her Hollywood comeback had come to nothing. Guess if I'd kept my relationship with you a secret and she hadn't asked for too much money we both might have kept our parts on that TV show."

"Shouldn't you be talking to Sid?"

"Letitia and Tiffany are doing enough of that. I don't want to overburden dad. I left a message." Rick halted on the grass. "Oh, my."

Alex shifted his vision to the plaque at their feet.

Natalie Wood Wagner - 1938 – 1981
"MORE THAN LOVE"

"Remember that crazy day Scotty roped us in to hang the painting of hers at the Wagners' new house?" Rick sadly shook his head.

"Yeah. And while the housekeeper went off to find an extension reel, I was alone in their kitchen when Natalie arrived home unexpectedly. I was lucky she didn't call the cops on me when she walked in."

"And then I was mouthing off when Scotty sent me downstairs to find out what was taking you so long. When I barged in and saw Natalie talking with you, I could've died. Then she remembered me from one of dad's parties. She was being nice about dad, and I got all sassy and disrespectful of him and his work."

"She put you firmly in your place."

"I behaved like a total brat. I did send her flowers and an apology."

"She was the one who gave me that guy's number at the marina. The one I chartered the yacht from to take you sailing on your birthday. She was a good woman."

"She was. None of us know what tomorrow will bring, do we?"

Walking onto the driveway, they meandered past the white marble crypts with black gates.

"Seeing the dates on Sid's gravestone made me realize I'm the same age as he was when he died," said Alex. "I always used to think of your dad as an old man. Funny how far off sixty-two feels in your twenties."

"Do we seem as ancient to the kids as dad's generation did to us?"

"Yes."

Alex's blunt answer cracked Rick up. "Shit, it's bad luck to laugh in a graveyard. I dunno, Tiffany and Tyler relate to us as equals. Patti, too, don't you think?"

"Or maybe they think we're dinosaurs and humor us."

"I don't think either of us look as old as dad did at sixty."

"You don't, but I do. And when my body aches, boy I *feel* old. And talking with young guys, like Jack, I realize that I *think* old. My attitudes are old."

"Jack's mid-thirties, he's not that young. Look, there's Marilyn."

"Who?" That startled Alex. Was Rick also seeing the shadowy figures?

"Monroe. In the open mausoleum on the corner. Second from bottom with the red and white flowers. See?"

Peering at the wall of crypts, Alex picked out Marilyn's tomb, the white marble discolored from years of lipstick kisses.

"Dad's got a good spot near Zanuck in the yard, but he'd have gotten a kick from being up here by Marilyn. He had a thing for blonds."

"That's true." Alex smiled.

"I did have my reservations about Jack, but the way he rushed to Tyler's side when he needed him was wonderful." Rick glanced back at the cemetery yard. "And he's been a real comfort to Letitia. Look, even Tiffany's let him put his arm around her now. It's a pity he and Tyler split." They carried on walking in silence along the driveway around the yard. "You were singing Jack's praises not so long ago. What changed?" Rick asked when Alex didn't respond.

"Jack's career isn't in music. He works in the sex industry."

"As a counter assistant in an adult store?"

"Uh huh. Adult videos, nude modeling. I was shocked."

"Me too! He's got his arm around my sister!"

"Stop. That's what I meant about my attitudes being old. It shouldn't be something to be shocked about."

"Shouldn't it?" Rick chewed his cheek.

"C'mon, we've looked at porn. And we both enjoy pictures of fit guys. And I don't mean ones wearing three-piece suits. Someone has to do that work."

"But not my brother's boyfriend! And they were going to get married. Well, it's a blessing that didn't happen."

"Not necessarily. They had an open relationship, but they loved each other. Ty had apparently considered getting into the adult industry too."

"What? Just as I'm about to be back on TV, can you imagine the fall-out if Tyler had actually done that? Some shady investments would be a non-event scandal story compared to my brother being outed as a gay porn star!"

"Knock it off, it's Tyler we're talking about."

"Jack's attempt to lure you into a threesome wasn't some delusion of yours then?"

"He apologized for that in the cafeteria. In trying to act cool around him and Ty, I inadvertently gave him the idea we were kind of open too."

"I'm beginning to think you're into this idea. Where's love fit in with a relationship like that?"

"For me, sex always followed love. But that doesn't mean it's the only way for everyone, does it? Jack clearly still has strong feelings for Ty. And he's here supporting the whole family, isn't he? That seems like love to me."

"To my mind, a relationship like Tyler and Jack's seems a risky basis for a long-term relationship. Can true love really exist like that?"

"Yeah, that's the problem Ty had. You see, the real reason behind their split was that Tyler had fallen in love. Deep love. But not with Jack … he'd fallen in love with me."

"Uh?" Coming to a full stop by the chapel, Rick confronted Alex. "That night you let Tyler sleepover, was it as innocent as you claim?"

"It was. But looking back, I think Ty sensed there was something wrong with him and was scared. That night could have been his last chance to ever feel the loving touch of another man. If he doesn't pull through the operation, would it really have been so bad if I'd given Tyler the comfort he needed?"

"Is that your ideal set-up? I scrub the sink, Tyler takes you surfing, and you fuck us both on a rota?"

"I didn't mean it that way."

With a thunderous expression on his face, Rick lowered his voice. "I sincerely hope Tyler makes it through, but now you've told me this I can't have him in the house. Or Jack. You may think cheating in a relationship's fine, even with consent, but I don't."

"When you were married to Giuliana you had affairs with men and so did she."

"That was different."

"And although me and Danielle truly loved each other, we both ended up having needs the other couldn't fulfill. Life isn't all black and white."

"Correct! Ours seems to be getting very gray." Breaking away, Rick strode across the yard to Sid's grave.

Taking a deep breath, Alex moved to follow. Setting foot on the grass, and keeping his eyes down, a shadow figure emerged from the haze on his right. A gust of wind swayed the cedars. Pop's shadow figure appeared in his eye's kaleidoscopic aura. He was sneering at him. Alex grounded himself on the solid earth. Why did he keep seeing these visions? Was he going insane? Or had that weird death dream in the hospital opened a portal to the other side? Maybe he'd briefly stepped through to the land after death and these spirits had followed him back. Willing himself to see only *real* things, Pop's ghost morphed into a woman with a smaller figure by her side. Alex wanted to weep as Danielle, holding a child's hand, walked towards him.

"Excuse me," said Danielle,

Alex raised his hand, desperately wanting to touch her.

"We're visiting my mother."

Moving his head, Danielle's misty figure solidified into a real woman in a pink sweater and blue jeans with a child. "I'm sorry." Alex snatched back his hand.

The woman murmured gently to her child as they bent to lay flowers on the stone he'd been standing beside.

Walking beneath a large tree's canopy, Alex leaned against its solid trunk to gather his composure. All the religious imagery, the hymns, the prayers, the weighing of souls, the last judgements - he couldn't bring himself to believe in that God. Yet in this time of need, he willed himself to believe that some higher power gave meaning to life. Closing his eyes, he bowed his head. Placing a blank canvas on the easel of his mind, he picked up his palette of memories and painted the Venetian twilight of a week ago. They'd spent last Friday visiting galleries and churches. Having had his fill of religious triptychs and dark Titians, he'd walked to dinner with Rick and Patti. The darkening squares and alleys suddenly opened out onto the wide lagoon and a sky ombréed from apricot to deep indigo. A constant point of light, Venus, burst from the darkness, followed by a scattering of stars. Crossing a canal, he'd looked down from the bridge to see a rat swimming from one drainpipe to another on the opposite side. That little rat, leaving a trail of perfectly formed V-shaped ripples in her wake, was determined to get someplace. The beauty of that plucky rodent, fulfilling some vital errand, struck him as worthy of wonder as the light from distant suns. That spirit of animating life was the power he found himself praying to, *'Dear God, please let Tyler be okay. If you let him be okay, I'll believe in you. Take anything you want from me, just let Tyler live ...'*

"Jack has to go, come say goodbye."

Alex raised his head to see Rick beckoning him. Joining the group around Sid's grave, Jack hugged each of them.

"Thanks for being here with us." Letitia rubbed Jack's arm. "I'll call as soon as I have any news."

Jack's chin crumpled, tears filled his eyes. "Tyler's a special guy. He must be, look how much love he's surrounded by. Sorry I can't stay, but I have to work."

"What a sweet man Jack is," said Letitia as she watched him depart.

Tiffany buried her face in her mother's shoulder.

Alex looked at Rick's face.

Rick turned away.

After one last farewell to Sid, they made their way to the west exit and grabbed a cab back to the hospital.

* * *

The gift shop shutters were being rolled down and the cafeteria lights switched off. As the hospital's night shift came on duty, Alex, Rick, Letitia and Tiffany sat in silence on the vinyl couches in the waiting area.

"I almost forgot, Luisa asked me to thank you for the flowers," Alex suddenly said to Tiffany.

"Can't she pick up the phone herself? That woman has no courtesy," blurted Letitia. "I know she's your mother, Ricky, but Luisa's always behaved like the Queen of Sheba."

Rick looked up from his phone. "No argument here."

"I'm glad she liked them," said Tiffany. "Matteo FedExed the master disc to me last week. Her commentary's wonderful."

"*Her* commentary? Hello, I was also part of it." Rick indignantly put his phone away.

"And you were terrific as well." Tiffany sipped her herb tea. "I watched the movie along with the track over the weekend.

Her Imperfect Past's one of dad's best films, if not *the* best. It's a shame that it was so poorly received at the time."

"Maybe it'll be re-evaluated when the Blu-ray comes out," said Letitia. "It's good that people will get to see it again."

Alex checked the clock by the admissions desk, nearly 9 p.m. "Fuck, I didn't bring my meds."

"Alex, Ricky, go home. You must be exhausted. It's truly been a comfort having you here, but …" Letitia pulled the tissue from her cardigan sleeve, "but it's been too long. Every minute more means it's less likely he'll be how he was."

Tears welled up in Tiffany's eyes. "I was so wrapped up in my problems that I got jealous of Tyler for being happy. I wish I could go back and undo all the mean things I said to him."

Rick went to the other couch, sat beside Tiffany and snuggled her. "Your mom's right, we bicker and argue but that doesn't mean we don't love each other."

"Ricky, have you kept in touch with Sid's other kids?" Letitia swept back her golden hair, struggling to maintain her composure.

Rick unfolded Tiffany, keeping his arm around her. "Sid's divorce from Deanna was nasty, and when there was no inheritance from dad's estate their boys cut off all communication. After Troy's overdose I heard Glenn took off up to Alaska. Sid and Helen's first daughter, Peggy, she passed on three years ago from pancreatic cancer. Eugene let me know. He and Darlene seem pretty well balanced and doing okay. We chat from time to time, but I can't say I really know them. You guys, Patti and momma are the only real family I have."

"I'm glad we were here for you when you came back to live here. Everyone needs a family. I can't take much more of this." Letitia clenched her fists. "Tyler, please wake up!"

"Someone's coming," said Rick.

Alex's knees were stiff from sitting. He had to use his hands to push himself up as a grim-faced resident in a white coat approached.

"Please." The doctor motioned them to follow.

Gathering their wits and belongings, they trailed behind her.

Everyone got into the large elevator.

Punching the sixth-floor button, the doctor nervously dug her hands in her white coat's pockets. "Apologies for taking so long to come get you. It was an extraordinarily complex procedure. We didn't want to be overly optimistic and give you false hope. That's why we waited so long before bringing you up. We're aware this is a most distressing time for the family."

Alex watched the numbers on the elevator panel pass by.

2.

3.

4.

5 ...

UNSEEN

6.

The elevator doors opened.

"You may be shocked by his appearance." The resident strode down the corridor and swung through the doors to the neuro-ICU. Alex, Rick, Tiffany and Letitia followed the doctor's flapping white coat past bays of wheezing and beeping machines hidden behind surgical curtains. Passing the buzz of frenetic activity around the nurses station, they went through two more sets of double doors. Their journey ended in a set of dimly lit bays behind white framed glass partitions.

"Only one of you may go in," said the doctor.

Letitia handed Tiffany her jacket and purse.

"But you can see him through the window."

Letitia exchanged words with the attending physician before approaching the bed.

Tiffany, Alex and Rick leaned their faces to the glass.

The bedside nurse in mint green scrubs faded up the light.

There was Tyler, oxygen tubes over his nose, drains, catheters and cannula drips stuck everywhere, a dressing taped around his head with scrappy tufts of hair sprouting from its right side.

Letitia spoke softly to him.

A ray of hope. His finger moved.

Tyler's groggy voice was followed by his mother's laugh.

Letitia murmured to Tyler for a minute or two longer before rejoining them. "He knows we're here. It was tough understanding him but he asked which of us brought the beers." Letitia gulped down a smile as she took her things from Tiffany.

The four of them restrained whoops of joy until they were out of the neuro-ICU.

In the elevator, Letitia and Tiffany let out relieved sobs on each other's shoulder. Sniffling, Letitia patted Alex and Rick's arms. "He's got a long way to go, but he made it through, thank God."

Alex also silently thanked the power he'd prayed to. Then he reasoned a skilled surgical team using state of the art medical technology had removed the aberrant conglomeration from Tyler's cranium. It could only be his ego needing to pat itself on the back to believe his plea could have had any impact on Tyler regaining consciousness.

"Take your mom home," Rick ordered Tiffany. "Do not let her stay here all night."

The elevator opened. Letitia, Tiffany and Rick got out.

Stepping forward, Alex rebounded as his right shoulder hit the frame. Throwing out a hand to steady himself, he rubbed his shoulder and walked on. A nauseating darkness covered the waiting area. The splotch in his right eye had grown. It was now blanking out the entire central portion of his right eye ...

★ ★ ★

Alex was in his studio mounting one of the paper 'hole' pieces on its display box, when the misty gray figure drifted from the gold metal panel's central slit. "I haven't got time for you. Go haunt someone else. Shoo!" Alex flapped his hand at the panel.

Kent shot a nail into the right-angled joint of the cuboid frame he was assembling. "Who was it this time?"

"Fog guy."

Kent swung his eyes towards the metal panel. "You're gonna get me thinking I see them."

"I should keep it in my head, I know, but I found verbalizing chases them off more efficiently …"

After the massive deterioration in his vision on the night Tyler came out of surgery, first thing next morning Rick had rushed Alex to the Eye Institute. They'd had to wait three hours before Dr. Kastani re-examined his eye. Two new blockages had formed and, perhaps due to flying, swelling had re-occurred at the original site. These new blockages and relapse of the earlier one meant monthly checkups would be needed for the foreseeable future. More time and money spent on medical procedures was exactly what he didn't need. They'd hung around for another couple of hours so Dr. Kastani could treat the areas with a series of mini-intravitreal injections.

"Will this give me enough improvement to drive?" Alex had asked while waiting for the numbing anesthetic on his eye to kick in. The idea of being an eternal passenger was too depressing to contemplate on top of everything else.

"The vision in your left eye is in good shape, so technically you can drive now if you want," said Dr. Kastani.

"I hear what you say, and it's true I can see, but I don't trust my eyes. I see things that aren't there. Well, I hope they aren't. If they are then I'm being haunted."

"What type of things do you see?" The doctor arranged the cover over Alex's eyes.

"People. Faces. Dead relatives. Sometimes misty gray or black figures. It's unnerving. I wasn't going to mention it, but I'm afraid I'm losing my mind."

"Does this happen all the time?"

"Mostly in low light, or when there are moving shadows, glittering reflections or a lot of visual detail."

"Ah," said Dr. Kastani, "sounds like Charles Bonnet syndrome."

"This is actually a condition?" Alex heard Dr. Kastani's nurse preparing the injections.

"It generally affects older people who suffer a massive and sudden visual decline. The brain attempts to fill in the gaps by generating its own images, often best guesses of what's likely to be there. But as every human being's a unique combination of physiology, chemistry and experience, there's no set pattern for what people may think they see. You're young for this condition but being an artist your brain may be more attuned to seek and process visual information. Your right eye's dominant, which means information from that side's perceived faster than the left. That could account for your creative brain leaping to rash and fanciful conclusions."

"How do we treat it?"

"Drug therapy may be considered for severe cases. But acknowledging the illusions can educate your brain to separate fact from fiction. For example, touching the hallucination proves it's not there. Try changing the variables, like turning the lights up or down, or moving your eyes to shift your focus. This should clear up once your vision improves."

"And what if it doesn't?"

"Your brain should learn to ignore any blank spots which persist. There, we're ready now. Pressure coming on your eye …"

When Rick had brought him home from the eye clinic, Alex went to lie down in the bedroom with the blinds lowered. His eye was sore and throbbing, his vision a total blur. Staring up at the dark ceiling, a dainty woman had glided to his bedside and peered down over him. "Hi, Mom. You always did hover by my bed when I got sick … Yeah, I feel like I got punched in the face. Don't worry, Mom, Rick's here. Thanks for checking in on me."

"Who are you talking to?" Rick asked nervously from the doorway.

"Turn on the lights."

Rick did so.

The ceiling lit up. Mom disappeared. "Dr. Kastani recommended this technique to get rid of those visions I told you about. I'm talking to them to prove they're not there."

"Is it working?" Rick asked dubiously.

"I'll keep you informed. Turn off the lights."

"Dinner will be ready in an hour."

Hearing Rick's footsteps return to the kitchen, Alex had relaxed. Okay, so Mom's bedside visit was a hallucination, but imagining he'd seen her had made him happy. That was a month ago. Now, instead of being alarmed by visions of the dead Alex found himself communicating with them ...

The *bang, clink!* of the nail gun snapped Alex back into his studio. Kent was attaching the glossy white panels to the top, bottom and sides of the skeleton cube he was assembling. Alex laid his hand on the 'hole' piece he'd just mounted. Through the punctures and rips in the Hollywood Map to the Stars and excavated layers of supermarket tabloids, he squinted into the hollow display box beyond it.

"Knock, knock." Rick entered the studio. "Hi, Kent."

"I just got the title for these," exclaimed Alex, "*Bucato!*"

"Say what?" asked Kent.

"Italian for laundry, but it literally means holes or punctures," Rick explained. "Nice idea," Rick said approvingly. "Where's Suki?"

Taking the mounted piece off the workbench, Alex set the next cubic frame Kent just finished in its place. "She's got a meeting with a gallery interested in showing her work." He picked up the next *Bucato* to mount.

"But Al!" Rick gasped on seeing it. "That's one of your watercolors."

"Yep." The topmost layer of this piece was a plein air sunset of his. The under layers were made of Monopoly money.

"But that was beautiful." Rick inspected the punctured, ripped and sanded holes in Alex's painting which exposed glimpses of pink, green and orange toy bills with 5, 20 and 500 on them. "Destroying your own work is sacrilege!"

"It still exists, doesn't it? Just differently. It isn't destroyed, it's transformed."

"If you say so. Okay, I'm headed off to another day in the salt mines of Bel Air with my lovely and not so lovely *Belles*."

"Who's not so lovely this week?" Alex positioned the watercolor sunset over the front of the hollow cube. "The dynamics change so frequently on that show I struggle to keep up."

"I'm still less than enchanted with Cristina for not stepping down from the Conservatory Board like she promised to. She claims she can do more good by staying on to convince the remaining trustees to vote off Hulton when the chair comes up for renewal, but I'm not convinced. She's coveted a Board position for so many years I think she'll do anything to keep it. And although no-one can prove how stories about Augusta's philandering husband, Joli's DUI and Vanda's secret affair with a daytime soap actress got out, manicured fingers are all being pointed at Cristina. Seriously, every day some new tittle tattle to do with the show breaks on the internet."

"What motive would Cristina have?" Alex jiggled the *Bucato* piece on the frame. "Kent, this is a little tight. Can you sand down those two edges?"

Kent inspected the frame, then carried the cube back to his workstation.

"That kind of gossip's unpleasant for the cast but great free publicity for the show," said Rick. "And remember, Cristina's one of the producers and our season premiere's two weeks away."

"Do you believe she's behind the leaks?"

"I'm not sure. Once Ellery's husband proved a banking error caused the delay in the withdrawal of the Raban's funds rather any irregularity, Ellery and Cristina made up. She's given Cristina the benefit of the doubt. Even so, I'm careful about what I tell Cristina now."

"That's a shame. I was almost beginning to like her."

"Well, one more shooting block and I'm done. It hasn't been the fun I'd hoped for but the money's come in useful to help

Letitia. I wish she hadn't had to borrow against the house but the intensive therapy's showing an improvement. Tyler's walking with crutches now."

"I told you I'm happy to help out financially with Tyler's rehab."

"With what, Al? Monopoly money?"

"I can borrow against this place again. Or sell the Ken Price."

"We'd get more for Rod's *FREEDOM* painting."

"Rod gifted that to me, I couldn't sell it. Let's hope Chen gets buyers for the last of the abstracts he took."

"Or you could paint him some new ones?"

"I don't like the idea of painting to order, but maybe I'll have to. Anyway, I gotta finish up everything for Neroli's show. And my vision needs to clear more before I can paint again." Alex flapped his hand to his right. "This fuzziness is throwing my creativity totally out of whack."

"Have you tried wearing the eyepatch I got when you're working?"

"Yeah, and it didn't help. Just made me feel like I was missing my parrot and a gold earring."

Kent sniggered as he brought back the adjusted frame.

Alex concentrated on mounting the piece over the hooks on the cube's front. A golden dog twizzled in circles by his ankle. He flicked out his leg. "Shoo, Bella!"

Rick looked at Kent, who shrugged in response as they exchanged weirded out glances.

"I saw that, you two," said Alex tartly. "Don't judge me, it works."

Rick kissed Alex goodbye and headed off.

"Another one bites the dust." Alex wiped his hands on a rag. Lifting the cube with the watercolor and Monopoly money piece attached on its front, he stacked it along with the four others they'd done. His mind was riffing on the best way to wire the backlights in these *Bucato* pieces when his iPhone buzzed.

Tossing the rag aside, Alex put on his glasses. Not recognizing the number, he answered with a gruff, "Y'ello?"

"Am I speaking with Alex Morgan?"

"Yeah."

"Thom Hannay."

Giving it a moment's thought, Alex remembered he was the journalist who'd done the interview at the Carlyle. "Hey, Thom. How's it hangin'?"

"Good, thanks. Listen, our photo editor's been working with Elio Toscani in Rome. There's a buzz going around about his photos and Zorzi's angle on the *Corriere della Serra* article you're featured in. In light of that, the magazine's pulled your interview from the September issue."

Alex's chest tightened. "Is this to do with gay marriage?"

"Yeah."

"Well, I'm disappointed but not surprised." Alex couldn't fathom what Luisa's motivation had been, but her spectacularly mistimed public approval of their relationship had now got the biggest publicity coup of his artistic career bounced from one the world's most revered magazines. "See why I keep my private life private? Everyone acts like the world's so open in these allegedly enlightened times, but here's a prime example of even a quality publication being afraid to stoke controversy. It was nice meeting with you —"

"Whoa, whoa, not so fast," Thom cut in. "The interview you gave me was good, but at the time my gut told me you've got a bigger story to tell. The magazine wants me to revisit the article with an eye on publication in the October issue. I'm in LA this week. Would you talk with me again? Not only you, but Rick too? I want to put your career in context with your relationship and your sexuality, also with history. Would you be up for that?"

About to rule it out, Alex stopped himself. He'd just been outraged because he thought the magazine wanted to drop the article because they considered his lifestyle 'unsuitable.' Maybe his problem was deep down he was uncomfortable publicly acknowledging that he was a man who loved men. Alex's heart thumped. His chest tightened. "Thom, may I call you back? I need to talk this over with Rick."

* * *

"Mr. Alex!" Manuela settled the frail fellow resident she'd been helping into a chair before greeting them. "Such beautiful flowers!" She beamed at the orange dahlias Rick held out.

"We thought they'd look nice in your room," said Rick.

"They will. I have a beautiful room. But everything here is beautiful," Manuela said proudly.

Alex had been dreading driving down to Rancho del Rey to pay this visit, not because he didn't want to see Manuela but because he feared she may be unhappy living in an elder care facility. Seeing how contented she was lifted a huge weight from his shoulders. Her arrythmia had abated, so he hoped Jorge had found a retirement apartment for her to move into.

The home's different wings were constructed around courtyards planted with lemon trees and colorful shrubs. Combined with its stucco-clad walls, wooden beams and red tiled roofs, the greenery lent the place a vacation atmosphere.

Manuela slowly walked them to her room. A journey made even slower by her obsessive compulsion to tidy the leaflets and wipe dust from every console table they passed.

"It must be nice having your son near to you," said Alex.

Arranging the dahlias in a vase, Manuela stared into the distance.

"This home is near to Jorge's home," said Alex trying to glean some information.

"It is?" Manuela placed the vase in front of the window onto the courtyard. Taking a duster, she wiped imaginary dirt off the windowsill. She moved the trinkets Alex recalled from her apartment at the Venice house to dust around them. "Where is Miss Danielle? Is she working today?"

Rick shot a questioning glance at Alex.

"She's at the studios," said Alex. "She sends her love."

Manuela picked up a porcelain cat decorated with flowers and birds. "Miss Danielle gave this to me. She is so kind."

Alex and Rick nodded.

"Does Jorge visit you often?" Alex asked, pushing the question. "Will he be coming today?"

"Jorge is a very busy man," Manuela said dreamily. "And Rancho del Rey is a long way away ..."

Alex knew there was no point reminding her they were in Rancho del Rey. As their visit continued, the rapid decline in Manuela's cognition became evident. Ending the visit with hugs, Manuela became tearful and clung to Alex. He kissed her, assuring her everything would be fine. Leaving her watching hummingbirds on the feeders in the courtyard, her distress had passed.

"I should have chased this up sooner. Do you think Jorge's not paying her the attention he should, or she's forgotten he's visited?" Alex asked Rick as they walked from Manuela's room to the entrance.

"Hard to tell. But she's clearly not capable of living alone."

"Maybe that's why he hasn't bought the apartment for her yet."

"If she's not going to be able to live alone you ought to ask Jorge for the money back," said Rick.

"I don't want to be an Indian giver."

"But babe, Manuela's situation has totally changed from when you made him that offer."

With the question of Jorge's visits rankling him, Alex knocked on the manager's office door.

"We've just been visiting with senora Alvarez," he said to the lady in a floral tabard apron sitting behind the desk. "Manuela used to be our housekeeper."

"You must be Alex. She speaks fondly of you and your wife. I'm Griselda Medina."

"My wife died seven years ago. This is my partner, Rick."

Griselda stapled some papers and dropped them in her out tray. "Senora Alvarez finds comfort in the past. If it makes her happy, we don't challenge it." She smiled sympathetically at Rick.

"Thank you for taking good care of Manuela," said Alex. "She looks well. But I'm concerned she didn't mention her son's visits. Jorge does visit her, doesn't he?"

Getting up, Griselda hastily closed the office door. She dropped her glasses on the gold chain around her neck and folded her fleshy arms. "The day Jorge Alvarez checked in his mother and unpacked her belongings was the last we saw of him."

"What?" Alex's chest constricted. "The whole reason Manuela moved down here was to be near her family. Don't worry, I'll call Jorge and read him the riot act."

"I hope you have a different phone number to the one we do. Our billing department gets a number out of service message and emails and letters go unanswered. If senora Alvarez's account isn't settled on a regular basis we won't be able to continue providing her care."

"But she has her benefits, savings and pension fund. And I gave Jorge a lump sum to buy her a retirement apartment. The fees shouldn't be a problem." Alex's heart fluttered.

"Jorge also assured us that was the case, but senora Alvarez has placed her son in sole charge of her funds. If we don't receive payment and her next of kin doesn't respond senora Alvarez will become a ward of the state."

"That's out of the question. Send any outstanding bills to me and I'll deal with them. And please direct all communications about Manuela's care to me from now on."

"But Mr. Morgan, you are not a relative —"

"I'll talk to my lawyers and deal with that," said Alex determinedly.

Driving around pretty roads lined with palms and pepper trees, Alex thumped the SUV's steering wheel. "I'm going to wring that little weasel's neck. How could Jorge do that to her?"

"Would you like me to drive?" Rick nervously asked from the passenger seat.

"No. I can see fine." Alex ground his jaw together. Swinging around a corner, Pop's mocking face loomed from a dark bank of bushes. Lifting his right hand off the wheel, Alex flung it around. "Outta my way, Pop! Yeah, I'm a trusting fool, I don't need you to remind me." His hand passed through the false vision and Pop's face melted into the weeds of a shabby house's front yard with a realtor's FOR RENT sign on it.

Pulling up, Alex despondently rested his forehead on the steering wheel. "Jorge's not gonna be here, is he?"

Rick stared up at the empty house. "Maybe the neighbors will know where he's gone?"

Climbing down from the jeep, Alex and Rick trudged up the overgrown pathway to Jorge Alvarez's last known address, both knowing they were on a fruitless mission.

✱ ✱ ✱

"We visited the County Clerk's office and got the license."

"We just haven't gotten around to the getting married part yet," said Rick with a laugh.

"We will. As soon as my new show's opened," Alex said as he guided Thom Hannay around the house.

"The sculptures and three-dimensional pieces you just showed me in your studio, these signal a radical change in your work," said Thom. "What's the reason?"

"It wasn't premeditated," Alex said with a dry laugh. "Or even premedicated. I turned down a new road and kept going. Maybe I took a wrong turn. It happens."

Thom switched his attention to Rick. "What do you think of Alex's new direction?"

Taking a moment to think it over, Rick said, "It's a risk. But what's art without risks?"

"You support him on this?" asked Thom.

"Totally."

"Thanks, babe," said Alex with a smile.

Thom flipped his notebook closed as they walked into the living-room. "Have you always been this happy together?"

"I haven't given it much thought," Alex laughed.

"Thom," said Rick. "Excuse me for asking, but are you gay?"

Thom swept his floppy black hair off his forehead and dipped his eyes. "I am. I just haven't had an emotional connection with a man like you guys have as yet. Finding the right someone who can push you and challenge you and support you isn't so easy. Your relationship gives me the hope to keep on looking."

In the living-room, they stopped in front of the mantel. *The Boy on the Beach*, Alex's painting of Rick from the seventies, was hung where Danielle's portrait used to be. The nude male life studies were grouped around it.

Thom sipped his wine as he perused the graphite framed pictures. "Beautiful drawings. Sensual, strong, dignified. Why weren't these in your retrospective?"

"Somebody else asked me that. Honestly, I suppose I felt ashamed of my male figurative work. Like it was too intimately revealing of myself. And in regard to our relationship, I guess I got caught up editing the picture of us we present to the world, so I hid that as well. When you've been hurt, humiliated and publicly shamed for doing nothing more than being in love, you get protective. The wounds of seventy-four still haven't fully healed."

"These drawings have given me the idea of the photo we need of you two for the article," said Thom.

Alex laughed, "But Thom, they're nudes."

Thom sipped his wine, a knowing glint in his eyes. "Precisely."

✶ ✶ ✶

Having drawn enough life models, being one was a totally new experience.

Standing under the studio lights in their robes, Alex found it hard to believe that in a couple of minutes they would drop them. And a camera would record an image of his and Rick's bodies. Which would then be printed in a magazine for world-wide distribution. This image would be out there forever to accompany the article titled 'The Unseen Alex Morgan.'

Rick had a flesh pouch taped over his groin for modesty. A pose had been decided on. They would both be facing left, Alex pressed up close behind Rick and Rick's leg angled to give the impression they were both nude. The plan was to crop the photo at hip height for publication.

There was no hair stylist, no makeup. No overly flattering lighting or soft focus. No attempt to disguise the bullet's scar on Rick's shoulder. No digital retouching.

"When you're ready," said Thom.

Taking off their robes, Rick and Alex handed them to an assistant.

Standing naked in front of Thom Hannay and the select studio team didn't feel alarming or odd to Alex. He and Rick had already bared their souls to Thom in the most brutally honest and revealing interview they could have given. They'd told Thom about the travails which tore them apart in the seventies, the intervening years of living a lie as married men and potential hurt that caused to their wives and families, and the joy of now being able to live openly and proudly as a legally married couple. Talk of Alex's art had taken a back seat to his personal journey of discovery and coming to terms about being totally open in his sexuality.

Alex pressed his face into Rick's head, his eyes closed, losing himself in the vanilla coconut scent of Rick's hair as the photographer snapped away.

"Alex, put your hand on Rick's shoulder," said Thom from the darkness behind the spotlights.

"My right hand? It's so ugly." This did make Alex feel shy.

"This photo's the truth, it's realism. I want to show you, the whole you," said Thom.

Seeing how he and Rick had already placed themselves in Thom's hands in the most intimate of ways, Alex acquiesced. He rested his misshapen fingers on Rick's scar.

Liberation and freedom flooded Alex's being. Here they were, two older gay men, open, unashamed, no longer needing to hide their love. He surrendered to the moment, let go of his gut and wondered if he was making the biggest mistake of his life.

✷ ✷ ✷

Suki stuffed her hands in her dungaree pockets. "Jess says I should channel my energy into making my own art rather than someone else's."

'*You haven't been making my art, you've been assisting me to make it,*' was what Alex wanted to say, but "I'll miss you. You must do whatever's best for you," were the words he said.

When Suki arrived for work this morning and said she needed to speak with him he never imagined it was to hand in her notice.

"I've finished everything you wanted in the upstairs studio. All your stock orders, filing and cataloging are up to date. Would it be okay if I go now?"

"Now?" Alex's heart did a somersault.

"Jess says we need a bigger apartment with studio space for both of us. She wants to go look at places today." Suki couldn't meet Alex's eyes.

"If I've done something to upset you, please tell me so I can make it right. We've been together over twelve years. I've come to depend on you."

"I know." Suki gathered her belongings from the trestle table and packed them in her bag. "But when you have a show or sell a painting or do an interview, the only name mentioned in connection with your art is Alex Morgan. I want people to know Suki Mihara's name. That won't happen unless I make this leap. You've been good to me. I've learned a lot here, and I'll miss you and Kent and the studio, but if I stay any longer, doing the same thing day after day to support your work, I'm afraid I may never get to make my own name known in the art world."

Suki's words pierced Alex's heart like daggers. "Is this what you feel or what Jess feels?"

"I felt it, Jess helped me voice it. So may I go now?"

Alex shrugged. How could he say no? "One thing I ask, please don't tell anyone about my new work in the upstairs studio. I want first sight of it to be first sight."

Fastening her bag, Suki nodded. "Tell Kent I'll call him."

Their last goodbye was sadly cool.

Once Suki had left, Alex stood alone. The twelve giant metal panels, all sprayed in metallic and flesh tones with glossy, blood-red lacquered undersides, were regimented around the studio's perimeter like an ominous army. The *Bucato* pieces, all now mounted on their hollow cuboid boxes, stacked like building blocks in the corner.

Scratching his chest, processing the enormity of suddenly no longer having Suki's help, he saw a woman walk in through the frosted glass window. She tossed back her hair. It was Danielle. Alex laughed. If only it was … "Have I been exploiting Suki and Kent?" he asked her out loud. "I always paid them well and thanked them, didn't I?" Danielle floated past the metal panels. He looked away from her to stare at his hands. "I'd do all the work myself if I could." Wanting to see Danielle clearly once more, he moved his eyes to look directly at her.

Too late. She'd gone.

Wandering to the Mac, he put on his glasses and opened the workbook with his projected expenses. Large numbers rippled before his eyes. Struggling to see them clearly, Mom appeared behind the Mac's screen by the stacked *Bucato* pieces. "I gotta pay the movers to deliver all this to The Copley Gallery," he told Mom across the dim studio. "Then I have to cover the hire of lighting and AV equipment. Neroli's given me free rein to do what I like with the gallery space as long as I pick up the extra expenses." Mom hovered in the background as he scrolled down the worksheet. "Then I've got to pay for Brian's legal work to regain control of Manuela's finances." Pop's face overtook Mom's dainty body. "Yeah, I was a fucking idiot not to have drawn up a contract with Jorge. Dumb trusting sucker I am, green lighting putting half a million dollars into his personal account with no paperwork. I'm a fool, I know." Alex lashed out at Pop's distorted visage which slipped away. Taking off his glasses, he looked for Mom again.

She'd gone.

Putting his glasses back on, Alex closed his financial spreadsheet and opened his email. Wracking his brain for former assistants he could ask to come back, he swung around on his chair as the emails rolled in. One from **E. KLOTTE** with the subject: "**CHEN**" caught his attention. He spun back to the screen and clicked the message ...

Great to catch up in NYC. Loved the show. Xander Chen's bombarding us with queries about Agua Nexus. He's got a buyer keen on it and says we should come to him first if we want to sell. I hear from the Hambletons and Rhonda Bigelow that Chen's been pestering them about selling your pieces they'd loaned to MOMA. Can you tell Chen to quit bugging us? We got no desire to sell. Take care, Alex. We're on our way to Art Basel. Neroli Copley sent us an invite for your new show. If we can make it, we'll be there. Mia says hi! Eli K

Alex shut down the Mac. Shit. The money was going out left, right and center, he'd lost Suki and maybe this was the best the vision in his right eye was ever going to get. He'd been grateful for the cash from the abstracts Chen had sold, but it passed through his checking account without touching the sides. Once Chen had taken his commission, at least the rest of the money had come to him though. But selling his old works on the secondary market would put big commissions into Chen's pocket and bring nothing to him.

His right eye felt sore and tired. As a test, he removed his glasses and blanked out his left eye with his palm. A misty spider's web covered the studio. Through the web in his eye, Dora's gray curls and crocheted shawl materialized. "Grandma, I've done everything wrong. I thought this year would make me a star and instead it's turned me into a joke. I should've stayed in Ohio. Then I'd never have messed up everyone's lives. Danielle would have had a family with someone who loved her equally, Rick would've been a TV star and Manuela wouldn't have wasted her life looking after a man who let her work herself into the ground. What did I do it all for grandma? To call myself an artist? I don't even know what that means anymore. What a mess I made of my life. And everybody else's. Just go, grandma. Leave me like the rest of them. You're not really here with me anyway

…" Alex waved his hand over his eye's web to make Dora's image disappear.

"Aw, pudding, I'm always here with you." Dora's kindly eyes crinkled in a smile. "And if you'd stayed in Ohio I wouldn't have had the years with you I did, and my life would have been so much the poorer for that."

Alex unfurled his fingers and reached to his grandmother, willing her to be real, desperately wanting to feel her loving touch once more. A deep, sad longing for the past constricted his chest.

His fingers touched Dora's illusion.

But she didn't vanish.

Dora's image hung in the air.

She reached out and stroked his hair.

He felt her hand touch him.

Alex clutched his chest, knowing his heart had stopped beating. The paint splattered concrete floor hurtled towards his face as he fell from the chair and the material world slipped from his grasp.

KA-BOOM!

Nurse DeLano checked the monitor's readings. "Good news, your EKG readings are normal and stable. Blood pressure elevated on admission but now down. Bad news, looks like we don't get to keep you for a sleepover."

"That's it. I can go?" Alex asked incredulously.

"I need your bloodwork back before completely ruling out a cardiac event, but if it's clear you're good to go." Nurse DeLano removed the electrocardiogram pads from Alex's chest, arms and legs. "You had another panic attack and fainted."

Alex shook his head in disbelief.

"Disappointed?" Tearing off a wadge of blue paper, Nurse DeLano mopped the conductive gel off Alex's chest.

"More like foolish. I thought I'd died."

Nurse DeLano draped the gown across Alex's chest and set about wiping the gel off his calves with fresh paper towel.

Alex massaged his wrist.

"Do you need to get that checked out while you're here?"

"It's fine. Just banged it when I fell."

"Lucky you didn't hit your head."

"That would've been the cherry on the icing of my day. How come you're not working on the ward?"

"Some cranky old guy complained about my bedside manner. The hospital sent me on an advanced pillow plumping course but —"

"You flunked it and wound up in the ER dishing out nitroglycerine pills and sass."

Nurse DeLano gave Alex more towel to wipe the gel off his arms. "I got my master's last year. A nurse practitioner vacancy opened up in cardiac emergency and here I am."

"I wouldn't have dropped by just to say hi, but I'm glad to see you doing so well. How long will the bloodwork take?"

"Another half-hour."

"Would it be okay for Rick to come wait with me?"

"Sure. I'll go find him."

Alex finished wiping gel off his arms and neck. He lay back listening to the background chatter in the Cedars-Sinai ER. Footsteps approached the bay, they sounded like a woman's high heels. A familiar cough accompanied them.

"Here are your friends." Nurse DeLano rattled back the blue curtain.

"Thank goodness you're okay." Rick's soft shoes padded to the gurney.

Scotty's heels clicked close behind.

"Hey, babe." Taking Rick's hand, Alex asked Scotty, "What're you doing here?"

"Checking off another of the city's medical facilities. The Eye Institute's color scheme made a far bolder statement but the coffee bar's better here."

"When Kent found you on the floor, I was scared this was the big one." Rick averted his eyes. "I didn't want to be alone if the worst happened so called Scotty for backup."

"False alarm." Alex smiled apologetically at Scotty. "Sorry you had a wasted trip."

"The Beverly Center's next door. Figured I could go shopping whichever way it went down."

"I'll be back when the bloodwork's in. Keep him calm," Nurse DeLano warned Rick and Scotty as he swished the curtain.

"Did you hear what that nurse said?" Scotty glanced over her shoulder before zeroing in on Alex. "Friends. Here are your *friends*!"

Flexing his wrist, Alex winced. "So?"

Scotty jabbed an accusing finger. "You could have had a massive heart attack and be lying there dead right now!"

"You haven't got the hang of this hospital visiting thing, have you?" Alex huddled the surgical gown around his chest.

"I'm a friend, but Rick's your husband to be! Okay this was a false alarm, but imagine if it wasn't? And suppose you weren't in any state to grant permission for Rick to have information about your condition or even visit you."

"Yeah, yeah, I know," said Alex resignedly.

"You should be married by now, then he'd be your next of kin without question," said Scotty firmly.

"Soon," added Rick. "We're going to do it soon."

"Uh huh." Scotty clapped her hands then spread them wide. "I'm staging a wedding intervention."

Alex and Rick exchanged wary glances.

"I made an emergency dash to buy the ring for the proposal, but the way you two are going about it the getting-married part's never going to happen. Organizing weddings is my trade. The nurse told me to keep you calm so that's what I'm going to do. I shall lift every stress about getting married from your shoulders so you can concentrate on your new show. I'll take charge of every detail."

"Actually, this isn't keeping me calm …" muttered Alex.

Scotty whipped her leatherbound planner from her bag. "Dates. People need time to arrange travel and accommodation."

"What people?" asked Rick.

"Guests."

"We were planning on something small and quiet," said Alex. "Look, as soon as we find a Justice of the Peace —"

"Or Salvation Army Captain or Medicine Man …"

Scotty and Alex raised quizzical eyebrows at Rick.

"They can perform marriage ceremonies as well as officiated celebrants," said Rick proudly. "I Googled it."

"Anyway," Scotty said, returning to her planner, "I'm looking at mid-October. That's enough warning for people coming from overseas."

"Overseas?" Alex was glad he wasn't still hooked up to the EKG. "Apart from who the heck says *overseas* these days, who have you got in mind here?"

"You'll want Patti to be there, won't you?" Scotty phrased the question to Rick like an order.

"I guess," mumbled Rick.

"And if you invite Patti, you must also invite Luisa."

"I can't see her coming. And, if in a moment of madness, momma did accept, she's so frail the journey could kill her."

"That's putting a positive spin on it," muttered Alex.

"If you invite one member of family the correct etiquette is to invite all family, whether or not you think they'll accept," Scotty stated.

Alarmed at the speed events were escalating, and Scotty using her *Miss Manners on Weddings* voice, Alex said, "We aren't in the best financial state. We can't afford a big event and —"

"It's my gift," Scotty cut him off.

"I didn't think you were exactly rolling in cash either."

"Rod's hooked me up with his investment manager. This Madoff guy's a genius. I'm already getting dividends," said Scotty.

"How come Rod's giving you financial advice?" asked Alex.

"He came to cry on my shoulder at the *Conceptualism in California* opening. He'd bought Galina the wrong color Mercedes. Since she'd been with him for six months she was devastated he didn't know her better. She ended it on the spot and flounced off in a huff."

"Along with the Mercedes?" asked Rick.

"And the five-carat diamond ring and French bulldog. To teach him a lesson she had the Mercedes resprayed and charged it to him," said Scotty.

The curtain swished back. A grinning Nurse DeLano entered the bay. "All clear. You're a free man."

"Just to point out ..." Scotty turned to Nurse DeLano. "Rick is not Alex's friend, his correct status is fiancé. They're getting married next month. I need you to be a witness."

"At the ceremony?" Nurse DeLano asked with a frown.

"You're more than welcome, but I need you to witness they've committed to this date." Scotty displayed the circled day to the three men. "Agreed?"

Alex and Rick nodded mutely.

"Congratulations. I'll get your discharge papers issued. And remember calm, Mr. Morgan must remain calm," Nurse DeLano told Scotty.

"Yeah, yeah. Give me your contact details in case I need this legally enforcing." Handing Nurse DeLano the planner and pen, Scotty turned her attention to Rick. "There's not much time, we need to think about venues ..."

Scotty took back her planner then everyone left the bay for Alex to get dressed. A couple of hours ago he thought he was dying. Oddly enough the vision of Dora which caused him to faint had led him here to the ER and a date for the wedding - a date now carved in marble thanks to Scotty. Grateful to be surrounded by people who truly cared for him, both living and dead, he buttoned his shirt and listened to Scotty's voice depart through the cardiac emergency suite, wondering what on earth he and Rick had let themselves in for.

* * *

09/13/2008
Client – Alex Morgan
20 x 48" LCD Displays @ $75 x 70 days = $105,000
30 x HD video cameras @ $25 x 70 days = $52,000
Standing spotlights and small focus spotlights – selected by client – lease period as agreed = $30,000
Installation, concealed wiring, radio control switching board = $10,000

Daily maintenance, emergency call-out & immediate like for like replacement of faulty equipment included in terms of lease.

Fine Art Movers – Packing, haulage, delivery, insurance and unpacking on site of 12 x cast metal sculptures, 15 x framed artworks mounted on timber boxes, 15 x blank media and boxed supplies from client property to Copley Gallery. Estimate = $10,000

And the big numbers kept on coming ...

The Treasury's bail out of Fannie Mae and Freddie Mac had dealt another brutal blow to his investment pot but Brian held firm to his advice not to raid it in desperation. With his liquid assets running on fumes, Alex had no choice but to take out another loan against the house to fund the new show. It would've been cheaper to buy the flatscreens and cameras outright, but what would he do with all that equipment after the show? The quantity of cash hemorrhaging out of his bank account was so eye-watering that when *The Belles of Bel Air* production office had contacted Neroli about featuring his exhibition's opening night on their season finale, and contributing $10k for the privilege, Alex had reluctantly agreed.

So, following two non-stop grueling days of marshalling gallery staff and video and lighting technicians to ensure his work was displayed exactly the way he wanted, his new show was ready to open. He stood in The Copley Gallery's foyer at 7 p.m., still in his work clothes of denim shirt, neckcloth and grubby jeans. With his grown-out shaggy hair and thick stubble, this wasn't the new improved Versace jacketed Alex Morgan of his MoMA opening, this was the old Sunset Cove version.

And he felt all the more comfortable for it.

Although a follow-up treatment was scheduled with Dr. Kastani, he'd come to terms with the fact that his right eye's vision was as good as it was going to get - and that wasn't very good. On a positive note, if he kept his fully functioning eye pointed towards the wall the fuzzy blurriness of his right meant he could remain splendidly oblivious to the opening night arrivals. Neroli had gone to town with the invitations and a sizeable throng had already packed into the lobby. *The Belles of Bel Air's* two mobile camera crews were busy lensing background footage.

"All miked up." Adjusting the microphone's power pack down the back of his dress pants, Rick snuck into the secluded corner where Alex had set up base camp.

Alex swiveled his good eye towards Rick's butt. "Stick it down the front and you'll get more camera time."

"And risk getting my balls electrocuted." Rick flicked back his hair. "Thanks for letting them shoot here tonight."

"The fee from your show's paid for the food and drink. Make sure you get our money's worth."

Rick grabbed a Sea Breeze off a circulating tray. "The gals on our show can drink any bar dry. And the producers love it when they get drunk and let rip." He slapped his hand over his silk shirt's open neck. "Shit," he whispered, "I hope my mic's not live. Speak of the Devil, *The Witches of Eastwick* are here."

Alex swung his working eye towards the gallery's front doors. Cristina, Ellery and a woman whom he vaguely recalled from the lunch at the house and assumed was Augusta, made their entrance. Cristina wore a white pants suit with diamante trim, Ellery was in a nude toned figure-hugging dress and Augusta was in a plunge neck jungle print blouse with hot pants. All of them wore vertiginously high heels, too much makeup and icy expressions. Alex felt a pang of nostalgia for the opening night faces of yesteryear. Wealthy Beverly Hills matrons like Monica Aigner and Autumn Thayer, with stunning estates and dubious couture, had been the champions and supporters of many young LA artists. Rosemarie Harrington was the last survivor of those formidable women. "Do you need to go over and say hello?"

"They'll find me when they're ready." Rick scanned the crowd. "Ooh, Rilke Rocha from *Art Unlimited* just rocked up. And Jauncey Hernandez from *Art and Artists* is with her."

Alex recalled Jauncey's particularly snide review of his MoMA show. "Quit with the running commentary on the critics. Leave me happy in my ignorance."

"My, my, they sent Roberta Smith," murmured Rick.

"Not Holland Cotter?" Despite not wanting to know about the critics, Alex was disappointed *The New York Times* hadn't sent their most revered arts correspondent.

A familiar cough approached from starboard. "You gotta lay off the smokes, Scotty," Alex said without turning.

"It's true, being blind does heighten the other senses." Scotty greeted Alex with a kiss.

"I'm on her back about that," said Rod coming up.

"I'm quitting, okay?" Scotty snapped back at him.

Rod's watery blue eyes pierced her. "Yes, you are, missy."

Alex noticed Rod place a protective hand on Scotty's waist. Also clocking it, Rick raised a knowing eyebrow.

"Sponsoring that Pavilion for your MoMA show must've cost 'em more than planned." Rod's white teeth gleamed in vicious delight.

Alex didn't understand. "What?"

"You broke the bank! Lehman Brothers declared Chapter Eleven this morning. Meanwhile, in London, the first night of Damien Hirst's sale topped seventy million. Art's looking like the safest investment you can make these days," said Rod smugly.

"But if all the rich folk go broke, Rod, who's going to be the buyers?" Rick countered.

"Yo!" Cayde guided his wife, Brooke, both with welcome drinks in hand, through the crowd. "Auspicious night to open a show. Wall Street's in meltdown!"

"You're very chipper about it," Scotty said to Cayde as the group greeted one another.

"All our money's in bricks and mortar," said Cayde with his arm around Brooke's slim shoulders.

"We're lucky." Brooke, so diminutive she could be mistaken for a child, stared up at them. "But people who depend on their investments for an income could be completely wiped out. It's scary."

"October twenty-nine all over again," said Cayde.

"Welcome to The Copley Gallery," Neroli Copley's voice came over the PA system. She stood in front of the double doors to the three chambers housing Alex's work. Neroli wore a black boat-necked blouse accessorized with a spiky coral necklace. "I'm thrilled tonight to be giving you first sight of Alex Morgan's new solo show *Empty Spaces*," Neroli said into the microphone. "My association with Alex spans over thirty years, so it pains me that this will be our last show together. The Copley Gallery will permanently shutter its doors at the end of November." A murmur of shock ran through the crowd. "I have a passion for discovering, nurturing and bringing new talent to your attention. I intend to keep doing that, but on a smaller scale. Next time we meet, and I sincerely hope we do, I may be showing you my latest discovery's work in my living-room or garage. Or even the back of my car!" Laughter. "I'm often asked what's kept me motivated over all the years I spent running this gallery. My answer? The constant surprise and invention from the artists I represent. I'm proud to have provided a safe space for those wonderful artists to share their vision because, believe me, when an artist shows new work they're putting their raw bleeding heart on display and standing naked before you. Now, Alex?" Spotting him, she asked, "Would you care to say a few words?"

Whether he'd care to or not, a forceful shove from Rod sent him lurching forwards. Throwing a reproachful glance behind him before acknowledging the applause, faces and TV cameras in front, Alex hissed at Rick, "Babe, can you make sure I don't trip over anyone's feet?"

Taking his arm, Rick guided Alex through the congested foyer.

Safely delivered to Neroli's side, Alex accepted the handheld mic and Rick stepped back into the crowd. The camera crew's shotgun booms and mobile spotlights moved in. "I always struggle to know how honest to be in situations like this." Through the webbed mist of his right eye, he hoped to see Danielle, or Mom, or Dora, but his good eye showed him the critics, collectors, friends, enemies, people who came to openings to be seen and the cast of Rick's TV show here due to contractual obligation. As he'd literally posed naked for the *Vanity Fair* photoshoot, he figured he may as well put the raw bleeding heart on the line too. "Okay, you're gonna get honest. When I used to lecture on art I'd tell my students not to edit themselves, not to be polite in their work. I realize what a hypocrite I'd become. I've been editing the picture of myself, giving people the 'me' I thought they wanted to see. The one that wouldn't offend, that would sell. But something happened to change that, I began having problems with my sight. Apologies if I snub anyone, but I've lost most of the vision in my right eye." Alex raised his palm to curb a sigh of concern. "I'm not looking for sympathy, just to explain how the weird shit going down in my eye provided the inspiration for this show. It's about how we see and how we're seen, and the layers we hide beneath our public faces. It wasn't easy to be an openly gay young man in the sixties, even the seventies. I'd like to think I haven't lied about or hidden my sexuality, but I guess I have. There's no one-size-fits-all rule for who you can and can't fall in love with, but there is a rule that you shouldn't hide or apologize for who you do love." Extending his arm, Alex grabbed Rick from the crowd. From his left eye he was aware of the mobile TV cameras and lights getting closer. Through his fuzzy right eye, Pop's faint shadow figure hovered in front of the audience. Alex directed his gaze at Rick to make Pop disappear. "I've always loved Rick Stradman, but I haven't been as transparent about his meaning in my life as I could. In May of this year, California's Supreme Court ruled that the statutes barring same-sex marriage were unconstitutional. So, to publicly cement our bond, one I plan on carrying us through the rest of our lives, I asked Rick to marry me. And he said yes. Cool, huh?"

Warm applause came from the opening night guests, Scotty's whoops audible over the top.

Alex noticed Augusta and the raven-haired woman with huge lips who'd joined her didn't look so enthusiastic. Only when the mobile camera swung around for their reaction shots did the two women smile and clap. "Rick and I don't take for granted those who've fought and lobbied for this right of equality. We also know that this right could also be taken away. Please make your vote count in November, so other late-to-mature dudes like myself may continue to have right to call the man they love their husband. Thank you."

Neroli glanced towards the gallery's entrance as a departing couple made a statement by allowing the front doors to slam on their way out.

"You can't win 'em all," Alex joked in response.

Taking back the mic, Neroli finished thanking the necessary people as Alex and Rick rejoined their friends.

"Great speech," said a man who rushed up.

"Alex, you remember our producer, Lyle Colquhoun." Rick indicated the crop-haired guy who'd intercepted them.

"Hi, yeah. Thanks." Eager to move on, Alex accepted Lyle's compliment.

"Your wedding would make a terrific second season opener." Lyle included Alex along with Rick in this.

"The show's been renewed?" Rick held Alex back.

"Enjoyment levels were through the roof at the test screening. If the ratings are as good as predicted, it's a given."

Cristina was suddenly at their side. "Alex! What a moving speech. And a wedding! Rick, you kept this a secret."

Rick deflected. "We're still making plans."

"Neroli's about to open the show. Catch up with you later. Excuse us," Alex said to Cristina and Lyle. "You didn't tell the girls we're getting married?" he asked Rick.

Covering his mic, Rick said, "Someone on the show's leaking to the media, I got burned by that once before."

Catching up with Alex and Rick, Scotty, Rod, Cayde and Brooke formed a protective phalanx around them. Neroli threw open the double doors. Moving forward as one with the opening night guests, they filed into the first room.

The buzz of excitement dissipated when the guests saw flat screen TVs in gilt frames and not paintings were hung on the white walls. Catalogs weren't being given out until the exit. With no guidance, the gallery goers were disorientated. A floor to ceiling floating panel masked the second room's entrance. The TV screens were the only things here to look at.

The guests dutifully prowled around the gallery, trying to work out what they were looking at. Static images on the screens appeared to come from behind ragged holes. An unvoiced anticlimax of 'is this it?' emanated from the viewers.

"NBC's Monday night line-up's lamer than ever," declared one comedian.

"Pass the remote," quipped another.

Keeping her cool, Neroli serenely rounded up the art critics and writers to usher them around the floating panel into the second room.

Movement appeared on the flat screens. Amusement broke out as everyone realized they were watching the people who'd moved on to the second room peering through the holes. Jauncey Hernandez's boggle eyed face filled one entire LCD flatscreen and received a belly laugh as he recoiled with an expression of grotesque distaste.

"Hilarious," declared Cayde. "The critics have become the show!"

More laughter ensued as the expressions on the faces of the viewers in the second room changed when they realized cameras behind the holes were relaying their reactions to the first room's screens.

"Delicious," purred Rod. "Is this your comment on the art world's zoo-like nature?"

"I made the art, it's up to the viewer how they interpret it." Clasping Rick's hand, Alex led him to the second room.

This next room housed his works created with the paper layers and the ruptured metal panels. The cubes with the 'hole' pieces mounted on their fronts protruded from the walls. Mini spotlights inside the cubes glared though the holes and cameras transmitted images of the viewers looking in. The back lighting turned the punctures and rips of the *Bucato* works into luminous trails, like bleeding rainbows. Shock, followed by ironic laughter, erupted as close inspection of Alex's defiled sunset revealed the Monopoly money with tiny dollar signs beneath it.

"I wanted to use actual dollar bills," Alex confided to Scotty, "but apparently it's illegal to use real money in art."

"The Federal Reserve, such philistines," tutted Scotty.

The standing metal panels, arranged in an outward facing circle in the middle of the room, elicited awe-struck murmurs. These eight-foot-tall monoliths with their metallic rips, slits and tears possessed a Stonehenge quality. A tower of dazzling spotlights and cameras in their central core shone out through the holes and relayed images of the viewers looking in. The blood-red undersides of the brown, tan, pink, olive, polished gold, silver, platinum and copper metal panels lent their explosive wounds an unnerving, visceral quality.

"Organic, dangerous and truly, truly odd," cooed Cayde.

The critics and writers moved beyond the next floating wall and filtered through to the exhibition's third room.

"This last room's where the real fun is," Alex told Scotty.

"Don't tell me, a bounce house?" she laughed.

The canvases, boards and stretched watercolor papers hung on the third room's walls were totally blank. Palettes, brushes, paints, water jars, oil jars, mixing pots, and all the other paraphernalia of an artist's trade were displayed, like in an art store, beneath each blank medium. Beside each blank was a miniature reproduction of one of Alex's art works. With Rick at his side, Alex stood before the one with the catalog photo of

Marooned on Red by it. This large white canvas had a yellow sticker with $25.99. Every tube of red paint, every brush, the jars of linseed oil, thinners and varnish, every single item had a pricing gun's yellow sticker with their value on it. "A visual guide to the cost of producing art in nineteen seventy-four." Alex slyly grinned at Cayde and Rod. "Know how many lifeguard shifts at the country club I had to pull to buy this shit?"

Four video cameras were positioned in this gallery's corners. Because everyone was now aware their reactions were being beamed to the TV screens in the first room, people were guarded in their physical responses. The outrage, confusion and amusement remained behind their eyes.

"Everything's here to recreate an exact duplicate of my pieces depicted. The costs clearly labeled on each element with the exact amounts used to originally make them," said Alex.

"And there's nothing to stop anyone opening a tube of paint and putting it on the canvas," added Rick.

"But what if they actually do put paint on one of the canvases?" Rod asked with genuine interest.

"It remains," said Alex. "My artistic directive for these pieces is to let anything happen to them. If the paint tubes dry out from not being used, or if someone throws water or writes obscenities, or comes back day after day to reproduce my work, or creates a masterpiece of their own, so be it. Who knows, maybe someone else can do my work better than me? And if no-one touches them, if the canvases remain blank, gather dust or grow mold, so be that too. They're not to be conserved, degeneration is their life."

Bold, stenciled words on the walls between the works declared TRY, EXPERIMENT, FAIL, HOPE, DESPAIR, CREATION. And Alex's hand painted words by the exit doors were …

FILL THE EMPTY SPACE

"That's it." Alex led Rick together with his pals out into The Copley Gallery's concrete rear courtyard covered by a latticed metal roof supported by iron girders. Attendees who'd sped through the exhibition were enjoying drinks and canapes from the serving carts dotted around. As filming was forbidden inside the gallery, the camera crew had cut around to set up out here. Alex spotted the mobile camera's lights on Cristina, Augusta and the raven-haired lady he figured must be Joli. The ladies were engaged in a heated, white wine fueled interaction before the cameras.

"Challenging work. Feathers have been ruffled." Cayde glanced at the knots of arts critics and writers also having heated discussions. "Wish Allen could've been here."

"His show's opening in Toronto. He sent me a good luck message," said Alex.

"Can I get you guys a drink?" Rod listened as Scotty gave her order first. Cayde went along to assist while Brooke departed to mingle with Neroli and other art world acquaintances.

"Last I heard, you thought Rod was a misogynistic dinosaur," Alex said to Scotty.

"Rick, could you come have a little talk with us?" The lady in hot pants with unfocused eyes interrupted them.

"Uh, sure. Everybody, this is Augusta Kramer," said Rick,

"We've met," said Scotty.

Augusta curtly acknowledged Scotty before dragging Rick over to where the TV cameras were set up.

"Rod's not so bad, and we have history," said Scotty picking up on Alex's comment. "Bob left me a decent inheritance, but that was three years ago. Life's expensive and getting more expensive by the day. That night Rod cried on my shoulder I did my share of crying on his. I was worried about money. He didn't make fun of me, he sympathized and helped me out with some of his contacts. And Galina really hurt him when she left."

"Scotty my darling, how are you?" Ellery, mineral water in her wine glass, stopped beside them. "Alex, I'm thrilled, truly thrilled about your marriage. Couldn't have happened to two nicer guys."

"You know each other?" Alex asked Ellery and Scotty.

"Scotty's arranged numerous events for my family." Ellery and Scotty exchanged air kisses. "And done them brilliantly, I may add."

Raised and slurred voices from *The Belles'* cast echoed across the courtyard.

"How come you're not with them?" Alex asked Ellery.

Ellery cupped her hand over the lavalier mic in her décolleté. "They've all had too much to drink. Because he's so popular, Augusta and Joli are scared Rick's going to dominate the edit. 'The show's called *The Belles of Bel Air* not *The Fags of Fairfax*' was Joli's choice comment. Hope the bitch's mic was live for that. They're causing drama to get the focus back on them. Thank the Lord they've thrown their McCain fundraisers, because when this show goes on air those two examples of Bel Air high society will be lucky to raise a nickel. They're ganging up on Cristina about the press leaks and now they've dragged Rick into it."

"I thought you weren't happy with Cristina over the leaks either?" queried Alex.

"Cristina's a good person and a good friend. Sometimes misunderstandings take place between good people and good friends have disagreements. But they're not usually broadcast and picked over in the public domain. I don't see why grown-up educated women can't behave politely, but apparently that doesn't make for good TV."

That sounded so sensible Alex was confused. "Then why are you doing the show, Ellery?"

Ellery considered Alex's question. "Because if I wasn't here, I'd be waiting for my husband to come back from wherever it is he's meant to have been, all alone in my big beautiful empty house full of big beautiful empty things." With a shrug, Ellery uncupped her hand from her mic and stalked back to the increasingly noisy fray.

"At least Ellery doesn't have to worry about financial crises," Scotty said to Alex. "She made her money the old-fashioned way. She inherited it."

"But I didn't!" Cristina's high-pitched voice pierced the courtyard as Rod and Cayde arrived back with drinks.

People stared over their shoulders at the noisy reality TV crowd. Neroli, mixing with the collectors and critics, caught Alex's good eye and issued a warning glance.

"I need to put a lid on this," Alex said to Rod and Cayde. "Excuse me."

"… she has a history of selling stories," Augusta slurred. "Rick said so, didn't he?" Augusta looked to Joli, who vigorously wobbled her overly plump lips in agreement.

"I didn't say Cristina definitely did. All I said was I had a suspicion she did." Rick's voice wavered.

Cristina recoiled, the hurt in her eyes directed at Rick. "I told you I never leaked that story about you in seventy-four!"

"Rick said she lied about stepping down from the Conservatory Board as well," Augusta shouted.

"I told you why I stayed on the Board, Rick. I want to redress the wrong done to Thaddeus and all the other Board members, including me, insulted by that horrible memorandum." Cristina blinked back tears.

"You're so fake, Cristina," Joli pitched in, "with your fake accent and your fake name."

Stepping into the fray, Alex adopted his masterful expression, which usually worked on Rick. "Hey, hey. Everybody calm down." He looked to Lyle for assistance in shutting down the altercation, but Lyle stepped back and let the cameras keep rolling.

Augusta carried on ranting. "Cristina's a producer on this show! She doesn't care who she hurts to boost ratings. The woman's a total user and —"

"Cut!" Lyle moved in. "You talk about interpersonal relationships on the show, *not* the show," he warned Augusta.

Augusta tossed a surly snarl Cristina's way.

The heat gone from the confrontation, everyone stepped back.

"Time to call it a day," Alex firmly told Lyle. "I know you've got your show to make but tonight's *my* show. Our friends are waiting." Alex extricated Rick from the group. "That was pretty intense," he said on their way back.

"You're telling me," Rick muttered.

"I'm hurt you said those things about me." Cristina chased them. "I've enjoyed having you as a friend again, Rick. You too, Alex. Don't let lies destroy that."

Rick stopped. He fixed his x-ray blue eyes on Cristina. "Stories leaked to the press about my relationship with Alex destroyed my career. And the papers publicly blamed me for the shame of discovering I was gay killing my father. That was a total fabrication, but because it was printed and repeated and is still on any database or microfiche for anyone who cares to look, it's taken as the gospel truth. Being sacked from a TV show that was created for me paved the way for *you* to take over the starring role. I always thought it was that mad woman from Sunset Cove who gave that story to the press. But looking back, I'm not so sure. The truth is, who had anything to gain from that malicious story except you?"

"Correct! You and Haran say you do everything in the name of charity, Cristina, or whatever the fuck your real name is," Joli inserted herself in the conversation, "but you claim every expense and recharge all the limos and fancy hotels to the charitable foundations you pretend to support. You fund your lifestyle from fake humility! You nouveau riche bitch, you'll never be a part of our world!"

"If that means being a grade-A bitch and a homophobe then I'm glad I'm not!" Cristina retaliated.

Joli spun on her ridiculous high heels, raised her glass of red wine and hurled it at Cristina.

Like blood, the wine splattered over Cristina's white suit.

Mortified, Ellery rushed in and hurried Cristina away.

Lyle riffled his hand through his cropped hair. "That was gold, and the cameras weren't running. Fuck, fuck, fuck!"

Everyone went back to their conversations.

"Was that tonight's performance art?" Rod asked as Alex and Rick rejoined the group.

"Takes me back to the old days of Kaori burning cardboard planes in concrete courtyards," Scotty added.

"Excuse us, hallo," came a man's voice.

"Gerhardt, Ilse, *guten Abend*!" said Rick brightly. "Alex, you remember the Kleinmans?"

"We liked your show." Ilse tapped Alex's arm. "We are not knowing much about your work in Europe. The retrospective made a nice introduction, but this is so different. Your metal sculptures are …" Ilse clasped her throat.

"Do you make us a discount to buy more than one?" asked Gerhardt.

"They should be shown together. Their power is together." Ilse and Gerhardt nodded with each other.

"Are you thinking of them for Berlin? They'd be stunning in the environment you described. How's the construction going? I'm certain Neroli can come to an arrangement. Excuse us …" Rick said to their group as he led the Kleinmans to Neroli.

"The Kleinmans are converting a military bunker in Berlin into an art gallery," explained Alex.

"Whereas we build art galleries here to look like military bunkers," commented Scotty.

While the old gang joked and laughed, out of his good eye Alex couldn't help seeing Cristina's pain and humiliation as she came back outside with Ellery. Augusta and Joli had ripped off their radio mics and teetered off to find their limos. Having linked up the Kleinmans with Neroli, Rick returned. Bumping into Cristina, he gave her the cold shoulder. Since it was a night of being honest, Alex couldn't allow this to go on.

Alex pulled Rick aside. "I haven't been Cristina's biggest fan, but she doesn't deserve you treating her like that. She didn't leak the story that led to you being fired from the TV show, your mother did."

Rick pulled back his chin.

"After I told her the truth about her health, Luisa confessed she gave that story to the press. If you knew what she'd done she thought you'd walk away and never speak to her again. She said it was her gift to me, a means of getting her out of our lives for good."

"Why didn't you tell me?"

"Because it would've hurt you and be a horrible end to her life. I said she had to tell you herself if she wanted you to know."

"After all the terrible things momma's said and done to you, you were still willing to protect her?"

"I did it to protect you, not her."

"Momma's change of tune about you makes sense now. Was approving of our relationship some kind of repayment?"

Nausea gripped Alex stomach, fearing Rick was about to turn on him. "I wasn't prepared to be a pawn in Luisa's game."

"You mean she actually told you she wanted to destroy my career?"

"No, she thought if you saw rumors in the press about you being gay, you'd break up with me to protect your job before they got any bigger. But when Sid died, the story took on a life of its own. To be honest, I didn't tell you because I wasn't sure I believed her. I think she just felt guilty about how she'd acted back then."

Thinking it over, Rick chewed his lip. "Momma's pulled that confession crap before with Patti and Giuliana. Not using that angle but with other things."

"I didn't protect her to get something out of it, I thought it was the right thing to do. If I was mistaken, I'm sorry."

Rick gave Alex a half-smile. "You're such a beautiful soul. This is why I love you."

Alex's heart eased. "You say Luisa's pulled the confession thing before, do you think she could have been testing me?"

"Maybe. Momma's pathologically incapable of normal human interactions."

"Things seem to be so much better between you and her. I hope this doesn't ruin that."

"Perhaps her public approval of our relationship in Venice was to make amends for the past. If I had gone on to become a star and we'd set up house together and been open about our relationship, a story like that would've come out sooner or later. It just wasn't possible to be openly gay on mainstream TV back then." Rick let out an exasperated sigh. "You'd think by the age of sixty I'd be over all this crap with momma by now. Shit!" He hastily covered his shirt collar with his hand. "I still have my mic on." Rick flicked his eyes at the headphoned technician in a shadowy corner. Seeing him look her way, the sound engineer averted her eyes.

"What're you thinking?" Alex heard the cogs whirr in Rick's head.

Rick uncovered the mic. "That even if Lyle upped my fee to thirty thousand dollars per episode, I wouldn't sign for another season. Tiffany was right, I can do better than this." Unhooking his mic, Rick pulled out the power pack and carried it to the sound recordist.

"This man needs a drink." Rod handed Alex a beer.

"Where'd everybody go?" While Alex had been occupied with Rick, the crowd had drastically thinned out.

"Hernandez and Rocha went back inside for a second look," said Scotty.

"Everyone else rushed off to call their stockbroker or jump out of a window," said Cayde.

Brooke spanked her husband's arm.

"With all the money I shelled out to put on this show I might do the same." Alex swigged his beer.

"You live on the ground floor," said Scotty, "I'm in a sub-penthouse."

While he chatted with his friends, Alex spotted Rick with Cristina and Ellery. Hugs and tears took place before Rick arrived back at their group.

"Everything okay?" Alex asked Rick.

Rick picked up the glass of wine he'd left beside Scotty.

"That'll be warm," said Rod. "I'll get you a fresh one."

"There's no proof Cristina did anything underhanded. As with all things, I guess the truth lies somewhere in the middle. Sometimes you have to take things on faith. We kissed and made up," said Rick.

"If that's high society I'm glad we're dead-beat artists," added Cayde.

"I'll drink to that," Alex clinked his bottle to Cayde's. As he drank, Alex wondered if he'd make any sales from this show. A financial crisis had just gripped the country, he was going blind in one eye, he no longer had gallery representation in LA, his housekeeper's son had stolen half a million dollars from him, his fiancé's invalid half-brother was in love with him, and his mother-in-law-to-be was a difficult woman who in her dying breaths was probably cooking up some scheme to puncture their happiness. Overall things couldn't get much worse.

Or could they?

SUCCESS D'ESTIME

'Challenging.'
'Cheeky.'
'Monumental.'
'Legendary."

Alex had to reread the reviews, then have Rick read them out loud to make sure his good eye wasn't deceiving him. Not a single negative comment. Even Jauncey Hernandez, after taking a second walk through the exhibition, saw the amusing side of his initial reaction being observed on camera. Hernandez's review stated, 'Alex Morgan's new show, *Empty Spaces*, seamlessly blends his unquestionable technical proficiency with the conceptual and political firepower to land a sock-in-the-jaw statement on the commercial value of art. Morgan also pokes a stick in the eye of the type of gallery goer who gets off on being seen looking at the art rather than actually looking at it.'

If only sales had been equally stellar.

The Kleinmans struck a deal with Neroli to purchase all twelve metal panels. The price paid factored in the astronomical cost of shipping to Berlin and import duties. Taking off Neroli's commission, Alex was pleased to have broken even and taken a modest profit on them. Although not compelled to do so, the Kleinmans phoned to let him know how they intended to show his work. Using Rick as their German/English translator where necessary, they outlined their plan to install his panels behind the slit windows running up the sides of their new gallery. Daylight through the brutal punctures in the metal pieces would mirror the wartime bullet wounds on the former bunker's exterior brickwork. From the outside, their red lacquered undersides would resemble a column of blood. Giving his pieces architectural as well as artistic integrity, Alex wholeheartedly approved of their suggestion.

 A well-respected collector and Oscar-winning actress purchased *Bucato #5,* the one with the Hollywood star map, for fifty thousand dollars. That was the sum total of sales by the end of the show's third week. *Empty Spaces*, however, had generated a deafening clamor in the press and social media. Neroli reported record attendances. No-one had dared paint on any of the blank canvases as yet. Alex's new show having received unanimously positive word of mouth, Xander Chen's phone call wasn't unexpected.

 "Spectacular feedback!"

 "Thanks." Cradling the phone in his neck, Alex distractedly scrolled through his account sheet's scary figures on the studio Mac. "That mean you'll be taking something from the new show to Art Miami?"

 "That style of work doesn't sit in context with my other artists. I'll level with you, your work has two desirable and saleable periods. The *Red* series and your early nineties abstracts. They're recognizable, collectable and sought after."

 "I guess those are the pieces you've been chasing for resales. Eli Klotte told me you'd been calling around. Those owners are good friends, I'd appreciate you not bugging them."

 "People look at those works and immediately know they're by Alex Morgan. And I represent you." Chen's tone hardened. "If you're not producing new work I can sell, what choice have I got but to pursue your old pieces to maintain interest?"

 "Choice?"

 "I invested heavily in you. I lobbied MoMA for your retrospective then contributed a sizeable amount of cash for the show. Not to mention the million dollars plus I paid for *Sphere 4* at Christie's. I'm building your brand. I need a return on my investment."

Alex's spine stiffened as he looked away from the computer screen. "You bought *Sphere 4*?"

"With a buyer's confidentiality clause, of course. If that piece hadn't achieved a good price at auction your values could've collapsed. Don't worry, it's safe in storage until the time's right to put it out there again … You still there?"

"Yeah, yeah."

"Your vision problem's actually heated up your prices. And thankfully the *Vanity Fair* interview hasn't dented your desirability as much as I feared. What I'm saying is, this would be an excellent time for you to produce some classic Alex Morgan-style work."

Alex took the phone from his ear, thinking he'd misheard. "Say what?"

"I sincerely believe a million plus would be achievable for any new *Red* paintings. The markets are turbulent, but there's still money looking for safe havens. Give it some thought, Alex."

"No, what you said about the magazine article. What did you mean about it denting my desirability?"

"I banked on that interview being about Alex Morgan the artist. Instead, it became about nineteen seventies prejudice and your struggle to come to terms with your homosexuality. How did that come about?"

"From Thom Hannay's desire to tell the truth about my struggle to be an openly gay man, not only in my life but also in the art world."

"And where did you and Rick being photographed naked and mauling each other come from?" Chen took an audible breath. "The art market's moved on. A lot of investors in new territories with big money don't share the same liberal attitudes we do."

"Well, they should."

"I didn't make the world the way it is. If you want to be in the major league play to your strengths. I can't sell blank canvases, light-box collages and conceptual art. Give my buyers the style of original paintings they want from you and don't rock the boat. Do that and I can achieve the prices your work deserves. I can make you rich, Alex. Think about it."

Ending the call, Alex finished scrolling through his accounts. It was too depressing. He turned off the Mac and flexed his knuckles. Picking up the canvas pliers and staple gun, he went back to stretching fresh canvas over a frame. In the old days he'd have knocked off a job like this in half an hour, but lack of dexterity and lack of practice made for slow progress.

"*Morgen waschen Sie die Böden im Wohnzimmer und in der Küche*!" Rick's voice echoed across the pool. Having liquidated his few stocks which hadn't sunk to zero, Rick was picking up the tab for their new housekeeper, Idabelle. This mature German lady, in her tan lace-up shoes and white bib apron, arrived on the bus from Mar Vista at ten, efficiently vacuumed, polished and laundered until four, then got the bus home. Rick was thrilled she stored the pots where he wanted and didn't put his knitwear in the dryer, but Alex missed Manuela.

"*Natürlich, Herr Rick*!" came Idabelle's reply.

Alex wondered if Idabelle was deaf because Rick had taken to instructing her in German … loudly. In return, Alex wondered if Idabelle presumed Rick was hard of hearing because she'd taken to responding equally loudly … in German.

"*Danke, Idabelle*! *Bis morgen*!" said Rick.

Alex gritted his teeth. He'd need to wear ear plugs if this carried on.

Rick tapped on the studio door. "Can I come in?"

"Yeah." Alex put down the canvas pliers and massaged his right hand with this left. "Rosa Klebb finished for the day?"

"I've told you not to call her that."

"It always sounds like the two of you are about to set the dogs on an escaped prisoner. Can you decrease the decibels or stick to English?"

"Sorry. I'm just over excited. It worked, my plan worked!" Rick jiggled a large manilla envelope in Alex's face. "I got a reading for a pilot. And not playing the shlumpy best friend, it's the lead!"

Alex smiled. Rick was practically jumping for joy. "That's great, babe."

"It's like the *Vanity Fair* article, the *Corriere della Sera* spread and the TV show all came out together at the right time." Rick swished the pages from the envelope. "It's a terrific part. Listen to the character description, 'Lyndon Lincoln. Super sleek advertising exec. Late forties, yet boyish in spirit and appearance.' It's like it was written for me!"

"Late forties? What kind of show is it, science-fiction?"

"Ha ha. It's a comedy and I can play that age. And the character's gay! They only sent the sides for the audition scene but it's real funny. If the rest of the show's as good it'll be a winner." Rick sighed. "I probably won't get it, but it's nice to be asked to read for a lead after nothing but crumbs."

"Yeah, it is." Alex pulled Rick to his chair and rested his head on his chest.

Tossing the script aside, Rick stroked Alex's hair. "What's brought this on?"

"I needed a hug." Alex sat back and rubbed his eyes. "I have these two big studios, but I can't do big work. My hands don't work like they used to, my knees don't work like they used to and now my eyes don't work like they used to. I can't afford to keep shelling out on assistants to do the grunt work if I'm not making sales. And Suki was right, she should be making art of her own not digging the foundations of mine. And Kent's too talented an artist to get stuck in the rut of doing my carpentry." Alex picked up the pliers. "I laid him off."

"That was rash, wasn't it?"

"I figured I should go back to making all my art myself." Alex held up his hands. "Except I'm not sure I can anymore."

Rick picked up the canvas Alex just finished stretching. "You did this, didn't you?"

"It's taken me four hours. And I'm no good with the technology. Suki did all my cataloging and ordering." Alex stared gloomily at the Mac.

"I can take over that side of things. And I can help with stretching canvases and building frames. We'll find a way to make it work."

"*Sphere 4* fetching over a million at auction gave me the confidence that someone out there thought I had value. I just found out that person was Chen. He bought it to control my market prices."

"Oh, babe."

"And he hated the magazine article. He thinks publicity like that could put his clients off buying my work. This could be the only window left in my working career to earn enough money to buy you a house in Malibu or a place with marble floors and gold faucets." Alex gestured to the fresh canvas. "I should paint something in red for Xander Chen. The only truly commercial period of my work in his eyes. An Alex Morgan in red. How many would you like, sir? Hell, I could probably spray a canvas red, sign it on the back and he'd try and sell it. And knowing Chen he'd succeed."

"Why don't you?"

"Yeah, why don't I?" Alex pulled Rick close and silently clung to him. Burying his face in Rick's chest, through his eye's dark mist he hoped to see Dora, or Danielle, or Mom, or even Pop. He needed someone to say, 'do this' or 'don't do that.' But no-one came. Just when he'd been tempted to believe in spirits, guardian angels, even God, interrogating his illusions had chased them away.

"Okay." Rick rubbed Alex's back before stepping away. "Go to the house and put on your board shorts. I need to get some things together then I'm taking you out."

"Where to?"

Rick smiled mysteriously. "The beach."

* * *

On the scrubby grass under the fan palms, Alex wriggled to get comfortable in the folding chair Rick had carried down to the boardwalk. Around them, other artists were working on field easels or canvases propped up against the trees. "I thought you were going to pull on a wetsuit, grab the boards and bring me surfing."

Rick opened up the little watercolor paintbox he'd dug out of a drawer in Alex's studio. "This'll be safer."

Sitting in the folding chair beside Alex, Rick clipped the compact paintbox to the watercolor pad. "Have you got everything you need? Sketchpad, paint, brushes, pencil, rag, blotter. Great. And perfect timing, the sun's going down."

Rick rested the watercolor pad on Alex's knee. "I'll hold your water jar. Oh, wait." Rick fished the eyepatch out of his shorts pocket. "Put this on."

"Uh," Alex grunted. "I tried that. It didn't help."

"It's not for your bad eye." Rick put the water jar on the ground. "I'm covering your good one." Alex jiggled the watercolor pad as Rick positioned the patch over his left eye. Rick picked up the water jar.

"I told you I don't see detail through my right eye. It's all blurry colors and dark patches. This is hopeless."

"You don't just see black, do you?"

"No, just fuzzy colors."

"Describe them."

"Er, the sea's a cool blue with spackles of gray. Then there's a purple haze. Above that it's apricot and watermelon, then a smoke pink bleeding up to a yellowish blue. But I'm not even sure those colors are there. The purple haze might be my brain filling in the empty patch. Let me check." Alex went to uncover his left eye.

    Rick slapped his hand down. "Don't check. Paint what you feel and don't worry if it's real or not. You want a pencil?"

    "Nah." Taking a medium size brush from Rick, after missing the water jar on his first attempt, he wet the brush and began mixing colors on the palette's lid. Using the periphery of his sight, he blended yellow and red. "This is pretty basic."

    "Experiment with what you can do rather than fixating on what you think you can't."

    "Okay." Forming a mind map of the palette, Alex mixed orange top left, some blue top right, a pink blush bottom left, purples bottom right. Taking a fresh brush from Rick, he gave a large square on the paper a few water washes.

    "I've been thinking a lot about Tyler," mused Rick.

    Painting with one poorly functioning eye was like working with one hand tied behind his back. "And?"

    "Living back home with Letitia's making him depressed. A few months ago he was an independent man. Now he's back to being a kid. He's getting physically stronger but losing motivation to keep pushing through his rehab."

    Working in a fog, Alex slammed in an apricot wash. Getting things quickly onto the paper, he laid in the purple hazy horizon. "It's tough for him."

    "It is." Rick paused. "Look, I was thinking of letting Tyler move back into the pool house. He'd have his independence and we'd be on hand to keep an eye on him."

    "But you said you didn't ever want him in the house again." Staring at the blurry view, Alex could glimpse the palette in his peripheral vision, but what he was getting onto the paper remained somewhat of a mystery. Swinging his eyes around, he momentarily saw purple on the page bleeding into the apricot. It wasn't unpleasant. "But would you trust him there being alone with me?"

"I trust you. Knowing how Tyler feels about you, I'm worried it might be unfair on him though. You'd need to have an honest talk, you know, set some boundaries. What do you think?"

Using instinct rather than intellect, Alex worked what he hoped were bluish-purple clouds into the watermelon sky. "I think it would be good for him. What made you change your mind? Clean brush."

Rick swished a fresh brush in the water, then exchanged it for the one in Alex's hand. "Getting all possessive and making ultimatums and casting people out, having talked it through with Dr. Susskind I realized I was behaving the way momma used to. Then we posed naked in front of a photographer in the name of art and our picture's in a magazine. I judged Jack unfairly. And Tyler can't go back to work yet, but maybe he could help you around the studio? You're an irritating pair of goofballs when you're together but Tyler needs to laugh again. And what's the point of saving his life if he's miserable all the time?"

"You'd really be okay with him moving back in?" From the top right, Alex picked up some blue to make the sea. It was strange not worrying about detail just using color.

"I hope so. I can't blame Tyler for falling in love with you. I suppose I'm afraid you might fall in love with him rather than me. But, at the moment, Tyler's need takes priority over my fears."

Dashing off a few indigo strokes on the horizon's bend, Alex was done. "Finito."

Putting down the water bottle, Rick took the brush and sketchbook from Alex.

Alex sensed an entity in the beach's blurry haze beyond Rick. He vaguely wondered if a boardwalk acquaintance had dropped by to say hi. In the misty twilight, a fresh-faced surfer boy with curly brown hair, a younger version of himself with a hint of Danielle about his demeanor, materialized. The boy grinned at him and Rick. Alex pulled off the eyepatch. The surfer boy's image resolved itself into the palm trunks. No physical body was present, but a tug in Alex's gut told him some spirit was there. He acknowledged the invisible youth with a laid-back smile, sensing a new harmony in the world.

"It's pretty!" Rick admired Alex's watercolor sketch as he unclipped the palette.

"Really? It's such a little nothing."

"It reminds me your grandmother's watercolors from the beach house. They possessed this other worldly feeling."

Taking back the pad, Alex appraised his work with his good eye. It was raw and messy, but an impressionistic quality about it pleased him. Above their heads the sky was darkening to navy blue, and the nighttime boardwalk hustle was livening up as his fellow artists packed up for the day. "Kind of nice sitting here on the beach like this, just a couple of creaky old guys on folding chairs watching the sun go down."

"One creaky old guy and one 'still boyish in spirit and appearance' guy," corrected Rick.

"Gee but you're full of it! How many more sessions does Dr. Susskind need to cure this Peter Pan syndrome of yours?"

"I'm going to stop seeing Dr. Susskind. He helped me put some things in perspective but he's real expensive. And I've come to the conclusion forgetting past hurts and pains is better than rehashing them over and over. I need to accept that being a total fuck up's more of my doing than anybody else's."

"You're not a fuck up, quite the opposite. Wanna grab a bite on the way home?"

"Let's." Rick gathered Alex's painting kit, folded up their chairs and they strolled to Martin's on the Beach.

Walking in, Alex got a blast from seeing his huge yellow canvas with the red circle dominate the far wall. "At least giving Martin that painting's covered our checks here for the next year," Alex said as they slipped into their regular booth on the terrace.

"I'm having an appetizer then. Think you can barter that other giant painting to cover our garage bills?"

"Worth a try, but I doubt it. It'll find a home one day."

They ordered food and drink and chilled out in the restaurant's evening chatter. Sitting with Rick on the beach while doing a little sunset watercolor had made Alex happy.

And if you had to make a choice between being happy or rich, wasn't happy better?

✷ ✷ ✷

"Do you think Tiffany's acting weird?" whispered Alex.

"Want to put a start date on that question?" Rick asked.

"Can I have another Coke?" Jay stuck his head around the door.

"No. Only one a day," Rick replied.

"What happened to the lizard?" asked Jay slouching into the kitchen from the living room.

"Have some water." Rick filled a tumbler. "What lizard?"

"The sick lizard we put in the hospital box. Did it get better?" Jay took the water from Rick.

"Oh, that lizard. He's hunky dory. Running around out there right now," said Alex.

"Take this to the patio." Rick handed Jay a platter of cut fruit.

When Jay left, Alex guiltily confessed, "The lizard died."

"Why didn't you tell Jay?"

"He and Maddy thought they'd helped it, why bring them down? No, Tiffany … she's listening to everything we say like she's writing it down in her head. And she seems, I'm almost afraid to say this," Alex glanced over his shoulder, "happy."

"Maybe it's this new writing partner. What's his name? Gregg? She's getting reacquainted with sharpening a man's pencil."

Alex sniggered.

Taking a fresh bottle of wine from the fridge, they went outside to rejoin Tiffany, Tyler and the kids.

Sitting down, Rick filled his glass. "I really was blown away by the script. It's seriously funny."

"See the benefit of writers? You get wit and structure, not the ad hoc mudslinging of reality TV," said Tiffany.

"They've offered a salary increase and a step up to main cast if I sign for another season of mudslinging," said Rick.

Tiffany shook her ginger blond curls in disgust. "You're not selling out to them, are you?"

"We could use the money," conceded Rick.

"Let's pray you get this pilot then. When's your reading?" asked Tiffany.

"Next week at Disney Studios."

"Terrific. We can meet for lunch." Tiffany speared a pineapple slice off the platter.

"I forgot that's where your show shoots," said Rick.

Alex felt Tyler's silence across the table. The stutter left by the surgery had made him self-conscious about speaking. Needing to broach the subject of moving back into the pool house, Alex thought it best to make sure the discussion took place away from young ears. "Hey Ty, feel like taking a walk?"

"H … h … how far are you talking?"

"Just to the beach," said Alex.

"Can I come?" Maddy skipped around the table and tugged Alex's arm.

"No, stay with Rick and your mom and work out want you want to wear for the wedding." This excitement distracted Maddy. Jay was in the meditation garden's hammock happily reading his book. Assisting Tyler from the table, Alex handed him his crutches. Seeing Tyler with short hair was strange, although it had grown into a cute ginger brown crop.

"I w … w … warn you. It c … c … could be slow g … going." Tyler gave a self-deprecating laugh.

"That's cool, we got time."

Rick helped Tyler through the doors onto the street, then Alex and Tyler ambled down to the boardwalk. Passing the coffee shop and tattoo studio, they navigated through the ragtag tourists browsing t-shirt and souvenir stalls. Alex guided Tyler to a concrete bench beneath the palms.

"I had a long talk with Jack in the hospital," Alex said as he sat down.

"About?"

"A few things. His work for one."

"G ... g ... guess we should've been open about that." Lowering himself, Tyler rested one crutch against the bench and steadied his right side with the other.

"Why weren't you?"

"I thought it might b ... be too much for mom to handle. I f ... f ... figured once she got to know Jack better, she wouldn't think b ... bad of him for it."

"I must admit I was a little shocked. But that says more about me than him. Jack's a good man. When you were scared and alone in the hospital, you called for him and he came without a second thought. That's pretty special."

"I know."

"He told me something else, that the reason you split was because you'd fallen in love with me."

Tyler traced a pattern in the sand with the tip of his crutch. "I wish he hadn't. N ... n ... now I've fucked things up b ... between us. I j ... j ... just feel so easy being around you. You're m ... m ... my hero."

"Well, you're pretty darned special to me. But, you know, the thing about romantic love, no matter how deep it may feel at the time, there's always a chance it may end. For all the people who fall in love, there's a goodly proportion who fall out of it. This is something I don't tell many people because it still breaks my heart, but a few years after Danielle and me got married she fell pregnant. Our love was deep and pure, but not always passionate. Having a baby wasn't something that had ever occurred to me, or her. But once we got our heads around it, we were both pretty stoked. We were going to be a family. But it didn't work out ... Guess the little guy was too beautiful for this rough old world. His heart didn't beat enough times for us to convince him our love would be enough to protect him from it. And it wasn't just a baby we lost, something in Danielle died with him. We were never the same again. You see, Ty, what I'm trying to say is, I've grown to think of you as the son I never had. Romantic love can end, partners may split and separate, but family ties, both the good and the bad, never leave you. So I figure loving you as my son will last forever, which maybe's a better deal than that other kind of love. Could my loving you that way work for you?"

"Would I have to call you d ... d .... dad?"

"Leave that for Sid, stick with Uncle Al. If you feel we could have that kind of relationship, and if you'd like to, Rick and I thought it would be good for you to move back in with us. You got the pool at the house, a gym down the street and the beach right here. We've always got yardwork that needs doing and I could seriously use help in the studio and some laughs. So, what do you say?"

Tyler bumped his shoulder to Alex's. "G ... guess we could give it a try."

"And to sweeten the pot, would you be my best man and stand by me at the wedding?"

"Does that m ... m ... mean I'd have to take c ... care of the ring? You willing t ... to risk I won't lose it?" Tyler gave his lopsided grin.

"Scotty's in charge of proceedings so there's zero risk of that. You'll be sworn to secrecy and probably be required to attend a training camp at an undisclosed location."

"O ... kay."

"Fantastic." Alex put his arm around Tyler and life on the boardwalk carried on behind them.

Back at the house, after Tiffany had taken Tyler and the kids home and he and Rick had cleared up before going to bed, Alex ducked into the study and dashed off an email.

Dear Xander,

Thanks for everything, but I've decided my future direction is not aligned to your market. Therefore, as we agreed either party could sever exclusive representation at any time without fault or blame, I'd like to make this the official end of our alliance. If anyone's looking for me I'll be down on the boardwalk painting watercolor sunsets.

Best regards,
Alex Morgan.

Alex's finger hovered on the mouse.

There'd be no going back.

The dream of art mega-stardom would be over.

He hit 'send.'

WHITE SHIRTS AND PROMISES

"Wait!" Alex shouted on hearing Rick's bare feet pad out of the bathroom.

"We should be dressed by now. Any deviation from Scotty's masterplan heralds disaster and may split the earth in twain," came Rick's voice from behind the closed door.

"Hold on!" Being careful not to snag the jacket and cursing his less than nimble fingers, Alex managed to work the garment bag's zipper shut. "Okay!"

Rick slid back the pocket door to the master suite's walk-in and dressing area. "What are you doing?" Warm from the shower, bergamot scent suffused the air as he came in massaging lotion into his throat and chest.

"I don't want to wrinkle my jacket. I was putting it in a cover."

"Why the big secrecy then?" Rick opened his underwear drawer.

"Bad luck to see what we're wearing before the wedding, isn't it?" asked Alex standing in only his boxers.

"Since when did you get superstitious? And I've seen you wear that Tom Ford brocade before."

"Yeah, but not like this."

"Whatever. We need to get moving. Any moment now one of Scotty's flying monkeys will frog-march us to the limo whether we're dressed or not." Rick slung his towel over the clothes rail.

"Surprise birthday parties are one thing, but a surprise wedding? That's a new one on me," grunted Alex.

"Watergate was shrouded in less secrecy than Scotty's wedding preparations. I'm amazed she actually let us meet the officiant in daylight rather than a darkened parking garage." Rick stepped into a pair of his skimpy European briefs.

The fuzziness of Alex's right eye and faint shimmer in his left, which he first became aware of late last week, combined with the soft lighting in the dressing area to lend Rick's moist skin a flattering glow. He stopped Rick from taking his white silk shirt off the hanger. "I need one more look at you."

"You'll make us late …"

Following it with his relatively good eye, Alex trailed his finger over the scar on Rick's right shoulder, resting momentarily on the dip in his flesh from the gunshot wound. Then he traced his hand down Rick's chest, studying how the light brown hairs, and a few white ones, edged the pink nipples and covered the swell of his pectorals. Alex pressed his chest against Rick's. "There's still time to back out," he murmured.

"Thanks for the reminder, but why would I?"

"I got the better deal." Alex brushed Rick's hair off his forehead. "You're as handsome as the first day I set eyes on you. Still fit, firm and gorgeous."

"Your vision's seriously on the fritz. I'm crepey, saggy and jowly."

"Crepey, Saggy and Jowly was one helluva law firm till Jowly quit to go solo." Alex absorbed every freckle, line and pore of Rick's face. "I'm painting your portrait." He tapped his finger to his brow. "A map to guide me home when the fog blinds me."

"Breakthroughs are being made every day to treat your condition. Stem cells, lasers, new medications. And it's only affected your right eye. Your other one's perfect."

Alex held back from voicing his fear it wasn't. "You're right. Today, I see. I walk, talk, breathe, taste, smell and love. Fuck tomorrow." Realizing Rick was studying his body with equal intensity, Alex folded his arms. "We should get dressed. This clunky body of mine's better covered up these days."

"I disagree." Rick circled him in appraisal. "You're in terrific shape. Dropped a little weight?"

"I have now you mention it." Alex waggled his head in pride. "Been putting in extra hours at the pool."

"It paid off, very sexy."

"Do the Chippendales need a senior member?" Alex suggestively bumped his hips.

A no-nonsense rap on the door from the hallway interrupted them. "Two fifty-seven!" Cayde bellowed from outside. "Need you guys out here on the double!"

"Hold the booty shaking for later." Rick slapped Alex's butt.

They finished dressing at speed. Alex tugged on a white band-collar popover shirt as Rick dashed back to the bathroom to fluff his hair with the blow dryer.

"*GQ* photoshoot this way." Cayde appraised Alex's pristine outfit as he opened the door. "The limo's here with its motor running. Rick needs to get his ass out on the double, I got a wedding planner reaching critical mass on the line." Cayde waved his cell phone.

"Stash this in the trunk, will ya?" Alex unhooked the garment cover from the doorframe. "Rick, car's here! Move it!"

Cayde grabbed the garment bag. "See you outside."

"Coming, coming." Rick grabbed his candy-striped blazer as he hustled through the walk-in. He followed Alex around the house, locking doors as they went before ending up on the sidewalk by the white stretch limo.

"10-4, control," Cayde barked into his phone, "Yogi and Boo-Boo entering vehicle. Will confirm when motorcade is 10-74." Ending the call, he slipped the phone in his pocket.

"Yogi and Boo-Boo?" Alex questioned as the liveried chauffeur opened the door.

"Your code names." Cayde smirked. "And I'm not saying which is which. Dang, I wish Scotty had gotten me one of them microphones with the curly wire that goes up your sleeve. I always did want to use one of them doohickeys."

Alarmed by how efficiently Scotty had drilled her team, Alex allowed the driver to assist him into the limo while Rick climbed in from the other side.

"Now you gotta keep these on till you get there," said Cayde.

Alex recoiled as Cayde fastened a blindfold over his eyes. "Hey, I don't see great at the best of times."

"Quit struggling, don't make me taser you," said Cayde.

Alex grudgingly relented.

Once Alex's blindfold was secured, Cayde scampered around to Rick's side. "Delroy's under strict instruction to make sure neither of you peek."

Alex heard the driver get into the limo then Rick's mumbled complaints about flattening his hair as Cayde blindfolded him.

"This is less like a wedding and more like a kidnapping," grumbled Rick.

"God speed!" Cayde slapped the limo's roof.

"Memorize the highway sounds and any other noises we may need to lead us back to the mastermind's lair," Rick muttered as the car set off.

Alex chuckled. "This is nuts."

"We haven't turned yet so we're headed south. Am I correct, Delroy?" Rick asked the driver.

"Apologies sir, but that's classified information," Delroy replied in all earnestness.

The limo then made several right and left turns in succession. Alex suspected Delroy had driven around the block a few times. Rick's sense of direction wasn't great when he could see, so being blindfolded Delroy's gambit totally succeeded in throwing him off the scent.

After they'd driven another ten minutes, Rick spoke. "You know the horrible feeling I've got?"

"That Scotty's holding the wedding on the *It's a Small World* ride at Disneyland?" Alex felt Rick's hand grip his.

"That something terrible's going to happen."

"Like?"

"A tsunami, or an earthquake … or a sniper in the crowd."

"Why does your mind work that way?"

Rick emitted a snorted laugh. "Maybe I have a fear of happiness. Like I don't deserve it."

"You deserve it. We deserve it."

A change in the road's noise distracted Rick. "Ooh, that was a bridge. Or was it an intersection? It sounded hollow."

"Tsunamis don't worry me. I'm more concerned about the guest list." Alex's heart skipped a beat, suddenly worried about whom Scotty may had invited.

"There can't be that many people coming. It was generous of Scotty to do this for us, but she can't have spent a fortune because she doesn't have one. And we don't know enough people to fill the Kodak theater. Tyler, Tiffany, Letitia and the kids are givens. Patti too. Although she was very evasive last night when we spoke after she'd checked into her hotel. I got the feeling she wasn't alone."

"You don't think Luisa's with her, do you?"

"No, but it'd be kind of nice if she was, wouldn't it? But momma couldn't come. Like the doctors said, the journey could kill her."

"But did they specify the outward or return trip?" The prospect of Luisa showing up jangled Alex's nerves. Although a sort of truce had taken place between them, he wouldn't totally trust her to hold her tongue when 'speak now or forever hold your peace' was said. His stomach tied itself in knots. This was real. He was about to marry Rick Stradman in a solemnized ceremony complete with vows and rings before friends and family.

"We're slowing, we're slowing," said Rick.

Delroy hung a right.

The highway's roar faded. The sound of surf and smell of ozone seeped into the limo.

"My orders are to make sure you keep the blindfolds on till you're told to take them off. I'd be grateful if you do. I need the tip from boss lady," said Delroy with a smile in his voice.

The limo made more winding turns. The surface beneath the tires changed to shale. Alex heard waves and seabirds. Delroy stopped the vehicle and got out. The door beside Alex opened.

"May I help you, sir?" asked Delroy.

The limo driver's strong hand pulled Alex from the vehicle. His knees had seized up during the ride, so he was glad of the assistance.

"Hi, hi, hi!" Scotty's voice trilled from Rick's side. "No peeking around the blindfolds. Alex, stay where you are! I need you side by side for the reveal. I'm bringing Rick to you."

"This is like a revival of *The Miracle Worker*," Rick grumbled as Scotty guided him around the limo.

Alex heard Scotty warning Rick to take care, footsteps on gravel and a murmur of voices in the open air. He sensed people gathering into position.

"Everybody ready?" After a pause and more shuffling steps, Scotty shouted, "Many thanks to all of you for keeping this location a secret! The time's come to let Alex and Rick in on the secret. Guessed where you are yet, boys?"

Alex heard Scotty whispering orders to someone then felt her fingers take hold of his blindfold.

Scotty cried, "Five, four, three, two, one!"

The Velcro rip behind his ears was followed by wincing pain as sunlight dazzled him. "Shit!" Alex clapped his hand over his eyes. On his left, Rick emitted similar sounds from the sudden switch from blackout to light. The background soundtrack was cheers, applause and a clanging bell.

"Oh, sorry. You okay?" asked Scotty.

As his eyes grew accustomed to the light, Alex's heart nearly stopped. Directly in front of him stood the dark blue trellis around the Beachcomber's front deck, it was festooned with white ribbon bows. The Stars and Stripes fluttered on the flagpole above the bar's green roof and grinning faces beamed from the wooden staircase and around the limo.

Clang! *Clang*! *Clang*! Rod rang the gold bell on the bar's deck.

"You can't ring the martini bell! It isn't five o'clock yet!" Alex yelled in mock outrage.

"They set the clocks forward for you," laughed Scotty.

Tingles ran up and down Alex's spine as the pastel-colored beach houses, green cliffs and homey sounds and smells of Sunset Cove came into focus.

"Thought it only fitting," Scotty whispered, "to hold the ceremony where you two began. I have to get everyone in place. Wait here, I'll be back."

"Yo, Al!" The wallop of Tyler's slightly uncontrolled arm slapped around Alex's shoulders. "This is where you hung out b … b … back when you were my age then?"

"Half your age," laughed Alex.

"Wanna g … g … go surfing later?"

"First things first," said Alex. "Got the ring?"

Tyler patted the pocket in the loose linen pants he wore with a coral batik shirt. "See you d … d … down there, Uncle Al." Tyler limped away, now only needing one underarm crutch to support his right side.

Alex swung around to find Patti fussing with Rick. "Hi, darling," he said as Rick pressed a box into Patti's hands while issuing last-minute instructions.

"What a beautiful place. And this was your home?" Patti kissed Alex Italian style.

"Yep, I lived on and off in grandma's beach house for over ten years. That one there." Alex pointed along the track to Dora's cottage, now painted ivory with French navy trim. Recovering from the shock of being back in Sunset Cove, Alex spotted a slatted walkway laid across the sand. It led from the Beachcomber to a decked area on the beach. Rows of beribboned white chairs were arranged on either side of a central aisle and tropical blooms covered an arch over a raised dais. Piano music played from speakers concealed in the flowers. Guests dressed in fondant colors were drifting down the walkway. Poised on the dais, the officiant, his purple robes flapping in the wind, greeted them as they found their seats. Perceiving more detail from his good eye, Alex spotted a woman swathed in white in a wheelchair amongst the seats. Trying not to let the realization that Luisa had made it here alive kill the moment, he pulled himself together.

"Well, here goes," said Rick.

"Yep, here goes," said Alex. "Delroy, I need my jacket from that garment bag in the trunk."

After another kiss for luck from Patti, she left to assume her place in the ceremony.

"Here you go, sir." Delroy swished the white jacket from the carrier and held it out behind Alex.

Rick's eyes popped out as he watched Alex pull up the jacket over his shoulders. "So this is the reason you've only eaten lettuce for two weeks."

Alex extended his arms and pivoted from side to side, allowing time for Rick to savor seeing him in the white linen jacket with nipped in waist, super wide lapels and double rear vent. "A tad snug under the arms but not bad otherwise."

"I bought him that jacket from Giorgio Beverly Hills over thirty years ago!" Rick told Delroy.

"And I finally got a good reason to wear it! Thanks for your help, Delroy."

"Have a wonderful afternoon, gentlemen." Delroy's eyes fell on Scotty striding up the walkway over the sand. "She's coming. I wish you both well."

Alex inhaled to calm his heart as Scotty approached. In a soft pink wrap dress, her hair held in a French twist by a comb of miniature roses and a hint of blush on her cheeks, except for the silver streak at her temples Scotty hadn't aged a day over the years.

A car door slammed up the track. Cayde scurried past. "Yogi and Boo-Boo have landed! Mission accomplished. Special ops signing out!"

"Thanks, Cayde!" Scotty gave him a wave as he raced down the walkway while wriggling into his seersucker sports coat. Once Cayde had squeezed into his seat beside Brooke, Scotty turned to the grooms. "Everyone's in place. All we need now are the two leading men."

Scotty was about to guide them to the walkway when a long-restrained sob burst from Alex's chest. He bit on his fist to dam it.

"Is it your heart?" Rick asked in alarm.

"Nurse DeLano's here if you need defibrillating." Scotty stroked his shoulder. "Want me to call him over?"

"No, I'm good." Alex gulped for air. "Just emotion."

"Ready to go then?" asked Scotty.

Alex nodded. "Thanks for organizing this. You're a true friend."

"Yes, thank you Scotty," echoed Rick. "It's magical. You've done a sensational job."

"A warm wind's blowing from the hills and the first gold of evening's breaking through. The day's smiling on you." Scotty led them to the beach.

As Alex and Rick reached the wooden steps, Maddy carefully climbed down from the Beachcomber's front deck. She wore a cute floral dress with pink satin sash. Using one hand to steady herself on the handrail, she carried a wicker basket of rose petals in the other. Safely at the bottom, Maddy waved shyly. Rick and Alex mouthed 'hello' to her. With a whisper and a gentle push, Scotty set the flower girl in motion. The petals

Maddy strew before them fluttered like butterflies on the sea-wind.

Alex controlled his nerves as they followed Maddy towards the floral arch framing the crystal surf. Blurry smiles and genuine warmth emanated from guests on either side. He wasn't able to make out the faces on his right, but Cristina and Ellery were seated to his left. Neroli was with the woman in the wheelchair. Wary of meeting Luisa's gaze and being turned to stone, Alex forced himself to confront the gorgon. When he did, relief overwhelmed him …

The woman in white was Rosemarie Harrington! She gaily waved her lace hanky at him. Thaddeus Boudreaux sat on Rosemarie's other side holding her hand. In the front row, beside Letitia and Jay, was a handsome dark-haired man he didn't recognize at all. He and Rick halted before the officiant, who Alex suddenly realized was a dead ringer for Stanley Tucci.

Tiffany beckoned Maddy to sit with her.

Tyler got to his feet and limped to stand by Alex while Patti assumed her place beside her father.

"Dear friends and family," declared the officiant, "we are gathered here today to witness the union of Alex Morgan and Rick Stradman. This is not a celebration of the beginning of what will be, but a glorification of what already exists. The wonderful and joyous occurrence of these two men's love has already taken place. This ceremony is to publicly acknowledge that love, to confirm their wish to dedicate themselves to one another, and to spend the rest of their lives honoring that commitment." Via the sound system, the officiant's voice clearly projected over the rolling surf and gulls' cries. "Just as it is with the ocean's tides, the fortunes of our lives ebb and flow. The footprints we leave in the sand will be washed away, but the love we give and receive remains indestructible and immutable, a safe harbor in times of storm and a haven of comfort and peace when seas are calm …"

Alex savored the officiant's words as he continued the welcome and invocation. They'd met with him last week to make sure his words echoed their sentiments. Alex obviously hadn't wanted a religious ceremony, nor had Rick, but they both desired an element of spirituality. Scotty's secret plan to hold the wedding on the beach was the perfect location. As he'd told Rick on Torcello, the beauty of the natural world was the work of the God he believed in. And with Rick gazing adoringly at him, his sandy hair ruffling in the wind and golden sun light flickering on the ocean beyond, Alex couldn't be any closer to that God than where he was right now. Sunset Cove would forever be his true home. His mind clicked into gear as the officiant reached the serious part of the service …

"Now comes the time to pledge your intentions to be united in marriage. Please face each other and join hands."

Rick and Alex followed instructions, eyes glistening as they met.

The officiant continued, "Do you, Alexander Nathanial Morgan, pledge to you, Ricardo Ettore Durazzo Stradman, that your love and loyalty will weather the storms of life? That you will respect his needs and concerns, that the decisions you make about the direction of your lives will be made together, and that once your course is set you will sail it as one in good grace and harmony."

Alex cleared his throat. "I do." He listened as the officiant repeated the words for Rick.

"I do." Rick had a catch in his voice as he answered.

"Alex and Rick, you will now exchange the tokens which represent your eternal love, outward and visible symbols signifying the unity of your beings in marriage …" The officiant carried on with the words Alex had to repeat.

After Alex had said those vital words, Tyler opened the box and held out the wedding ring. Doing his utmost to mask his lack of dexterity, Alex concentrated on taking the ring from Tyler and placing it on Rick's outstretched hand without dropping it.

When the officiant had spoken again, Rick repeated his words. "I, Ricardo Ettore Durazzo Stradman, give you, Alexander

Nathaniel Morgan, this token as a symbol of my commitment to you, as powerful and enduring as the sea."

Patti opened the velvet box and lifted out two silver pendants on chains.

Rick showed one to Alex. "I had these cast from the broken eternity pendant. See, they join together." Rick took the other chain with its curving half pendant. "Each of them's beautiful in their own right, but they don't make total sense until they come together." He twisted the two pendants together. Like a puzzle, they linked to form the flowing curves of the infinity symbol. He twisted them apart again. "One for you." Alex ducked for Rick to drape the chain over his head. "And one for me." Rick offered the other chain to Alex.

Accepting it, Alex gently draped the chain over Rick's head and let the pendant fall against his heart. The open necks of their white shirts framed each half-pendant on their tan chests.

"By virtue of the authority vested in me under the laws of the state of California," said the officiant, "it gives me honor and pleasure to pronounce you husband and husband. Congratulations, you may now kiss."

Alex, his heart pumping with love, pulled Rick to him. 'Oohs' and 'ahhs' and warm applause welcomed their embrace, along with the whirr of the circling photographer's camera.

First time ever I saw your face ...

The folky tone of a female vocalist with guitar accompaniment came from the speakers as the legal business took place. The officiant signed the license and got the witness's signature, then he instructed them to file the document where the license was granted within ten days.

With the legal work done, Rick and Alex walked into the congregation. Guests gathered around, showering them with rose petals and snapping photos of their own.

The sensory overload was too much for Alex. From every side people were hugging and kissing and patting him on the back. Rod dragged Allen over. They pointed out that the guitar and vocals were courtesy of Kaori and Hank. Alex squinted at the rear of the seats, wishing he could see everything more clearly. Kaori's corkscrew curls were silvery gray and Hank's long hair, tied back in a ponytail, was pure white. Kaori wore a floral smocked dress and lots of turquoise jewelry. Hank was in a fringed suede vest with multi-colored bead bracelets. Alex's heart overflowed with joy to see them, still the same old hippies they always were. Kaori blew him a kiss and carried on singing, not missing a beat.

Until the end of time, my love ...

"Alex, this is Vincenzo," said Patti breathlessly.

"Catch up with you guys later." Alex excused himself from Allen and Rod. "Nice to meet you at last." Alex shook hands with the handsome man.

"Is my pleasure to be celebrating with you on this happy day," Vincenzo said with a dazzling smile.

"Your ship came in?" Alex hoped Patti understood his cryptic way of asking if Vincenzo was now free from his marriage.

She did. "*Si*! You will soon be coming to another wedding." Patti snuggled into Vincenzo's shoulder.

Scotty was buzzing about, alerting everybody that food and drinks were being served up in the Beachcomber.

A small pair of arms wrapped around Alex's waist. He looked down to find Jay hugging him. "Hey, mister. How you doin'?"

"Does this make you my uncle for real now?" Jay's solemn eyes stared up through his Harry Potter glasses frames.

"I was before," said Alex, "this just makes it official."

"Congratulations." Tiffany kissed Alex. "It was a beautiful ceremony. You both look so handsome."

Alex angled his eye to take a good look at her. He wasn't sure if it was the relief of Tyler surviving the operation or that the TV comedy she'd co-written was going to pilot, but a lightness radiated from her he'd never seen before. Her coral chiffon midi-dress, along with the honeysuckle florets braided in her hair, were a world away from her usual gray cardigans. "You're looking pretty darned good yourself, Tiff."

"We got a shooting date! It's all systems go and —"

"Alex?" A crackly woman's voice came from behind Tiffany.

"We'll go get something to eat." Smiling politely at the elderly lady, Tiffany held Jay's hand and led him away.

Rick might have been correct when he said something bad was bound to happen. Pop's judgmental face hadn't appeared in his blind spot for some time. But just when he thought he'd banished those negative illusions for good he had to be confronted by this real judgmental face from the past. The hyacinth foulard dress worn with a short white jacket made the old woman appear frigidly cool, even in the encroaching sunset's glow.

"Roy forbade me to come, but I had to witness this for myself."

Alex angrily shook his head. "What're you doing here?"

"I was invited."

What Scotty said about the correct etiquette of inviting every member of family if you invite one flashed through Alex's mind. His blood pressure hit the stratosphere and a scarlet drum pounded behind his eyes. "Go ahead, give me the lecture. Shocked. Disappointed. Cowed by the public shame of your queer brother who deserted the family. I've heard it all before, Myrna. You're too late to save my soul cause I'm not about to repent. You should leave before you get caught up in the hellfire and brimstone by association."

Myrna covered her gasp with a liver spotted hand. "Why must you always think the worst of me?"

"Because you've made it abundantly clear in the past you don't approve of my life choices."

Kaori and Hank wound up their set. The few people still on the beach applauded. Kaori and Hank nodded their appreciation then a technician scuttled in to remove their microphones.

"Why travel half-way across the country if not to berate me?" asked Alex angrily.

"My God, that was Kaori singing!" Rick rushed up. "Scotty needs everyone in the Beachcomber so they can dismantle the deck."

"We'd better jump then seeing how Scotty's pulling all the strings," said Alex. "Rick, my sister Myrna. I'm sorry Myrna, but Scotty had no right to invite you."

"Don't blame Scotty," said Rick, "it was my idea."

"Well, it was a bad one. You'd better get out of my way too. Why not show Myrna to the bus, she was just leaving."

With a shaking arm, the old woman offered Alex a floral tote bag. "For you." Her lined and careworn face looked from one man to the other. "I hope you'll be happy together."

"I can't accept your gift." Alex shoved the bag back at her.

"They're the family photos. You forget we did have happy times before Mom's accident."

"Accident? Mom didn't fall downstairs, Pop shoved her! And when she wasn't around to hit anymore, he hit me. I came to you for help, but you denied me and said I was lying!"

"Alex, don't do this here." Rick looked around nervously.

"Why not? Cause people will see? Isn't this what that reality TV shit you've been shoveling's all about? Ugly confrontations at pleasant events. Where's the fuckin' cameras? This would make a real ratings grab."

"Pop's letter's in there. The one he wrote you before he died." Myrna gave the bag to Rick. "Take this for him."

"I've told you before and I'll tell you again, I never want to read that letter of his!" Alex snatched the bag off Myrna and hurled it across the beach.

Myrna let out a sob.

The sun was sinking. Fiery tendrils of orange, cerise and lilac underlit the clouds. Two technicians in blue overalls lingered on the deck's perimeter, itching to dismantle it once Alex, Myrna and Rick had vacated the area.

"You've no idea what coming here's cost me." Myrna regained control of her voice. "And I don't mean in money. Mom married a man who was like her father, and I made the same mistake. I know Pop hurt you, but he hurt me too, although it wasn't his fist he used to control me." Myrna shamefully dropped her eyes. "When you have the same narrow views and old lies rammed down your throat every day of your life you start to believe them. I didn't know things back then that I do now. I let you down when you were a boy, I know. And I have to deal with that just like Pop had to deal with his guilt. Our father died a broken man. I don't know what made him the way he was, but, although it was hard, I forgave him. At the end he wanted to make peace with you."

"Tough," barked Alex. "No-one should treat a kid the way he treated me. He made my life a misery."

"I was just a girl! He robbed me of my childhood too! I just didn't realize it at the time. I try to talk to you, but you've built a wall of anger around yourself I can't break through. You had the courage to break away when you were young. I'm only finding the courage to do it now. My life back home will never be the same after today." Myrna stared wistfully out to sea.

The boiling rage in Alex's veins subsided.

Stepping out onto the beach, Rick picked up the floral bag and brushed the sand off it.

Alex pointed at the three beach houses at the foot of the hill. "That one in the middle was grandma's house. I loved her. Our family disowned her because she was different."

"Different can be very threatening to people who live in a place where everybody wants to be the same. You may choose not to believe me, but I'm proud of the man you've grown to be." A flash of fierce, genuine love passed behind Myrna's milky eyes. "People can't change unless you let them, Alex. I wish you'd let me show you that I have." Taking the bag back from Rick, her cheap white shoes sank in the sand as she trudged towards the track up to the highway.

No sooner had Myrna started walking than the workers moved in to dismantle the deck.

"Well, it wasn't a tsunami," said Rick. "Don't blame Scotty, I gave her Myrna's address."

"I overreacted. I shouldn't have lost it like that."

"No, it was my fault. I thought this might be the last chance for you and her to find some kind of peace." Rick looked towards Myrna's forlorn figure diminishing into the dusk. "She's your sister, your family, please don't let her leave this way. May I go after her to see if I can get her to stay? At least until someone can give her a ride into town. May I, Alex? Please?"

Alex chewed it over. "Okay. Go on."

Rick smiled with relief. "Now we've got the fighting out the way it's time for celebration! I never knew Kaori could sing like that. Do you think she and Hank have got another performance lined up for later?"

"Who knows? But check on the location of the fire extinguishers just in case she has."

Rick's heels kicked up sand as he chased after Myrna.

Alex walked towards the Beachcomber, where the festoons of colored lights around its deck had just lit up.

Rick swung around and yelled, "Good wedding!"

"The best!" Alex yelled back. He glanced over his shoulder at the sun about to sink into the ocean. "Yeah," he said to himself with a smile, "it was."

*　*　*

"This is harder work than an opening night," Alex hissed as Scotty raced off to grab more guests for them to be photographed with.

"Keep smiling, babe," Rick whispered through his grin.

The white Giorgio jacket was too restrictive once they'd gotten inside. Alex had happily zipped it back into the garment bag. Rick had also shucked off his blazer and rolled up his shirt sleeves.

... and put 'em in a tree museum ...

Kaori and Hank had taken up residence on the small stage and were delighting the crowd with more music. Maddy was by Kaori's knee, swaying and tapping a tambourine.

Rick gulped a hefty swig of champagne. "It's a shame Jack's not here. He could've entertained with the flute and pole dancing."

Alex shot Rick a sidelong glance. "There's the Catholic coming out in you again."

"I was kidding. Jack's a nice enough guy. But Tyler could do with someone more ... more *dedicated* to him."

Jack and Tyler had picked up as 'close' but casual friends after Tyler moved back into the pool house. Although he didn't say it out loud, Alex agreed with Rick. There hadn't seemed that many guests out on the beach, but the Beachcomber felt packed to the rafters now everyone was inside. Everything in the bar, the fishing nets studded with seashells and glass floats and wooden beams with tumbling ferns in macramé potholders dangling from them, hadn't changed a bit from when he'd lived in Sunset Cove. He almost expected to see Julie, the waitress who used to work here, sashay from behind the counter to take their order.

Rick put down his champagne as Scotty dragged Cristina and Ellery, both tipsy and overdressed, in for photos.

"That was a beautiful ceremony," said Ellery.

"You should've let us film it for the show," slurred Cristina. "Great publicity. And you'd have gotten paid for it!"

"Thanks, but one season was enough fun for me. And I can do without publicity like, 'Rick Stradman, is he still sexy at sixty? Star's true age shocker!' appearing on *Radar Online*."

"I told you, we let that sketchy sound recordist go. And her replacement will definitely *not* be eavesdropping over hot mics to sell gossip," said Cristina. "But the important part is they called you a star!"

"And your *true* age wouldn't have been a shocker if you hadn't sworn on camera you were fifty-five," Ellery added with a cheeky laugh.

"Who's gonna replace Augusta and Joli?" Rick asked while the photographer lined up the shot.

"Oh, we signed them for another season," said Cristina. "They're total cunts but good for the show."

"Smiles! Say cheese," said the photographer.

"Cheese? This is a gay wedding." Cristina squeezed Alex's waist, tossed her head back and laughed. "Say, 'penis!'"

Ellery and Rick took Cristina's suggestion to heart while Alex forced a smile.

"That'll be nice for Myrna to tell Roy about when she gets home," Alex muttered as an aside to Rick as the *Belles* moved on. "Where is she anyway?"

Rick squinted through the shoulders of lively partygoers. "She's got a drink and talking to Patti and Vincenzo. Let me go over and check they're okay."

Scotty looked around to check she hadn't forgotten anyone. "Lettie! We need Tiff, Ty and the kids in for a family shot."

Letitia signaled that she'd gotten the message and went to round them up.

"You're still alive! I can leave happy in the knowledge you made it through in one piece." Nurse DeLano, out of his scrubs and wearing a cinnamon silk shirt, chino pants, gold chain on his bronzed chest and tousled black curls, greeted Alex.

"Thanks for coming!" Alex greeted Roberto with a hug. A passing server topped up Alex's champagne.

"Go steady on that," chided Roberto looking at the glass. "I know you're a fan of our cardiac suite's five-star service, but we don't encourage guests to rack up loyalty points with frequent stays."

"I won't undo all your fine work in healing me. Promise," said Alex.

"Keep hold of Tyler while I go find the others." Letitia hustled Tyler next to Alex before diving back into the fray.

"Roberto, meet Tyler, my nephew." Alex frowned at Tyler. "Seeing how you're Rick's half-brother, technically that makes you my half-brother-in-law, doesn't it?"

"B … b … better stick with nephew. Easier t … to say. Hi." Tyler gave Roberto a lop-sided grin. "H … how'd you know my uncles?"

"I cared for Alex when he was in the hospital. I'm a nurse," replied Roberto.

"Cool. I w … w … wouldn't be here today if it weren't for g … guys like you," stuttered Tyler.

"Ty had a brain tumor removed a few months back," Alex said. "It's been a rocky road but he's doing great now."

Roberto's limpid dark eyes stared up at Tyler. "Glad to hear."

"J … j … just wish it was quicker so I could g … get back to work."

"What kind of work do you do?" asked Roberto.

Scotty scuttled through to them. "Alex, go say goodbye to Rosemarie. She's out on the front deck waiting for her transport. Where'd Rick go?"

"He's over with Patti," said Alex.

"Patti needs to be in here for the family shot," muttered Scotty, "jeez, this is like herding cats. Tyler, once your mom's got the whole family together don't let anyone go! Okay?"

"I'll be right back." Alex pushed through the drinking and laughing crowd to the entrance. Although it was bedlam, the joyous atmosphere in the Beachcomber was wonderful.

Outside on the deck, beneath a swag of colored lights, Rosemarie sat in her wheelchair, a blanket over her knees. She was gazing out at the orange and violet dying sun.

"Thanks for coming," said Alex placing his hand on her shoulder.

Looking up, Rosemarie patted his hand. "Wild horses could not have stopped me being here."

Alex steadied himself on her wheelchair's arm to creakily kneel by her side. "I wouldn't have the career I do today without you. I owe you so much, Rosemarie."

"Talent and hard work built your career. I nudged you along the path, that's all. Now you and Rick, I need you to look after one another. I'd love to stay and keep an eye on you both myself…" Rosemarie gave one of her tinkling laughs as she gestured to the uniformed caregiver coming up the steps. "… but I have another party to get to." Rosemarie's cool fingers stroked Alex's cheek as she took a last long look at him. "See you there later."

The caregiver kicked off the chair's brake and wheeled Rosemarie to the steps. The retirement home's ambulance was parked at the bottom of the track. Its driver helped take her wheelchair down. As Rosemarie was carried into the night, she raised the back of her hand in farewell.

"Scotty's looking for you," shouted Rod sticking his head onto the deck.

The bar had warmed up considerably when Alex got back inside. Trays of little pizzas, mini-hamburgers and crab cakes with lime mayonnaise were going around.

"Babe, there you are! We need you." Rick was in the center of a line-up with Scotty organizing people around him.

… winter, spring, summer or fall …

Kaori's sweet voice over Hank's chords filled the room.

Rick grabbed Alex's arm. "This is the last photo then I'm getting drunk."

"Jay, Maddy, get in the middle so we can see you." Scotty arranged the kids with Rick and Alex.

After more stage management, jiggling heights around and stepping back and forth to fit everybody in the frame, the photographer asked, "Is this all the family?"

Alex checked. The kids were down front, Tyler beside him, Tiffany, Patti and Letitia next to Rick. About to say yes, he hesitated. What the heck, this was a day for love. "My sister," he said, "we need my sister Myrna in. Where is she?"

There was some head turning and looking around before Myrna haltingly stepped from the crowd.

... and I'll be there, yes, I will ...

Taking her hand, Alex sandwiched Myrna's fragile body between himself and Tyler.

Everyone smiled.

The photographer clicked.

The Morgan and Stradman households were officially joined and a photo had been taken to commemorate the event.

"That was a nice thing you did," Rick said once the photos were over, Scotty had gone off duty, and he and Alex could relax.

"Myrna went out on a limb to offer an olive branch. I was the one who caused the scene. Maybe the anger about Pop I can't let go of is I recognize part of him in me." Alex drained his glass. "Wanna come take a look at the old beach house?"

"You bet. I thought you'd never ask!"

Music and laughter from the Beachcomber blended into the surf as Alex and Rick scuffed along the track behind the restored beach houses, now short-term vacation rentals.

"Hey, they got rid of the lot in the dunes." Alex still saw an outline memory of his battered green Chevy parked up there and an echo image of Luisa getting out of her white rental to come say that if he truly loved Rick, and didn't want his TV career blighted by scandal, he should let him go.

"See what they've done to the Waverley's place," said Rick studying the house next door. "Not sure I care for the yellow clapboard and red roof."

A vivid replay of Gloria Waverley hurling pot plants and insults at their kitchen door after she'd accidentally seen him fucking Rick projected from Alex's eyes onto the wall. He turned to the house on the other side. "How they've made over the Piper's place is sympathetic though. They've matched the green paintwork to how I first recall seeing it." Dora and Mrs. Pipers' shadows having a conversation over the picket fence appeared+. All the years he'd known Mary Piper as just the kindly neighbor, never realizing she and Dora had once been lovers and came to Sunset Cove in the '30s to live openly together without shame or judgement. Behind these familiar windows new people turned on the lamps, wandered through the rooms and dreamed in the beds.

Did they ever glimpse the lives gone before?

Ambling back along the shale track to the Beachcomber, Alex noticed movement in the shadows at its rear. Moments later, Scotty and Rod walked into the light. Rod's jacket was draped around her shoulders, her hair was down, her lipstick smeared. They all bumped into each other at the foot of the wooden steps. "You'd go to any length to make her quit smoking," Alex said to Rod.

Tucking her hair behind her ear, Scotty looked away.

Rod flashed his super-white teeth. "Tried and tested method. Replace one addiction with another."

"I hear nicotine gum also works," added Rick.

"But it's not as much fun." Rod allowed Scotty to lead their way up the steps.

Alex and Rick hung on the deck, looking at the beach before the sky faded to black.

"Hey," said Rick, "I see two guys taking a stroll along the shore. Well, one's strolling. The other one's limping."

"What? Roberto and Ty?"

"No, Thaddeus and Ty. Duh! Yes, Nurse Dreamy and Ty. I hope Tyler's crutch doesn't rust in the salt water."

Going inside the Beachcomber, Kaori and Hank had wound up their final set. But just as Alex was wondering if the party was over, the swirling strings of *Love's Theme* swept over the sound system.

"Disco!" cried Rick. "Time to show off your booty shaking!"

Everyone stepped back to let Rick drag Alex onto the dancefloor. And as The Love Unlimited Orchestra with Barry White's smoky vocals wrapped around the partygoers, a roar of approval greeted the happy couple's first dance.

* * *

The party moved to the house after the Beachcomber. Tinkling glasses, smoky jazz and carefree laughter filled the wood paneled rooms and spilled out onto the patio. The October night's temperature had plummeted. Those outside availed themselves of woolen throws and the patio heaters. Inside, Alex lit a fire in the living room's rarely used fireplace. Rick broke away from chatting with Kaori and Hank to wave their empty wine bottle in Alex's direction.

Needing water to take his evening meds anyway, he went to get a fresh bottle. In the kitchen, Neroli and Thaddeus were in deep conversation. They stopped talking the moment he walked in. "Why so serious? Have you found the officiant was a fake and we need a do-over?"

"Let's not end a beautiful day on a sour note." Neroli tossed her wrap around her shoulders. "I'll tell you tomorrow."

Alex pondered the fridge's wine selection. "Oh, get it over with. Tell me now."

Neroli exchanged glances with Thaddeus. "Someone defaced *One Hundred and Fifty-Six Dollars* last night."

"Defaced?" Alex chose a bottle.

"They opened two tubes of red paint, scrawled 'Homo Scum' on the blank canvas and then squirted the rest of the paint over the other tubes," said Neroli.

"Perhaps they were trying to write 'Homos Cum' and got confused?" Thaddeus mused with a hopeful shrug.

Neroli sighed. "I'll have the canvas and paints replaced tomorrow."

"But you mustn't." Alex set the wine bottle on the countertop. "The materials are there for anyone to use. It's a dare. We can't censor what people do if they take us up on it."

"But those words are offensive," said Neroli.

"People can paint over them if they think that too. Or write something else. The *Work in Progress* pieces are organic. Like I said, what happens to them happens."

"You're meant to be getting a fresh bottle not fermenting the grapes." Rick entered the kitchen, empty glass in hand. "Uh oh, what's up?"

"The blank canvases are no longer blank. Someone used the red paint for *Marooned on Red* to write Homo Scum." Alex handed Rick the corkscrew. "You'll be quicker than me."

Neroli picked up her purse. "The *Vanity Fair* article and Rick's TV show have put your relationship, particularly your marriage, under public scrutiny."

"Don't forget my Twitter account." Rick pulled out the cork. "I only opened it a week ago and I've already got over three hundred followers."

"Seeing words like that graffitied on a street corner's bad enough, but I was horrified at seeing them in my own gallery," said Neroli. "What's wrong with people?"

"Rather than hiding or downplaying this," said Alex, "we should be totally transparent. Publicize it, even. *Empty Spaces* is about the way art's valued and appraised. One hundred and fifty-six dollars is how much the materials to paint *Marooned on Red* cost me back in seventy-four. Each piece's title is the base cost of the materials used in the original. That's their intrinsic value. What are you asking for this new piece, Neroli?"

"One hundred thousand's my territory for all your *Work in Progress* pieces. Depending on the buyer." Neroli smiled awkwardly at Thaddeus.

"Don't mind me," said Thaddeus. "I'm well aware of the mechanisms of commercial galleries."

"Notoriety's a valuable commodity these days. Let's see what effect word of mouth has on its desirability and asking price. You know what we should do? A Polaroid of each mark made on the canvas." A thrill of excitement buzzed through Alex. "Then mount the photos around the piece to document its progression. That'll create a new artwork in its own right."

"Must they be Polaroid photos?" asked Neroli.

"Absolutely," said Alex, "instant, honest, with no hint of Photoshop or digital manipulation."

"Okay. I'll send Tad out tomorrow to get a camera and some film. I suspect they'll be expensive."

"Put it on my tab," said Alex drily while visualizing even more financial outgoings.

"I'll leave the piece the way it is then." Neroli's tone brightened. "Well, it was a wonderful day, I'm so happy for you both." She picked up her purse and kissed Alex goodbye. Having parked off-street in the space between the main house and the small house, Rick accompanied her to raise the roller door.

"You okay for a drink?" Alex asked Thaddeus.

"Fine, I must be going."

"I hope there was no awkwardness having Cristina there today. I'm afraid the guest list was out of our hands," said Alex.

"Cristina's been good to her word about effecting change on the LACoMA Board. Her new cabal wants me back. And not just for my collection, they want me for Chair."

"That would make a real statement."

"Would it? By replacing a right-wing bigot like C.Z. Hulton with a black man the Conservatory thinks it can rehabilitate its tarnished reputation? I don't want to fight for respect, be given a consolation prize or be used as a bumper sticker to telegraph their newfound political correctness. That memorandum from Hulton insulted me, and the museum ownership's silence on the matter condoned that insult. I'm through with that place and I've no intention of returning on any basis. I'm moving my loan to *The Harrington Collection*. They've lost trustees and funding in this wretched financial turmoil, my donation will give them a much-needed boost." Thaddeus drained the last of whatever exotic cocktail it was Rick had mixed for him, put down his glass and tweaked his bow tie. "Our freedoms and rights are incredibly fragile. For all those who've fought for them, there's always someone else who'd happily take them away. Acceptance and toleration are different to being treated as an equal, we must never let politeness prevent us from taking a stand against injustice."

Alex nodded, knowing only too well how true that was.

One by one, or as a pair in Scotty and Rod's case, guests made their exits. Hank and Kaori left to crash out in Manuela's former apartment as they had to hit the road back to Oregon early in the morning. Maddy and Jay, thrilled to be allowed to stay up super-late, were in the den watching *Enchanted*. The remaining adults, Tiffany, Tyler, Patti, Vincenzo, Letitia, Cayde, and the newlyweds, had kicked off their shoes and flopped on the living room's sectional couch and comfortable chairs.

Nestling in Vincenzo's arms, Patti stared into the crackling flames. "This feels like Christmas," she said, finishing her red wine.

"Thanks for liaising with your grandmother on the commentary track." Tiffany leaned across and refilled Patti's glass. "Criterion's booked me to produce the special features on their next two Blu-rays of dad's movies on the strength of that package. And I got a pilot getting ready to shoot. Things are finally looking up for Tiffany Stradman."

"You're going back to the family name?" asked Rick in surprise.

"The marriage to Pav didn't work out so it's dumb to keep his name. The Stradman name used to stand for something in the entertainment industry, I'd like to make it that way again."

"Me too. Especially if you write more great parts for me," said Rick brightly.

"I didn't write that part *for* you. I created a character you're suited to play," corrected Tiffany.

"C'mon, 'Late forties but still boyish in spirit and appearance.' The minute I read that character description I said, 'This writer's a genius!'"

"Sucking up won't get you the job. I'm just the writer. Co-writer at that."

"You really had no idea it was T... T ... Tiff's script t ...t ... till you were at the reading?" asked Tyler.

"My agent only sent me the sides for the scene. It wasn't until I walked in and saw Tiffany at the production table I even knew she was involved."

"You gave a terrific reading," Tiffany said to Rick. "I can give them my opinion, but final casting isn't in my hands."

Hearing a barrage of annoyingly loud beeps from her phone, Patti jumped up to find her bag.

"I've never seen your house look as lovely at it does tonight," Letitia said to Alex.

Scrolling through her phone, Patti's expression grew concerned.

"Make the most of it. Unless some financial miracle occurs, we're going to have to sell. Those hideous new apartment buildings couldn't have topped out at a worse time," said Alex. "I cannot imagine who'd buy a place in anything so ugly."

Patti went and whispered to Vincenzo. They quietly excused themselves and went outside.

"Confession." Cayde sheepishly raised his hand. "Brooke and I have bought a unit in one of them for Leland."

"That wouldn't be the unit whose balcony overlooks your putting green by any chance?" asked Alex.

"You know what they say, keep your enemies close and your family closer."

Tyler yawned.

"You're beat, honey," said Letitia. "Time to turn in. Need me to help you get ready for bed?"

"No, m … m … mom." Not using his crutch, Tyler steadied himself on furniture and the door frame to leave.

"How come you have the cash for that when everyone else is selling the family silverware?" Alex asked Cayde.

"I diversify. Leland's coming in with me on a start-up to supply large scale art to corporate buildings. We're looking into delivering it via giant screens in digital format."

"TV art?"

"Even when times are tough there's money to be made," said Cayde. "Digital's the future."

Hearing Tyler stumble into something on the patio, Letitia jumped to her feet.

"You stay and relax. I'll go check on him," said Alex.

Crossing the patio, Alex saw the glow of Vincenzo's cigarette tip and Patti's phone screen in the meditation garden. He knocked on the pool house's kitchen door. "Thanks for being my best man today."

Sitting on the bed, Tyler raised his eyes from his phone. "N … no worries, Uncle Al."

"Didn't Roberto want to come back with you?"

"I d … d … didn't ask him."

"Why not?"

Tyler despondently tossed his phone on the bed. "He spends all d … day with sick people. Needn't do it all n … n … night as well."

Saddened that romance didn't seem to have blossomed between Tyler and Roberto, Alex closed his door. Going back to the house, he found Patti and Vincenzo coming across the red bridge.

"My phone has only just picked up messages." Patti's voice trembled. "I need Papa."

"Come on in then," said Alex.

Patti shook her head. "Ask Papa to come out."

Vincenzo sat down at the patio table, dragged an ashtray across and flicked ash off his cigarette.

Alex leaned into the living room. Rick, Cayde and Tiffany were chuckling away. "Rick, you're needed out here," he said.

Rick, still giggling, stumbled outside.

"Have you checked your email today?" Patti asked Rick.

"Er, no. I've been a little busy getting married."

"Sister Marta's been trying to reach us all day." Patti shivered in the night air. "Nonna Lu has left the institute."

"What do you mean left it?" asked Rick. "How?"

"As soon as I was out of the country nonna called in her notary. She has sold the Ca' dei Venti to a private investor. Then, yesterday, a private ambulance took her to Nicelli airport. A plane had been chartered to take her to Zürich." Tears welled up in Patti's eyes. "There is only one reason dying people go to Switzerland."

Vincenzo didn't rush to his feet to comfort Patti, he carried on smoking, staring at the table.

Alex instinctively stepped forward, enfolded Patti in his arms and let Rick stroke her back as she sobbed on his shoulder.

In typical fashion, Luisa was having the last word yet again.

LETTING GO

"Sorry, but no way am I gonna be home in time," the harassed airline pilot, who had the look of a more mature Jamie Foxx, said into his cellphone. A jet's hull was visible through the large airport window. Disgruntled passengers silently lugged shoulder bags and roller cases off the jetway. A paramedic assisted a limping flight attendant with her arm in a sling.

"And there's not a spare part in the whole of Sydney?" Rick was speaking on the handset of a wall-mounted phone in a stylish kitchen.

"It's a 747 babe, not a Ford Falcon."

"And there's no work around?" Rick loosened his necktie and undid his designer shirt's collar.

"There is. But crossing the Pacific with duct tape holding a jet engine together's not recommended airline procedure." Audience laughter greeted the pilot's rising annoyance. "We're waiting on a replacement plane from Singapore. You'll have to play alongside Jaxon at the family soccer game."

Rick's eyes widened. "Soccer game?"

"Shorts, jerseys, players kick a ball and score goals," said the pilot. "Ring a bell?"

A nine-year-old boy, clearly the pilot's son, with Harry Potter glasses and carrying a book came up and tugged Rick's shirt. Rick covered the mouthpiece. "Hi, hon. I'm starting dinner. Get a snack if you're hungry."

The boy put down his book and crossed to the double-door refrigerator.

Rick resumed his call. "But Ken, tomorrow night's the Advertising Awards Gala. After four years of being runner up, I'm finally in with a chance of bringing home the best direct print award in the product category. Have you any idea what that means?"

Captain Ken grimaced. "Not really." Audience laughter. "But I know it's important for you. This'll be the first game I've missed since Shanice passed. You'll have time to make the award show after the game. And we don't want Jaxon to be the only kid playing without a parent, do we?"

Without turning, Rick covered the mouthpiece "Carrot sticks, not chocolate cake!"

With a long-suffering eyeroll, Jaxon put the cake back.

Indulgent laughter.

"You're right," Rick said on the phone. "I'll make it work."

"You're the best, babe. Make sure to get a photo of yourself in those soccer shorts." Ken smirked.

"You're real funny." Rick gave a wry laugh.

Jaxon dragged a stool to the counter and reluctantly picked at the carrot sticks.

"Hi, hi!" An elegantly dressed and splendidly coiffed blond woman made a grand entrance through the back door from the yard. She held the hand of a four-year-old Vietnamese girl. Vivid splotches of blue, green and red paint covered the little girl's smock.

"Gotta go, Leona just brought Kelsey home. Take care, darling." Rick hung up. "Hi, mom." He gave the girl's smock a quizzical glance. "So what did you two get up to today?"

"We took in the Warhol exhibit, discussed Nietzsche and pondered humanity's place in the universe." Leona greeted Jaxon with a kiss.

"Really?" Rick lifted Kelsey onto a stool and undid her smock.

"As if," said Leona, "I went to Elizabeth Arden."

"And I ate paint!" Kelsey declared proudly.

Lots of laughter.

"Non-toxic," Leona added once the laugh died. "It was the museum's 'Free Expression for the Under-fives' day."

Rick held up Kelsey's paint splattered smock. "If she'd thrown up, I guess you could always have passed it off as a Jackson Pollock." Tossing the smock aside he clattered pots and pans out of the cupboards.

"You seem more agitated than usual, darlin'." Leona poured herself a glass of wine.

"Ken just called with some bad news." Rick put down a cooking pot and turned to Jaxon. "Your dad's not going to be home in time to take you to the family soccer game. His plane had a major engine failure. He had to abort take-off and declare an emergency. A passenger had a heart attack, a flight attendant broke her wrist and one of the fire trucks crashed into one of the ambulances. The chaos shutdown all air traffic for over two hours. Your dad's stranded with four hundred and seven irate passengers, not enough hotel accommodation, complaints about missed connections and everyone's baggage is stuck in the hold until they can tow the jet off the runway."

Jaxon slapped his palm to his forehead. "Why does everything happen to me?"

Hearty laughter.

"But never fear." Rick puffed out his chest. "*I* shall be taking you to the game."

"You play soccer?" Jaxon raised a skeptical eyebrow.

"Sure." Rick busied himself with food preparation. "Of course, that was back when I was in high school."

"And when TV was in black-and-white," added Leona.

This got a warm laugh.

"Thanks, mom." Rick gave Leona the side-eye. "Actually, I was rather good."

"Well, we look forward to seeing you in action then." Leona helped herself to a carrot stick.

"You're coming to the game?" Rick asked in surprise.

"You bet. Kelsey and I would not miss this for the world." Leona raised her glass. "Ra, ra, ra!"

Rick's expression grew tense as he chopped vegetables.

Brrrrrring! A loud bell sounded on the soundstage.

"That take went better," Letitia whispered to Alex. "Tiffany and Gregg seem happy."

"Moving on!" a disembodied voice announced.

Thumping music faded up over the speakers. "Whoa, some delay for Captain Ken!" A spotlight hit the warm-up guy with hand-held mic in the audience bleachers. "Any of you guys fly here? Anybody on vacation? Shout if that's you!" The lights dimmed on the kitchen set as the actors cleared. The four cameras and two sound booms rolled to a locker room set with a black curtain obscuring its central section. "Louder, I can't hear you!" urged the warm-up guy.

Alex was relieved that he, Letitia and Tyler were seated in the roped off section down front, somewhat removed from Lewis, the warm-up guy, who kept the audience energized during lulls in taping. Angling his head to watch the overhead monitors with his left eye was giving Alex neck ache. The central portion of his right eye's vision was virtually non-existent, but even with 20/20 vision he'd have struggled to see the live action on set due to the cameras, monitors and crew in the way.

On his left, Tyler's knee jiggled impatiently. Although this was a multi-camera sitcom, the shooting process was the same agonizing stop-start affair Alex recalled from watching single-camera shows being filmed. The cast had done a dress rehearsal that afternoon, also in front of a live audience. This evening's taping had begun at seven. An hour and a half later and they were only a third of the way through the twenty-one-minute episode. The warm-up guy was conducting a noisy competition to find the audience member who'd experienced the longest flight delay.

"Jesus, this is agony," Tyler muttered.

"Yeah, the legroom's tight," Alex whispered in reply.

"I wasn't t ... t ... talking about the seats," said Tyler.

Alex stifled his laughter. Letitia shot them a glare from his right.

Hollers of joy greeted the lucky audience member who'd sat on the tarmac at JFK for eleven hours on an iced-up JetBlue with a blocked toilet. Catching the t-shirt Lewis hurled her way, she triumphantly waved her prize. The pounding music faded out, the studio lights faded up. The actors and background artists hit their marks on the locker room set.

"Okay," said Lewis. "Time for the family soccer game! How'd you think Lyndon's gonna do? Let's find out as we return to *The Homing Instinct*!"

"Rolling." The second camera assistant held up the digital clapper board. "Scene four. Take one. Cameras A, B, C, and X. Common mark." She clapped the slate. "Action!"

Tyler's fidgeting rattled Alex's seat as the scene began. A dialog interchange took place between Jaxon, in his soccer outfit, an uppity kid and uppity kid's uppity father. No big laughs, just titters. Jaxon turned to give his line to Lyndon. The black masking curtain rose silently. The reveal showed Rick tugging down his extremely short soccer shorts while tying his shoelaces. The contrast between Rick's smart suit and uptight manner in the opening scenes and his discomfort in this alien situation triggered a knee-jerk belly laugh.

Stuck between Letitia purring with pride whenever Tiffany rushed on set to pep up a joke and Tyler squirming with boredom, Alex's concentration drifted. While more flight delays for Captain Ken, prejudice from uppity kid's father, and the twist of Rick's character, Lyndon, being a killing machine on the soccer field played out, Alex was mentally checking off the tasks to be accomplished now he'd accepted a low-ball buyer's offer on the house. Brian had suggested leasing out the place or 1031 property exchanges, but it all seemed too complicated. The time had come to move on from one dream to a smaller, more manageable dream – one with less property tax.

To say the three months following their marriage had been stressful would be an understatement. The day after the ceremony at Sunset Cove, while Rick and Patti were embroiled in getting to the bottom of Luisa's sudden flight to Switzerland, Alex had lured Scotty into rushing him to the eye clinic with the promise of a third checkmark on her medical facilities of SoCal tour. As suspected, his left eye was experiencing the same issue as his right. Steroid injections, more bloodwork and modifications to his RA meds to address clotting side effects followed. If the prospect of gradually going blind in both eyes hadn't been sobering enough, when he got home from Dr. Kastani's Rick's news had been equally devastating.

 Apparently, once Luisa learned the truth about her health, she'd covertly contacted lawyers to wind up her affairs. In her final phone conversation with Rick, the full content of which he still couldn't bring himself to divulge, she revealed Ileanna Souter had arranged the flight and accompanied her to Zürich. They received Ileanna's call the following afternoon telling them that Luisa had died in the night. Her remains were cremated within twenty-four hours. Although aware it was inevitable, the manner of Luisa's passing was unexpected, and all the more distressing for being shrouded in secrecy. Ileanna had given the nuns a cover story that Luisa was being rushed to a Swiss clinic for a miracle cure. Because of the legal ramifications, no-one voiced the fact Luisa had chosen to end her life on her terms. And her timing wasn't malicious, she'd done it while Patti and Rick were out of the country so they couldn't talk her out of it or be implicated. No Last Rites and no Funeral Mass for Luisa. Rick and Patti wept uncontrollably for two solid days. And, despite his checkered past with Luisa, Alex shared their grief. Details seeped through of Luisa's bequests. Her art collection, in its entirety, was to go to the Museo del Novecento. The proceeds from the sale of the Ca' dei Venti were to go to the same institution to build a wing to house her collection in the name of her father, Barone Ludovico di Durazzo. The Lido house was left equally between Patti and Rick, the Milan apartment went to Patti, and Rick was to get the lake house in Bergamo. By the time debts, loans, taxes, and bequests to loyal staff were disbursed,

Patti and Rick would receive modest sums. Although the money would take many months, perhaps even years, to materialize. Alex noticed Vincenzo's ardor for Patti cool with each revelation of her diminished wealth. As Patti left the Venice Beach house to return to Italy, Alex felt as though he were sending his own child off to an alarming unknown future …

Back on the soundstage, after nearly four hours of taping, the wise cracks, raucous laughter, Tyler's squirming and Lewis's grating jokes reached their conclusion. Lyndon Lincoln missed out on collecting his advertising award to celebrate their school team's first win in five years. Pilot Ken came home to find Jaxon in awe of his other dad's sporting prowess and witty tongue which had put uppity kid and uppity kid's dad in their place.

Lewis whipped the audience up for the cast's final bow. "Loretta McKee as Judge Wanda Starr! Morgan Fairchild as Leona Lincoln! Terry Diggs as Captain Ken Andrews and Rick Stradman as Lyndon Lincoln! You have been a terrific audience! Good night and thank you!"

The music pumped up. Rick and Terry shared a smooch, grooved with the kids, then Rick picked up the little girl playing Kelsey and they all boogied off the set. A front cloth with *The Homing Instinct* logo dropped in, the work lights came up, the doors were flung open, the audience flooded out.

Letitia sniffled beside Alex. "I wish Sid could have seen Tiffany and Rick working together. He'd be so proud."

Tiffany picked her way over the cables to the audience bleachers. She pointed out her co-writer, Gregg Masters, who waved warmly to the family from the studio floor. After a swift backstage post-mortem, cast and crew were meeting at a nearby bar. Tiffany told Alex and Tyler to go grab a table, and she and Rick would catch up with them. Letitia congratulated Tiffany then headed back so the sitter could get home.

Leaving the Radford studio complex, Alex and Tyler crossed Ventura Boulevard, Tyler walking unaided with a slight limp. Expecting some swanky wine bar, they found The Laurel

Tavern to be a laid-back gastropub with Craft Beer specials on chalkboards. The jazzy patch in the inner field of Alex's left eye meant Tyler had to read the specials out loud. Tyler went to the bar while Alex groped his way to a corner table.

"What did you make of that?" Alex asked as Tyler brought their drinks to the table.

"It was okay. But not real life." Tyler shuffled into a seat.

"Well, it is a sitcom." Alex gulped his Californian Pilsner, which was extremely good.

"Exactly. Non-problems in a pretty box, all wrapped up and t ... t ... tied with a bow in t ... twenty minutes."

Alex grunted noncommittally, realizing he'd had the same thought. "But for what it was, Tiffany did a good job."

"I guess." Tyler sipped his diet Mountain Dew. "But a mixed-race same-sex couple assembling a rainbow family to fulfill their need to nurture? You think America's ready to welcome that into their home Thursdays at nine, eight Central? T ... Tiff and her new boyfriend have cooked up a fantasy of how they'd like the world to be rather than how it is."

"You're being too hard. Prime Time TV's never seen a family like this. Change is in the air. Obama's in the White House, The United States voted in its first President of African American heritage. A country can't go backwards after that, can it?"

"D ... d ... don't forget, the same night Obama took the White House, California voters sanctioned Prop Eight. Fifty-two percent of the state v ... voted against marriage equality."

"But a show like this can change attitudes. Same-sex couples have the same issues as any other couple. And why shouldn't two women, two men, or two people of whatever orientation, gender or race who love each other be seen as great parents and role models?"

"But isn't this show also saying gay relationships are only valid and non-threatening if the t ... t ... two guys are pushing strollers, shopping in Ikea and bickering over who takes out the garbage? What about guys who just want to hang out and fuck other guys? Where's our representation?"

"Is that what you really want, Ty?"

Tyler shrugged. "When you love someone deeply, and they can't, sorry, d …d … don't love you back, it stings. Better to keep things casual. Life's not about what you want, it's about making the b … b … best of what you get."

They drank in silence for a few minutes.

"You still keep up with Jack?" Alex asked.

"He's doing great in San Francisco. I'm thinking of moving up there t … too."

Alex put his drink down so fast he almost missed the table. "What about your business? You're getting your fitness back. You can drive again. Isn't it time to pick up where you left off?"

"You guys are selling the Venice house. Tiffany's career's on a roll and mom's running her fan club. I'm gonna be out on my own. I'm grateful to the doctors who took that thing out my head, but since the operation I feel different. I feel like … like I'm *less*. And I keep wondering if coming b … b … back was a mistake."

A cold presence brushed past Alex. "Back from where?"

"Wherever it was I watched the surgeons open up the back of my head and touch my brain. Someplace not in me. It wasn't scary, and I could've stayed. But I hesitated and something pulled me back down. The next thing I remember was pain like a freaking ice p … p … pick behind my eye. I knew then I'd blown my chance to escape."

Alex maneuvered his head to get a good angle on Tyler's green-gold eyes. With his short hair, hollow cheeks and a couple of seasons of not working outdoors, Tyler's face possessed a pale, haunting beauty.

"We joked about it in the p … p … past, Uncle Al, but there is something beyond. The spark inside us carries on, I know it." With a sad laugh, Tyler finished his drink. "Just wish I knew what the fucking p … p … point of it all is though."

"Maybe there isn't one? Maybe life is one colossal cosmic joke?"

"What, it's all a sitcom and God's the warm-up guy?" Tyler laughed. "The winner of the shittiest time on earth gets a t-shirt." Riffing on the comedic aspects of the meaninglessness of life, Tyler and Alex were chuckling away when a flurry of activity erupted in the entrance. "Here's Tiff and Rick." Tyler leaned to Alex. "Don't t … t … tell them about the other side stuff. You know how Tiff makes fun of me."

"I won't," said Alex.

A million people poured into the bar.

Rick swept up to their table with a post-performance glow of adrenalin and sweated-off makeup.

"You were sensational." Alex heaved himself up to plant a congratulatory kiss on Rick's cheek. "Nice work, Tiff."

"Yeah. Well done, sis." Tyler warmly hugged Tiffany.

A slew of introductions followed as people joined their group. Alex gave up trying to match names to blurry faces and grinned benignly. More drinks were ordered and chairs and stools got pulled up to adjoining tables.

"We were seriously worried this afternoon," said Tiffany as Gregg passed her a mineral water mixed with juice. "That audience was not prepared for the gay theme."

"I was dying inside. I thought no-one was ever going to laugh," added Rick, "but we won them over by the end."

"Lewis tweaked his welcome speech for tonight's taping. He explained the show's premise and had Rick and Terry chat with the audience to build some history," Tiffany explained.

"It worked. Tonight's crowd were along for the ride from the get-go," said Alex.

"Hey, 'show' husband!" Terry, who played Captain Ken, swung by their table. "That was a blast. What say we do it again?"

"I say, yes." Rick put his hands together in prayer. "Let's hope the network does as well. Terry, this is my real-life husband, Alex Morgan."

On his bad side, Alex fumbled finding Terry's hand to shake it. "Nice meeting you. Good show."

"And this is my and Tiffany's brother, Tyler." Rick gestured across the table.

"Wow, sensational looking family!" Terry bent across to shake Tyler's hand. "Are y'all the result of some supermodel cloning experiment?"

Tiffany glanced at Terry, Rick and Tyler joking and laughing with each other. "Guess Terry wasn't including me in that comment," she murmured in Alex's ear. "It's cool," she added before Alex could respond. "I've gotten used to Ty parading his peacock feathers." She looked at Tyler, grinning bashfully in response to Terry's rapt attention. "I'm happy he's alive and well. Anything Tyler does from now on is cool with me."

Alex wondered how cool she'd be about Tyler's proposed move to San Francisco. From his left eye, Alex noticed Tiffany was on juice and water, not wine. "You're not celebrating?"

"I have to knock two *Mothers, Wives and Sisters* scripts into shape this weekend. I'm praying this pilot goes to series so I can wave goodbye to those frickin' nuns. It'd also be great for Rick's career. Apart from recommending him for casting I didn't pull any strings. Rick got this part on his own merit. Of course, your gay marriage coverage in the media and outrage surrounding those homophobic slurs at The Copley Gallery helped too."

"Ironic, isn't it?" mused Alex. "In nineteen seventy-four Rick got canned from a TV show because of being gay, and in two thousand and nine he gets a leading role because of his authenticity."

"Any more news on that *Red* canvas?"

"Only that it's on its way to Amsterdam. I'm still blown away the Stedelijk museum bought it. It's a shame people painted over the 'Homo Scum.' Leaving it that way would have sat well beside the 'Fagots Stay Out' sign in the Barney's Beanery installation at the Stedelijk. The last Polaroids Neroli took before

One Hundred and Fifty-Six Dollars got shipped showed the canvas was almost entirely covered with paint. The insults, the retaliations, the slurs, the praise, all those red words rendered invisible in a sea of red paint." Alex took a drink. "I never thought a blank canvas, red paint and an open invitation to use it could create such controversy."

Sipping her juice and water, Tiffany placed a protective hand across her stomach. "Ah, the thrill of creation. Making something which didn't exist before then watching it make its way in the world." She smiled warmly at Gregg across the bar.

Without needing to see, Alex sensed Tiffany and Gregg's next project was going to be more ambitious than creating a hit TV show.

"Thanks for coming." Tiffany kissed Alex on the cheek. "And if the show gets picked up and we need plot ideas, I'll send Jay and Maddy and any new additions over to you guys for the weekend."

An hour of banter, laughs and good humor slipped by. Cast and crew vowed to keep in touch before wending their separate ways.

Stepping onto the crosswalk over Ventura, Alex felt Rick take his arm on one side and Tyler take his arm on the other. Rather than making him feel elderly, the care surrounding him made him feel safe.

Their SUV was parked in a reserved space beside the stage. As they got in the jeep, the show's set was being unloaded from Stage 14's elephant door. Rick had been drinking and the blur hadn't cleared from Alex's left eye after Dr. Kastani's last set of shots, so Tyler took the wheel.

Although it was late when they got back to the Venice house, Rick was still on a high. Tyler parked the jeep in the garage. As they emerged from the door to the pool, two bundles of white fur with wagging tails raced madly towards them. Bippy and Boppy jumped up at Alex, Rick and Tyler in hysterical welcome.

"We've been around the block, peed, pooped, and sniffed hydrants." Scotty stubbed out her cigarette.

"Terrific, how about the dogs?" asked Alex.

"Them too." Getting up from her seat under the pergola's heaters, Scotty lifted a bottle of champagne from the ice bucket. "Congratulations to Rick!" She popped the cork.

Alex picked up the ashtray and rattled the stubs in it at her. "Does Rod know about this?"

"My last ever, promise. I came across a pack Vincenzo left behind in the small house." Scotty handed Rick a glass of champagne. "How'd it go?" She was filling the other glasses, but Tyler declined and went to the pool house.

"I can't speak for anybody else, but I had a wonderful time." Rick flopped down on a seat and kicked off his shoes. "I was nervous about working with a live audience, but know what? I loved it! Hearing the laughter and applause was such a rush. I didn't think I could handle stage work but maybe I shouldn't rule it out. I can't count on this pilot getting picked up and we need some cash coming in."

"We'll be okay, babe. LA Modern Auctions has accepted ten of the male nudes for sale and I'm waiting on Christie's to get back with an estimate for the large-scale abstract," said Alex.

"You're doing a Damien Hirst and bypassing the dealers to go direct to auction?" asked Scotty.

"Just seemed like the right time to put the nudes up for sale. If anyone's going to profit from my press attention it might as well be me. Rick's been contacting the new Indie galleries too. Figure I'll drip out whatever unsold work I have through them until I can see well enough to paint again."

Tyler came out from the pool house holding a lite beer.

Rick tapped Alex's hand. "You take your evening meds?"

"Yeah, Ty reminded me during the taping break. And once this place is sold we can buy someplace smaller and clear our debts."

"About that." Tyler hovered by the table with his drink. "You guys helped p … p … pay for my rehab. I got a plan to pay you back. Jack knows people who can get me work in San Francisco. More money that I c … c … can make here and —"

"Uh huh." Rick shook his head.

"What d'you mean, uh huh?" Tyler asked.

"You have work to do here," said Rick.

"I've lost clients. People are c … c … cutting back on maintenance."

"Only last week Thaddeus told me he needs a new landscaping contractor. And Cristina's house has overgrown tree canopies which are a fire hazard and need cutting back. You've got the equipment, your truck's fixed and —"

"I'm not a k … kid! I'll pay you back for the truck too. It's better for me t … to make a clean start and —"

"This isn't about payback," said Rick.

"Then why shouldn't I go? What's keeping me here?"

Putting down his glass, Rick scraped back his chair and stood. "Until Alex's eye responds to the new treatment he can't drive. I have auditions lined up and need to find work. I won't be around to take him to his doctor's appointments. We need to go to Italy to deal with momma's estate and scatter her ashes and someone has to look after the dogs. We're moving out of here, but we'll find a new house with room for you. A place we can be together but separate. Take six months to get back to work and build up your funds. Help me and Alex through this next phase of our lives and I'll give my blessing to whatever you decide to do after that. I don't want you to go to San Francisco because I need you here. *We* need you here."

"If you put it that way, I guess I g … got no choice." Tyler relaxed with a lop-sided grin.

"That's settled then." Rick wrapped his arms around Tyler's waist and hugged him. Leaning back, he looked up. "Considering you're my little brother you're freaking enormous! Did you grow in the hospital?"

"Maybe you shrank? I hear it happens as you get older."

"Very funny. Tiffany should write you into the show as a comedy sidekick," said Rick playfully slapping Tyler's shoulder.

Laughing, Tyler finished his beer and crunched the can. "I'm b … beat. See you in the morning." Tyler went to the pool house. Bippy and Boppy chased after him. Once they were all safely inside, Tyler shut the door.

"Nice work, babe," Alex said softly to Rick as he sat back down. "Moving to San Francisco wouldn't be right for Ty."

"Had to think on my feet," Rick replied equally softly. "But it's true, we've got the dogs to think of now. Those two furballs were a truly unexpected part of momma's legacy."

"We couldn't have left them in Italy," said Alex. "Patti and Vincenzo are out all the time. The poor things would've gone nuts couped up all day."

"How's Patti doing?" Scotty asked.

"Working hard overseeing the decommissioning of the Ca' dei Venti. It's been tough, but as the Museo del Novecento's made her chief conservator for momma's collection she hasn't really said goodbye to the pieces she's watched over for years." Rick took the bottle from the ice bucket. "Just said goodbye to the fat salary she'd gotten used to collecting and an unlimited expense account. Though I suspect Vincenzo will miss those things more than she will."

"I don't like to say this." Alex prevented Rick from filling his glass beyond halfway. "But I don't like Vincenzo."

"You know what?" Rick topped up Scotty's and his own drinks. "Neither do I. While we're in Italy I plan on speaking with Giuliana about strategies to terminate that relationship."

"You can't mean that?" Scotty gasped.

"I do. I'm not going to just stand by and let her marry him," Rick declared.

Scotty focused on Alex. "And how'd you feel about that?"

"I'm with Rick on this. There's something about Vincenzo I don't trust." Alex waved his hand over the cigarette packet and lighter. "Look, he's not even here and he's leading you astray."

"And how do you propose keeping Patti and Vincenzo apart if they want to be together?" asked Scotty.

"Now Patti's income is diminished, Giuliana can put pressure on by not helping maintain the lavish lifestyle she's grown accustomed to. Let's see what effect that has on Vincenzo. And Aldo, Patti's grandfather, can be extremely persuasive when he needs to be."

"Well, dragging ourselves out of *The Godfather, Part Three*, here's to Rick." Scotty raised her glass and they clinked, although Alex missed. "And here's to me!"

"You're celebrating losing a million dollars?" Alex mopped his spilled champagne off the table.

"You're a fine one to talk about losing money to fraud." Scotty narrowed her eyes at Alex. "Anyway, it sounds like us Madoff investors will get our investment back if nothing else."

"Good news for Rod as well," said Alex, "although getting conned out of a million dollars when you have twenty million more in the bank's not quite so bad as the hit you took."

"Tell me about it." Scotty sighed. "I wasn't expecting to be nearly bankrupt at sixty."

"You're welcome to stay in the small house for as long as you need. While we still own it, that is," added Alex.

"Thanks, but I'll be moving out next week." Scotty reached for the cigarettes.

Spotting her from the side of his eye, Alex batted her hand away. He pushed the cigarettes and lighter out of reach.

"Did a vacancy open up at the Priscilla Hotel for Single Young Ladies?" Rick slyly asked.

"No, a nice house up on Mulholland. It's really a share. The owner's a very successful artist." Scotty finished her drink.

"Sounds like Rod got himself a new chick," said Rick.

Scotty tossed a haughty look their way. "That'll be Mrs. Chick to you. Night boys, see you in the morning."

Alex placed his hand over the cigarettes as she kissed him and Rick goodnight.

When Scotty had gone through to the small house, Rick cleared up.

"Go to bed. I'll do that," said Alex.

"Sure?"

"I'm not totally incapable yet."

"Thanks." Tiredness hitting, Rick dragged himself off to the master suite.

Alex turned off the patio heaters, emptied the ice bucket into the pool and picked up the glasses and bottle. After carrying everything inside, only bumping into the doorframe once, he tidied the kitchen. Having set the dishwasher in motion he killed the lights and crossed the dining room.

The family photo album Myrna had brought to the wedding sat on the table. Having shied away from revisiting his past for so many years, the very real prospect of blindness had led him to leaf through its pages late at night. Putting on his glasses, he picked up the album and moved to the lamp which illuminated Rod's word painting, *FREEDOM*. Alex opened the album. Warm light fell on the page holding the photograph of himself, aged two, along with Myrna, who would've been nine then, Mom, Pop and the family dogs. Alex studied the square black-and-white image held by age-yellowed photo corners. The family was out in the yard. Mom, Pop and Myrna were laughing because little Alex, wearing a jaunty felt cowboy hat, was trying to ride one of the dogs. He adjusted his vision to get a clear look at Pop's face. Pop's laughter was different then, laughing with his son, not at him. Exploring his storehouse of repressed memories, Alex recalled a time when Pop had been warm and kind. A time when Pop's masculine hand would ruffle his hair or squeeze his shoulder, not slap his face or punch his gut. Alex had a good look at Mom too. He'd forgotten how much she resembled Dora. Mom seemed genuinely happy in this photo. What happened, he wondered, to make it all go wrong? What were the hurts, the disappointments, the fear that led Pop to tear this happy family apart? Or maybe something bad had been done to him ...

Alex closed the album. He was putting it back on the shelf when something dropped. Thinking the brittle cellophane corners had given up the ghost and photos were falling out, he bent to pick it up. It wasn't a photo. It was his father's letter. Myrna must have tucked it deep between the pages. He held the sealed envelope up to the lamp. 'To Alex, my son,' was scrawled in discordant lettering on the thin stationery mottled with age. Taking off his glasses, Alex rubbed his eyes. Should he read Pop's final letter while he still could?

Pop's mood turned on a dime. He recalled Pop's pleas for forgiveness after a bout of cruelty which only held good until his next onslaught of viciousness. Which Pop wrote this letter? Was this an admission of his brutality and a plea for absolution? Or was it an accusation of Alex's wickedness for having brought the punishments upon himself? Was this letter Pop's justification for knocking the sensitive, artistic gay boy out of Alex and turn him into a man? Or did it say, 'I love you eternally my beloved son. I was wrong. I'm sorry.'?

And would either sentiment make anything better now?

'You won't move on until you let him go ...'

Recalling Kaori's fondness for using the transformative and elemental beauty of fire in her performances pieces, Alex took the letter out to the patio. He picked up Vincenzo's cigarette lighter. His thumb's lack of dexterity made it hard to flick the wheel but, after a couple of attempts, the lighter burst into life. He put the flame to a corner of Pop's last letter.

The fire took hold.

The old paper burned fast. Alex dropped the letter in the ashtray. Specks of ash whirled in the air as flames consumed Pop's handwriting. Whatever Pop had written no longer mattered. Alex thanked his father for the gift of life and the chance to walk on this beautiful earth and forgave him.

"Everything okay out there?" Rick yelled from inside.

"Fine," Alex called back, "on my way." Watching the fire die, he fingered the half-eternity pendant around his neck. How do you know what to let go of and what to hold on to? Who is right, who is wrong? There were no absolutes, you just had to trust your gut and believe.

Making sure the letter's charred remains were totally extinguished, Alex dumped the ash in a planter and went to join his husband in bed.

WHEN THE EVENING COMES — OCTOBER 2019

Blu di cobalto in alto a destra.
Rosso permanente chiaro in alto a sinistra.
Giallo primario nell'angolo inferiore sinistro.
Terra di siena naturale a basso in destra.

That's how he worked these days, thinking in Italian, using only blue, red, yellow and brown, and relying on their location in his palette to know which was which.

Pure and transparent, Alex loved those qualities of this Italian brand of watercolor. White paper gleamed brightly, like light, through the pigment. At least he expected it still did from the memory of when he last saw it. Likewise, he couldn't be sure if the dusk colors above the lake were real or memories. And until Rick or Jay gave their feedback on what he'd painted this afternoon, he wouldn't know if he'd got anything coherent on the page at all. Not that it mattered anymore. Since losing his vision, he no longer practiced his art for an end result. Rick would usually help him down to the lake but today, Jay, visiting the Bergamo house on a break from studying history and politics at Cambridge, had done the honors of setting up his field easel, putting his paints in the right place, making sure his water and brushes were precisely where he needed, laying a blanket over his knees and leaving him alone to commit his illusions to paper for a few hours. This was his daily ritual. Whether at their ranch house in the Valley, the apartment in Venice or the lake house in Bergamo, the habit of practicing his art simply for the sake of it gave Alex great comfort.

A skid on the lake was followed by a splash, quack and flap of feathers. Alex loved how the birds lowered their webbed feet to the water's surface to reduce speed for landing. Fall was the time of year the goldeneye ducks arrived from northern Europe. Some years they'd stay around on the lake until spring. But if the winter was harsh, as the coming one promised to be, they'd only stay for a few weeks before heading farther south. The goldeneye flicked crystal drops of water off its black and white feathers, its bright yellow eyes gleamed in its greenish black head. The bird was beautiful. Or rather his memory of a goldeneye duck was beautiful. It was peculiar, but as his sight had faded to indistinct blurs, the memory of how things used to look grew more vividly detailed. The colors of the past glowed inside his head.

The crack of a stick hitting the ground startled him. He moved his fingers. They were stiff and painful.

Fuck ... he'd fallen asleep and dropped his brush. Had he dreamed the duck? He wasn't prepared to lean over to retrieve the paintbrush. Last time he tried that he'd toppled out of his chair and lay sprawled on the deck for half an hour. That had been September, the day after they'd arrived in Bergamo and summer's dying warmth still clung to the air. He hadn't shouted for Rick to come down and help him up. He just lay there musing on the day he'd never get to his feet again. Still, he wouldn't want to be lying on the ground out here as this cold fall night descended.

Up in the house, Rick was having one of his ninety-five decibel, rat-a-tat Italian conversations with Jay. Rick swore he wasn't deaf and was far too vain to succumb to a hearing aid even if he discovered he was. Having spent so much time over here in Italy with him and Rick, Patti, her husband Mauro and their two kids, Jay's Italian was practically fluent. Because they were so loud, Alex heard Rick and Jay were discussing the far-right 'Italy Pride' rally which had taken place in Rome last weekend and the alarming rise of nationalism and intolerance, not only in Europe but also back in America. Alex accepted other people held different views, but the current political climate of his homeland did not sit well with him. He'd always had faith the world would become a kinder, gentler place as modern communication led people to realize they all wanted pretty much the same things - freedom, equality, mutual respect and to live with their loved ones in peace and harmony.

But it seemed that wasn't to be.

The damp evening air caught in Alex's throat. His chest felt tight. He coughed. He was on the verge of yelling for Jay or Rick when a creak of the door to the kitchen's verandah was followed by footsteps crunching down from the house.

"*Cosa ti è successo?*" asked Jay as he came closer.

"*Lasciato cadere il pennello,*" Alex replied. English and Italian had become interchangeable in the household and his head. Alex heard Jay pick up the brush.

"There's another brush in the jar," said Jay.

Alex felt Jay guide his hand to the table on his right, but he pulled it away. "Nah, I've done enough today. Tell me, how'd it come out?" There was a long pause as Jay studied his watercolor on the field easel. "That bad, huh?"

"Every day you paint the same lake and sky, Uncle Alex, and every day you paint it differently. Today your sky's red, orange and yellow. It's nicer than reality. And you put a sailboat on the water." Another pause. "And there's someone on the boat."

"It's me ... wishful thinking." Alex extended his hand and tapped the place Jay's arm should be. "Tell me, are there ducks on the lake?"

A pause as Jay looked out to check. "Yeah, there are a couple in the reeds."

"Goldeneyes?" asked Alex.

"The mist's coming in, I can't see from here. Why?"

"Just wanted to know if they were real or if I'd imagined them."

The sounds of Jay packing away his field easel, paints, other bits and pieces, were followed by the latch's click after he'd put the watercolor board in the wet work carrying case. "Uncle Rick's starting dinner."

Alex felt Jay help him from his chair. "No, you go on up, Jay. I'm gonna sit out here a while longer."

"Don't be too long, Uncle Alex. It's getting cold."

Tucking his hands under the blanket, Alex heard Jay's footsteps crunch back up the path to the house. He felt a glow of pride. Jay was such a kind young man. And so bright. Although Alex suspected his choice of studying at Cambridge was because of his love for the Harry Potter books and the University's resemblance to Hogwarts as much as for its educational pedigree.

Alone, Alex stared up in the direction of the sky. A lone bird's call echoed plaintively across the lake. Allowing snatches of the golden sunset from the extreme periphery of his vision to bleed and fill the canvas of his mind, his perception did its usual trick of turning the shadows and fog into something meaningful. In this case, the golden mosaic of the ancient Santa Maria Assunta cathedral's dome on Torcello projected into his head. A shadow crossed his memory's recreation of the Virgin Mary, in reality the shadow was a bank of raincloud or flock of migrating birds crossing the setting sun. The phantom faces and figures which at first disturbed him, then comforted him, had faded as his sight declined. They'd now taken on flesh and blood and lived in his head. As his health failed more each passing day, he sensed himself on the brink of two worlds. One realm of the living, populated by people he could no longer see, and one realm of the dead, populated by those who'd passed yet he saw distinctly. In that world of the dead, the old, like Dora and Rosemarie and Luisa, were young again. And the young, like his infant son, Tyler and Danielle, had grown mature. Alex recalled Tyler wondering if he'd made a mistake by not staying in the peaceful place during his brain surgery rather than returning to this world of pain.

Tyler obviously decided not to make the same mistake again when they operated on a secondary tumor. Alex figured the trees and plants on the other side would be growing more beautiful with Tyler's tender care.

Alex's doubts and fears about that other side had vanished. He'd be making the voyage there one of these days. At sunset, he'd climb onboard his sailboat, a twenty-two-foot sloop with a yellow hull, cast off and head out to sea. Well underway, he'd look back at the receding shore and see those he was leaving behind wishing him luck and waving farewell. Then, as an east wind filled his sails, he'd peel his gaze from the sad faces and look towards the crimson horizon. The land beyond that horizon was unknown, but he felt a sense of expectation growing over there. Dora, Mom, Danielle, Manuela, Tyler, his son who'd grown into a man, Myrna, Sid, Rosemarie, Luisa, perhaps even Pop would have put on his Sunday best and a smile, were gathering on the harbor and staring out to sea, waiting for their first glimpse of his mast and topsail. At night, he could almost hear their excited whispers, 'We shall see him soon. Our boy's coming home. Any day now!'

"Alex!" Rick's yell from the house brought Alex back to the deck beside the lake.

"I hear ya!" Alex yelled back.

"Dinner's ready! Do you want me to come and get you?"

"Nah, I'm okay! Coming!" Picking up his walking stick, Alex threw the blanket aside and arranged his tired and painful old bones into an upright position. Slowly, he made his way up the path to the house. The dents and stones along the way were his signposts. The scent of hot bread, meat sauce and red wine spurred him on. Nearly there, and exhausted, Alex climbed the last two painful steps up to the verandah. He paused, listening to the clatter of dishes and cutlery and Rick fussing around Jay at the table on the other side of the door. Alex extended his gnarled fingers to the place he knew the handle would be.

Although he'd miss this world, he was getting excited about his last solo voyage. Flying high alongside the gulls, he would look down and watch himself making that trip. A strong young guy, his long dark hair flowing in the wind, his firm hand on the tiller and hope in his eyes. And after he'd arrived in that land without pain and been welcomed by those who had gone before, he would wait alongside them on the harbor for Rick to get there. The two halves of the eternity pendant would be joined, and they'd be one again. Rick still had many years of work ahead of him in this world, but Alex knew his own departure would be soon …

But not tonight!

Smiling inwardly, Alex went into the house to take his place at the table, ready to enjoy a wonderful dinner with his family.

Howard Rayner

Other works by Howard Rayner

<u>Novels</u>

That Summer of '74

<u>Books for Young Readers</u>

The House of Dolls
Dawn Over the Outback
A World Behind the Sky
The Wardrobe / The Noisiest Family
Knights
The Medusa Disk

<u>Screenplays</u>

Taxi
Losing the Plot
Guarding Angel

Printed in Great Britain
by Amazon